WOMAN OF THE APOCALYPSE

Riley Parra Season Five

Geonn Cannon

Supposed Crimes LLC • Matthews, North Carolina

This book is a work of fiction. Names, characters, places, and incidents are products of the author's imagination or are used fictitiously. Any resemblance to actual events or locales or persons, living or dead, is entirely coincidental.

Published in the United States.

ISBN: 978-1-944591-96-0

www.supposedcrimes.com

This book is typeset in Goudy Old Style.

TABLE OF CONTENTS

Woman of the Apocalypse	5
Wrestling with Angels	32
The Starry Cope of Heaven	59
Among the Faithless	87
The Mercy Seat	114
Wandering Steps Through Eden	140
Farewell Happy Fields	165
Hail Horrors	192
Easy is the Way	219
These Troublesome Disguises	247
Wormwood	272
Spiritual Warfare	298
The Never-Ending Flight of Future Days	33?

WOMAN OF THE APOCALYPSE

TWO YEARS. Seven hundred and thirty days. Not even that, not exactly. Riley remained in the car for a long moment, staring at the street outside the window as she contemplated what Priest had told her. There was a version of this morning that included Gillian's death. To ensure that didn't happen, Riley made a deal to sacrifice her life for Gillian's. She would do it again if she was given the chance.

"There's no way out of it?"

Priest shook her head, hands resting on the bottom of the steering wheel. "I know that we've avoided the hangman so many times. Ridwan brought you back from the dead, and I sacrificed my divinity to do the same. Marchosias turned back the clock so you could make a different decision about the end of the war. But this time there's no..."

"It's okay. I don't want to change it."

"What? Riley, this is your life~"

"No, it's Gillian's life." Riley's voice was soft, sympathetic. "She's alive right now, and according to Otheriley, she shouldn't be. I'll pay any price for that. And so I'm going to die in two years. The only difference is that now I know it. Before this happened, I could have been killed today or tomorrow. This way I'm guaranteed to die saving Gillian's life. Two years." She looked down at her hands. "It's a nice number. A lot of time left to do what needs to be done, and to appreciate what I have."

Priest shook her head. "It's not enough time."

"How much time would be enough? Five more years? Eighteen?" She smiled ruefully. "It doesn't matter, Priest. Unless I live to be eighty or ninety, it'll never be enough time. And a cop working in a town like this, who moonlights as its champion... I was never going to make it to eighty or ninety. I'll have two more years with Gillian, and then she can be free. She won't be the champion's wife anymore, and the demons will leave her alone. And she'll be alive, Caitlin. So yeah. I'd say Otheriley got the better part of the deal."

"I'm still sorry."

Riley nodded and furrowed her brow. "I'm surprised I'm not angrier. There should be seven stages of grief, right?"

Priest thought for a moment. "No. You're relieved because you've been waiting for this moment since you were fifteen. You could have died at every step. Now you know it's two years away so you're able to relax."

Riley smiled. "Huh. You have a point, I guess. No more looming doom to worry about. But do me a favor... I don't want to tell Gillian."

Priest's eyes widened. "Riley, that's~"

"If I have to die, I want everything to be normal. That includes fights, her being angry at me, butting heads... if she finds out I'm going to die she'll change. She'll start mourning me immediately and that wouldn't be fair to either of us. I'm sure it'll come out eventually, but I don't want it to affect what little time we have left."

Priest pressed her lips together and then nodded.

"What did you do with her? Otheriley?"

"She died in the battle against the demons sent to kill Gillian. I did as she instructed. I used a pallet to create a pyre and placed her body upon it."

Riley raised an eyebrow. "That didn't cause any problems? A body being immolated on the waterfront at dawn?"

Priest's smile was weak and short-lived. "Oddly, it seems no one noticed."

"Odd." Riley smiled at the mysterious ways of her partner, but then her eyes flashed with anger. "Marchosias..."

"No."

"I don't care about rules right now, Priest. He~"

"Helped you. The other you." Riley frowned at her and Priest shrugged. "Otheriley swore to me it was so. I'm inclined to believe her since she would have no reason to lie about something like that.

She named the demons and in doing so gained a measure of power of them. It's what allowed her to destroy them even as they were killing her. The names could only have come from Marchosias or the person who sent them."

Riley shook her head. "Why would he help?"

"I doubt we'll ever know."

"I don't accept that. I'll make it my job to find out." She got out of the car and Priest joined her on the sidewalk. "I'm serious, Priest. Not a word about this to Gillian."

Priest nodded reluctantly. "It's your place to tell her, not mine. I'll keep your silence. But Riley, she deserves to know. She has the right to say a proper goodbye to you."

Riley sighed. "I know. I'll give her that time, I promise. But for now~"

"Normalcy."

"Right. Come on up. Gillian or I will make you breakfast."

They went back into the building and Riley led the way upstairs. Gillian was once again dressed for work in baby blue scrubs, her hair pulled back and held with a clip. Riley paused in the doorway, the needle that had been waiting to pierce her heart chose that moment to plunge, and she choked down a cry. Gillian glanced up as they came in before she went back to what she was preparing. The look was too quick for her to notice the emotion raging on Riley's face.

"Hey, Caitlin. Are you staying for breakfast?"

"If it isn't an inconvenience."

"Never. Pull up a chair." She looked at Riley again and smiled. "Are *you* planning to stay?"

Riley nodded, having taken the brief interaction with Priest to compose herself. "Right. Yeah, I'm..." She shut the door and followed Priest into the kitchen. She put her hand in the small of Gillian's back and pressed against her, bowing her head to kiss Gillian's neck.

Gillian chuckled. "Honey, we have a chaperone."

"Let her watch." She kissed Gillian's ear and slid her hands to rest on Gillian's hips. The position was reminiscent of one they had frequently taken in bed and she felt Gillian take a single heavy breath as she remembered it. She turned her head to see Priest at the table studying the folded newspaper.

"Do I have to spritz you with the sink thingie?" She chuckled as she pushed Riley away with her hips. "What's gotten into you this morning?"

"I just want to make sure you know you're precious to me."

The smile faded from Gillian's face as she turned to meet Riley's eye. "Of course I know that. Is everything okay?" She cut her eyes toward Priest and then back to Riley. "What happened? Was there a development in the case, or~?"

"No. I just wanted to make sure you knew." She kissed the corner of Gillian's mouth and stroked her cheek before she stepped away. "I'll be good. No peep show for the angel."

Gillian still looked wary, but she went back to her cooking. Riley sat at the coffee table and took the part of the paper Priest wasn't reading.

"So much for normal," Priest muttered.

"Quiet." Riley unfolded the paper. "Was there anything on the case?"

Priest shook her head. "I haven't heard anything."

Riley grimaced. They were in the midst of three major investigations, none of which looked to be closed any time soon. An undercover detective named Wanda Kane had been murdered in a nightclub and, when the SWAT team arrived to arrest their suspect, they found that every single person in the club had been killed. Meanwhile, at approximately the same time, one of the Good Girls had been stabbed. A few hours later Gillian identified a mutilated body as that of the city's disgraced former mayor, a man Riley herself had arrested only a few days earlier.

Riley was assigned to Wanda's case and Priest was working with Aissa to find the Good Girl's killer, but the commissioner had assigned the mayor's case to a detective named Benjamin Harding. Riley was still trying to figure out a way to get in on his investigation, but she had her plate full just trying to figure out how to work her own job. She was certain the new mayor, and Marchosias' new champion, Lark Siskin was involved with Wanda's murder but she was going to have a hell of a time proving it.

Gillian turned away from the stove, eyes cast toward the window. "Is that thunder?"

Riley heard it a moment later; a dull and hollow roar that was steadily growing louder. Priest stood quickly. "That's not thunder."

Riley stood and crossed the kitchen in a single step, grabbing Gillian and holding her tight as the apartment began to shudder and shake around them. The pan danced on the stove, clattering against the burner, and everything around them seemed to have suddenly come to life. Everything that had just a moment ago been solid was now moving and liquid. Riley's hand on the back of her head kept Gillian's face against her shoulder and she hunched her shoulders in an effort to further protect her from any falling debris.

When the world settled again, the silence was filled by shrieking security alarms and blaring car horns. It was only a moment before wailing sirens joined the cacophonous chorus. When Riley was sure the shaking was done, she looked over her shoulder and saw Priest had vanished from the kitchen. She focused her attention on Gillian.

"Are you okay?"

"Yeah. I'm fine. Go."

"I don't~"

"We're both probably going to get calls any second now, so we're both going to have to go. You seem very..." She searched Riley's face as if the answer was written on it somewhere. "You seem odd this morning. I don't know why. But I'm giving you permission to leave me and go where you're needed."

Riley squeezed Gillian's shoulders and kissed her. "I love you."

"I love you too. Go on. You're needed."

"I'll take you in with me. Odds are they'll need both of us."

Gillian nodded, but Riley tightened her grip.

"Be careful today. Promise me."

"Scout's honor."

Riley nodded and finally let her go to get her badge, gun and wallet. Gillian dumped the scrambled eggs she had been cooking into a coffee cup and handed it to Riley as she hurried past. Gillian followed her out the door a moment later. By the time they got downstairs to the car, Riley's phone was ringing. She answered it, knowing who would be on the other end without looking.

Lieutenant Briggs began talking without preamble. "Where are you?"

"I'm at home, almost in my car. Where do you need me?"

"Not you. Sorry, Riley. I didn't hear you answer. Hold on." Her voice became more muffled. "No, I need you on Truman. Yes. Thank you. Okay. Riley, you're at home?"

"Yeah. Priest was here a second ago. I'm sure wherever she is she's already busy."

"Right. Okay, come down to the station. We'll figure out where to send you from here. Oh, is Dr. Hunt with you?"

"She's right next to me."

"Can she explain what the hell happened in the morgue this morning?"

Riley looked at Gillian, who returned her stare with the blankness of someone who was only hearing half a conversation. Riley instinctively knew that whatever had happened between Otheriley and the demons had occurred in the morgue. Odds were no one had taken the time to clean up the mess.

"I don't think so. Why? How bad is it?"

"It's pretty bad. We can deal with that later. For now just get down here, both of you. We need all the warm bodies we can get."

Riley hung up and pocketed the phone as she started the car. She put the small red dome light on the dashboard so they could get through any road blocks.

Gillian waited until they were underway before she spoke. "How bad is what?"

"The damage at the station. Apparently, they were closer to the epicenter than we are."

"Riley. Why are you lying to me?"

There wasn't any anger in the question, but Riley almost wished there had been. She sounded scared; more scared than she'd been before she fled the city and went home to Georgia. Riley didn't know how to answer. Revealing she was dying wouldn't exactly set her mind at ease. She sighed heavily, driving slowly to avoid the people who were moving through the streets to assess the damage.

"If I'm lying, you know there's a good reason. Right? It's not because I don't trust you, and it's not because I'm trying to deceive you."

Gillian nodded slowly. "Whatever it is, I'm here when you're ready to tell me."

"I know. Thank you." She put her hand on Gillian's knee and squeezed.

Priest stood in the morgue and tried not to be ill. Blood pooled on the tile, following the grout lines until they reached the charred remnants of bodies that had once hosted demons. She stepped around one of the beds and saw an organ, fat and sickening, lying on the floor like an alien being. Some instinctual part of her, a part of Zerachiel rather than Caitlin, knew that it belonged to Riley. When she looked back she saw the sigils encircling the doorframe. Her mind did the proper calculations and she realized what they were for.

Riley trembled despite the warmth of the newly-risen sun. Blood soaked her clothing but she didn't seem to notice. She sat with her knees drawn up, her arms around them as if she was trying to hold herself together.

"I went to a bad place, Caitlin. You and I..." She looked at Priest, who winced at the effort it seemed to take her to make such a simple gesture. "We weren't friends at the end. It's nice to sit with you and see compassion in your eyes." She held out her hand, and Priest took it. Riley's blood smeared on her skin and she shuddered. "I'm sorry."

"You didn't do anything to me."

"Just take the apology. You don't know how bad things got."

"I accept your apology, Riley Parra. And I grant you absolution."

Riley faced the water again and closed her eyes. A moment later she did something that stunned Priest to her core.

She cried.

Now Priest knew exactly how bad things had gotten. She could feel the gravity of spells which had been spoken only a few hours ago and knew Riley's first gambit had been to torture her enemies. She had trapped herself in a room with two demons that had arrived with murderous intent, and once they were locked in the room she had enraged them even further.

She didn't have time to marvel at the evidence surrounding her. There were people in need, and soon the morgue would house more than its share of anguish. She crouched in front of the main entrance, her back to the swinging doors, and put her fingertips against the cold tile. She steepled her fingers and closed her eyes.

The air around her crackled with released energy, her ears filled with the sound of electricity muffled by water. A quiet sound of constant tearing, an echo of metal crumpling, and then silence.

When she opened her eyes again, the room was pristine. She stood and walked to the far end to make sure all of Otheriley's sigils had been erased. When she was content that there was no evidence of what transpired remaining, she slipped away as effortlessly as she had left Riley and Gillian's kitchen earlier.

There was much more work to be done before she could rest.

Muse Skaggs jogged to the end of the street and paused to look both ways before opting to go left. The houses in this neighborhood were always one good wind gust from collapsing, and the earthquake had been more than enough to send a half dozen crashing to the ground. Dust was still swirling in the air as he approached one pile of debris by crossing an overgrown lawn. The surrounding streets were still alive with the sound of chirping and shouting car alarms as he reached the former front stoop. He heard movement inside and braced one hand against a strut that was still standing to peer inside past cracked and crumbling drywall.

"Yo! Anyone alive in there?"

A woman answered him. "We could use a hand!"

Muse stepped back and eyed the home like the world's most intense game of Jenga. If he pulled the wrong thing, it might send the whole works crashing down on the people he was trying to save. He looked toward the garage and craned his neck, stepping off the porch. The garage was still standing but the door was severely warped. He put one hand on the building and the other on the door, gritting his teeth as he pushed the gap wide enough to slip through. He slipped past two large trucks to the interior door, opened it, and breathed a sigh of relief when he saw a clear path into the kitchen.

"Comin' in! Where are you?"

"Where are *you*?"

"Garage. In the kitchen now."

The resident coughed. "Go straight through the door to the left and into the living room. We're in here. By the far wall."

Muse followed the directions. The back door was blocked by a collapsed section of ceiling that had also destroyed a dinner table. When he reached the living room he spotted the woman crouched against the back wall tending to a man with drywall chalk all over his face. It made him look deathly pale, an image helped by the sight of bright red blood trickling down one side of his face.

"He's hurt," the woman said.

"I can see that." Muse picked his way across the devastation to kneel next to her. The man's leg was pinned under a beam. "That's bad."

"Oh, good. I got a doctor. I know it's bad, you son..." The woman sighed and pushed her hair away from her face. "Sorry."

Muse waved off her apology. "Day like this, you're entitled to be a little grouchy." The walls groaned around them and Muse looked warily at the ceiling. He could see patches of sky. "Look, I think we gotta choose between staying here and possibly making things worse by movin' him out of here."

The woman nodded. "Yeah. I know... we have to get him out."

"Okay." Muse undid his belt and slipped it off, looping it around the man's leg above the wound. "My name's Marcus."

"Irene. This is Roger."

Muse smiled at the man. "Hey, Roger. I'd ask how it's goin', but that seems kind of stupid right now. What we're about to do might hurt you, but it's better than the alternative." At least he hoped it was.

He managed to lift the beam while Irene pulled Roger free. He suddenly came to life, moaning low in his throat and then clutching at Irene's arms.

"Hold on, buddy. We'll get you out of here as soon as we can." To Irene he said, "Help me get him up."

They moved slowly through the destruction as the house continued to protest. He had just helped Roger into the garage when someone knocked on the garage door.

"Anyone in there?"

"Yeah! Could you maybe get the door open a little so we can get this dude out?"

A tall athletic girl dressed in a ragtag assortment of secondhand clothes moved into the gap between the door and the wall. She had blonde curly hair that was pulled back so it would stay out of her face, and she her hoodie was zipped up to her throat. When she gripped the door he saw that she was also sporting a pair of thick work gloves. She used her entire body as leverage and furthered the already warped door. Muse helped Roger through and the girl took him, twisting to motion at someone in the street to come join them.

Muse let Irene go out first, then followed her. He saw the blonde handing Roger over to an EMT who had apparently come from a white van that was idling at the end of the block.

"You got an ambulance to come down here?"

"Just a white van. Chuck's a real EMT, though. He's close enough in a pinch." She took off her gloves and held out her hand to him. "Aissa."

Muse smiled and shook her hand. "Aissa Good. Yeah, I've heard about you. Been doing a lot down here past few months."

Aissa shrugged. "I do what I can. Is that everyone who was in the house?"

"This one, yeah. Whole bunch of other ones out there. How much medicine and stuff you got in that van?"

"Not enough. I have people out looking for more."

Muse raised an eyebrow. "You got people?"

Aissa shrugged humbly. "I have a few people. Want to be one of them? Looks like you know what you're doing."

"I'm my own man, Ms. Good." He backed away toward the sidewalk, still smiling at her. "But I'll keep my eye out for you. No reason we can't help each other out from time to time. Name's Muse! Remember it."

When he passed the white van, he waved to the driver and motioned for him to roll down his window. The man did so warily, making sure that Muse could see the stun gun resting on his lap. Muse kept his distance and held his hands out to show he wasn't a threat.

"What are you low on? Priorities."

"Gauze and aspirin. Any kind of generic painkiller. We're just patching things up so people can manage until the real doctors get a chance to look at them."

Muse made a mental note and tried to think of where he could go to get the supplies. He had a few options that he doubted even someone with Aissa's connections could reach.

"Okay. Where will you be in about an hour?"

"Do you need anything?"

"Will you stop asking me that? I'm not an invalid."

Kenzie tightened her jaw. "I'm just asking, sweetheart. Don't bite my head off."

Chelsea took a slow breath and then reached for Kenzie's hand. "Hey. I'm sorry. I don't need anything." She didn't want to admit how frightened she had been for the first few minutes after the earthquake. Kenzie had been on a stakeout and the phones were down, so she'd spent a harrowing ten minutes unsure if her partner was hurt or not.

Chelsea could still see vague shapes, could differentiate shadow and light, but her rising panic caused her to rush when going down the stairs. She'd missed a step and fallen, and now she was reclining against the wall next to the stairwell as they waited for a doctor. Considering all the calls to 911 and all the sirens filling the air, they both knew Chelsea's ankle was a low priority. It could be hours before anyone showed up. Kenzie was seated beside her, keeping her twisted ankle elevated.

"How does it look?"

"A little swollen. I don't think it's too bad." She looked toward the door, glad that Chelsea wasn't an emergency but still annoyed she was in pain and couldn't get help. "We'll just keep the ice on it until someone shows up."

Chelsea rested her head against the wall. "You don't have to sit here with me. There's nothing you can do, and there are a lot of other people out there who could use your help."

"I don't care about the other people. I only care about you. I'm staying until someone with training shows up to take over for me." Chelsea squeezed Kenzie's hand. "I love you."

"I love you, too."

The front door opened. Before Kenzie could get her hopes up about the ambulance, she recognized Priest's voice. "Kenzie? Chelsea?"

"Over here, Caitlin."

Priest came into the office and crossed to where they were sitting in a single step. She dropped to one knee.

"What happened?"

"I slipped. Fell down the stairs." Priest rested her hand on Chelsea's ankle. "Ah! Oh, that's..." She slowly rotated her foot and smiled. "Oh, that's better..."

Priest smiled. "Angry muscles are easy." She squeezed Chelsea's foot and then stood to help her and Kenzie onto their feet. Chelsea favored her injured side for a moment before she finally put her weight on it.

Kenzie said, "How is everything outside? I saw some heavy damage when I was getting over here."

"It's pretty bad. No Man's Land was hit incredibly hard, as you can probably guess. I'm running around trying to put out the small fires before I focus on the big one."

Chelsea tilted her head to one side. "Big one? Do you know what caused the earthquake?"

"I might. There's a chance it was caused by something Riley did."

"Inadvertently, right?"

Priest hesitated. "No. She just wasn't aware of the far-reaching consequences. She did the right thing, but now there are some very heavy costs."

Kenzie said, "If either you or Riley needs help, call. We're here for you both."

"I know. Thank you." She kissed them both on the cheek. "I have to go. Are you sure you're both all right?"

"Yes, now," Chelsea said. "Thank you again. Come by when this is all settled down and we'll thank you properly."

Priest blushed and averted her gaze. "I would enjoy that. But for now, duty calls."

"See you later, Supergirl." Kenzie nudged her. "Go save the day."

Priest narrowed her gaze. "Shouldn't it be Superwoman?"

"Preaching to the choir, angel."

"Okay. Stay safe." She waved goodbye and left the room by more supernatural means than she'd used to arrive.

A small vestibule separated the mayor's loft from the private elevator. A man in a dark suit occupied a small desk in front of the door and straightened his posture when the bell chimed to announce a new visitor. The doors parted and Marchosias moved forward with purpose. The attendant stood to block his progress but was shoved aside without a glance. He fell over his chair and only hit the ground after the demon was well into the loft.

The spacious living room was to his left, all the furniture situated around the floor-to-ceiling windows. The immaculate kitchen to the right was softly lit and seemed like a museum display rather than a place where meals were actually prepared. Marchosias paused in between the two, listened for a moment, and then continued forward to the bedroom at the back of the space. The double doors were closed but provided no obstacle to him. Both doors slammed against the walls to either side and he stepped into the doorway.

"Lark Siskin."

Her armchair was pulled away from the wall, turned so she could face the bed. She wore a dark gray suit over a black blouse, one leg draped over the other, her hands resting lightly on the arms of the chair. Her ash blonde hair was pinned back and hung in a solid sheet over her shoulders. She didn't turn her head when he spoke her name, but her lips curled into a smile. Whether it was because of his arrival or timed to something that had occurred on the bed, he couldn't tell.

"When you are summoned, you are expected to respond."

"Something came up."

Marchosias looked at the bed and sneered. Lark's twins, Abby and Emily, were currently engaged in a position that seemed like something cut from the Kama Sutra. Their identical faces were locked on Marchosias with a combination of shame, guilt, and embarrassment.

"Oh, relax," Lark sighed. "They're not actually related. They're only twins because I paid for the similarities."

"I'm not here for that. Gillian Hunt."

Lark glanced at him and shrugged before returning her attention to the bed. She casually snapped her fingers. "No one told you to stop." The women on the bed went back to what they had been doing before the interruption. "You told me Dr. Hunt was off-limits. As far as I know she's still alive. Has that changed?"

Marchosias clenched and relaxed his jaw. "I know what you tried to do. Through some miracle you failed, but there must be consequences. You've disobeyed me, and that makes me very unhappy."

Lark rolled her eyes. When she spoke, her voice was carried on an indulgent sigh. "And what exactly are you going to punish me with this time? I am your champion. I have been branded with your sigil and to remove me now would be to announce a forfeit. Do you really want Riley Parra to defeat you *twice*?" She smiled and shrugged. "Do what you wish, and then leave my home. You're interrupting our time together."

Marchosias held his hand out toward the bed. He flicked two fingers and one twin was suddenly tossed toward the headboard. She yelped in surprise as she was dropped onto the pillows, while her partner was yanked from the mattress by an invisible force. Lark rose to her feet, eyes flashing with anger as her girl hit the floor.

"What are you doing?"

The twin was naked and sweaty, her skin flush and her head bowed as Marchosias grabbed a handful of discarded clothes and hurled them at her.

"Punishment, Lark Siskin. I cannot remove you as champion, but your twins are expendable. Since you ensured Detective Parra saw the wound on Abigail's hand, she will be our sacrificial lamb. She will bear the punishment for your crimes." He looked at Emily, who was clutching a pillow to her chest. "Next time I will not be so lenient. Disobey me again and I swear you will know the true extent of my wrath."

Abby looked up at him and then quickly turned her head when Marchosias fixed his gaze on her. "Dress. Now."

Lark stood and glared at him. "You~"

Marchosias stepped around Abby and placed his hand on the side of Lark's head. Her lips widened into a silent O, and her knees buckled.

"You will keep a civil tongue when you speak to me. You are a mortal and I am a demon, and I know ways to tear you apart and rebuild you in a more pleasant image. If you disobey my orders again, I will do it slowly and I will do it with pleasure. Do you understand me, Madam Mayor?"

"Yes."

She collapsed when Marchosias removed his hand. Abby now wore a blouse and her underwear, but Marchosias was done waiting. He grabbed her arm and led her out of the room, partially dragging her out of the loft. The attendant was back on his feet and seemed torn between standing back and trying to stop him. Marchosias made the decision for him; he flicked two fingers and both of the attendant's legs snapped. He fell, howling, as Marchosias shoved Abby into the elevator.

She retreated to the far corner as Marchosias shut the doors. He turned his back to her, unconcerned as she finished dressing with trembling hands.

"Wh-what happens now?"

"Now you are going to tell a little story and end your former employer's ridiculous plan once and for all."

Riley learned a lot of news without asking a single question, absorbing the facts from everyone around her. The earthquake measured 6.7 on the Richter scale. Most of the damage was in the outskirts of the city and, therefore, inside No Man's Land. Half a dozen deaths were already confirmed, while hospitals and free clinics were being overrun with people in various states of distress. The last time she ventured downstairs she saw first aid tents set up in the lobby and out on the sidewalk but she hadn't seen Gillian anywhere.

Riley spent most of the morning staying out of everyone's way and doing whatever was asked of her. It was a strange day of temporary assignments and being quickly trained to fill in for someone who was unavailable. Gillian spent much of her time outside the morgue, doing triage with people hurt in collapses or car accidents. Briggs asked where Priest was soon after Riley's arrival, and Riley simply shrugged and gestured vaguely. "Other business." Briggs nodded her understanding and let the matter drop.

Kenzie and Chelsea arrived a little after noon to offer their services. Briggs welcomed them and, a testament to how bad things were, none of the other detectives took issue with Chelsea temporarily rejoining their ranks.

At a little past one Riley took a five minute break to splash water on her face and get something to eat, then decided to go down to the morgue to see if they needed her for anything. She had just started downstairs when Priest caught up with her.

"There you are. I'm on my way to see if Gillian needs any help." Priest put a hand on Riley's arm. "Wait. There's something you need to know, and it involves the incident you asked me not to reveal."

"Otheriley?"

"Yes." They moved to one side of the stairwell. "I've determined that the epicenter of the earthquake was in the exact center of the city. The shockwave grew more powerful as it spread, which is why the majority of the devastation is in No Man's Land."

Riley said, "The center of the city. The Ladder?"

Priest nodded. "Otheriley didn't give me much to go on when I asked how she came back, but it makes sense. She used the Ladder to take her appeal to the highest court. But accessing a power that large creates ripples. You... she..." Priest grimaced, frustrated at trying to make sense of the situation. "Otheriley couldn't have known what awaited her on the other side."

"It didn't matter to her." Riley shrugged. "Two years without Gillian. Either walking into the Ladder would let her speak to someone with the power to change things, or it would have instantly burnt her to a crisp. After two years, I wouldn't care anymore which one it was."

"Right. How are you coping with the knowledge? It can't be easy."

"That's just it. I feel fine. I'm calm and relaxed, even today of all days. I know how it ends. If anything I'm worried it will make me lazy. Knowing I'll live for another two years might make me take crazy risks."

Priest shook her head. "Don't test the fates. If you get hit by a bus today, you could just linger in a coma until the appointed time. Or you could lose a limb, be rendered brain dead... there are many things worse than death that leave you breathing."

"Point taken. So opening the Ladder caused all of this devastation?"

"Yes... but you can't carry the blame. If~"

"I don't. I'll do what I can to help people, but that's my job. But I won't beat myself up over something that's already happened."

Riley started to walk away but Priest grabbed the lapel of her jacket. "You're concerning me. I tell you that your days are numbered, and you shrug it off. I tell you that the pain and suffering in No Man's Land is due to your actions, and you're unmoved. And in another timeline, this is the morning that you and I broke. She told me that we had become enemies, Riley."

"In another timeline, this is the morning my wife was raped and murdered. But instead she's downstairs, healthy and intact and completely unaware of what we're talking about. That's the only thing I'm thinking about, Caitlin. Gillian is alive because of what I did. That outweighs everything. When the adrenaline wears off, yes, I'll feel sad about the people who are hurt or dying or lost everything. I'll sit in the dark and shudder uncontrollably when I think about how little time is left to do everything I want. But right now I'm going to go kiss my wife and hold her. That's all that matters to me right now. Okay? Can I just have a little time to enjoy the fact that for once, I got the happy ending?"

Priest released Riley's jacket, shame writ across her face. "I'm sorry, Riley."

Riley managed a smile. "It's fine. The benefit of happy-go-lucky me is that I'm not holding a grudge." She kissed Priest's cheek. "You're looking out for me. I appreciate that."

"You're welcome."

"Come on." They started downstairs. "So where have you been all morning?"

Priest sighed. "All over the city. Checking on Kenzie, Chelsea, and Aissa..."

"Kenzie and Chelsea are upstairs... how is Aissa?"

"Her day has been hectic, but she's performing remarkably well. I planned to give her assignments so she didn't feel helpless, but I had to track her down. She commandeered a white van, found medical supplies, and press-ganged a group of medical students to assist her in finding people who needed aid. I've never doubted your choice of successor, Riley, but today especially she has proven herself worthy."

"I'll be sure to mention that next time I see her." Riley's expression darkened slightly and she paused on the last step. "I guess we got lucky that I've already chosen someone to follow in my footsteps."

"We'll need to ensure she's really ready."

Riley nodded. "In good time." She paused outside the morgue doors. "This... Briggs said something happened in here, but someone cleaned up the evidence. You?"

"Yes."

"This is where Gillian was..." She swallowed hard. "And it's where Otheriley..."

A long pause, and then: "Yes."

Riley took a deep breath and exhaled slowly. "Okay." She opened the door and stepped inside. Priest followed a moment later. Gillian was holding court like a general, issuing orders to soldiers in baby blue scrubs. She glanced up when Riley and Priest arrived, offering them a weak smile as she adjusted her horn-rimmed glasses and motioned for them to follow her to her office.

Riley held the door for Priest and then closed it behind her. Gillian stood at the desk and bent down to type something on the computer.

"What happened to your contacts?"

"Hm?"

"You put in your contacts this morning. Why are you wearing glasses?"

Gillian frowned at Riley, then touched her face. "Oh. God. I don't know." She took them off and hooked them on the collar of the gray T-shirt under her scrubs. "I picked them up for something earlier and I never even thought about it."

Riley stepped behind Gillian and began rubbing her shoulders.

"Oh-ho." The tension immediately released its hold on her neck and shoulders. "Please hand in your resignation for the day so you can follow me around all day doing that."

Riley smiled. "I'll give you a quickie now and the real thing when we get home tonight."

"It's a date."

Priest said, "How have things been here?"

"I've been in and out, but we're holding our own. People are understandably anxious about coming to a morgue for medical care, so we've been seeing patients in the garage and outside. And considering the fact I'm a medical examiner, having even one patient get up off the table is a wonderful day."

"But not unprecedented," Riley said.

Gillian smiled and touched Riley's hand. "No, thankfully not unprecedented. It's just so bizarre. I've been asking around and no one remembers an earthquake ever hitting here before. Have you found anything about what caused this?"

Priest said, "Marchosias' new champion attempted to

circumvent the rules of combat. Our side retaliated, and it caused some unforeseen damage. The plan was thwarted and the war will continue as before, but the earthquake was simply..."

Riley offered, "The thunder that happens when a cold front and a warm front slam into each other."

"Ah." Gillian shook her head. "Seems ridiculous that so many people have to suffer to make things right."

"Well..." Riley glanced at Priest and then kissed Gillian behind the ear. "At least you're around to make things righter for whoever you can."

"Righter?"

"More rightly?"

Gillian chuckled and patted Riley's hand. "Thank you."

Riley gave Gillian another squeeze before she let go. "We'll let you get back to saving lives. I'll see you at home."

"You'd better. Bye, Caitlin."

Priest smiled and opened the door so Riley could lead the way out. "Where do you have to go next?"

"I've made the rounds, so I'm free. I'll stay by your side."

"Thanks. Right now I'm just an extra pair of hands wherever someone needs them. I offered to get lunch for Briggs when I had a minute. Want to go with me, see if we can find somewhere that's actually open?"

"Sure."

They arrived in the shantytown of the lobby and started for the door, but they were stopped by the desk sergeant. Riley almost didn't recognize him out from behind his bulwark, and his normally pristine uniform gave away how busy he'd been.

"Detective Parra. I have someone here you need to speak with."

"Can it wait?"

He hesitated. "Maybe. But I don't think you'll want it to."

She nodded and gestured for him to lead the way. The bench where suspects usually sat handcuffed to await processing was empty except for a single person. Her clothes were wrinkled and wrongly-buttoned, her red hair hanging limp and tangled to obscure her face. Her hands were between her knees, shackled by shining handcuffs. The woman sensed their approach and, when she looked up, Riley recognized her as one of the new Mayor's twin aides. She tensed and looked at Priest, who had confirmed the night before that Mayor Siskin was Marchosias' new champion.

The woman's right hand was bandaged, and Riley remembered

the tell-tale wound. "Abby Shepherd. Surprised to see you here."

She tightened her jaw and straightened her shoulders. Riley braced herself for the possibility the woman would try to run, but eventually Abby's shoulders relaxed as if she was suddenly resigned to her capture.

"I want to confess to the murder of Annora Good."

Riley glanced at Priest. "Okay. We'll~"

"And the murder of Wanda Kane. As well as the murder of the previous mayor, Dominic Leary. I killed all three of them."

The confessions stunned Riley so much that she couldn't speak for a moment. "You were a busy girl."

Abby met Riley's eyes. "I killed them."

"Okay." She motioned for the desk sergeant to move forward. "Take her upstairs and put her in an interrogation room. Make sure she's guarded at all times." He made a sound of disbelief but Riley cut him off. "Right. I know. Priest~"

"I won't let her out of my sight."

"Thank you." She leaned forward so that she could look into the redhead's eyes. "Why are you taking the fall? Yeah, I believe you killed Annora, and for that you're going to jail for a very long time. But the mayor and Wanda? What's your angle?"

Abby pressed her lips tightly together like a petulant child refusing her vegetables, so Riley straightened and motioned for Priest to take her away. She took her wallet out and handed money to the sergeant. "Find someplace that has lunch. Lieutenant Briggs hasn't eaten all day; a hamburger, a fish sandwich, a damn hot dog, whatever you can find."

He nodded and headed out on his mission. Riley looked around the lobby to see if there was anything she could do, and then she headed upstairs.

Twenty minutes later, Lieutenant Briggs was already halfway through the chicken sandwich the desk sergeant had delivered to her. She used the wrapper to keep her fingers clean, holding the sandwich in one hand as she rested the other on her hip. She was with Priest and Riley in the observation room, where a bank of cameras showed Abigail Marlene Shepherd from four different angles. Her cuffed hands were resting on the table in front of her, her eyes locked on the wall directly ahead. If not for the gentle rise and fall of her shoulders with every breath it could have been mistaken for a photograph.

Her fingerprints had returned a criminal record, which provided them with her full name and a photo of someone who bore very little resemblance to the woman currently waiting in the small interrogation room. Riley looked from the print-out to the screen like she was playing the easiest game of "spot the differences." Dark brown hair, a wider nose, brown eyes, rounder cheeks, plumper lips...

"I wonder if they made her look like the other one," Briggs said, "or if they both just got adjusted until they looked the same."

Riley said, "I'll add it to the list of things I want to ask when I get in there."

Briggs looked at her. "Did you speak with Harding? What are the odds she's telling the truth about doing all three murders? I mean look at her. I'll buy that she surprised a Good Girl and got the drop on Wanda. But the mayor was a big guy."

Riley shrugged. "Big guys have the same weakness as little guys. And she is attractive. All she had to do was get him to drop his guard." She shook her head. "But I don't see it. Wanda was killed right around the same time Annora died. She would have had to fire the gun, slip out of the club without being seen, race across No Man's Land and find a Good Girl to attack."

"The last part wouldn't be that difficult," Priest said. "Until Annora was killed, it was impossible to go three blocks without seeing two of them."

Briggs said, "What about the slaughter at the club? Is she confessing to those, too?"

"She didn't mention it. That'll be the first thing I ask." She stepped around Briggs and motioned for Priest to stay behind. She picked up Shepherd's file and carried it with her to the interrogation room.

Abby looked at her as she entered but made no other indication of awareness. Riley dropped the file on the table, turning it so Abby could look at the picture as she sat down.

"How many surgeries did that take? Ballpark. Had to be a really long recovery time." She affected a casual pose. "I'm not saying it was a waste of time. You're much prettier now than you were then. No offense." She smiled. "But that's a lot of dedication. If you're willing to do that to yourself for someone, I can't imagine what else you would do. All they have to do is ask, and you'll jump. So, Abigail. Who told you to take the fall for these murders?"

"No one. I killed those people."

Riley raised an eyebrow. "Really." She turned the file back around. "Aggravated assault, drug charges, domestic violence, theft, grand theft, breaking and entering... I admit you were a bad girl. But there's bad girls, and then there's mass murderers." She looked at Abby's hands. "How's the cut on your palm? Happened cutting a bagel, right?"

"No. That was a lie. I cut it when I shoved the knife into the Good Girl's stomach."

Riley's stoicism wavered. "Her name was Annora."

Abby shrugged. "I don't care. All that matters was the robe. I was told to kill a Good Girl, so I did."

"Right. And who told you to do that?"

Abby lifted her chin, defiant. "Gail."

Riley's mind tossed up an image of Gail Finney's face, throwing her. "Gail? Who is Gail?"

Abby moved both her cuffed hands and tapped a finger on the picture. "That's Gail. The girl I destroyed. But she didn't stay gone. She's still in here. And she's mad, Detective. She's mad that I buried her alive. So she makes me do things. She makes me do bad things all the time. She made me seduce the mayor and then do those awful things to his body. Then she told me to kill that police woman. I tried to run away, but she saw a Good Girl. And I killed her, too."

"You just happened to have a gun and a knife on you at the same time?"

"I also had a garrote. Gail regrets that I didn't have the occasion to use it. Once I stabbed the Good Girl to death, she was appeased. I went home and went to bed."

"What about the people in the club? How did they all die?"

Abby shrugged. "Gail has friends."

"What does that mean?"

"Demons, Detective Parra. Hellspawn. When Gail killed the police officer, they were unleashed into the club. Why shouldn't they have their fun?"

Riley said, "Who helped you transport the mayor's body?"

"No one."

"You're tougher than you look."

Abby leaned forward, smiling. "Want to see how tough I am?"

"No thanks. What about the mayor's head and hands? Where did you put those?"

"Ashes. Have you ever watched the face of someone you know

burning? Have you ever seen a person you knew very well turned into a thing, and then just watched them melt? It awakens you. It shows you that we're all just things, inanimate husks moving through this world. We were awoken by some cruel joke and, eventually, we return to being things."

She glanced toward the camera and smiled before meeting Riley's eye again.

"How is your wife?"

Riley returned the stare, holding her best poker face. "She's well. A little tired. It's been a busy day around here."

"Hm." Abby made it sound like a quiet laugh and then looked down at her hands. "I would like to go to my jail cell now. I had a very busy evening and I would like to sleep. Do you have everything you need?"

There was a knock at the door. "Sit tight." Riley ignored Abby's put-upon sigh as she left the room.

Detective Benjamin Harding was waiting outside for her. "Heard you got someone in my case."

"We have someone who confessed."

"About five-eight, redhead, gorgeous?"

Riley frowned. "Yeah. How'd you know that?"

"I found a witness. Claims the late mayor was carrying on an affair with someone matching that description. Driver said he dropped the mystery lady off at the mayor's place night he went missing. He figured it was a little pick-me-up after the house arrest. If she confessed, I'm inclined to believe she did it."

"Anything to close the case, huh?" She stepped to one side and pointed at the one-way glass in the window. "Can you picture a woman that size cutting off Dominic Leary's head and hands, then dragging his body to a vehicle to dump it? Doing all of that without leaving a trace of evidence?"

"You hear about women lifting cars to save a baby. Maybe it goes the other way, too. Women get really strong to pull off bad stuff."

Riley rolled her eyes. "Wow. Of all the times for you to support the idea women can be as strong as a man..."

"Equality, Detective Parra. Gotta take the good with the bad, right? It ain't all equal pay and voting rights." He pointed at the window. "We have a confession and we have a witness that puts her in the right place at the right time. Briggs told me she has a cut on her hand that corresponds to the wounds on Annora Good. I get the feeling when you finally get off your ass and do a little police work, you'll find security cameras that put her at Speakeasy around the time Wanda got killed."

"Why? Did you plant them?"

Harding smirked and walked past her. "Watch it, Detective Parra. You just closed three big cases without doing any work. Play this right and you can keep on coasting without ever straining yourself."

Riley resisted the urge to tackle him, settling for an ugly look at the back of his head. Briggs came out of the observation room, watched Harding disappear around the corner, then approached Riley.

"What do you think?"

Riley sighed. "I hate it. But I think Marchosias is going to a lot of trouble to make sure this is the only conclusion we can reach. If we keep investigating he's just going to route us back to Abby. Harding found a witness in the mayor's murder, and he's right... Abby *did* kill Annora. I'm sure of that. So Gillian is going to match the wound on her hand to the same knife that was used on the girl. The DA will be thrilled to have such an open-and-shut case."

Briggs nodded. "And with the earthquake, we're stretched thin as it is."

Priest was watching Riley. "Are you okay?"

Riley looked back at the glass, watching Abby as she calmly waited for the next visitor. "We'll get justice for Annora Good now, and we'll have to settle for getting Wanda justice later. As much as I hate it, and as bad a taste as it leaves in my mouth, I think we have to take what we can get."

"I concur," Briggs said. "It's nowhere near ideal, but it's the best we can hope for. I'll find someone to take her down to holding."

Priest joined Riley at the door after Briggs was gone. "You're certain she killed Annora?"

"That, I actually am certain of."

"Then I'll find Aissa. I'll let her give the news to Cerys."

Riley nodded. Priest started to turn away, but Riley stopped her. "You did well today. Really well. You made me proud, Cait."

"Thank you." She smiled shyly, then followed Briggs down the hall.

When Riley looked back at the glass, Abby had turned her head to look at her. The woman smiled and Riley held eye contact even though she knew Abby couldn't actually see her.

The apartment doors were standing open, too damaged to fully close. The attendant escorted Riley inside and then returned to his desk. The sun was setting, casting golden light across the polished surfaces so that it looked as if the room was glowing. Riley took a moment to examine the furnishings before she focused on the woman standing a few feet away.

Mayor Lark Siskin was standing at the windows with her back to the room, dressed in silk that looked like liquid onyx. Her hair was down, looking even whiter than usual against the black of her clothes. She sipped her drink before she spoke.

"This is not exactly the view I expected to have. Such devastation. People are hurting so badly right now." She turned to face Riley. "It's so refreshing to know we have someone like you on the side of the angels, working to make amends. Very heartening."

"Your aide is in jail. She confessed to three murders, including the murder of your predecessor."

Lark pursed her lips. "My, my. You cut right to the marrow, don't you, Detective? May I offer you a drink?"

"No. Did you put Abby up to it?"

"To what? Murder or confessing to it?" She waved her hand dismissively. "Never mind. The answer to both is no. I first heard of her deeds when she revealed she was going to confess. Terrible business. We'd been concerned about her mental health for some time."

"We?"

"Me and her fellow aide, Emily Simon."

Riley nodded. "Right. Well, you give someone thousands of dollars' worth of plastic surgery so she'll be identical to her coworker... it's bound to give anyone problems."

Lark smiled. "I merely paid for the operations. Abigail and Emily wanted the operations before they met me. I simply provided the means, and they are working off their debt to me. Abby seemed to underestimate the mental strain that went along with losing the face she was born with. She invented an entirely new personality for the woman she had once been. Named her Gail... I thought it was merely a coping mechanism. I wish I had seen the signs."

Riley stepped further into the room. "Why are we doing this?"

"Doing what, Detective?"

"Pretending like you're the mayor and I'm just a cop. We both know what this is, so stop playing games."

Lark put down her glass. "I don't play games, Detective. I wage wars."

"Looks like you just lost one of your soldiers. Abby is going to prison for the crime she did commit. I have a feeling she really did play a part in the mayor's murder. Wanda, though... I assume Emily was the trigger woman there. I can't prove that, of course, and with everything that's going on, no one is going to let me pursue an investigation to prove the murder was actually committed by her identical twin."

"You seem to think Abby's confession was part of my plan. It wasn't." She faced Riley fully. "Abby was coerced into confessing by Marchosias as punishment for my true plan. I arranged for your wife to be murdered. I don't know how or why it was thwarted, and I won't risk another punishment by trying again. So you can rest assured she's safe for the time being. But this was just the opening gambit, Detective Parra. I'm making my presence known. You should be prepared to face a true adversary."

"Oh, I'm ready. You went after my wife, Lark. You intended for her to die in an agonizing manner to send a message to me? Well, I got the message. I'm not going to back down. I'm not going to cower in fear. No games. No taunting. The gauntlet is down. Just remember that I already won this war once."

"A war you've been waging for four years now. You're the weary veteran and I'm a new recruit."

"I'm not going easy just because you're a rookie."

Lark smirked. "I will remember that when you're pleading for mercy."

Riley turned and walked back toward the door. "Make sure your next scheme gets approval before you put it in action. I'd hate for your demon-daddy to be forced to give you another spanking."

Lark laughed, but her smile faded as soon as she heard the elevator doors close. Emily came out of the bedroom where she had been listening. Her hair was wet from the shower, her face devoid of makeup. She wore a black robe, suitable for mourning her loss, and curled her bare toes in the carpet.

"What are we going to do now?"

Lark seemed to ignore the question, staring at her wet bar before pouring herself a new drink. She took it in a single draught, smacking her lips together when it was gone. Still holding the empty snifter she turned and stared out the window at the sun setting over the devastated city.

"Now we move on to the next engagement. Our war has been declared. The time has come to begin claiming ground."

Riley was finally finished with paperwork and processing at ten, having been called away to other emergencies no fewer than five times in the course of her work. The initial panic after the earthquake was fading. People were still being rescued and dust was still settling, but the infrastructure was intact. Like bees in a hive that had been kicked, the initial burst of blind scrambling had been replaced by an orderly response. Downstairs the injured that could be moved were being transferred to hospitals that had found space for them.

Riley went down to find Gillian leaning against a wall, too exhausted to even search for somewhere to sit. Without saying a word Riley slipped under Gillian's arm and took her weight, walking her to the garage and placing her in the passenger seat. Gillian melted into the seat, already drifting off as Riley pulled out of the crowded garage.

"Food?" Riley asked.

"Later."

She had to agree with that. She was hungry, but sleep was a more pressing concern.

By the time they arrived home, Gillian had found enough energy reserves to get upstairs under her own power. Riley climbed up behind her, one hand on Gillian's hip to keep her steady. Gillian toed off her shoes in the doorway of the apartment, sighing with relief as she wiggled her toes in their socks. Riley nudged the shoes out of the way and escorted Gillian down the hall to their bedroom.

They didn't turn on any lights, giving up on undressing halfway through the process. Gillian stretched out in her scrub top and panties, hands on her stomach as Riley settled in next to her in jeans and an undershirt.

"Busy day," Gillian said.

"Tomorrow's probably going to be bad, too."

"Not just tomorrow." She sighed heavily. "We'll make it, though." She reached out and found Riley's hand. She brought it to her lips and kissed the knuckles. "You were different today."

"I'm not used to doing damage control."

"No, I mean..." She smacked her lips, eyes still shut. "You seemed calmer. More relaxed. You were like one of those soldiers who kept their cool when everyone around you was losing their heads. It kept me calm, knowing you were there. Like an eye in the storm." She smiled sleepily. "You keep me grounded, Riley. I don't know what I'd do without you."

Riley's heart seized and she forced herself not to clutch at it. "I'm not going anywhere, sweetheart."

Not yet, anyway.

"I think..." Gillian's voice was drifting, a mere echo of its former self. "I think I'm going to try to get some sleep."

"Okay." Riley turned her head and kissed Gillian's cheek. "You've earned a little rest. I'll be right here when you wake up."

Gillian smiled. "Good..."

Soon Gillian's breathing became steady and even, and Riley watched her sleep. At some point, when Riley's eyelids drifted down, they remained down and she joined her wife in slumber.

WRESTLING WITH ANGELS

IN THE back of her mind, the voice that was never quiet often chided her for what it called "bad habits." She picked them up even before her brief sabbatical as a mortal; the charade of sleeping every night, of eating and drinking twice a day, bathing and laundering her clothing. None of it was necessary once she was reunited with Zerachiel's divinity but Caitlin Priest appreciated the routine. She even had a theory that bathing was less about cleanliness and more about taking a respite and clearing her mind at the end of a long day.

She stood under the spray, letting it plaster her hair against her skull as she contemplated her hands. Her fingers were long and slender, the nails pink with just the right amount of distal edge extending from the cuticle. She cupped her hands under the water and watched as it pooled, crystal clear and cold as it traced the lines of her palms. She splashed her face and then dragged her hands down to her breasts, over her stomach, and between her legs.

Priest put off sexual gratification - another affectation left over from her time as a mortal - and finished bathing. She soaped her arms and hands once more before she turned off the faucets and stepped out of the stall. She toweled herself off and wrapped the towel around her neck. She had cut her hair short a year earlier, a hack job with her sword that had been smoothed out by Gillian Hunt's scissors, and she had grown accustomed to it. She looked at her reflection in the mirror, turning her head one way and then the other to admire how it fell over her ears. She didn't need to maintain the hairstyle, she just had to decide that it was the proper length and it wouldn't grow any further.

She wanted to get a haircut. She wanted to fumble with fingernail clippers to trim her nails to the right length. She wanted hangnails. She leaned forward, her pubic bone pressed against the edge of the sink as she examined her reflection up close. She was human, down to the veins and capillaries and the small cells making up the blood that ran through them. But she was also more.

With a sigh she left the bedroom. Her sleepwear was a simple pair of cotton trousers and a white V-neck shirt. She walked barefoot to the window and rested her palm against the glass. She closed her eyes and knew Riley's exact location. It wasn't information she ever had to seek; she always felt Riley's presence like a quiet and unobtrusive hum in her consciousness. When it changed, even a fraction, she felt it like a jolt.

Currently, Riley was asleep but agitated. No... not agitated, but she was active. She felt the world shift around her and opened her eyes to see Riley and Gillian's bedroom. She was standing at the foot of their marriage bed; Riley had migrated toward the other side of the bed and Gillian had twisted to face her. Both were still fast asleep, but they had reached out for one another in the night. Riley's legs were wrapped around Gillian, gently thrusting against the curve of Gillian's hip.

Priest departed before her presence could disturb them, feeling like a voyeur as she moved to another familiar site. In sleep, Kenzie Crowe's hair had fallen away from the burns that she believed marred her features. She was curled on her side, knees drawn to her chest, one hand under the pillow. Beside her, Chelsea was sitting up and reading. Her right hand skimmed the Braille on the pages as her left hand idly stroked her partner's hair. She paused in both and lifted her gaze to where Priest was standing.

"Caitlin..."

"Sh. I was just checking in."

Chelsea smiled and spoke in a low voice. "We're fine. You're welcome to stay the night if you want."

"Thank you. But I think I will let you both get your rest." She bent down and kissed Chelsea's lips, then kissed the corner of Kenzie's mouth. "You have both earned it. Pleasant dreams. I'm sorry for disturbing you."

"You're always welcome in this home, Caitlin."

Priest smiled and touched Kenzie's cheek soft enough that she wouldn't be disturbed. She wished Chelsea a pleasant evening and then returned to her own home.

She went to the bed and drew back the blankets. As much a ritual as bathing, Priest had come to appreciate the joy of preparing for bed and resting her mind. She smoothed the blankets over her legs and folded her hands on her stomach. It was a form of meditation and drew the line firmly between one day and the next. She remembered her first days as a mortal and the utter exhaustion that had overtaken her when she went a mere thirty hours without sleep. Now even when it wasn't necessary, taking to her bed at least once a day made her mind sharper and made her feel as energized as attending a prayer meeting.

As she drifted off, she felt Zerachiel's presence looming to fill the unconsciousness with her own mind. Zerachiel always came to the forefront when Priest slept.

The angel was never far away.

Priest liked suits. She understood the appeal of comfortable clothing, and she wore loose-fitting cotton when she wanted to relax, but her preferred work garments were three-piece suits. During her first year on the mortal coil Zerachiel had simply manifested the suits, but Priest eventually started to buy the real thing. She liked the feel of them, savoring the smell that filled the closet when they hung together as she ran her fingers along the sleeves.

Today she wore a light gray suit over a robin's-egg blue Oxford shirt. Since Riley had forbidden her from driving until she passed the test, Priest walked to Riley's apartment and accepted Gillian's invitation for breakfast. The earthquake still dominated the news; the situation had progressed to rebuilding and recovery but there was still much to be done. The Red Cross had set up safe places every few blocks, taken the place of the ever-present Good Girls who seemed to have vanished from the city overnight.

When she finished her breakfast - which she only ate to be polite to the effort Gillian put into cooking it - she stood and preceded Riley to the door so the couple could have a private moment to say goodbye.

Priest waited until they were in the car to speak again. "How was your evening?"

"Fine. Jill rented a movie."

"Have you told her...?"

"No." Riley cleared her throat, uncomfortable with the topic. Priest watched her hand flex on the steering wheel. "When is a good time to tell her? Right before I head off to work? After we have sex? Should I just leave her a memo on the fridge door?"

Priest pressed her lips together. "Of course not. But she has to be told eventually, Riley."

"I know. I'll tell her. I just want~"

"Normal. Right."

Riley nodded.

They were still only a few blocks from Riley's apartment when Riley's phone rang. She transferred it from her pocket to a dashboard dock and turned it on speaker.

"This is Parra."

A dispatcher responded, her voice tinny and mechanical over the radio speakers. "Detective, we have a report of shots fired near your home address." She gave an address Priest recognized as an apartment building she had walked past on her way to Riley's. "Any chance you could swing by and take a look?"

"Yeah. Priest is with me and we were about to head out anyway. We'll check it out." She disconnected the call and shook her head. "The downside of being a famous detective."

Priest smiled and braced herself as Riley executed a quick turn and sped to the north instead of east. They passed Gillian driving the opposite direction, and Priest saw her twist to watch them before returning her attention to the road. Priest pulled out her cell phone and sent a text to explain to her what was happening so Riley could focus on driving.

"Thanks," Riley said.

"It's what I'm here for." She reached into the backseat and retrieved their bulletproof vests. She only wore hers for show, and because every time she put it on made Riley pause long enough to put hers on as well. Riley parked, the vest hanging unsecured off her shoulders as she rounded the front of the car. She tilted her head back to look at the building as she secured the Velcro straps and took her gun from the holster.

"Be careful, Riley."

"I'm always careful."

"Yes. But this is the first time we've encountered a dangerous situation since you acquired your... deadline. I don't want you to feel you're invincible simply because you know when you're supposed to die. You could still be paralyzed by a bullet to the spine. Don't think you're invincible."

Riley nodded. "Noted. Are you ready?"

Priest gestured for her to lead the way. The lobby had exterior doors at the front and back, both currently standing open to create a cross-breeze. The call had come from Apartment 2-B, so Riley moved to the left and looked up the stairs. One of the ground floor apartments opened and a shaggy young man stuck his head out. Priest motioned for him to go back inside, and he retreated as he pointed toward the back door.

"About two minutes ago."

Priest looked at the door, then nodded her thanks. Riley gestured for Priest to check it out as she started up the stairs. Priest crossed the warped tile of the lobby and stepped outside, looking first to the right and then over her shoulder to the left. Both directions had narrow and dark walkways that led back out to the parking lot. Straight ahead was courtyard that contained a swimming pool that was gated shut until summer.

She assumed that someone fleeing would continue straight out of panic, even if that path would take them into an enclosed area. She entered the courtyard cautiously, sweeping her weapon one way and then the other to make sure the shooter wasn't hiding in a corner.

"This is the police," she said. "Show yourself."

She was near the swimming pool when she heard sounds of movement coming from the other side of the fence. An ancient patio chair had been pulled close, and she saw a pristine shoe imprint in the grime that covered the plastic seat. To preserve the evidence, Priest crouched and gently propelled herself into the air, hovering just high enough to step off the top of the fence. She landed on the other side, just ahead of a pile of dead leaves.

Before she could even examine the area, a man in low-riding jeans and a hoodie came out from behind the small wooden lifeguard perch and raced toward the opposite fence.

"Police!"

He twisted and swung his right arm up across his body. Priest saw the gun and simply reacted, raising her gun as well.

Priest pulled the trigger.

The man's shoulder jerked backward and his knees buckled, his aim wavering as he fell back toward the fence.

She didn't know how much time passed before she heard Riley calling her. She snapped out of her fugue and stepped back, then ran around the empty pool.

"I'm in here, Riley!"

She knelt beside the man. He'd dropped his gun, his hands resting palm-up on the dirty pavement. He was trembling, his shirt soaking through with blood. Priest heard Riley scrambling over the fence but couldn't take her eyes off the suspect. His eyes were wide and frightened, his bottom lip trembling as if he was trying to speak. She rested her hand on the wound, applying pressure as she tried to undo what she had done. Nothing happened, and she cried out in frustration as the blood continued to pool around her fingers.

"I am sorry. I am so sorry." She heard Riley landing on the concrete behind her. "We need an ambulance."

Riley was a few feet away, making the call, but Priest kept her gaze locked with the man she had just shot.

She was still looking into his eyes when he died, the ambulance sirens echoing off the brick walls of the building.

The room was bland, gray, cold. Priest sat on the wrong side of the table, the side normally reserved for criminals, and tried to figure out what to do with her hands. She finally pressed them together and bowed her head in prayer for the soul of the man she had shot. The door opened and she raised her head to see a man in a rumpled suit carrying two cups with one hand, the other hand lugging a pitcher of water.

"Hi. Sorry. Hope you haven't been waiting long." He kicked the door closed and put his load down on the table. "Would you like some water? Fresh and ice-cold."

"No. Thank you."

"Well, it's there if you want it." He sat down and pulled a small device from the inside pocket of his coat. "I love these things. Used to be we had to haul around big manila file folders and flip through the pages. Now I just have to jab the screen and scroll around to find what I want. It's amazing, don't you think?"

"I don't know."

He met her eye and took sympathy. "Don't worry. This isn't a game of good cop, bad cop. I'm not trying to be your friend just so you'll give yourself up. We're not looking to get you on anything. We know what happened, and we understand."

"I killed a man."

He nodded. "Yes. You did." His chubby finger scrolled a bit on the screen. "You killed a man named Jeremy Howard. He lived with his grandfather, who was eighty-seven years old this morning when Jeremy decided he'd lived long enough. So he tried to strangle the old man in his sleep. Turns out, Grandpa was a veteran. You know what they say about soldiers. They don't die, they just fade away. Well, Gramps wasn't faded yet. He fought off the kid and tried to call 911. That's when ol' Jeremy pulled out a gun and just shot the old man."

Priest remained frozen during the story, staring at her hands.

"Jeremy had a criminal record. He had a history of beating on his girlfriends and getting them to recant when the cops showed up. He did drugs. He couldn't hold down a job."

"So he deserved to die?" Priest's voice was hoarse.

The man closed the file and put his device down on the table. "No one deserves to die, Zerachiel. They all die anyway, and nothing can be done about that. Jeremy Howard was a bad young man. He should have died a long time ago, but he's a rare case in which the person goes on living after their soul withers. It was a diseased husk inside of him and it made him a dangerous, angry person. No one deserves to die, but if someone was due to die this morning then Jeremy Howard was the best choice."

"I didn't have to pull the trigger. If he had shot me, it would have hit the vest. Or even if it didn't, I could still have survived. I didn't have to pull the trigger..."

"No, you didn't. You could have let him shoot you and then arrested him. When he was eventually released back into the wild, he would have been a much worse creature. You did the world a favor by removing him from it. I know that you can't see it right now, Zerachiel, but you did not commit a crime today."

"I must be held responsible."

"Not by us." He slipped the device back into his pocket as he stood. "Feel free to partake of the water before you return. It really is quite good."

Priest waited for him to go and then closed her eyes. The temperature dropped as the air in the room changed. The dim glow of artificial light transformed into the warmth of natural sun. She blinked her eyes back into focus and found herself sitting in the backseat of a squad car, turned so her feet could rest on the pavement. Riley was standing a few yards away talking to an officer.

"Riley."

She turned and excused herself from the conversation. "Cait. You okay? You looked like you'd gone away for a while there."

"I did. They took my gun. That's normal, right?"

"Yeah. There's going to be an investigation, but it's not going to last very long. You'll get your gun back once they verify the shooting was justified. And they definitely will. We have the grandfather's testimony that the kid tried to kill him."

Priest blinked. "The grandfather is alive?"

"The bullet just grazed his arm. I found him in the bathroom dressing it himself." She glanced over her shoulder and then crouched. "Are you sure you're okay?"

"I don't know. Zerachiel spoke with someone and they agree that it was the proper course of events. Every death is a tragedy, but Jeremy Howard's death was an acceptable loss. I'm not sure I understand that. I don't understand why my hand was the one that pulled the trigger. I killed him, Riley. Ended his life. How can I live with that?"

Riley squeezed Priest's hand. "You just... do." She winced and wet her lips. "Wow, sorry. That sucked. I'm sorry, Caitlin, I'm not good at this sort of thing. First time I shot at someone, I got lucky. He was charging at me with a knife, completely insane on PCP, and I knew that short of getting back in my car and running him down I was going to be killed. So I pulled the trigger. In a situation like that, you don't doubt whether or not it was the right thing. It was him or me."

"But that's not what happened to me, Riley. If he had shot me, I would have gotten right back up. Actually, no. It might not even have phased me. I didn't have to pull the trigger. I didn't have to kill him and he didn't have to die."

Riley tried to think of the right words, but they wouldn't come. So instead she put her hand on Priest's shoulder, squeezed it, and crouched in front of her to wait until someone came to tell them they could leave.

Briggs debriefed them both in her office, getting Riley's report before listening to Priest's. Once she was finished Briggs nodded. "Okay. We'll have to find a way to fudge your aerial acrobatics a little, but it's not as bad as I thought. You identified yourself, you gave him a chance to surrender peacefully, and you only fired when he brought his weapon up. Internal Affairs isn't going to find anything to make them antsy."

"But I wasn't in fear for my life. The self-defense claim is flawed."

Riley closed her eyes and leaned forward. "You want to play what-if? What if you'd just let him shoot you? I've seen you get shot before, Priest. It might not kill you or cause permanent damage, but it knocks you down. Angel or not, you would have been off your feet. Jeremy would have taken that opportunity to get away from you. If he could have gotten to the parking lot or the street, you think the guy who had just tried to kill his grandfather and a cop would hesitate to shoot some woman going out for groceries so he could use her car to get away?"

"She's right," Briggs said. "We're just providing the cleanest version of events to keep anyone from looking too closely at this incident. If a different pair of cops had responded to the call, the situation could only have ended worse. It's due to your angelic nature that you got into the gated area so quickly. Anyone else would have been forced to search for an entrance. Jeremy could have taken that time to escape. Don't spend too much time flagellating yourself for this, Caitlin. There isn't a way this could have gone better, and that is on Jeremy Howard's conscience. Not yours."

Priest nodded hesitantly.

"Good. Now go home. You're not suspended, but you won't do yourself any good sitting at your desk doing paperwork. Relax."

"I'm not sure how I'm supposed to relax."

Riley said, "You'll think of a way. There has to be a church in session somewhere. Go top yourself off with some prayer." She patted Priest's arm. "If it's any consolation, I wish I'd let you go upstairs while I went after the shooter."

Priest smiled. "Thank you, Riley. I think I'll take the suggestion and take some time."

"Leave your phone on. IA may want to speak with you, but this should be cleared up very quickly."

"Yes, ma'am."

Riley followed Priest out of the office. "Want me to drive you home?"

"No. Thank you. I prefer walking. Besides, there's a stop I have to make first. I apologize for leaving you without a partner."

"It's fine. You just hold me back." She winked and patted Priest's shoulder. "Go on. I'll call you later on to see how you're doing."

Priest nodded her thanks and went downstairs to the morgue. She paused at the door without announcing herself, watching as Gillian performed an autopsy. Her back was to the door and she was dressed in scrubs, her hair bound underneath a loose cap. The overhead lights reflected off the plastic visor she wore and obscured her features from view. Priest was accustomed to seeing Gillian with Riley, rarely on her own, so she savored the moment.

Gillian glanced over when she finally approached, pausing in her examination. "Caitlin. I heard about what happened. Are you all right?"

Priest opened her mouth to respond and surprised herself by sobbing. Gillian quickly put aside her instruments, called over another doctor to take over for her, and quickly stripped off her gloves and apron. She put a hand on Priest's arm to guide her into the office. She shut the door and let her take the chair while she crouched in front of it.

"I'm sorry." Priest wiped her cheeks. "I seem to be feeling particularly mortal this morning. Zerachiel doesn't know how to deal with what happened this morning so she seems to have just retreated to hibernation."

"It was a traumatic experience. I'd be worried if you didn't have some kind of emotional breakdown. Is there anything I can do?"

Priest shook her head. "No. I want help, but I don't know that anyone could do anything to make this better." She swallowed hard and looked toward the window between Gillian's office and the morgue. "Everyone keeps telling me that Jeremy Howard deserved to die."

"That's not true. No one deserves to die, and no one is beyond redemption." Priest was startled at how closely Gillian echoed the angelic representative's words. ÒBut from what I've heard, I think that Jeremy was in a spiral this morning. He wouldn't have listened to reason and he couldn't have been eased off the path he'd already started down. He needed to be stopped before he caused damage that couldn't be undone."

"But why did it have to be me?" Tears rolled down Priest's cheeks again.

Gillian reached for a Kleenex and dabbed the moisture away. "I don't know. But maybe..." She thought for a moment. "Riley said that he tried to kill his grandfather this morning. It seems to me that should be indicative of his family situation. Maybe Jeremy Howard was destined to die this morning, maybe some grand scheme said that this was the last day he would be alive. And if he was estranged from his friends and family, if he was all alone in the world, then maybe you were put in that place so he would be treated with compassion in his final moments and only an angel could have provided him with that solace. Maybe involving you was a kindness."

Priest blinked rapidly. "Do you think that's possible?"

Gillian smiled. "I know it is. Jeremy Howard burned all of his bridges and destroyed any goodwill his loved ones might have had for him. Your paths crossed, and the last face he saw was compassionate and loving. He saw someone who truly cared about him in the last moments of his life. I don't know if that made a difference or not, but I know it had a better chance of saving him than anything else. You weren't put there to end his life, Caitlin. That would have happened regardless. You were put there so that he would see someone cared about him."

"Thank you."

Gillian nodded. "Of course. If you want to stay in here for a while, you can crash on the couch and I'll put out a Do Not Disturb note. You may not be mortal anymore, but today you're more Caitlin than Zerachiel."

"I think I'll take you up on that."

Gillian smiled and stood up, offering a hand to pull Priest out of the chair. She took a blanket out of the bottom drawer of her file cabinet. "Don't tell anyone I have this stashed here." She winked and spread it over Priest's lower body, tucking her in.

"May I ask you something?"

"Of course," Gillian said.

"You spoke of Jeremy being destined to die, that a grand scheme was at play. Did Riley talk to you?"

Gillian frowned, confused. "About what?"

"Nothing. Never mind. It was just a discussion we were having recently."

"Okay. Try to rest. I'll check on you in an hour." She kissed Priest's forehead. "You gave him peace, Caitlin, whether he wanted or deserved it. Now you need to take some of that peace for yourself."

Priest smiled. "I'll do my best. Thank you, Gillian."

"Of course. Rest well."

She turned off the lights as she left the office. Priest settled onto the couch, light coming in through the blinds in thin slats. She didn't know if she would be capable of sleep and didn't even really feel like trying, but before much time had passed she found her mind drifting and soon she was fast asleep.

"I know it's not much. The wiring is bad and there's some kind of mold growing in the bathroom." The man trudging up the stairs ahead of her recited the litany of demerits with the resignation of someone who was being forced to speak against his will. Most likely the building managers had forced him to disclose any problems to all potential tenants to protect them from a lawsuit. Zerachiel was uninterested but, for the purposes of her subterfuge, she simply nodded as she followed him to the landing.

"I'm certain it will be fine."

The super unlocked the door and shoved against the protesting hinges. He sighed heavily as he walked into a living room musty with the scent of abandonment. The ad indicated the apartment would be furnished, but the couch and chair were only present because the previous owners couldn't be bothered to drag them curbside.

"Oh. And sometimes you get bleed-through from the church downstairs. Music and hall-yay-you-juhs, that sort of thing. Usually you can ask 'em to keep it down or put on headphones until the service is over."

Zerachiel nodded absently. *"I'm sure I won't be bothered."* She went to the kitchen to give it a cursory examination. Crossing the windows to see the view, she tried to think of what other things mortals would concern themselves with when buying a new home.

"So what do you do?"

The angel turned. *"Do?"*

"For a living. Job, work... you know. Income."

"I'm a police officer."

His eyebrows rose. *"Really. No offense, but you may want to keep that information from some of your neighbors."*

Zerachiel walked toward the bedroom and looked inside. *"Why? Police officers enforce the peace and protect the innocent."*

"People around here aren't exactly innocent. Just... you know, don't make a lot of noise and no one will bother you too much."

"Thank you." She turned to face him again. *"This will be suitable."*

He slapped the fist of one hand against the palm of the other and snapped his fingers. *"Well, all right. Just have a few papers for you to sign and this little slice of the world will be all yours. Well, for three years anyway. That's, uh, standard lease length."* He kept his eyes on her as he turned, waiting to see if she protested the terms. She remained silent so he nodded once and pointed back to the stairs. *"I'll go get the forms. You keep getting acquainted with your new home."*

Once he was gone, Zerachiel walked to the window and looked out again. It was odd to be mortal. It was odd to be female, to be breathing and standing and speaking. But Riley Parra was facing a tremendous trial, and she required someone physical to lean on. For her sake, Zerachiel was willing to make the sacrifice of self. Pride was a sin, after all, as was vanity. She would do whatever was necessary to serve her charge.

She rested her palm against the glass and felt the outside temperature. It was cool, and the air was humid after the brief thundershower that followed Samael's death. Her clothes felt unusual on her skin. She rolled her shoulders and looked at the buildings across the street.

"Officer Priest?"

She hesitated before she turned; she would have to get better at responding to the name. "Actually it's Detective Priest."

"Oh. Sorry about that." He held up a thin sheaf of papers. "Got your lease."

"Excellent."

She joined him at the counter and took his pen. She signed her name for the first time, watching as the letters appeared in the world: Caitlin Priest. She would have to learn how to act more human before she approached Riley. After the situation with Samael, Riley would be reluctant to trust another angel.

Zerachiel knew that if she was going to make any headway with Riley, if she was going to become a partner, confidant, friend, she was going to have to succumb to her humanity more than she was comfortable with. It would be fine. She had no doubt she was strong enough to reassert control if necessary.

She signed the last page and, when she looked up, she was smiling. She could feel the rigidity evaporating from her posture as she relaxed. She was comfortable in this place, comfortable in her skin, as she slid the paper back across the counter. "Here you go."

The super took the lease and thumbed through it to make sure she hadn't missed a signature or an initial. "There I go. Thank you very much, Detective."

"Please," she said. "Call me Caitlin."

Priest woke before Gillian came to check on her. She left the office, pausing to make sure Gillian knew she was leaving. "Are you sure you're okay?"

"I will be. Thank you for your words, and for watching out for me."

Gillian lowered her voice. "Just because you're a guardian angel doesn't mean you have to do all the watching out. You keep Riley safe. I owe you a little protection."

Priest tried not to flinch. "I'll do what I can."

"That's all I ask. Come over for dinner. You've had a rough day."

"I'll have to consider that. I'll call you if I decide for sure I'll come, but right now I think I just want to be alone."

Gillian nodded. "Call regardless. Let us know you're okay."

"I will." She kissed Gillian's cheek. "I love you."

"I love you too. And Riley does, too. It's just..." She chuckled. "It's hard enough for her to say it to *me*."

Priest smiled. "It's okay. I know."

She left the morgue and descended the stairs to the lobby. There was still evidence of the provisional hospital that had occupied the ground floor of the police station immediately after the earthquake that devastated No Man's Land. She adjusted the collar of her jacket as she stepped outside. She felt like she was abandoning Riley, felt like she should shove through whatever maelstrom occupying her mind so that she could lend a hand. But she knew she would be less than useless for the rest of the day.

Convinced that staying would do more harm than leaving, Priest turned away from the station and resumed her walk toward home.

MacKenzie Crowe's fingers were in her hair, and Priest tensed as their lips touched. They were in her bedroom, standing beside the bed, both fully dressed. Priest kept her eyes open and her hands hovered in the air on either side of Kenzie's torso without making contact. To her left she could see Chelsea Stanton between them and the bed. Kenzie's tongue teased Priest's lips but she didn't allow it entrance so she withdrew. She kissed the corners of Priest's mouth before taking a step back and looking at her girlfriend.

They gave her a moment to catch her breath before Chelsea leaned in. Kenzie put a hand on Chelsea's cheek to guide her, and her thumb was caught between their lips as they kissed.

Priest had asked for this. She had seen how being with Gillian changed Riley, had made her more complete. Riley's energy was electric, but Gillian seemed to center it. She had seen a toy once with jagged sparks dancing along the inside of a glass globe. Touching a finger to the outer surface gathered all the energy into a single spot. Watching Riley with Gillian was like that, and Priest had to admit she was envious.

First she considered watching Riley and Gillian making love, but she couldn't bring herself to want it. She was far too close to Riley to feel comfortable, and they had been together for long enough that their lovemaking was an act of communion rather than debauchery. But Kenzie and Chelsea were new to each other. She could watch the progression of sex as it went from a primal need to an emotional urge.

Priest's lips parted when Kenzie's thumb brushed it, and Chelsea took it as an invitation. Her tongue slid across Priest's lips and into her mouth, and she had no choice but to meet it with her own. As she stumbled backward, Kenzie moved to stand behind her. Kenzie's hands stroked her shoulders before moving to the placket of her shirt. She undid a button and pulled the material apart to stroke the skin underneath.

She had watched them make love a handful of times, had locked eyes with Kenzie while Chelsea was between her legs, but Kenzie had finally suggested they turn it into a true threesome. Priest demurred, citing her virginity, and Kenzie had agreed to go at her pace. So they kissed, they touched, and now they were preparing to take it to the ultimate level. She moved her arm back to smooth her hand against Kenzie's hip, curling her fingers in the rough denim as she curled her other arm around Chelsea's waist to draw her closer.

In the past eighteen months she had become more comfortable with her humanity. Caitlin Priest was no longer just a name she used to disguise her divine origins. She had developed likes and dislikes, and she had emotional responses to the smallest, most inconsequential things. She laughed. She wept.

She desired.

She turned her head and Chelsea's lips dragged across her cheek. It was hard for her to draw breath; not normally a problem but she was following the commands of her mortal body now. Her face was hot and she wet her lips as Kenzie finished unbuttoning her blouse. She hunched her shoulders and let Kenzie take the shirt off of her.

"I want you..." It was a gasp, a sudden declaration that she hadn't intended to voice. She didn't even know which of the women she was speaking to. She wanted them both. She kissed Chelsea's throat as her bra was undone and Kenzie's thumbs hooked in the straps. Chelsea pulled it down and then pressed her palms against Priest's breasts.

Earlier, Kenzie had asked if Chelsea was sure about going through with their plan for the night. Chelsea had kissed her and said, "I need someone to tell me how beautiful you are when you come. Caitlin... I want you there. But I want you to be my eyes. That's my only stipulation. I want you to tell me how beautiful Kenzie is while we're making love to her." Priest had agreed.

Now partially undressed, Chelsea's lips on her neck and Kenzie stroking her back as she knelt, Priest doubted her ability to remain coherent. Her pants were unbuttoned and slid off her hips, left to fall on their own as Kenzie drew down her underwear. Priest shivered despite the warmth of the room and gasped when Kenzie placed a kiss on either cheek of her ass and stroked the inside of her thighs.

Normally Zerachiel maintained the mechanisms of Priest's body. Her heart rate, respiration, body temperature, and everything else that came with the human machine were kept at a steady rate. But now Zerachiel had retreated and Priest was on her own. She found it difficult to stand, not that there was a risk of falling pinned between her two friends. Her skin was slick with sweat and her heart was thumping against her ribs so hard that she feared one or the other might fail and cause permanent damage.

When Kenzie's fingers moved inside of her, Priest was unprepared for how it would feel. She had touched herself sexually, of course. Her human nature demanded exploration, but it was nothing compared to two of Kenzie's fingers brushing against her sex. She bit off the cry of surprise that broke from her, pressing tighter against Chelsea as she arched her back. She bent her knees and pointed her toes. Her hands flattened against Chelsea's back as Chelsea licked the shell of her ear.

"Tell me what she's doing to you, my angel."

Chelsea's voice was like a physical caress, and Priest shivered in response. "She's touching me."

"I want details."

Gathering her strength, Kenzie's fingers stroking her vulva in anticipation of pushing inside, Priest found her voice and began to speak softly into Chelsea's ear.

Chelsea Stanton was in the office alone when Priest arrived, tending to the white roses in the greenhouse that abutted their main workspace. She paused in her work, head tilted toward the door with a smile playing at the corner of her lips. She wore dark purple lenses in silver frames that hid her eyes, but Priest knew that the sight-deprived investigator was looking directly at her. Due to her divinity, even Chelsea could see Priest with clarity. She had once described it as seeing a lighthouse through a fog bank.

"Am I interrupting?"

"Not if you want to help." She gestured vaguely toward her tools.

Priest took off her jacket and rolled her sleeves to the elbow. She picked up a pair of snips and moved to stand next to Chelsea.

"What are we doing?"

"We're making clones." Chelsea smiled. "We're just taking a piece of one plant and cultivating it to grow another one. I can show you how if you're interested."

Priest nodded slowly. "Yes. I am."

Chelsea was an excellent teacher. Patient and calm, she explained the steps and guided Priest's hand for the first few cuts. When she was convinced she had the hang of it, she returned to her own plant.

"I'm surprised you're not at work. Even Kenzie is lending a hand at another precinct. I would be there myself if..." She didn't need to finish her reasons, stopping her hand as it rose to adjust her glasses. "Is Lieutenant Briggs rotating detectives to avoid exhaustion?"

"No. That's a good idea, though." She wet her lips. "I'm temporarily suspended."

"You? What in the world are they investigating you for?"

Priest's hands went still, the blades of her tool standing open around the stem of a rose.

"Caitlin?" Chelsea touched her shoulder, her voice softer now. "What happened? Tell me, sweetheart."

"I shot a man. He died."

"Oh, Lord." Chelsea turned her around and embraced her. Priest held her hands out behind Chelsea's back, unwilling to smear dirt on her blouse. "Hug me properly, you stupid angel."

Priest smiled despite herself and tightened the embrace. She sagged against Chelsea, who took her weight without protest. Safely in Chelsea's arms, Priest recounted what had happened. Reliving the details dulled them somewhat, and sharing the information relieved it of some weight. It made it easier for her to bear.

When she was finished, Chelsea kissed her cheek. "Are you okay?"

Priest nodded. "I will be. Everyone has been treating me so wonderfully. Gillian watched over me while I napped in her office. Riley is being so understanding, as is Lieutenant Briggs. They're willing to give me time to deal with it, which I appreciate more than I can say. I ended a man's life. It's very difficult for me to accept my part in that."

Chelsea leaned back and brushed her thumbs over Priest's cheeks. "When I was still in uniform, I responded to a domestic violence call. When we arrived the man was standing at the top of the stairs shouting obscenities at me. I tried to talk to him, but he brought his hand up and aimed something small and black at my head. I shot him. Later we discovered it was a cell phone."

"How did you cope?"

"I didn't cope. I felt guilty, but the burden wasn't on me. The man, consciously or not, made the decision to die. He made me his method of execution. When he raised his hand, I didn't know if he could have killed me or not. I didn't know if my partner was in danger. I had to make a decision in a heartbeat. I don't know if I made the right decision or not. If I had it to do over again, knowing what I do now, I wouldn't pull the trigger. But in the moment you can't debate, you can't question, and you cannot hesitate. In that moment you weren't an angel and you weren't mortal. You were a police officer."

Priest lightly kissed Chelsea's lips. "Thank you."

"Go upstairs. Sleep. Gillian had the right idea, but you need real rest in a real bed. I'll send Kenzie up to check on you when she gets home."

"Okay. Will you be all right alone with the flowers?"

Chelsea smiled. "I always am. Sleep peacefully, Caitlin."

Priest thanked her again and left the greenhouse. Weariness gripped her as she ascended the stairs and went into the loft apartment Kenzie and Chelsea shared. She always felt comfortable in their home; it had been one of the few places she'd felt comfortable during her time as a mortal, and returning there calmed her frayed nerves like a balm. She only realized she had left her jacket downstairs when she began undressing, but by that point she was too weary to even consider going back for it.

In just her sleeveless undershirt and panties, she crawled into the bed she had once shared with Kenzie and Chelsea, taking the time to gather the pillows to her chest before drifting off.

The glass was cold against her palms. So cold it felt like burning, but she didn't notice. Tears cascaded down her cheeks, plummeting from her chin but she didn't care. Riley was dead. She had died violently, and so suddenly, and she was gone. And she hadn't been there to help her cross, to ease her passing. Zerachiel finally pushed away from the glass and turned around to see Michael standing behind her. His shirt was a drab brown, his trousers a brown-white desert camouflage pattern.

"I've come to see you away."

Zerachiel wiped the back of her hand over her cheeks. "Where?"

"A child is due to be born in three days. You will be assigned to her."

"No."

Michael stared at her. "Your charge has passed, Zerachiel. She is beyond your help."

Zerachiel straightened. She could tell that the thoughts roiling in her head weren't her own, or they were her own but they were born of the emotion and frailty in her human shell.

"There is more I can do."

His eyes widened and he shook his head slowly. "I know what you're considering, and you must stop. It can't be done. You'll only succeed in destroying yourself."

"I have to try. Her death is my fault. I owe it to her to try putting it right."

She started past him, but Michael gripped her arm and squeezed. Caitlin Priest acknowledged the pain as his fingernails dug in through her sleeve, but Zerachiel was beyond noticing pain. She tugged her arm free, his nails scraping the flesh underneath hard enough to draw small beads of blood.

"You would sacrifice your entire existence for one person?"

"I would risk it for Riley. She is vital."

"More vital than the one who came before her? More vital than your first? Zerachiel, we have all felt the need to do something more. But mortals are frail. Even if we protect them from everything the world throws at them, they will still one day fade."

Zerachiel said, "It's my job to protect Riley. Instead I colluded with the Angel Maker and I stood aside while she put herself in danger. If I had been present I could have saved her without resorting to desperate measures. I cannot stop now, or my time as Riley's guardian will have been for naught. I can't allow her to die like this."

"It is not your place to decide."

"I'm making it my place."

Zerachiel left the apartment, expecting to hear Michael pursuing her down the stairs. When his footsteps didn't come she slipped through the ether to arrive instantaneously at the morgue. She walked to the table where Riley's body had been lain, nude but for the thin sheet covering her from chest to mid-thigh. She put her hand on Riley's shoulder.

Their last words had been angry. Riley had died furious at her, and Zerachiel didn't know how she could bear that for the rest of her days. She remembered days when she had guided Riley into an alley so a rapist wouldn't see her, the nights when she stood between Riley and a group of thugs who intended to do harm to the first person they came across. And the difficult times, when she had to allow a broken arm to prevent a cracked skull, or when she had been forced to stand aside while horrible things were done to Riley with her father's blessing.

All the bad things she had allowed to happen in her time as Riley's supposed guardian... she hadn't possessed the power to change any of them. She had been told there was a plan, and she believed it. But what plan would allow Riley to die like this?

She wasn't aware of how long she had been standing there, staring at Riley's lifeless corpse, before she was startled by a side door opening. Gillian emerged fresh from the shower, her hair wet and the collar of her scrubs damp. She stopped and stared for a moment before she spoke in a cold voice.

"She wouldn't want you here."

"I know."

"Then get the fuck out." The words should have been angry, but instead they were nearly a plea. Zerachiel understood she was intruding on a sacred, painful moment and wished there was a way for her to apologize. The best option was to just do what she had come to do.

"I just... there's just one thing I have to do."

Now Gillian's anger emerged. "What? Do you have to steal her tattoo for the next champion? Do you have to do some damn ritual to pass it on? Part of your damned war? Well do it. And then I never want to see you again."

Zerachiel put her hand on Riley's chest. She met Gillian's eye. "I don't know what this will do. Only one person has done it before, and he was more powerful than I am."

Gillian looked exhausted. "Just get it over with."

Zerachiel closed her eyes. She heard Priest meekly protesting, insisting Zerachiel didn't have to do this. But Zerachiel knew it was the only way to make amends. She closed her eyes and corralled her essence into a single surge. It flowed through her like a stream, emerging from her hand like a honeyed glow. The pain was unexpected; she felt herself being torn away from her physical body. She forced the dissipating energy into Riley's body through strength of will, directing it like standing in the center of the Nile and changing its course by extending her arms.

When the last tendril of energy left her and filled Riley, Priest's body was physically thrown back in a burst of light. The shattering sound deafened her momentarily, but her hearing returned by the time she hit the floor with a bone-shattering impact.

Afterward she remembered pain and isolation, with a sense of loneliness that she hadn't expected crowding in on all sides. She opened her eyes and saw Gillian kneeling beside her. And then she saw Riley. Alive,

living, breathing, whole. And despite the agony she smiled.
It had worked.

She didn't know how long she had slept, but the bedroom was dark when she woke and someone was curled against her. There was enough light for her to see who it was, and that she had stripped down to her underwear as well. "Kenzie?" she whispered. There was no response, so Priest didn't try to wake her. Kenzie was lying on top of the blankets, her body curled in the fetal position against Priest's side. She shifted position so as not to disturb Kenzie, resting on her side so that they were facing. She rested her hands on Kenzie's hip and let herself fall back to sleep.

When she woke again, Kenzie was awake and watching her. She smiled once Priest's eyes were open and focused, and she began to move her hand in slow circles on Priest's hip.

"Hey. You okay?"

Priest nodded.

"Chelsea told me what happened. And Riley called to see if I would check in on you. Thanks for making it easy."

"My pleasure." She kissed Kenzie's lips, and Kenzie returned the kiss with passion. It hadn't been Priest's intention to begin anything sexual, but the feel of Kenzie's body against hers awoke a need she hadn't known she was fighting. She pushed down the blankets to get closer, Kenzie rolling onto her back as Priest straddled her. Priest sat up and slid her hands under Kenzie's shirt, cupping her breasts as she settled against Kenzie's hip.

"Yeah," Kenzie whispered, giving blanket consent to whatever Priest had in mind as she gripped the hem of Priest's undershirt. Priest wrapped her fingers around Kenzie's forearm and rocked her lower body forward. The bedsprings wailed, and occasionally one woman or the other would make a quiet noise of pleasure or permission. Clothes were discarded haphazardly, and Kenzie sat up only to have Priest shove her back down onto the mattress.

Priest closed her eyes, wishing she still had long hair to serve as a veil to hide her face as she grimaced through her climax. She tightened her thighs, closing Kenzie between them as she quaked and tensed. She lifted her weight off of Kenzie's hip and scooted down. She lowered her head, stretching out along the length of Kenzie's body and kissed her. She pushed the shirt up to kiss the multitude of shrapnel scars that she had only ever shown to two people. She ran her tongue to the curve of Kenzie's breast and took the nipple into her mouth, and Kenzie raked her fingers through Priest's hair.

"Lower," she gasped.

Priest obliged. She knelt between Kenzie's legs, feet crossed underneath her as she bowed forward like a supplicant. She guided Kenzie's thighs onto her shoulders and kissed the soft cotton crotch of her panties. Kenzie moaned, and Priest began to stroke with her thumb and forefinger. Her other hand cupped Kenzie's rear end and squeezed, digging her fingers into the soft flesh and pulling Kenzie closer to her.

"She's between my legs," Kenzie suddenly gasped, and Priest realized Chelsea had joined them. "Going down on me... her lips are so soft. God."

"Just her lips?"

"Fingers, too." Kenzie's voice was barely more than a whisper. Chelsea put her hand on Priest's back and stroked the bumps of her spine, making her shudder.

Chelsea said, "And what did you do for her?"

"She fucked me. Ro-oh..." She grunted. "Rode my hip 'til she came."

Chelsea's hand drifted down between Priest's legs, and Priest moaned as a slender finger pushed into her.

"Oh, yes... she is very wet." The hand was withdrawn and Priest knew Chelsea was sucking the moisture from her finger. She pushed the underwear aside so that her own middle finger could push inside of Kenzie. She moved her lips to cover Kenzie's clit, sucked it into her mouth, and within seconds Kenzie was in the grips of an orgasm.

"Don't forget to speak, darling..."

Kenzie cried out in frustration. "Finger. Sucking my..."

"Your clit?"

"Mm." Prolonged and tremulous, it was the only acknowledgement Kenzie could voice.

Chelsea's voice was a soft purr. "She's very good at that, isn't she?"

"Yeah," Kenzie murmured.

"Poor baby. Can barely speak. Maybe you can do something better with your mouth instead." Chelsea joined them on the bed and crawled on her knees, letting Kenzie guide her until Chelsea was kneeling on either side of her head. Priest closed her eyes and enjoyed the sounds as Kenzie gave as good as she was getting. Kenzie came first, freeing Priest to sit up and watch as Chelsea was pleasured.

When Chelsea came, she twisted and reached for Priest. They kissed as Chelsea rearranged herself so that she wasn't sitting on Kenzie's head. Kenzie pushed herself up and rested against the headboard to kiss them both.

Priest could feel Zerachiel trying to exert control, attempting to return her vitals to normal, but she pushed it aside. She wanted to feel the sweat drying on her skin, wanted her erratic heartbeat and her rushed breath. She watched Kenzie and Chelsea kiss in the dark, then kissed them both before she moved to the edge of the bed.

"You don't have to leave," Kenzie said.

Chelsea said, "Stay the night with us, Caitlin."

"Thank you. But I know what has been gnawing at me. I need to go speak with someone." She retrieved her clothes and dressed, then kissed both women goodbye. "Thank you. I had no idea I needed this so badly."

Kenzie's teeth flashed in the low light as she smiled. "Nothing like a celebration of life to end a day like today. Call us if you need anything, Cait."

"I will. I love you, MacKenzie. I love you, Chelsea."

They echoed her sentiments, both giving her a final kiss before she finally left. She waited until she was downstairs before she sat on the bottom step and put on her shoes. When she finished tying the laces, she looked down at her feet and tried to talk herself out of what she knew had to happen next. It was asking for an unnecessary conversation, changing a perfectly civil situation into a particularly argumentative one. She sighed, smoothed her hands over her slacks, and pushed herself up. The day had been full of mortality, raising her awareness that life could end in the blink of an eye. Her emotions about Jeremy Howard's death were true, but they weren't the true source of her emotional turmoil.

There was no getting around it. If she wanted to have peace, she had to confront Riley.

The sun rising over the water made the city beautiful, but Priest wasn't watching it. She had her eyes on Riley. She was only two years older, but she wore them like a decade. She obviously hadn't wasted much time sleeping, and her hair was going gray. Scars extended from under her collar and touched her neck, and Priest couldn't help but wonder how many more were hidden by her blood-stained clothing. Some of the blood was fresh, some not so fresh. Riley looked away from the sun and smiled weakly, as if she was out of practice.

"You're crying."

"Do you blame me?"

Riley reached out and brushed her thumb over Priest's cheeks. The gentle pressure made Priest's heart seize. She held Riley's wrist and kissed the moisture from the skin.

"What now?"

"Now... you have to burn me. Now..." She forced Priest to look at her again. "You know you do. If any part of me is left behind, it'll raise questions. Teeth, or bones, anything that could be used to trace DNA... you can't leave anything behind."

Priest sniffled and nodded.

"Cait. I love you. I wish I'd gotten a chance to apologize for everything I did to you... before. And I'm sorry I'm doing this to you now."

"I've protected you for your entire life, Riley. Why would I stop now?" She cupped Riley's cheek and chastely kissed her lips. "Rest for now. I'll stay with you until you pass."

Riley sighed and rested her head on Priest's shoulder. Priest stroked her hair and tried to keep herself from crying again. Her eyes burned and her body hitched a few times, but if Riley noticed she didn't mention it.

Riley's voice was so weak that Priest almost didn't hear it. "I spoke to Gillian."

"Oh?"

"First time in... two years. I forgot. How beautiful she sounds." She chuckled, but it rapidly turned into a groaning cough. More blood blossomed on her shirt. "I destroyed the world and went back in time, and I... slaughtered two demons. And I didn't even remember how much I loved her. I did that on a diminished amount of love." She laughed again. "Don't let me forget this time around. I need to cherish her."

"I swear."

Riley coughed again. "Hey, Cait."

"Yes, Riley?"

"You were a great angel."

Priest closed her eyes and let her tears flow free. One of them dripped onto Riley's face and Priest apologized, but Riley didn't respond. Priest held her tighter and watched the sun climb higher.

Riley answered on the third knock, already dressed for bed. The lights in the living room were off, but she could see down the hall behind Riley that the bedroom was lit. Riley's hair was down, which was enough of a rarity that Priest was momentarily thrown by the sight of it.

"Cait? Everything okay?"

"Is Gillian here?"

Riley nodded. "In the bedroom. I could get her..."

"No. I want to speak with you privately."

"Okay. Just... give me a second." She left the door open and pulled on her shoes. She disappeared down the hall and Priest heard quiet voices coming from the bedroom. When Riley reappeared, Gillian came with her. She stopped at the bedroom door, already dressed in her pajamas, and raised her hand in greeting. Priest returned the wave with a smile she didn't feel.

"Everything okay?"

Priest nodded. "Yes. I just need to speak with Riley."

"Okay. Don't keep her out too late."

"I'll try."

Priest led the way down the stairs and out into the building's underground parking structure. She walked ahead to make sure they were alone, then turned to face Riley as the doors swung shut behind her.

"Have you told Gillian yet?"

Riley didn't have to ask for clarification. "Not yet. I haven't found the right time."

"There will never be a right time, Riley."

"I know. But I can't tell her when we're making love. Or right before, or after. And if I tell her on the way to work... and when we come back from work~"

Priest interrupted by loudly barking, "And what about me?"

Riley was stunned by the outburst. "What?"

"What about *me*, Riley? Have you thought about how this is affecting me? You're calm and you're at peace with what's happening, fine. But you're going to die, Riley. I'm your guardian angel. You may have learned the day you'll die, but I learned the day I'm going to fail." Her voice cracked on the last word and she turned away. She longed for Zerachiel to hold back the tears, but the angel had been silent since Kenzie and Chelsea's bedroom. The tears burned, sitting behind her eyes like a ball of hot steam.

When she trusted herself to speak again, she kept her voice low and even. "I've lost every one of my charges. That's the nature of protecting humans. It doesn't matter how long they live, eventually something will take them and they will die. I remember all of them. Their deaths still hurt me when I think too hard on them. But I've never known any of them the way I know you, Riley. And I never loved any of them as much as I love you because I never loved with a human soul. I've lost you twice. I don't know if I can lose you again.

"I understand why you're focused on how Gillian will take the news. I know that she comes first, and that is as it should be. But this is hard for me, too. When you die, I'm not just losing you. I'm going to lose everything. Caitlin Priest won't be necessary anymore so she'll just... vanish. And I'll go on to my next charge, but I honestly don't know if I'll be able to handle it. I can't imagine feeling this hurt again. It's killing me to know that I only have two years left. And I've felt like I couldn't say anything because Gillian... of course Gillian is more important. But I have to know that you know I'm being torn apart at the thought of losing you. And it's worse because I saw you... the future you... Otheriley. I held her as she died and I saw her draw her last breath knowing that I'll have to do it all again in two years and it makes me ache."

The silence grew until Riley was certain Priest was finished. "Cait... I'm sorry. I never even stopped to consider..." She looked away. "Gillian may be more important, but you're just as vital. You saved my life countless times just by being around. When Gillian left me, sometimes the only reason I got out of bed in the morning was because I knew you'd come drag me out if I didn't. I had to strive to be a better person because I didn't want to disappoint you. I should have asked how you felt. I should have taken a few minutes to say this to you when we first found out. It's going to kill me to say goodbye to Gillian, but it's going to be just as painful saying goodbye to you. You've been more than my partner; you're my sister.

"I've only made it this far because you kept me going. I'm not talking to Zerachiel, although she's fine in my book, too. I'm talking about you, Caitlin. The flawed, funny, weird, infuriating, clumsy human that I fought to keep in my life when you gave up your divinity. I can't imagine a life without Gillian in it, but I don't want to try imagining a life without you, either."

Priest sniffled and faced Riley again. "I love you, Riley."

"I love you, too." Riley embraced her. Priest resisted the urge to collapse into the hug, tightening her jaw against the tears that threatened to flow freely.

After a long moment, Riley whispered in a shaking voice, "I'm scared as all hell."

Priest nodded. "I know. But I'll be here for you, Riley. Always."

Riley tightened her arms and held onto Priest, reluctant to let go. And Priest was content to let Riley hang onto her as long as she needed.

THE STARRY COPE OF HEAVEN

GILLIAN ROLLED over, dropping her hand on Riley's hip. Her hand molded to the curve and she pulled herself closer. Riley looked into her wife's face, the slack lips and fluttering eyelids, to make sure she was staying asleep before she returned her gaze to the ceiling. The apartment was warmer than she liked, so the blankets were pushed down around her waist. Gillian was swaddled in the excess length. She moved her head against Riley's shoulder and murmured in her sleep.

"Armph."

"Mm-hmm," Riley whispered. She had learned that if she didn't acknowledge Gillian's dream-speak she would often repeat the gibberish statement until the sound of her own voice woke her up. Gillian exhaled a sound like "Hah," and Riley knew she had just lost some imagined argument. She didn't mind.

Her right arm was pinned underneath Gillian's body, so she brought her hand up to stroke her back. The nightshirt she wore had ridden up, and Riley tugged it back down to cover the small of her back. There was a tattoo there, a drawing Priest had assured her would grant some of Riley's protection to Gillian. It turned out to be a lie, but a well-intentioned one. The well-intentioned ones were the worst, in Riley's opinion. They misled not only the person being lied to, but the person doing the lying. The only thing worse were lies of omission.

Otheriley told Priest that she was thirty-eight years, seven months, three days and four hours old when her death was set. The minutes hardly mattered. She had done the math and she officially had two years, one month, four days and however many hours left before her debt came due. She ran the numbers around in her head. Technically it was after midnight, so she had three days instead of four.

She tightened her hand on Gillian's back. Gillian tensed and furrowed her brow. "Sweep."

"I know," Riley said.

"Se-sey-sem."

"Yep."

Gillian chuckled softly and Riley smiled.

So far the only person who knew the truth was Priest. But a reckoning was going to come soon. She would have to tell Gillian, of course, but Lieutenant Briggs also needed to know. Chelsea and Kenzie would have to be told, and... Aissa. The poor girl was still learning the ropes of being a person outside of her monastery. She would only have three years of life experience before she was responsible for the well-being of an entire city against the forces of evil.

Gillian's breathing changed and she shifted against Riley's side. A few seconds passed when she could have fallen back to sleep, but instead she lifted her head slightly.

"Still awake?"

"Yeah."

Gillian kissed her jaw. "Poor baby. Want me to heat up some milk?"

"No, I'm fine. Go back to sleep."

"I would, but nature calls." She pecked Riley's cheek again and freed herself from the blankets. Once she was gone Riley shook her arm and flexed the fingers that had fallen asleep in its time trapped under Gillian. She sat up and tented her knees under the blanket to rest her arms on them. She could hear sirens outside and watched the curtains to see if they were washed with red and blue. When the sirens continued past the building, Riley smoothed her hand over her hair and stared into the shadows until Gillian came back.

"Have you slept at all tonight?"

Riley thought about lying, but she knew Gillian would see through it. "No."

Gillian settled in beside her and rubbed Riley's arm. "Does it have anything to do with whatever you and Priest are keeping from me?" Riley looked at her and Gillian smiled indulgently. "Something is going on, Riley. I trust you to tell me everything when you're ready. But I also know that keeping it inside is taking a toll on you. I hate seeing you like this. As much as I enjoy waking up to see you watching over me..."

Riley grinned. "I do like watching you sleep."

"If you start singing that Aerosmith song, I'm divorcing you." She brushed Riley's hair with her hand. "You have to decide if keeping the secret is more important than your health. As bad as it is, we can deal with it together." She kissed Riley's cheek. "And I can handle whatever you have to say."

"I'm sure you can," Riley said. "Doesn't make it any easier to talk about." She checked the clock. "How tired are you?"

"Please, in med school I would have begged for four hours of sleep. Do you want to get up and talk for a while?"

Riley hesitated and then nodded slowly. "Yes. Get dressed... I want to go for a walk."

"It's three thirty in..." She caught herself. "All right. A walk." She brushed Riley's arm and squeezed her bicep. "Thank you."

"For what?"

"Trusting me."

Riley smiled and kissed Gillian before she got out of bed and started to dress.

In addition to the beds that normally filled the room, they had found space for cots and sleeping bags so that most of the aisles were congested with sleeping bodies. Aissa knew that Eddie didn't like overcrowding the shelter like this, but there wasn't much other choice. Thirty-eight percent of the people in the neighborhood had either lost their homes entirely or the buildings were rendered uninhabitable by the earthquake.

Aissa wore a sweatshirt from somewhere called Stan Ford with sleeves that she had to constantly push up to her elbows so they didn't fall down over her hands. She carried a canvas bag with the strap across her chest, its bulky body bumping against her hip with every step as she surveyed the sleeping quarters before continuing to the kitchen. Anita Cashion was still cooking despite the late hour, since some of their guests were on a different clock than others. Her hair was limp and dead as she moved from one burner to the next, barely glancing up as Aissa entered.

"How are you coping?" Aissa asked.

"I'm hanging in there. This is the last batch, and it'll go into the fridge so anyone who wants something can get it."

Aissa put her bag on the counter. "I found some more supplies."

"Found?" Anita's skepticism was weary as she began going through what Aissa had brought her; she couldn't afford to be picky about how they kept the shelves stocked. "You got some good stuff this time. Beef stew..."

"I heard someone asking for that yesterday."

Anita smiled. "I didn't know you were listening. Thank you, Aissa. Just so long as you didn't rob Peter to pay Paul." Aissa stared at her without comprehension. "It means you're taking from one needy person to feed another. I don't want this if any of it came from someone's pantry."

"It didn't. At least no one who will miss it."

She kept her supply raids to the center of town, the neighborhoods less affected by the earthquake. She further narrowed her scope to homes purchased with ill-gotten gains. Drug dealers, people connected to the Five Families. Everyone she stole from could count on a steady income and a full larder. The people of No Man's Land, the people her so-called victims exploited, didn't have that luxury. She felt no guilt over repurposing a few cans of beans and some stew. She didn't tell Anita or Eddie any of this, knowing they would have to remain in the dark for deniability if the police ever caught her breaking in somewhere.

She helped Anita stock the shelves. "We don't have much in the way of bedding, but there's a couch in Eddie's office you can take..."

"I'm not sleepy. If you don't need me here, I plan to head back out."

"Aissa, you've done enough for one day. And I'm talking the day that started three hours ago." She put her hand on the girl's shoulder. "Have you slept in the past twenty-four hours?"

"Of course I have."

"More than a catnap, Aissa."

She sighed. "We were trained for long hours of worship and training. I'm not used to setting aside eight hours a night for sleep. And you need the help."

"Well, I can't argue that." She ran a hand through her hair and looked around the kitchen. "Can you cook?"

"All of the sisters are trained in the culinary arts. Would you like me to take over here?"

"Yes. Unlike the Good Girls, I was brought up on eight hours of sleep a night. And I kind of like to see my husband once a day."

Aissa smiled. "Say hello to him for me."

Anita kissed her on the cheek and untied her apron. "Call me if you need anything. I'm serious. We're all pulling double duty around here after the earthquake and I'd rather feel tired than guilty." She passed the apron to Aissa, who put it on and took Anita's place at the stove. Anita told her what was nearly done, what steps were required on other things, and made sure the fridge had everything she needed.

Finally, Anita left and Aissa was alone in the kitchen. She appreciated the silence, the still air that reminded her of being home with her sisters and her Mother. She missed them terribly but knew that this place was her calling now. Even without the tattoo on the back of her neck identifying her as Riley Parra's successor, she would have remained when the rest of the Good Girls went home. Well, most of the Good Girls. Cerys was still here, mourning the loss of the sister she had loved more than the others.

Cerys wasn't adjusting to secular life as well as Aissa. She still wore her white robes, changing to more modern dress so she could wash it in the laundry room of her building every night. Aissa's robe was reverently hung in the closet of Eddie's office and worn only for her daily prayers. She didn't have an official residence, choosing instead to sleep in whatever beds the shelter could spare. It was as close as she could get to the communal feeling of sharing a room with her sisters.

When the food was finished cooking, she transferred everything to Tupperware dishes and put them in the fridge for later in the day. She cleaned up the counter and washed off the utensils, wiping her hands on a towel before she turned off the lights and left the kitchen. She was a little tired, now that the subject had been broached, but there weren't beds to spare. And there was always the possibility that someone might need the couch in Eddie's office more than she did.

If sleep wasn't possible, she would wake herself up with activity. The nights recently had been unseasonably cold, so she paused to put on a jacket before she went out. One of her new friends, a homeless veteran who was trying to overcome a speech impediment, had given her an olive-drab military cap. She put it on and tucked her hair behind her ears as she stood on the sidewalk, her hands in her pockets. She walked to the curb and stood silently.

She never consciously chose which direction she walked when she left the shelter. Sometimes she would hear a siren, or a screech of tires would draw her attention. Sometimes there would just be a feeling that drew her east rather than west. She waited, lifting her eyes to the clear night sky, alert to the world around her as she waited.

She had heard people calling her the Scarred Detective. She didn't mind, except insomuch as it made it more difficult for her to blend in when she wanted to go undercover. There was a half-moon chalked on the door, almost invisible in the dark thanks to the recessed entryway. Kenzie looked over her shoulder to make sure she hadn't been followed as she walked into the alley. A knit cap was pulled low over her ears, and the collar of her oversized military jacket was turned up to further obscure the scar tissue. She had to get the jacket from a surplus military supply store; the jacket she already owned fit her too well for her purposes.

This week's signal knock was a rapid-fire staccato rhythm that left her knuckles sore. She stepped back to the middle of the alley as she'd been instructed and waited for a response. No one ever came to the door in the first minute after a knock, working on the assumption that anyone who wasn't supposed to be there would get bored and wander off in that time.

Finally the door opened to reveal a man who looked like a ferret standing upright. His clothing was third-hand, at best, and lank brown hair hung down on either side of his hatchet face. He sniffed loudly then leaned out to look past her.

"Yeah? What?"

"I'm McKenna. I got some stuff for you."

He stared at her again and worked his lips against his teeth. Finally he stepped back and motioned for her to come inside. Kenzie looked down the alley once more, then went into the back room of the shop.

"You got a wire?"

Kenzie unbuttoned her jacket and held it open to reveal her heavy plaid shirt that was purposefully buttoned wrong over a white T-shirt. "That's as far as I'm going for you, pal. Your boss wants security, he can see it for himself."

"Nah, nah." He opened a door that looked as if it should have led to a closet but revealed a steep, narrow staircase. "Up the rabbit hole."

Kenzie looked up toward the landing and stayed where she was.

"Problem?" the man sighed.

"Mama always told me not to get into coffin-like spaces with weird men who smell like frying meat."

The gatekeeper's lips twisted. "Bet you do lots of stuff your mama told you not to."

"Lead the way."

He entered the space and Kenzie gave him a few inches before she followed. The angle of the stairs made her feel as if she was climbing a ladder that had slipped just a little, tilting her perspective so that when she was back on solid ground there was a moment of vertigo. The ferret man took advantage of her disorientation to quickly pat her down. He slapped her hips, the outside of her thighs, and the small of her back before he declared her safe.

"Buy a girl some dinner first, Fess."

"Sorry, boss. You said to be sure."

Kenzie looked toward the new speaker. The room was full of tall metal shelving with milk crates arranged like safe-deposit boxes. The boss was standing at the head of one aisle, dressed in a rust-red jumpsuit unzipped enough to reveal a relatively nice shirt underneath. He was handsome in a grease monkey sort of way, with thick black hair and a smile that would be charming under different circumstances.

"You must be McKenna."

"And you must be Graham. Is that a first name or a last name?"

"Both and neither. You told my friend downtown that you had access to some material I might be interested in obtaining. You understand, though, it's a buyer's market these days."

Kenzie nodded. "Right. Why pay more when there's always someone else willing to rob for a little less money."

Graham held out his hands as if helpless. "This is a business, after all."

"Right. Well, Mr. Businessman, I have a confession to make. My name isn't McKenna. I'm Kenzie Stanton. I'm a private investigator."

Graham rolled his eyes. "Excellent screening process, Mr. Fess." He advanced. "We're not interested in violence or making people like you disappear. So if you turn around and leave, and forget where this place is..."

Kenzie held up her hands. "I'm not here to shut you down. I have a client whose house was robbed. She doesn't care about the TV or the computer, but you - or one of your people, most likely - took a photo album that is irreplaceable. The money you would get selling the binder to a pawn shop is hardly worth the trouble it would cause to make me an enemy. So why don't you just hand over the album, I'll take it back, no harm and no foul. We walk away tolerant of each other's continued existences."

"Photo album." He rubbed his chin and scanned the milk crates. "I remember quite a few photo albums. I'm not exactly sure which ones were from which house."

"I have a description if that would help narrow it down."

Graham waved his hand dismissively. "Then I'd have to go through all this stuff... I admit we have a bit of an inventory problem. I want to help. I do. But I could just throw out the pictures and still get a good price for an empty album. I wish I could help you."

Kenzie closed her eyes. "Damn. Okay, make the call."

"I already made it, Ms. Stanton."

Fess pressed a gun against the back of Kenzie's head, just hard enough that she could feel it through her knit cap.

"It's Mrs. Stanton," she calmly corrected. "And I wasn't talking to you. Gatekeeper, what's your name again? Fess? Listen, Fess. In about three minutes, cops are going to break down that little door downstairs. They're going to come up the stairs and what they see depends on you. Are you going to be a go-fer who gets offered a deal to flip on the big fish, or are you going to be the fool with a gun?"

The pressure wavered. Graham was staring over her shoulder at Fess, urging him to pull the trigger. After a moment, Fess dropped his hand.

Kenzie shrugged. "I tried to play nice. You chose this outcome, Mr. Graham."

He reached into his jumpsuit but Kenzie was too quick for him. She twisted at the waist, took Fess' gun and shoved him away all in a single fluid motion. She flung herself toward the wall as Graham fired, ducking behind one of the shelves. She considered using the aisles as a maze, but there was a much more elegant solution. She gripped the far edge of the shelf and shoved. She wasn't strong enough to knock it over entirely, but she upset the balance enough that the boxes on the top shelf spilled their contents in a wave of electronics and jewelry.

Fess, rather than waiting for the best case scenario Kenzie had postulated, made a run for the stairs. He had only gotten halfway down before a group of police wearing body armor blocked the lower doorway. Kenzie heard his cry of surrender and picked through the fallen debris until she found Graham. She took his gun away from him and held both in the air by hooking her thumbs around the trigger guards.

The cops reached the landing and Kenzie made sure they saw her arms were up. "MacKenzie Stanton, Stanton Investigations. Mr. Graham is under this pile here. Gun in the right hand is mine, gun in the left is his."

The officer in the lead took the weapons from her. "You're good, Mrs. Stanton."

Kenzie dropped her arms and stepped out of the way. Half a dozen officers poured out of the stairwell to help clear the second floor. Kenzie descended the stairs to the antique shop that served as Wayne Graham's front. The front windows were awash with blue and red lights, and Detective Delgado was waiting for her by the alley access door. She took off her cap and unhooked the fiber optic camera from her ear. The wire trailed down the side of her neck, under her hair, to a pack hooked to her bra strap.

"They never check the hat," she said as she handed it over. "Hopefully the picture won't be too obscured."

"As long as the audio works," Delgado said. "Thanks for your help."

"Sure. Look... I know we had a deal, but the photo albums..."

"Sorry, Kenzie. You called us in before he handed them over. They're part of the crime scene now. They're evidence."

Kenzie grimaced. "I was kind of hoping to give them back to the Fergusons tonight."

"It's late and they're old... come by the station tomorrow morning and you can sign them out. You have my word. We're not going to prosecute Graham on sentimental charges, so I doubt we'll need them for court. You can come by any time after eight. Happy?"

"You're a peach, Thomas."

"Get outta here before my heart grows three sizes."

"Eight in the morning," she confirmed.

He waved over his shoulder and headed upstairs. Kenzie walked outside and fished her phone from the inner pocket of her coat. She turned off the speakerphone feature and brought it to her ear as she stood on the sidewalk. "Thanks for the assist, babe." She waited for a response and then smiled. "Chelse, turn off the mute."

"~mn it. Can you hear me?"

"Now I can. Did you hear Delgado?"

Chelsea said, "Eight o'clock. Come on home and go to bed. I'll pick up the album and you can give it back to the Fergusons after you've gotten some rest."

"I'll go to bed, but do I have to rest? I was thinking a celebration might be in order." She smiled as she walked. "Did you hear how I introduced myself?"

"I did." Chelsea chuckled softly. "First time you've said it out loud. How did it feel?"

Kenzie thought for the right word. Then she chuckled. "It felt right. Almost twenty-four hours and I'm not having any regrets. Seems like it might stick."

"Well, then we'll have to apologize to Riley and Priest for not inviting them to the ceremony."

"Ceremony." Kenzie scoffed and stopped on a street corner. "I don't want to badmouth your wedding, but it was a formality. We just confirmed we're going to be together from now on. I didn't need a wedding to make it official... but I liked saying the words out loud to you. I'll never leave you, Chelsea. I'll never love anyone the way I love you."

Chelsea was quiet for a long moment. "Wow. I think you're sleep-deprived and saying things you're not thinking about."

"No. I'm saying things I'm always too anxious to say in person. No more. MacKenzie Stanton speaks her heart. Get used to it. I love you."

"And I love you, Mac."

Kenzie hated the name "Mac." When she was a kid, using it would lead to a punch in the arm if she liked you or in the face if she didn't. At the police academy, she had to constantly correct anyone who tried to go with the more common shortening of her given name. Once she joined the Army she just identified herself as Kenzie from the get-go and avoided the discussion. But Chelsea could get away with it. And when Chelsea said it, Kenzie got chills up and down her spine.

"I'll be home in about twenty minutes. Keep the place warm for me."

"I will."

She hung up and looked back to make sure none of the cops

had overheard her conversation. She was about to step off the curb and leave when she spotted a girl in a Stanford sweater and a ponytail of wild blonde curls emerging from underneath a military cap. She only saw the girl briefly before she disappeared down the alley, but she could have sworn she recognized her.

"Aissa...?"

She checked her watch. She had enough time to check it out and make sure the girl was all right before she went home. If Aissa needed help, Kenzie could always call Chelsea and say she'd be late. She would rather miss a little sleep than leave the heir to Riley's champion title alone in No Man's Land without backup.

"I'm expecting the worst... just so you know."

Gillian had her hands in her pockets, her left arm threaded around Riley's. They were hunched together, walking down the sidewalk close to the buildings so they would better blend into the shadows. Gillian's breath plumed out in front of her, forming the shape of her words in the air before evaporating. A friend had once told Riley that if she held her breath on a really cold night and exhaled as hard as she could, the resulting cloud would be equal to the size of her lungs. She had no idea how accurate his statement was, but she couldn't shake the dubious fact from her mind even all these years later.

"That's probably a good thing. I'm not even sure where to start."

"The beginning is always good."

Riley considered that. "There are two beginnings. I'll go with the one that's less confusing." She cleared her throat. "The day Lark Siskin 'announced herself' as Marchosias' new champion, she decided to make her presence known with three murders. She killed Annora Good, Wanda Kane, and~"

"The previous mayor."

"Right. But her original plan was for a fourth death, the day after the other three. She wanted to scramble us and then go for the crippling shot. She wanted..." Riley's voice trailed off and her eyes felt warm. "I heard all of this third-hand from Priest, so I'm not exactly privy to the exact details. Keep that in mind."

Gillian reached up and brushed away Riley's tears with the pad of her thumb.

"The fourth target was~ it was you. She wanted to kill you."

"Oh." Gillian tensed. "How did you and Priest stop it?"

Riley sidestepped the question. "She sent two demons to the morgue to wait for you the morning of the earthquake. The day I called you and kept you from going to work... they were waiting for you."

"My God." She tightened her arm on Riley's. "How did you know?"

"I'll get to that. Just imagine what would have happened if they succeeded. They didn't want to just kill you. Their plan was worse than death. It was a violation." She looked to make sure Gillian understood and then quickly looked away again. "They would have left you alive but trapped in the moment, reliving it, until your body shut down after hours or-or days of torture. If I found you, I would have been forced to... take mercy."

Gillian stopped walking. Riley faced her and Gillian cupped her face. "I'm sorry."

Riley nodded and kissed her. They held each other for a long, silent moment before Riley stepped back. She kept her hands on Gillian's shoulders and looked down at their feet.

"If that happened, I wouldn't have stopped at mere vengeance. I would have made every demon in this town pay for what those two did."

"But it didn't happen."

"This time it didn't."

Gillian watched her. "What do you mean 'this time'?"

"It happened. The first time around, it happened. I kill–" Her throat closed and she blinked back fresh tears. It was almost a minute before she was able to continue. "I went after them all. Apparently I turned against Priest and Kenzie, Aissa... everyone. I eventually made an agreement with Marchosias. He helped me find a way to come back using the Ladder. I spoke to someone on the other side and convinced them to give me another chance. So I came back. Well, she did. Priest and I have been calling her Otheriley. She called you, probably... to hear your voice again. Did you say you loved me when she called?"

"I don't remember." Gillian's voice was soft, frightened. "There's... another Riley Parra running around?"

Riley shook her head. "She stopped the demons Siskin sent for you, but the damage they inflicted on her was too much. She died after telling Priest everything I just told you."

"Oh, my God. And the Ladder... opening it must have caused the earthquake." She cupped Riley's face again, warming her cheek.

"That's what you've been holding back. Riley, the damage isn't your fault. The consequences aren't on you. Don't blame yourself."

"That's not..." She swallowed the lump in her throat. "Thank you. But that's not what we've been keeping from you. When you... died... in the original timeline, your death was set. It became a fixed point as the end of your life. As champion, my death has always been possible. Every minute of the day, I could die. So in exchange for coming back and keeping you alive, I made my death a fixed moment in time."

Gillian tried to say something, but no sound came from her moving lips. Only plumes of condensation that dissipated between them.

"In order for you to survive that day, I'll die when Otheriley did. She was two years older than I am now, so~"

"Two years?"

Riley flinched, Gillian's suddenly loud voice echoing in the canyon of buildings that surrounded them. She sobbed softly and touched her forehead to Riley's.

"Two years."

"Two years, one month, four days, and~"

"Nowhere near long enough."

Riley closed her eyes. "No." She put her arms around Gillian, holding her as she cried.

Emily Simon, Lark Siskin's only remaining assistant following Abby Shepherd's arrest, rarely slept. She was required to be available during business hours to answer calls and set appointments. At night she was responsible for security at the mayor's loft. She was allowed to change into sleepwear - black silk pajamas - but sleeping was forbidden. It had been easier before, when she could alternate shifts with Abby. Now it all fell to her, and the strain was exhausting.

She stood at the foot of Lark's bed, hands clasped behind her back as she watched her employer sleep. The deceptively frail-looking blonde wore white silk pajamas and a matching sleep mask, her right hand limp on the pillow next to her face. Somewhere in the city sirens sounded, and Emily moved around the side of the bed. Her bare feet sank soundlessly in the plush carpeting as she adjusted the volume on Lark's white noise machine so that the sirens wouldn't wake her. She reached out and gently stroked the hair away from Lark's face, her touch so tender that it wouldn't disturb her any more than the change in air pressure when the heater kicked on.

Emily loved Lark, as Abby had. They would do anything she asked them to. The surgeries were proof of that. Emily no longer saw her own face when she looked in the mirror, but she saw the face Lark desired. That was enough for her. And watching Lark slumber was more refreshing than eight hours of actual sleep.

Content that Lark was sleeping soundly, Emily left the room walking on the balls of her feet, her hands behind her back so that she had the proper shoulders-back-chest-out posture that Lark preferred. There was a small refrigerator in the living room and she crouched in front of it, opening the small drawer that kept her syringes nice and chilled. The only bright side to losing Abby was that now Emily had twice as much for herself.

The drug was her own design, a concoction of stimulants that helped keep her alert. She had created it in another lifetime, when she wore another face and had another name, before she met Lark. She held the glass vial in her hand, warming it just so, and then pushed up the right sleeve of her pajama top. She injected the crook of her elbow and gasped as the frigid medicine entered her bloodstream. Her hand, balled into a fist to raise the vein, relaxed until her fingers were splayed. Her lower lip trembled with relief and she exhaled sharply. It was like stepping into a cold room after wandering in the desert.

She was awake. She was alert. She was ready for a new day.

Emily stood and smoothed down the wrinkles in her pajamas before she closed the fridge. There was a noise from the corridor and Emily turned toward it. Lark was adamant about disruptions in her sleep schedule. If she woke, she would deal with the inconsiderate clod and then dole out punishment to Emily for not taking care of it before she was disturbed. Emily did not want to deal with another session so soon after taking her injection, so she moved to the door and silently slipped out of the apartment.

The desk between Lark's front door and the elevator was empty, as it always was between midnight and five in the morning. The computer was on, the screen glowing with the official seal of the mayor's office rotating in a field of blue. Emily didn't have to search, since the space was too short and narrow to allow any hiding places.

She put her hand on the seat of the desk chair and felt warmth. The keyboard was askew. Emily followed the logical conclusion and turned her gaze to the ceiling tiles. She picked up the desk phone and dialed direct to the lobby.

"This is Miss Simon. Lock down the building. All entrances and exits are to be sealed until I give the all-clear. Am I understood? And if a single alarm sounds, you will answer to me." She hung up the phone and opened the bottom drawer of the desk. Inside was a lockbox, the combination to which she had long ago memorized: it was Lark's birthday, a holiday to those in her inner sanctum.

She removed two guns from within and tucked one into the waistband of her pajama pants, wielding the other. She could have gone back to dress, but she doubted it would take long to deal with the intruder. From the desk, she - and it would have to be a she, due to the size and weight needed to accomplish the feat - had removed the tile and used the pipes to pull herself up into the narrow access space. Then she would have shimmied along to the elevator, entering the shaft. With the car stationed at Lark's apartment the intruder would only have had two options.

The elevator opened on an empty car. That left a single option: the intruder must have gone up. Emily stepped into the car and pressed the button to ascend.

She had to hurry. If Lark woke to find her gone, there would be hell to pay.

They sat next to each other on a cold stone stoop, Gillian's arms on top of her knees to cushion her cheek. Her eyes were still wet but the tears had stopped falling. Riley had one hand on Gillian's back, the other on her arm. After several minutes of staring into space, Gillian turned toward Riley, folding against her body in the instinctive posture of vulnerability. Riley held her, resting her cheek against the crown of Gillian's head.

"But you've been so happy. So calm. Is... is that denial?"

"Maybe a little. I accept it, though. I went through it all with Priest, the bargaining and looking for a scheme to get out of it. She said that there's no fix. We've screwed up the timeline before, brought me back from things I shouldn't have walked away from. But this time is different."

"Why? How can you accept it, Riley?"

She thought for a moment, trying to put into words something she'd been feeling since Priest dropped the bombshell on her.

"Ever since I was thirteen, I've known I could die. I would wake up and think one of my father's friends would get a little too rough, or I'd steal from the wrong shop, or I would just walk into the wrong bar wearing the wrong colors. Then I became a cop in No Man's Land, and I knew all it would take was a lucky shot to take me out. Death has always been right around the corner. I never cared until I met you, until I finally had something to lose."

Gillian lifted her head and kissed Riley's cheek. Riley stroked her hair.

"The first time I died, I got thrown off a building. An angel brought me back. Then the Angel Maker punched me with a knife in his hand, a lucky shot. Zerachiel brought me back."

"So... what? Third time is a charm?"

"No." Riley wet her lips. "I wasn't supposed to die those times. They didn't mean anything. This time, no matter how my heart stops, I'll be dying to save your life. I'll know that my sacrifice means you got another day. I can not only live with that knowledge, it's how I would choose to die. I only regret that I'll be leaving you behind."

Gillian looked into Riley's eyes. "I don't know what I'll do without you, Riley."

"Well. We have time to figure it out. I'm going to spend the two years I have left making sure you have a lifetime worth of love." She kissed Gillian's lips, and Gillian held her when she tried to pull back. The kiss finally broke and Riley smiled. "Wow. Yeah. Like that."

"Why didn't you tell me?"

"Because I wanted everything to be normal. Good and bad, ups and downs. I didn't want everything tinged with a ticking clock. But I had to tell you. I had to tell you so that you could decide for yourself what you wanted."

Gillian frowned. "What I want?"

"If you stay with me to the bitter end or... wean yourself off. Walk away while you can. The small pain now or a big pain later."

"It will never be a small pain, Riley. And if I only have two more years with you, I'm not going to waste a single second of it." She attempted a weak smile and touched Riley's bottom lip. "You gave your life for me. I always knew you would, in theory and hypothetically. But you actually did it. You love me that much?"

"More," Riley said. "We're just lucky the world gave in to my demands so cheaply."

"I don't want to live without you," Gillian whispered.

Riley's expression hardened. "Don't say that, Gillian. I gave my life so you could live on. Even if you have to go on without me. Your survival is all that matters."

"But I would do the same thing for you, Riley. If it meant you lived~"

"Sh. What's done is done."

"I can't die for you because you died for me first?"

Riley chuckled. "Something like that."

Gillian looked out into the street. A van was moving slowly down the street, tossing sheaves of bundled newspapers onto front stoops. Traffic had picked up slightly as people woke and headed to work before the rush.

"You know I love Priest... but I don't care what she says. So what if she says there isn't a loophole this time? She brought you back from the dead. You were a corpse, and she brought you back in one piece. You were thrown off a building and you came back. So the angels won't help you this time. Fine. It's the mortal's turn." She grabbed Riley's hand and squeezed hard. "You fought to save me. Now I'm going to fight to save you."

Riley kissed Gillian again. "I love you."

"I love you, too."

"C'mon. Let's go home and get some rest."

Riley stood and helped Gillian up off the stoop. She put her arm around Gillian's waist, already feeling calmer and more relaxed now that she had revealed her secret. She looked at her watch and sighed.

"You do realize we have to be at work in about an hour."

"Yeah," Gillian said. "Maybe we'll get lucky and it'll be a slow day."

Emily stepped out of the elevator with the gun at her hip, pausing to scan the room in front of her before she ventured out. The room was wide open, with no separation between rooms beyond furniture that demarcated different areas. Everything was leather and dark oak, and even her bare feet made a quiet noise against the hardwood floor. The room smelled of sex and oil, remnants of Lark Siskin's celebration from the night before. She had been officially named mayor, and the debauchery had only been muted by the absence of Abby. Emily forced herself to put aside her loneliness and focus on the problem at hand.

She blocked the elevator until the doors slid silently shut behind her so the intruder couldn't slip through. "There's no need to be afraid. Your punishment will be swift... I assure you, there will be no pain. It will be just like going to sleep." She moved into the room, scanning for movement in the shadowed corners. "You should take your punishment. You broke into this place, and you were caught. You've been bested, and it's only proper for you to accept your loss."

She pivoted on the ball of her right foot, spinning to look back the way she had come. The room was open, but there were plenty of places for a wily opponent to conceal themselves. She didn't have time for this. The sun would be fully up soon and Lark would awaken. Then Emily would have a punishment of her own to face. She set her jaw and turned in a slow circle.

"You will be found. The longer you make me search for you, the less inclined I will be to show mercy. I understand that a quick death is hardly incentive, but keep in mind that you are going to die regardless. You will never again going to breathe fresh air, and you will never see the sun. I'm giving you the chance to leave this world peacefully."

The intercom buzz, startling her. She growled and stalked to the panel, scanning the room as she held down the button.

"What?"

A guard from the lobby spoke, his voice echoing slightly but as clear as if he'd been in the room with her. "Ma'am, there are two people here who insist on speaking with someone in charge."

She pressed her lips together as she watched for any signs of furtive movement in the room. "Tell them to return during business hours. It's not even dawn."

"Yes ma'am, I've told them as much. They say they're investigating a break-in."

Emily considered that for a moment. "Continue the lockdown on the upper floors, particularly the Mayor's recreation floor. All security sensors should be activated. No security codes on this level should be accepted."

"Ma'am?"

"You heard me. Even if they're using an authorized code, don't accept it until you have confirmed the identity of the person using it. Tell our guests that I'll be right down."

"Yes, ma'am."

Emily called the elevator and faced the room again. "You'll not get out of this building. You've made me very angry, miss. Very angry indeed." She tapped the gun against her hip and stepped into the waiting car. She pressed the door close button and then, a moment later, opened them again. She stepped out and listened to the room. It was completely still. Emily smiled slightly, proud of her opponent for not breaking cover, and nodded. "Very good, little mouse. I'd have been disappointed."

She rode the elevator to the private floor, stopping just long enough to get a robe before continuing to the lobby.

There were two guards on duty, and both of them were hovering near the windows that fronted the building. They turned at the sound of her approach and Emily saw to whom they had been speaking. One was a woman in her late thirties, a shock of brown hair falling forward over her face in an attempt to hide the burns that marred her jaw line. She wore an army jacket so large that the sleeves covered her hands. Next to her was a young girl, barely into her twenties if she was even that old, dressed in a threadbare college sweatshirt and a military cap. Part of her surprise stemmed from the fact their early morning guests weren't Parra and Priest.

"Do you have any idea what time it is?"

"Yes, ma'am. Sorry." She spoke loudly to be heard through the glass. "My name is MacKenzie Stanton. I'm a private investigator. This is Aissa Good; she works at a shelter in the area. We have reason to believe that a homeless girl has gotten into your building through a wall in the garage that was damaged by the earthquake. She was just looking for a warm place to sleep and now we're afraid she's gotten trapped and can't get out."

"There are laws against trespassing." Emily tried to disguise her irritation; this private investigator and her friend from the shelter meant that she wouldn't be able to dole out the proper punishment even if she did find the intruder. "As it happens, I believe your little friend made it up to the mayor's private residence. I could have her arrested from breaking and entering."

"Please," Aissa said. "She didn't mean any harm. Whatever she did, I'm certain she was just trying to find a way out of the building. She's completely harmless."

An alarm chimed from the security desk, and one guard went to respond. Emily watched him go before focusing on the women outside.

"Leave your contact information. When we find this girl, we'll call the proper authorities and have them get in touch with you in regards to bail."

Kenzie glanced at Aissa. "Ma'am, maybe you want us to show

you how we think she got inside your building. Just so this sort of thing doesn't happen again."

It would be useful information to have, and it would save her time trying to find it herself. She checked her watch and saw she had forty-five minutes before Lark's wake-up time.

"Very well." She motioned for the guard to unlock the door, and looked back at the one who had returned to the desk. He gave her a thumbs-up and she nodded before stepping outside into the cold. It cut through her robe as if it wasn't there, the wind plastering the legs of her pajamas to her body. She cinched the robe tighter and gestured for their two guests to lead the way. They walked down the sidewalk, along the cement planters overflowing with leafy green shrubbery.

"We're very sorry to bother you so early," Kenzie said without looking back at her.

"Just consider yourself fortunate that you didn't disturb the mayor."

"Perish the thought," Kenzie said under her breath. Emily didn't like the woman's tone, but decided to ignore it for the time being. The sidewalk was freezing under her bare feet, but she forced herself to ignore it. It wasn't cold enough to be painful.

They entered the underground garage, which was kept open at all hours. Security lights burned yellow-orange at ten-foot intervals, casting eerie lights on the cars of building security. The kitchen staff had arrived and, she knew, were busy preparing the mayor's breakfast upstairs. The sight of their vehicles prompted another look at her watch.

"Who is this girl?"

"No one of consequence," Kenzie said after a moment. "She's a... runaway."

Emily said, "Why are you lying to me, Stanton?"

Aissa said, "Maybe because it's none of your business who she is."

Kenzie spoke the girl's name under her breath and Aissa turned away. "Sorry about her. The girl is a friend of hers."

"You should tell your friend not to violate private property. There are plenty of other places for her to sleep. Breaking into a building only means she'll be sleeping in prison." She smiled coldly. "The silver lining is that she will at least get three hot meals and a warm bed."

The woman put a hand on the girl's arm, apparently

forestalling a counterargument or an attack. "We'll definitely have a discussion with her. Miss... I'm sorry, I don't think I got your name."

"Emily Simon."

They arrived at the back of the garage, near the elevator banks. Sure enough there was a sizeable crack in the foundation. It wouldn't be large enough for most people, but Emily remembered that the intruder had apparently spider-crawled between a set of pipes and the drop-ceiling acoustic tiles. Their quarry must have been incredibly petite, or abnormally agile. Possibly both. Kenzie put her hand into the crack and nodded.

"This goes straight to the Underground. She came up, probably slipped into the maintenance hatch for the elevator, climbed on up hoping she could find an empty room where she could bed down."

"Seems like a lot of trouble when she has a friend who works for a shelter." She looked pointedly at Aissa. "Did you not offer your friend a place to sleep?"

"The shelters are overcrowded. Maybe you didn't notice the earthquake damage in No Man's Land was a lot worse than a little crack in the wall."

Emily said, "Oh, we noticed. The mayor is dedicated to providing assistance to each and every afflicted person." She paused. "Provided they go through the proper channels and submit all the necessary paperwork, of course."

Kenzie stepped between Aissa and Emily. It was a subtle move, but one that wasn't lost on either woman.

"You should get that checked out," Kenzie said. "No telling how much damage a bad foundation can do to the entire building."

Emily's eyes flashed. "What did you say?"

"A bad foundation?" Kenzie looked genuinely confused. "The... big-ass crack..."

"Yes. Of course, no." She nodded, putting aside a ghost of a memory. A bad foundation. She swallowed and nodded back toward the street. "I would thank you to leave now. The day is about to begin, and I have much to do."

Kenzie took out a card and held it out to her. "So you can have the police call us when you find our friend."

Emily took the card and glanced at the writing on it. Stanton Investigations. "Thank you for calling our attention to the foundation issues. We'll certainly amend this as soon as possible."

"Right. Come on, Aissa. There's nothing else to do here."

Aissa hesitated, but then followed Kenzie out of the garage.

Emily stepped forward and peered into the crack. It was wide enough for her to fit through, but only just. Her robe and possibly her pajamas would catch on the rough walls and she would be stranded. Even if the intruder was a child, she would have had to be incredibly determined to use this method of entry. Emily looked back at Kenzie and Aissa as they left the garage.

She knew they were lying. It was simply a matter of which part of their story was the lie.

Riley opened the apartment door and, as she stepped inside, felt Gillian press against her from behind. She was turned and pressed against the wall, too surprised to even cry out before Gillian's lips covered hers. She gave in as Gillian's tongue parted her lips, and she passively took it into her mouth as Gillian pushed up her brown leather jacket to grip the waistband of her jeans. Riley got her arms around Gillian to grab her ass and pull her close, approving of the situation physically since she couldn't speak at the moment.

When the kiss broke, Gillian gasped and brushed her lips over Riley's closed eyes. "I thought we could try to go back to bed, sleep for another hour or so, then get up for work... or I could take advantage of being awake with you." She kissed the corners of Riley's mouth. "How tired are you?"

"Sleep is overrated. But going back to bed..."

She tried to push Gillian toward the bedroom, but Gillian resisted. "No..." She pushed Riley against the wall, her hand against Riley's shoulder until she was certain Riley would stay put. She bit her bottom lip and sank slowly to kneel in front of Riley. The jeans were snug enough that Riley hadn't worn a belt, so Gillian simply undid the button and dragged them down her hips, pausing to pull the underwear down with them.

Riley flattened her palms against the wall and closed her eyes. Gillian ran the tip of her tongue over Riley's hips, then down into her pubic hair. Her hands brushed over Riley's inner thighs to ease them apart. Riley bent her knees and looked down, making eye contact just as Gillian's tongue pressed flat against her. She moved one hand up to find Riley's on the wall, and Riley threaded their fingers together as Gillian's other hand joined her tongue.

First there was just a teasing brush of knuckle, then Gillian moved her lips to Riley's clit and eased her finger inside. Gillian murmured, resting her lips against sensitive flesh so that the vibrations transferred to Riley.

"Good?"

"Yes..."

She barely moved her head away from Riley to speak, her breath warming the already hot flesh. "How good?"

"Amazing, Jill..."

"Mm, good." She curled her tongue against Riley's clit, and Riley's head thudded against the wall. "Sorry."

"Sh, don't... keep going..."

Gillian did as she was told, adding a second finger. Soon Riley's hand moved to the back of Gillian's head to hold her in place, and Gillian used her now-free hand to hold tightly to Riley's hip. She sucked Riley's clit hard and extended a third finger, teasing it against Riley's sex just as she began to come.

"Don't hold back, sweetie," Gillian whispered. She rested her forehead against Riley's stomach, watching as her fingers as she twisted her wrist and then pushed them deep. Riley arched her back and Gillian kissed her through her T-shirt, Riley's legs trembling as she rocked her hips forward against Gillian's hand.

"Good girl," Gillian whispered. "That's my darling girl..."

Riley shuddered as she exhaled sharply, sagging forward with her hips against the wall. She looked down at Gillian, face flushed and eyes half-lidded, and smiled.

"What was that all about?"

Gillian stood up, staying in contact with Riley as much as possible. "That was me, appreciating you while I can." She pecked Riley's bottom lip, and Riley teased her tongue into Gillian's mouth. She cupped Gillian's ass again and bent her knee, pressing her leg between Gillian's thighs.

"Settle..."

Gillian rested on Riley's thigh and they rocked against each other. "Ah..." Gillian rested her hands on Riley's shoulders for balance, both of them keeping their eyes open to watch the other. Riley used her hands on Gillian's ass to guide her thrusts, and Gillian let herself be maneuvered.

"Riley..." Her eyes drifted shut and Riley kissed her lips, muffling her groans as she came. Her fingers dug into Riley's shoulders as she tensed. Gillian's eyes snapped open and she focused on Riley, both of them perfectly still in the moments after her orgasm. Riley relaxed her grip on Gillian's ass, turning it into a caress as they kissed tenderly.

In the silence afterward, when Riley became aware of the sweat on her face and her burning ears, she kissed Gillian's cheek and straightened her leg to let Gillian stand. Gillian pressed against her and they kissed tenderly as she helped Riley pull her pants back up.

"We have two years together," Gillian said quietly. "I'm not going to waste them being mad because you made that choice, or because you kept the secret from me. I'm going to cherish the time we have. Life is literally too short." She brushed her thumb over Riley's cheek. "I'm honored you want to spend the last two years of your life with me."

"There's no one else I would rather spend them with."

"Come on... let's at least go lie down until the alarm."

"Time cuddling with you in bed? I'll take that." She slipped her hand into Gillian's and let herself be led down the hallway.

"What do you mean there wasn't anything there?"

"Just what I said, ma'am." The guard was trying to maintain his composure. "The alarm went off on the private floor, but our guys didn't see anything when they went up there to check. We had the entire floor locked down. No one came in or out of the building after you made your first call. If there was anyone here, they aren't here now. If you think that's impossible, then... maybe you were mistaken about someone being here in the first place."

Emily glared at his partner and then back at the man bearing the brunt of her wrath. "Cue up the security footage from tonight. All of it. I want it all sent to my office for review. If I find anything I don't like, I'll have more than your job. Am I understood?"

"Yes, ma'am."

He didn't sound wary, which meant he was confident she would come up empty. She didn't like that. "I want a floor-by-floor search before you lift the lockdown. The mayor and I will go to work, but no one else leaves until the building is secure."

The other guard said, "Ma'am, our shift ends in twenty minutes."

"Then you'll clock some overtime. Appreciate the paycheck; it will be your last day employed with us. Find this girl."

She walked away, infuriated by their incompetence. She stepped into the elevator and adjusted her robe over her pajamas, trying to figure out how the ghost could have gotten out of the building without being seen. The odd guests... MacKenzie Stanton and Aissa Good. Could they have anything to do with the escape?

She ran it over in her mind but couldn't imagine how. Both had been outside already, so drawing her attention couldn't have helped them get away. It was a question she would have to ask the bitch when they caught her.

At the apartment she walked quickly to the master bedroom, slipping through the door and closing it quietly behind her. She was so intent on resuming her position that she didn't notice the bed was empty before she was standing at the foot of it.

"No..." She looked around the room, half-frantic, and then went back out into the living room.

Lark was standing in front of the picture window, stoic and statuesque against the violet-blue of the sky. Emily shuddered violently when she saw her, terrified by the fact she had run right past her without noticing. She swallowed the lump in her throat and stepped furtively forward.

"Ma'am... I am sorry. I am so terribly sorry that~"

"I woke alone," Lark said. "I am displeased."

The mayor's voice was soft, and that only increased Emily's anxiety. She clasped her hands behind her back, trying to control her shuddering.

"My apologies. There was a situation in the building."

"Did you resolve it?"

Emily's teeth grinded together. "No, ma'am."

Lark sighed, and it was like sandpaper on the back of Emily's neck. Tears began to flow down her cheeks. "Please, ma'am... I'm sorry."

Lark turned to face her. "You know the rules, Emily. You must be punished."

"Yes, Miss." She got onto her knees and leaned forward until her forehead was touching the carpet. She closed her eyes, trembling and forcing back her tears as she waited for the punishment to begin.

The catering staff that made the mayor's breakfast stood in a row near the freezers. They were exhausted and irritated at the delay between the end of their work and their return home. Several of them had other jobs that were due to start soon. The supervisor quietly assured his people that it was only a temporary delay and looked hopefully toward the security guard that was going down the row checking off each member of the team.

"What's your name?"

"Cerys Good."

"How long have you worked for the company?"

"Only two weeks. I'm an apprentice. I just graduated culinary school."

The guard looked at her, gauged that she was young enough for this to be true, and looked back down. "What's your job?"

"I don't have a job. I mean, I just do whatever I'm told. Get stuff out of the truck, fill in at the omelet station, or make the gravy for the biscuits." She shrugged. "I'm being trained so I do a little bit of everything."

"Okay." He moved on to the next person.

Cerys leaned against the edge of the prep table and feigned boredom. She crossed her feet and kicked the heel of one non-slip shoe against the toe of the other. Being a go-fer meant that she could disappear for an hour or so without causing too much of a disruption. Anyone who needed her just assumed she was on an errand for someone else. She just had to keep her hands in her pockets so the guard wouldn't notice the burns she'd gotten clutching the elevator wires for the ride down. Her entire body ached from the gymnastics she'd put it through, but it was all part of a Good Girls training.

Before long the security guard confirmed everyone on the team was who they claimed to be and dismissed them. They filed out into the parking garage and began to scatter for their vehicles. Cerys started for the street instead.

Georgia, the member of the staff closest to Cerys in age, called after her. "You want a ride? I don't have anywhere to be."

"No, thanks. I think I'll walk." She smiled and waved, waiting for Georgia to turn away before she walked out of the garage. She reached the end of the block before she spotted Aissa and an older woman waiting for her. She slowed down but didn't avoid them. She stopped when Aissa was directly in front of her. "Who told you where I was?"

"One of the girls at the shelter mentioned you had gotten a job here. She asked how you were doing." Aissa looked disappointed rather than angry. "So? How did you do?"

Cerys looked down at her feet. "I didn't find anything."

"As I told you." Aissa sighed and put her hand on Cerys' shoulder. "The woman in custody killed Annora. Detective Parra is certain of it. Whatever else happens, Annora has received justice. The rest will follow in due course. I know you stayed to avenge what happened to the woman you loved, but there's no sense endangering yourself in the process. Swear to me you won't pull another stunt like this."

"I swear. I'm sorry, Aissa."

Aissa hugged her tightly. "You have nothing to apologize for. You're simply a woman who lost someone she loves. It would affect any of us the same way."

Cerys nodded, then finally acknowledged Kenzie. "Cerys Good, this is MacKenzie Stanton. She's a private investigator, and a friend. She's the one who distracted the guards and Emily Simon so you could slip through the security net."

Kenzie nodded a greeting. "I wasn't sure where you were in the building, but I thought a distraction might help. Nice to meet you."

"And you."

"That was a pretty slick scam, getting into the building like that. And getting away without being spotted? That took skill. If you ever need a little work, come by. Chelsea and I could use a few Bakers Street Irregulars." The girls looked at her. "Sherlock Holmes. It's a movie. Well, books and a..." She scratched her unscarred cheek and rolled her eyes. "You girls have a lot of catching up to do. For now, we all had a big night. How about I call my wife, see if she's willing to make breakfast for all of us?"

Cerys nodded. "That would be wonderful. Thank you."

Aissa put an arm around Cerys' shoulder and they followed Kenzie away from the mayor's building.

"When did you know you loved me?"

Gillian's head was on Riley's chest, her hair feathered across the blanket tucked under Riley's arms. Their plan to simply lie in bed and cuddle had turned into another quick lovemaking session, and she was still trying to catch her breath when Riley asked the question. She smoothed the blanket out against Riley's hip and thought about her answer.

"It was after I ran away, in Georgia. I decided I wasn't coming back. I never really liked this city all that much, and home was safe. It was a known quantity. I didn't have to worry about demons taking over my body or angels lurking on every rooftop. I thought I wanted the life I had before you came into it. But then one day I woke up and I hurt. I ached to come back. And I knew this city wasn't my home, and this apartment wasn't my home. My home was wherever you were. That's when I knew. When I was willing to walk back into Hell just to be by your side."

"I'm sorry."

"Don't be." She sat up and looked into Riley's eyes. Her hair was down, falling in waves over her left shoulder. With the blanket draped over her, she looked like a boudoir photograph. She touched Riley's cheek. "I was taking a backward step. I was running away and hiding. Coming back here to be with you made me braver. Made me a stronger person. Made me worthy of being with someone as brave and impressive as you."

Riley curled her fingers in Gillian's hair.

"So when did you know you loved me?"

"The first time I went up against Marchosias, in the hotel. His demons nearly flayed me alive. I couldn't hope... I didn't expect to survive those injuries. I was ready to give up, and at the time I wouldn't have minded too much. I didn't come here because you're a doctor, Gillian. That was actually the last thing on my mind when I made my way here. I came to you because I wanted to see you one more time. All the time I wasted... I wanted to see you again. And when I woke up the next morning, alive, in your bed, that was when I knew."

"Letting you in here that night opened the door to demons and angels and Heaven and Hell..."

"Like I said... sorry."

Gillian shook her head. "The only thing I'd change is that I would open the door earlier. I'd go back in time and grab myself the day we met and I'd shout at her to kiss you."

"Then I might be afraid of the crazy kissing medical examiner."

Gillian started to respond, but she was interrupted by the plaintive cry of the alarm clock. Riley reached over and silenced it, then looked at Gillian. It was the start of another day, one day closer to Riley's deadline. Gillian's smile faded completely and she blinked away her tears, lowering her head to Riley's chest. Riley held her wife and stroked her hair, closing her eyes when Gillian began to cry softly. She decided to stay in bed until hunger forced them to take breakfast.

Dawn was starting to break across the city, but the day could start without them, just this once.

AMONG THE FAITHLESS

THE BODY was spotted nine minutes after six in the morning. The first squad car arrived eight minutes later, and by ten-thirty the entire area was roped off and swarming with uniformed officers. Riley parked behind the Medical Examiner's van and climbed out into a cold drizzle. She flipped the hood of her jacket up over her head and looked across the car to see Priest doing the same. Their crime scene was a parking lot enclosed on three sides by tall brick buildings, forming a box with only one exit. Each building had a loading dock backed up to the parking lot, but currently it was full of emergency response vehicles. Riley saw a group of uniformed police officers speaking with obviously irate business owners whose deliveries had to be delayed due to the investigation.

One of the officers stepped forward to lift the yellow tape for them. She recognized him from other crime scenes and nodded in greeting. He looked miserable, his cap protected by a transparent plastic bag, his uniform draped by a navy blue slicker.

"What's the story on this one, Officer Patton?"

"Bakery truck saw him when he arrived. No idea how long he'd been lying there, but he said he didn't see anyone else around."

Gillian's interns had set up a white tent that covered the scene, protecting any evidence from being washed away. The body was underneath a brick overhang, but the tent prevented the drizzle from coming in at an angle. Gillian had her back turned when Riley approached, and she lightly touched the shoulder of her windbreaker. Gillian smiled but turned in the opposite direction, watching as Priest approached the dead man's feet. The killing wound was to his throat, a jagged red tear just above the collar of his shirt. His last outfit had consisted of a much-wrinkled shirt unbuttoned over a T-shirt. His pants appeared to be a faded black, but Riley looked closer and saw that the color was the result of many smears of white powder.

"Detectives."

"Doctor," Riley said. "Our man is a baker?"

"Astounding, Holmes. One of his employees identified him as Alex Baker." Riley raised an eyebrow and Gillian chuckled. "I swear, I'm not making that up." Gillian and Riley both moved to the left at the same time, inadvertently making it look like a choreographed motion, but neither noticed. "I have a preliminary finding to share with you, but I don't want you to overreact."

Riley looked at her, then looked at Priest. "I'm getting that 'uh-oh' feeling."

Gillian gestured for Riley to crouch and pointed with her pinkie. "Do you see the way his throat was cut? The power behind the initial strike, and the leverage necessary to pull the knife back after it was in... someone used their right hand to stab the right side of this guy's neck. Then they pulled it out."

Riley's stomach did a flip, but then she realized the significance. "Ah, damn. Just like that guy last week. What was his name?"

Priest knelt on the other side of the body. "Henry Winn."

Gillian nodded. "I'll have to get him back to the morgue to make an official connection, but the cut looks like it was made by the same knife. Everything else matches; the body was left in an isolated location, no witnesses, only one wound on the victim. I hate to say it, but I think it's another serial killer."

Riley sighed. "Well. We took down one of those before. Priest, don't help this one."

Priest flinched. "I..."

"I'm kidding. Gallows humor." She put her hands on her knees and pushed herself up. She scanned the parking lot, passing her eyes over a crack in the concrete before she went back to it. "Cait..." She motioned for Priest to follow her while Gillian remained with the body. The crack ran across the ground, its width alternating between paper-thin and wide enough for Riley to put her arm into it and feel a draft. Someone thin enough could possibly climb up from below.

"The last crime scene had cracks like this. Bigger, even. I didn't think anything of it because after the earthquake it seemed like everything had cracks. Last week Aissa and Kenzie found a crack like this in the underground parking garage of the mayor's building. She thought it went all the way to the Underground."

Priest looked to either side to see the origin and terminus of the crack. "It's certainly possible. There have been reports of sinkholes opening up entire sections of the Underground. You think the killer is using these cracks to escape unseen after the killings. Is it even possible to fit into that?"

Riley nodded. "Oh, yeah. Every summer people leave their garage door open a crack so it can air out a little, and intrepid thieves scurry underneath to make off with whatever they can carry. Something this wide? Even if they're crawling up instead of forward, I think it would be possible." She stood and looked around the parking lot. "The victim was a baker. Last week's guy was a... remind me?"

"A bartender."

"Two killings don't make a pattern, just like it doesn't necessarily make a serial killer. But I think it's pretty clear these people weren't targeted, they were just people who happened to be out and alone early in the morning." She resisted the urge to shudder, even though she could have blamed it on the drizzle.

Priest looked back toward the crime scene. Gillian was preparing the body for transport to the morgue.

"You think someone is killing just for the thrill of it?"

"I think that's rare," Riley said. "More likely there's a reason behind it that we're just not seeing, or the killing itself is the purpose. Right now all I'm sure of is that the killer is using the Underground to hide."

Priest frowned. "Why are you sure of that?"

"Because it's dangerous, and because I'm the detective investigating the murders. Of course it'll be in the Underground." She sighed. "I'm not being fatalistic. But seriously, the way this city screws with me?" She looked down at the crack and nodded. "Yeah. I'd bet good money I'll end up down there again. Come on."

Priest, obviously remembering the last time they ventured into the Underground, hesitated at the edge of the crack for a long moment before she followed Riley back to the car.

Their morning was spent gathering security footage from businesses near the crime scene, but as Riley predicted there was no sign of anyone joining Baker the Baker in the parking lot. Riley and Priest commandeered a side room at the precinct to scroll through the videos, giving themselves two hours on either side of Gillian's estimation for time of death. Baker's truck, a white Chevy, pulled in a few minutes before five. He reappeared to take out the trash, placing it in the alley before he went back out of camera range.

"Five-thirteen," Riley said softly, marking the last time Baker was shown to be alive. "That fits with Gillian's estimate that he hadn't been dead long."

Priest nodded. "Do none of the cameras have a more direct angle?"

"Why would they? There isn't another way into that parking lot, at least before that crack popped up." She leaned forward and ejected the final tape. "Okay, that settles it. No one else went in or out of that parking lot during the time of the murder."

"The killer could still have come through the buildings," Priest said. "There are other businesses with access to the loading docks."

"None of them were open at the time. Plus they were all eager to get their security tapes to us. We didn't even have to get a warrant." She sighed and rubbed her eyes, trying to undo the afterimages caused by fast-forwarding through all the tapes. "Someone came up through that crack, out of the Underground. We have Morlocks."

Priest searched her memory, but Riley took pity on her.

"It's an old science-fiction story. A guy goes hundreds of thousands of years into the future and finds that humanity has evolved into the soft, peaceful Eloi and the dark, beast-like Morlocks. The Eloi live aboveground and the Morlocks live in the dark underground. They come up during the night and eat the Eloi."

"That's disturbing."

Riley shrugged. "That's the sort of thing they wrote back then. But now we have a real-life variation. The earthquake gave them access through those cracks. But I don't think they're just coming up to kill for a lark. They've always had ways to get up here. Why would they start taking advantage of it now, just because it's slightly easier?"

"It could be that the person using the cracks isn't from the Underground at all. At least, not originally. Perhaps someone discovered they were an easy method of moving around without being seen."

"Kind of like a secret passage." She considered that. "Whoever was doing that would have to know the Underground pretty well to be able to move around without getting lost. You remember what it was like down there."

Priest tensed slightly. "Clearly. If Lieutenant Briggs does approve of us going down there, I recommend taking someone who knows the terrain."

"Radio."

"He was living down there when we met him. The people down there know him and trust him. Last I heard, he was still in town somewhere in No Man's Land. Kenzie or Aissa would be certain to know. And if he agrees he would be an invaluable asset to the investigation."

Riley nodded. "We can ask Kenzie where we might find him."

"Actually, there's someone else who might have a better idea."

The diner was typical of every other diner Riley had seen or eaten in during her lifetime. The counter was to the right, with a row of booths to the left. The only customers present occupied the two booths farthest from the door. Aissa was seated at the counter and turned as the bells over the door chimed. She straightened slightly when she saw it was Riley and Priest and knocked on the countertop. The short-order cook turned and smiled. He was a tall and muscular black man dressed all in white and he flashed a wide smile when he saw Rilye.

"Waiting on a friend?" Riley asked.

Radio put down the spatula he'd just used to flip a patty. "Back in the saddle."

Riley held out her hand, smiling as Radio took it in both of his. "Good seeing you again, Radio. Did you make it through the earthquake in one piece?"

He paused and took a slow breath. Riley was used to this when speaking to him. Post-traumatic stress had trigger an impediment where Radio was unwilling to speak without using song titles. He wet his lips, rolled his shoulders and then smiled. "We made it through fine. Detective Parra."

Riley's smile faded and her eyes widened. She looked at Aissa, who was smiling brightly. "What the hell was that?"

"Speaking. Aissa helps." He was speaking easily, but Riley could see it was still a strain.

Aissa said, "We met last year. We discovered that we had mutual friends in the Stantons, and Kenzie explained his situation to me. I tried to help him overcome the block."

Radio removed a pad from his pocket and held it out to Riley. "I write the songs."

Riley opened it and flipped through the pages of songs titled *Hello, Kenzie Crowe, Chelsea Stanton, Riley Parra, Caitlin Priest,* and various statements that otherwise would have been impossible for him to express. The lyrics were jumbled, with a lot of space-filler nonsense and simple rhymes. But if the process worked, that was all that mattered.

"This is fantastic, Radio."

"I don't even need songs. Not all the time. It helps, though. Sometimes I'll write the song in my head. Real quick. Just so it exists, even if it just exists for me." He took the pad back and tucked it into his pocket. "Helps with orders, too."

Riley smiled. "Speaking of which, we can wait until you're finished cooking. We don't want to get you fired."

"Be just a minute."

He turned back to the grill and Riley and Priest settled onto stools on either side of Aissa. Riley lowered her voice. "That was a really smart method. I never even thought about writing new songs with titles to fit odd situations."

Aissa shrugged. "It just occurred to me that he was the one who made the rules. It's not cheating. It's just finding a new way to work through the process."

"It's clever," Priest said. "Excellent work, Aissa."

"Thank you. He already knows that whatever you're here to ask him about could be dangerous. He's willing to help, whatever it is."

Riley watched Radio to make sure he wasn't eavesdropping. "Now I'm not sure we could ask. We didn't know how far he'd progressed. If this has a chance of causing a relapse, I don't know if it would be worth it."

"He wants to help," Aissa said. "He's not fragile, Riley. And he knows there isn't much point to getting better if everyone treats him like a child."

Radio had delivered the burger to his last customer and came back to stand across the counter from them. "I can help."

Riley looked at Priest, who nodded. The truth was they needed Radio's help, and it wasn't their place to make the decision for him.

"We're investigating a pair of murders that have occurred since the earthquake. We think the same person is responsible for both, and we have reason to believe that whoever it is used the Underground to escape from the scenes. I know the people down there are your friends, and we're not accusing them of this. For all we know the killer is someone from the city who just discovered the cracks were a convenient way to move around unseen. If that's true, the Underground citizens are in as much danger as anyone else. Lieutenant Briggs gave us the okay to go sniff around a little."

"What can I do?"

"We want you to clear a way for us," Priest said. "It will be hazardous enough venturing Underground with Riley's status as the champion."

Riley said, "You don't have to do this, Russell. We can find another way."

He had rested his hands on the counter with his head bowed as he listened. Finally, he looked at them again and shook his head. "No. I want to help. You went down there to save me. I can go back to help you."

"Thank you."

"That's what friends are for," he said. "When do we go?"

Riley said, "We'll let you decide that. If we go now, we might catch the majority of people down there when they're sleeping. But going at night, while more dangerous, might be more productive to finding the person we're looking for."

Radio gestured at the clock. "Nine to Five."

"We can wait until you finish your shift. Does it actually end at five?"

"Two," he said. "We're only open for breakfast and lunch."

Riley looked at the clock and checked it against her watch. "Okay. We can wait."

"I'll make you lunch. On the house."

"We appreciate it. Why don't you make up three burgers and some fries? We'll take it to a booth."

"Coming up."

They moved to the booth by the door, with Riley sitting across from Aissa and Priest. Riley smirked at them and shook her head.

"What?" Priest asked.

"Ten years ago, if someone said I'd be sitting in a diner with an angel and a former nun, I'd have sent them for a psych eval."

Priest smiled. "You've certainly grown a lot in the past few years."

Aissa said, "What is the Underground? I've heard several people discussing it, but none of them would tell me much."

Riley sighed. "First of all, don't go down there unless you absolutely have to. And even then you should take as much back-up as you can find. It's a... what did you call it?"

Priest said, "A forgotten realm. On the surface, Marchosias and his forces have to put on a show of humanity. Down there, not so much. They have free reign to show off their powers without consequence."

"Basically the Underground is a maze. Old buildings, former streets that got turned into passageways, and it all makes a labyrinth ruled by whoever happens to have the most power that day. The Underground is what No Man's Land would become if absolutely no one cared."

Aissa swallowed hard and smiled weakly. "If it's all the same to you, I think I'll skip going down there with you."

"That saves me the trouble of forcing you to stay behind."

"I'm sorry," Aissa said. "I'm still trying to take on the challenge of No Man's Land. By the time I have to take up your mantle, I know that I'll be prepared for whatever this city has to throw at me."

Riley glanced at Priest and then quickly away, hoping Aissa hadn't caught her guilty expression. She still hadn't told anyone but Gillian about her impending doom, and had no idea how she was going to begin breaking the news to everyone who deserved to know. Fortunately Radio chose that moment to arrive with their lunch.

He pulled one of the stools over and sat at the head of their table. "I know some people... we can contact... to make our... entry into the Underground easier." His speech was stilted, as if he had written several songs in his head and was piecing together the titles. "They won't be able to conceal... the presence of a champion and an angel, but hopefully it will expedite our passage so we don't have to spend any more time down there than necessary."

"Thank you again, Russell," Priest said.

"How to save a life." He smiled and gestured at their plates. "Enjoy your meal."

Riley picked up a French fry and popped it into her mouth,

already chewing before she realized Priest and Aissa were holding hands. Their free hands were extended across the table, waiting for her to take them.

"Oh. Seriously...?"

Priest made a 'come on' gesture with her fingers. "That's the price of dining with angels and former nuns."

Riley wiped her fingers on a napkin and took their hands so they could say grace. Aissa said the words quietly and, when Riley opened her eyes, she saw one of the other customers had gotten up to pay his bill and had been staring at them. She raised an eyebrow and took her badge off her hip so he could see it. "We thought we could use all the help we can get out there. Do you have a problem with that?"

"No, ma'am. Sorry."

She returned the badge to her belt and reached for the ketchup. "Hopefully Radio knows an Underground entrance that's near the two crime scenes. If someone is just using the Underground as a way station, I doubt they would want to spend much time down there if they could avoid it. I'm not waiting for a third body to show up just so we can triangulate better." She took out her phone and used the map to mark the two crime scenes. They were nearly two miles apart with nothing obvious to connect them. At least nothing aboveground.

They finished their meal and Radio locked the door behind the last customer. He untied his apron and left it on a hook, moved the money from the register to a floor safe, and then joined them in the booth. He sighed heavily.

"I'm not sure I want to go down this road again. But I'm sure you've done a lot of things you're not sure about to protect the people of this city."

"If you want to turn back at any time, we'll understand," Riley said. "We'll find another way to catch this guy."

He nodded. "Thank you. How much do you know?"

Riley showed him her map, and he pinched the screen to expand the area. He rubbed his thumb along his chin and closed his eyes. "That's the west part of the city. Not a lot of development over there. You have buildings, of course, but they're mostly blocked off. People used to get into them to sleep and stay safe. There's a really big courtyard here." He pointed to a spot on the map that, on the surface, was occupied by a storage facility. "Sometimes people would congregate there on the weekends." He looked up and saw Riley was smiling. "What?"

"Nothing. It's just weird hearing you speak like this."

"I could have lied."

Riley smiled. "Feel good about it."

He tapped the map again. "There are ways to get from the courtyard to both of the crime scenes. If someone is setting up camp in the Underground that would be an ideal location."

"Show me the way," Riley said.

Radio considered for a moment and then expanded the map and moved it down two blocks until he found a drainage ditch. He followed it back to where it disappeared under a bridge.

"There's sewer access in the tunnel here, and from there you can take a ladder down into the Underground. It's probably the least harrowing method."

"Lucky day."

He looked sideways at her, smiling. "I'm not alone."

Riley shrugged and nudged him with her elbow. "I get a kick out of you."

Priest glanced at Aissa, who was following the proceedings with confusion. Priest smiled. "Riley is speaking in song titles."

"Oh. It is well with my soul."

Radio winced. "Maybe we should head out before it spreads any further."

"Probably a good idea." She slid out of the booth.

Aissa stood with Priest. "What can I do? I may not be going Underground with you, but I can still lend a hand."

"Stay by the phone Gillian and I got for you," Riley said. "If we don't get in touch by midnight, call Lieutenant Briggs. Tell her to send a SWAT team to come get us."

"Isn't that a little excessive?"

Radio shook his head. "If we're still down there at midnight, we're going to need all the firepower we can get."

After dropping Aissa off at the mission, they stopped at Priest's apartment so she could pick up her knife. Since brandishing her sword a year earlier to free Riley from Marchosias, she had become taken with the idea of protecting herself with a blade. The knife was smaller than her sword, and completely mortal in origins, but it would do the trick. She ordinarily never carried it when she was on duty, but she had a feeling it would come in handy during their present excursion. They parked a few blocks away from the drainage ditch and walked to the bridge, pausing before they went down into the dark. Riley took the lead, with Priest in the rear. Riley eyed the graffiti on the tunnel walls and faced Radio.

"What kind of resistance should we find down there?"

"This early in the day, it won't be anything too overwhelming. Most people sleep during the day to be active during the night. Occasionally they leave a small group to watch the entrances, but they shouldn't put up too much trouble."

Riley nodded. "Okay. You might want to take the gun out of your pocket before we head down." He tried to look confused, then looked chagrined. "You'd be stupid not to bring a weapon. I know you know how to use it, and I want you watching my back. So take it out so you won't be fumbling for it in the dark."

He took out a small gun, most likely the weapon used for security at the diner. "I'm sorry. I should have known better."

"Don't relapse now, pal. You're going to need your wits about you down there."

"Right."

Riley looked at Priest, who nodded that she was ready. The trio walked under the arch of the bridge, the temperature seeming to drop several degrees as soon as they were out of the sun. Remnants of the morning's rain had left a trickle of oily water in the lower dip of the ditch. Riley kept on the right side of the water, while Priest and Radio walked on the left. When they were close to the sewer access they crossed over to line up behind Riley.

"Radio, Priest and I will go in first. Once we're clear, you follow. Understood?"

"Yes, ma'am."

She opened the door and stepped into utter darkness, pausing in the hopes her eyes would adjust. Small caged lights hung off the brick walls every ten yards or so, but their muddy orange glow didn't extend very far. Riley could just make out a wide, squat tunnel with walkways on either side of a slow-moving runoff. To her surprise the smell was actually bearable. Though she had a flashlight, she didn't want to risk using it until it was absolutely necessary. If someone was lurking in the darkness, she didn't want to give them a focal point to attack.

She stepped out onto the walkway to let Priest join her and then motioned for Radio that he could come through. "Which way?"

Radio pointed. "Just down here. You go about fifty yards and then there's an alcove."

"Okay. Stay close."

Their footsteps echoed off the curved brick, both succeeding in making Riley anxious and telling her that it would be hard for anyone to sneak up on them. Hopefully Radio was right and anyone that would give them trouble was down for a nap. When they reached the alcove Radio reached out and touched Riley's elbow.

"Someone's following us."

Riley stopped and only then heard the pad of bare feet on the walkway behind them. Whoever it was stopped walking when they did. She searched the darkness but couldn't see anything. She put her hand on Radio's arm and, as softly as she could, said, "Talk."

"Friend of mine?"

Silence, except for Radio's deep voice echoing down the tunnel and coming back to them.

"Do you really want to hurt me?"

This time there was the sound of a shuffling step. "Radio? Izzat you?"

"Jumping Jack Flash?"

A light snapped on. The boy carrying it was at least six feet tall, nothing but skin and bones in a dirty jumpsuit, and when he hoisted the flashlight to get a better look at them, in the backwash Riley could see that his face was still dotted with acne. His eyes widened and he broke into a wide grin.

"Son of two cousins... Radio!" He lunged toward them, and it was only Radio's gleeful laugh that kept Riley from firing on him. The kid wrapped his arms, thin as foal-legs, around Radio's bulk and squeezed him like a spider. Radio slapped the kid's back hard enough that it had to bruise. "What the hell are you doing down here, man?"

"Coming home," Radio said. "With a little help from my friends."

The kid looked at Riley and Priest and slowly nodded. "Well, any friends of Radio are friends of mine. You can call me Tarpon. C'mon, man. We have a lot to talk about." He moved into the alcove and swung open the door to lead them inside. Radio slipped back toward Riley and ducked his head down next to her ear.

"Citizen soldier."

Riley nodded. She took her badge off her belt and slipped it into the pocket of her jeans. Radio followed Tarpon while Riley conveyed the message to Priest.

"Are you sure?" Priest asked.

Riley looked at Radio's broad back as he disappeared through the door. "Radio is. This is his turf now. So we'll go by his rules."

Priest nodded and put her badge away. Riley patted her arm and followed their guides into the Underground.

The doorway led into a cramped tunnel that made Tarpon's lantern seem much brighter. He kept casting glances over his shoulder at Radio, the sharp lines of his face cut into deep shadows by his smile.

"People said you weren't coming back, man. And for good reason, you know? Most people find a way to get outta here, there's no reason to come back down." His smile faded. "Ah, man, I'm... is everything okay? Are you doing all right?"

"Life's been good," Radio said.

Riley eyed him, partially sure that he was just putting on a show for the kid given how quickly his regression had come on. But the mental and emotional effects of being back in the Underground had to be taken into account.

"Good, man, good." He looked past him. "So who're these, anyway?"

"A voice in the dark," Radio said.

Riley deduced his meaning. "We're here to speak for him when he can't. We've known him for a while. We're pretty good at figuring out his meaning."

Radio nodded and tapped Tarpon on the arm. "Heard it through the grapevine. For what it's worth. See my friends." He looked at Riley and repeated. "For what it's worth."

After a moment Riley had mentally accessed the song and figured out he was referring to the lyrics rather than the title. "Radio's heard some bad things are happening. He was afraid for some of his friends down here, so he thought he would check up on them."

Tarpon nodded. "Oh. When isn't it dangerous down here, man? You know how it goes."

"And so it goes," Radio sighed.

"Anything specific?" Riley asked.

"I don't like talking to you."

Riley said, "You're not talking to me, you're talking to Radio."

Radio nodded. "Two hearts beat as one."

"I don't even know this chick."

"That should make it easier for you to ignore me. I'm just a voice in the dark, like Radio said." Priest had stepped back, no longer illuminated by the lantern's glow. Riley had a feeling that Tarpon wasn't even fully aware of her presence. Priest had done that in the past, and Riley was always disconcerted by how fully blind the angel could make people. "Radio just wants to help his friends. He wants to make sure they're okay. With everything that's happening, he didn't want to waste time making people dissect what he was saying."

"Friends in low places."

Tarpon sighed as they reached the end of the tunnel, handing the lantern back to Radio before clapping his hands together as if he was about to lift weights. The door was blocked by a crossbar that the skinny man had to lift with both hands and then lean against in order to get it open. He was so slender that it almost didn't happen, but just as Riley was about to step forward and help, the door swung inward. They went through into a wide thoroughfare. Boarded-up windows to the left and right showed where businesses had once stood. A low ceiling had been put in, turning the long-ago street into a wide interior corridor. She heard furtive footsteps on the ceiling above and wondered if they belonged to demons or humans. The population was about sixty-forty belowground in favor of the imps.

"Everybody's talking," Radio said.

"We're hoping someone down here could be a little bit more specific," Riley added.

Tarpon shrugged. "We can take care of our own. Stuff's been happening since the earthquake, and things are changing, but it's for the good down here. People up top are just a little bit closer to being like us now."

Priest finally spoke up. "I don't know how that's good for you." Tarpon looked sharply over his shoulder her, confirming Riley's theory that he'd forgotten - or been made to forget - she was even there. "The people on the surface need food, shelter, supplies, energy, just like you. And now it's more difficult for them to acquire. They'll be infringing on your supplies. They'll be taking up space that was once your territory. Where once you had free run, you'll now be scrounging for a foothold."

Tarpon faced forward again. "Yeah. Well, they're used to having everything handed to them. We're used to fighting for what we have. We have the upper hand for once. Maybe they'll keep falling while we'll finally get to take their place up top."

"Who have you been talking to?" Radio said.

Tarpon chuckled under his breath and shook his head. "Man. You know more songs than anyone I know, Radio. That one doesn't even sound familiar."

Radio looked at Riley and she knew he had slipped. "It's by a Canadian band."

"Oh. Well, there is a guy. He came down here about a year ago. After Jeremiah died, we were all kind of drifting. Finn brought us back together."

Radio tensed, his eyes dark with pain. Riley wanted to feel bad for Radio, but she couldn't bring herself to feel too bad about the old guy. She knew he'd been Radio's friend, but the wily bastard had hit her with a pipe and tried to hand her over to the demons. She was more concerned by the name Tarpon had just said.

"You said his name was Finn?" Riley said.

"Finn Burke."

The name almost made Riley stop dead in her tracks. The Burke family had been torn apart and absorbed into a larger group a year earlier when a demon named Danny Falco tried to unite them all under his banner. Of course his actual plan had been to turn Riley herself into a demon, a plan Priest had brilliantly foiled, but the remnants of his machinations had to go somewhere. Riley never imagined any of the Five Families would try to make a name in the Underground, but it seemed as if that was exactly what had happened.

"Why are you following a Burke? He's from top-side."

"We were all from top-side once, lady. Finn had a few setbacks, that's all."

Riley would have classified the beheadings of two family members as a bit more than a "setback," but she wouldn't argue semantics.

"A place called home?" Radio asked.

Riley translated. "Where does he hang out?"

Tarpon glared at her. "I can figure some of them out on my own, lady."

She wanted to snap at him for calling her lady, but she'd never offered him her name. She shrugged instead. "Sorry. I didn't want to risk overestimating your intelligence."

"Thank you," he said, then squinted and stared at her for a long moment trying to decide if he'd been insulted. Finally he gave up and just continued forward. "The Courtyards. He and his pals hang out down in the Courtyards."

Riley raised an eyebrow and looked at Radio. "Good call on that." He nodded. "Can you take us there?"

"Where you think I've been taking you? My place for tea and strumpets?"

This time Riley didn't correct him because she liked his version better than the real version. "We're going to see Finn now?"

"He likes to see everyone who comes down here. He doesn't regulate, he just wants to make sure everyone knows right off who the one in charge is and make sure no one has any big ideas. You shouldn't have anything to worry about, though. Anyone down here will put in a good word for Radio."

Riley wasn't concerned about that; she was worried Burke or one of his cronies would recognize her as a cop. She glanced at Priest and saw she was thinking along the same lines.

"Sounds like he's kind of a tyrant."

"Tyrant's a word for y'all up topside. Down here people do what needs to be done. He keeps anyone up top from taking advantage of us."

Riley muttered, "Yeah, because he got to you first."

Tarpon stopped and turned, glaring at her before he looked at Radio. "I don't like her."

"She works hard for the money."

"You really want to make Finn work through Radio's manner of speaking? I doubt he's the patient sort."

Tarpon worked his jaw and then rolled his eyes. "Fine. But I can understand Radio, so from now on, you don't speak! I don't need you translating so just shut up."

"You got it, fish stick."

He actually took a step toward her for that one, but Radio put a hand in the middle of Tarpon's chest and pushed him back.

"Go your own way."

"Radio..."

"You heard the man," Riley said. "Walk away, Renee."

Tarpon growled, then spun on his heel and stormed off. Radio hurried to catch up with him while Riley and Priest brought up the rear.

Priest moved closer to Riley. "Why are you antagonizing him? He could have been an ally against everything else we have to face down here."

"I don't trust him, and neither does Radio. Why do you think

Radio is pretending he can't speak normally? Besides, a member of the Five Families comes down here and starts regulating passage, and he leaves *this* guy as the gatekeeper. There's more to him than meets the eye, and I'm just trying to figure out what that means for us. Hopefully I'll have a chance to get Radio alone so we can discuss how he knew Tarpon before he came down here."

"Well, if alone is what you want you may be out of luck. I can feel them. The demons... they know we're down here, Riley."

She was suddenly reminded of being a child, lying awake at night and hearing the sound that was conclusive proof that something was lurking in the shadows. Of course, thanks to her father, there really were monsters in her room when the lights went out. The monsters were really here as well, currently sniffing the air and catching the scent of an angel and a champion moving deeper into their domain.

"Let's cross that bridge when we get to it."

"I'm afraid the bridge may already be behind us, and that our enemies are in the process of burning it. Speaking of enemies, did I hear him correctly? Finn Burke is dead, Riley. We saw his body. He was decapitated along with his father, Liam."

"That's not the first time we saw Finn Burke's body. Remember when Raum tried to set the Five Families against each other? He killed Finn Burke then, too."

"How is that possible?"

"Liam and Finn Burke rule their family like it's their own personal kingdom. They're the king and prince of the realm, so they have to protect themselves." She looked to see if Priest was getting it. "Look-alikes, Cait. They set up a cousin or a nephew who looks just right enough to fool a stranger, gives him fake ID, and they send those saps into the dangerous situation. If it's a trap, then some nobody gets killed. We figure it out once the DNA comes in, but by that point the real Liam and Finn have had a few weeks running around like ghosts, getting retaliation. It took us a long time to get wise. They've fooled Jill twice. She is not a happy camper."

"I would assume not." She turned to look behind her, eyeing the darkness with the steel eyes of a jungle animal.

"Problem?"

"Not yet. Soon, though, without question." She pressed her lips together. "Riley, in a situation like this, where the danger is thick and escape isn't guaranteed, I want you to make me a promise. If I tell you to leave me behind, you mustn't question it. This is like the hellhounds all over again. If I tell you to run, you must run. Promise me."

Riley stopped walking. Priest hooked her hand around Riley's elbow and urged her forward.

"I'm not going to abandon you, Cait."

"I'm concerned that knowing the day of your death has made you reckless. Just because you won't die today doesn't make you safe. It only means that you'll be left alive for whatever happens. The people and things that make their homes down here are, I assure you, experts at keeping their victims alive for as long as possible. If we become trapped, I want your word that you'll abandon me."

Riley set her jaw.

"I'm your guardian angel, Riley. If Caitlin Priest dies to protect you, then she'll have served her purpose. Zerachiel may even choose to create a new form in order to interact with you."

"Like I said... we'll burn that bridge when we get to it, okay? Right now no one is talking about abandoning anybody."

Priest knew when she was beaten so she simply nodded. Radio looked back to make sure they were keeping up and Riley nodded to him. They were getting close to the spot he'd indicated on the map. Already she could hear voices echoing off the walls around them. The ground under their feet began rising and they followed the steady incline until they stood on the lip of what seemed to be a large crater.

Around the perimeter of the space Riley could see other corridors that ended at the common area. The ground was thick with people, reminding her of courtyards outside of business parks at lunch hour. The far wall of the space was a former apartment building with the windows knocked out so that they looked like small, perfectly formed caves.

Very few people noted their arrival, and those that did were more focused on Radio than the people he was with. Riley kept her head down and her eyes up, watching for anyone who might recognize her. Priest had moved to walk slightly behind her, offering protection without seeming to be. Riley looked back and nodded her thanks as Tarpon led them to what had once been the building's main entrance.

The front doors were replaced with a tall wooden gate. Two men stood on either side of the gate, automatic weapons casually slung over their shoulders like fishing poles. The taller one was leaning against the door, his gaze sleepy but not missing anything that happened in his scope. The other was solidly packed with muscle, his hair cut into a short Mohawk. He was the first to step away from the building as Tarpon approached, and the taller guard straightened to add a second line of defense.

Tarpon held up his hands to show he was defenseless. "I have guests to speak with Finn. One of them is an old friend. He'll want to meet him, I assure you." He looked back at Radio and winked, then faced the guards again.

The stone-like guard dialed his cell phone and spoke so quietly Riley couldn't hear him from five feet away. He listened, nodded, and slipped the phone back into his pocket. He and his friend stepped aside, which Riley took as a tacit invitation to enter. Tarpon patted the men on the arms as he walked past them, and Riley saw the barely-restrained contempt they both had for him.

The lobby had been transformed into a throne room. Riley stopped at the threshold to appreciate the sheer scope of it. A row of torches lit a path from the door to the chair, also providing just enough light to illuminate the writhing bodies of women dancing between the torches and the wall. Dozens of other people milled around the periphery, either getting high or enjoying the high off whatever they had taken earlier. Riley guessed there were about thirty people in the room, but there could have been more in the shadows she couldn't see. Framed artwork and vases and wall hangings that looked expensive decorated the walls, obviously taken from the house aboveground when Finn Burke made the descent to his underworld realm.

The man himself was seated in a throne where the reception desk had once stood. He was illuminated by bright halogen floodlights positioned around his seat of power, and he leaned forward with his elbows on his knees. He grinned, flashing perfect white teeth as he rested his chin on folded hands. He wore a pair of wraparound sunglasses and a floral kimono that draped the bottom of the throne. He was tall, slender, and shaved almost bald with just a thin peach fuzz of white hair on his bullet-shaped head. Riley wondered how he could see even with the torches flickering nearby.

Riley feigned a quake in her voice and quoted, "I was just thinking, fellas. I really don't want to see the Wizard so much. I think I'll just wait outside."

Finn clapped and stood up. He was wearing a dressing gown over what looked like pajamas, and his bare feet slapped the tile as he walked forward.

"My, my. This is an auspicious day. What guests I have been graced with! Tarpon, you did a wonderful job."

"You know Radio?"

"Hm? No. I don't care about him." He aimed a finger at Riley. "Detectives Parra and Priest! My daddy likes you! He likes you an awful lot. Tell me, did you ever find who killed me? Either time? Or was it demons? Because after my first death that seemed ludicrous. The second made it more likely. But since I came down here, the whole 'demons did it' accusation has a special resonance for me."

Tarpon had stopped paying attention when he heard their names. "Detective...?"

"Yes. Detective. As in police officers. You brought *police officers* into my home, Tarpon."

The guards from outside grabbed Tarpon. They had moved so quietly that when they took the tall, thin kid into custody Riley actually jumped back a step. She'd have felt embarrassed if Priest hadn't done the same thing. How could two men move so quietly an angel couldn't hear them? Riley had a sinking feeling she already knew the answer. She looked back at Finn, his eyes hidden by sunglasses.

"Actually we never properly introduced ourselves. It's not the kid's fault."

"We have high hopes for our goons. We gave him so many opportunities. His luck ran out. But since he brought me such a valuable gift, we'll leave him alive. For the time being."

The guards dragged Tarpon off, the kid too terrified to even protest as he was pulled toward the hall where the elevators had once stood.

Finn waited until they were gone before he turned back to them. He clapped his hands together and grinned.

"Well, well, well. The heroes have been captured by the villain. What a horrifying predicament. In the old movies, this is where the film would end to get the rubes back into the theater the next week. But I think we're going to see this to the end right here and right now. I've never been a fan of suspense. So... which of you wants to be tied to the train tracks, and which of you wants to be dangled over a shark pit?"

Riley said, "Were you insane before you got down here, or is it an acquired taste?"

He laughed. "Oh, I was insane a long time before I came down here. Do you have any idea how boring it is to be the real me?

Anything fun, anything vaguely dangerous, and dear old papa sent out one of my idiot cousins. I mean, sure, one of them was decapitated and the other was... um... what happened to the other?"

"His throat was slit."

"Right. See, my father thought that was evidence his little scheme worked. But I knew that if we'd been in the same situation, we would have prevailed. The imposters only died because they were morons. In their stead the end result would have been much different. But bygones. Weak genes out of the pool, more room for the grownups to swim." He looked at Radio. "Who are you?"

Radio didn't answer, so Riley spoke. "His name is Radio. He's a friend. So I guess you're the one who arranged for the murders on the surface."

"Initiation rituals. I have to be certain I can trust the people in my employ."

Priest said, "Which murder did Tarpon commit? The baker, early this morning? He's the only person I've seen thin enough to fit through that crack at the crime scene."

"Very good detective work, Blondie. Yes, that was poor old Tarpon. I did the first one. Can't ask my people to do something I'm not prepared to do myself, right? There will be more. Starting with two detectives who have been causing no shortage of trouble for my family." He seemed suddenly lucid. Riley looked back to see people had flowed in from outside to see what was happening. The door was now blocked by a crush of people.

Priest raised an eyebrow but Riley shook her head. She didn't want to resort to theatrics if she could avoid it.

"Okay, Finn. You want to tell one of your kids to kill a cop? Which one will do it? You said you lead by example, so... come on. You kill me, and then you can order someone else to take down Priest. If you're still standing, that is."

Finn raised an eyebrow. "Oh, my goodness, how delightful. The cop has gumption."

"The cop has a gun." She took it from her belt and aimed it at him. "Come on. How fast do you think you are?"

He stepped closer. "You're going to shoot an unarmed man? Please. No cop alive would risk that paperwork." He pressed his chest against the barrel and leaned into it. He smiled. "If you have the guts to cover up something like this, then be my guest."

Riley hesitated and then dropped her weapon. "Finn Burke, you are under arrest."

He grabbed the barrel of her gun, wrenching it from her grip. He brought his other hand up over his head and brought it down like a hammer toward her head. Riley ducked her head in a defensive posture, but the blow never came. She compared the odd sensation washing over her to the effect of standing next to a speaker at a rock concert, a concussive shudder that worked through her bones and made her hair stand on end.

When she opened her eyes, she saw Finn sprawled a few feet away with his arms spread out to either side. His glasses had been knocked off, revealing bright red eyes of a man possessed by a demon. He stared at her, his barely-sane mask forgotten as she stalked toward him. Riley suddenly realized why he'd been hurt for touching her, and understood that his insanity was definitely more than the garden variety.

"How did you do that?"

"You're a demon," Riley said. "You must have been possessed soon after you came down here. Did you even realize?"

He glared at her.

ÒDoesn't matter. You're a demon, and I'm the champion. I have a tattoo that protects me against unprovoked attacks by piss-ant demons like you."

Finn rolled onto his hands and knees, sneering at her. "Tricky. You may have protection against me, but how about all of these fine people? Get her!"

The wall of people around the edges of the room moved forward. Priest puffed out her chest and rolled back her arms, preparing to do battle. Riley spotted her gun a few feet away but knew that she would never get to it in time. Finn got back to his feet, swaying slightly from the force of her assault.

Radio stepped forward between Riley and the crowd and bellowed, "Stop! Stop this! Stop this right now!"

Enough people in the crowd seemed to know Radio that they were able to stop the forward crawl. They were staring at him in shock, some of them looking confused as they tried to think of a song with titles to match what he had just said.

"Isn't there enough to work against without creating enemies for ourselves? We have to fight just to exist, just to be alive. With the earthquake, it's harder than ever to make it through each day."

Someone near the back of the crowd said, "Finn helps us."

"Finn helps himself," Radio barked. "He uses you. He turned Tarpon into a murderer and, when he decided the boy was a disappointment, dragged him away. What will he have you do? What *will* you do to gain the favor of the man who would be king? Stop this. Stop bowing down to a man just because he has power. He only has power because you gave it to him. Take it back. You're the ones who have earned the power. Don't give it up so easily, and not to someone like him."

Someone said, "Who the hell are you?"

Another person, one close enough that Riley could see his face, said, "That's Radio. And he's right. You want her, Mr. Burke? Do it yourself."

Finn sneered and pointed at Radio. "He's a traitor. Someone... so-someone..."

"How much power can he have if he's always asking you to kill for him?" Radio said. "He's a weak man. Walk away from him."

To Riley's surprise, the crowd did indeed begin to disperse. Priest crossed the room and stood beside Finn, holding out her palm. He stopped trying to stand and dropped back to the tile with a pained grunt. A few people moved cautiously toward Radio to thank him and welcome him back. They gave Riley and Priest a wide berth, hiding beneath the brim of baseball caps or behind their hoods. Riley respected their privacy and didn't try to see them.

Once they were alone with Finn, Riley and Radio walked over to where Priest was holding him at bay.

"A champion and an angel." He laughed, though it sounded more like a wheeze. "Guess Tarpon was a bigger fuckup than I gave him credit for."

Riley said, "Shit... Tarpon."

Radio was already moving. "I'll get him."

"I'm a little rusty, but I think I remember how this goes. Cait, keep him down." She closed her eyes and remembered the phrases she had memorized to exorcise any demons she sequestered in the Cell. "*Modarum cui clines damnatrices.*"

Finn's back arched, his arms and legs rigid as black smoke poured from him. When it dissipated, he was left flat on the ground with his empty hands curled at his sides. He twitched a few times and then passed out, fully human and far beyond the point where he could have fought back. Priest knelt beside him to make sure Finn was okay as Radio returned with a half-conscious Tarpon draped against his side.

"Everything okay?"

Radio nodded. "Mr. One and Mr. Zero won't be running

anywhere any time soon, but I convinced them to stop the punishment."

"If only they could have heard your speech."

He smiled shyly and gingerly lowered Tarpon to the throne. The kid groaned, curled in on himself, and seemed to pass out.

"He'll be okay," Radio said.

Riley watched him and, when she couldn't bear the suspense any more, said, "Look. A couple of things were said about, uh..."

"Your partner is an angel. You're... champion? Whatever that means?" He smiled. "I figured something was up a long time ago. You walk into No Man's Land and the Underground like it's some holy endeavor. You don't hide behind your fear. Had to be something special about you, I just didn't know the right titles. You don't have to tell me anything. Actually..." He looked at Finn. "Is he out of commission?"

"Yeah. No more murder-runs up to the surface. We're taking him in." She looked at Tarpon. "I'm sorry, Russell, but..."

"I know. He killed someone. He's gotta pay for that."

"He was operating under the influence of someone he couldn't have hoped to deny. I'll see what I can do to get some leniency for him."

Radio sighed. "Doesn't help the family of the person he killed." He crossed his arms over his chest. "Thank you, though."

"Yeah."

Priest joined them, having handcuffed the unconscious Finn. "We should go before our luck runs out. The demons are trying to avoid Finn's territory, but they'll discover he's dead sooner rather than later."

Riley looked around the lobby. "Is there a way out of here without crossing back through neutral territory?"

Tarpon said, "Tunnels."

They looked at him and he sniffled, wiping his nose on his sleeve. "The cracks after the earthquake. They're bigger than they look. We could all fit through them."

"Not Radio," Priest said.

Radio cleared his throat. "I'm not going."

"What?" Riley stepped in front of him so he couldn't look away. "What do you mean?"

"I closed away my voice because I was scared of it. It failed me, and it failed the people I cared about, so I stopped using it. But now I found it again. I used it to save lives. They're going to need someone to watch out for them. They respect me... for whatever reason." He gave her a self-deprecating smile. "This is where I'm supposed to be."

"I'm not going to fight you on it. But you have to promise me you'll come back to tell Kenzie where you're going. She deserves to hear it from you, okay?"

Radio nodded. "I agree. I'll be up as soon as I can, once things have settled down from everything that just happened. For now, I think your partner is getting a little antsy."

"They're getting close," Priest said softly.

"Right." Riley hesitated for a moment and then hugged Radio. "You were never dull, Russell."

He laughed. "Coming from you, that means a lot. Now go on. If anyone gets the balls to come find you, I'll hold them off as long as I can."

"Billy, don't be a hero," Riley said.

"One tin soldier."

Riley smiled and went to Tarpon. She cuffed his wrists together and hauled him up. "Come on. Show us the back way out of this place. I'm already itching to see the sun."

Gillian glanced up from the table. "Let the record show my wife arrived at the morgue at six-thirty-two in the evening."

"Is that actually on the record?"

"No." Gillian smiled and reached out to tap the microphone hanging in front of her. "It's not on right now. So how was your day, dear? You look like hell."

Riley looked down at herself and had to agree with the assessment. Her blouse was ripped in several places, smeared with dirt on the front and back, and two buttons were missing.

"A little tip. If someone tells you something is a tight squeeze but you should fit, hold your breath anyway."

"Duly noted."

Riley stepped around the table. "Can I contaminate you?"

"Yes, please."

Riley embraced her and kissed the back of her neck. "I have good news. No serial killer, and we caught the guys responsible for the two similar crimes. They're downstairs being processed right now."

Gillian turned around and kissed her properly. "Well done, sweetie."

"And I have better news. One of them is Finn Burke."

Gillian's eyes widened. "Alive?"

"Alive, and double-checked with fingerprints and photo identification. It's definitely, without a doubt him this time."

"Hallelujah. I was so sick of that guy turning up on my slab. So... two cases closed. Looks like I married the hotshot of the homicide department. I better watch my back. The groupies are going to be all over you."

"Groupies don't have anything on you, hot stuff." She slid her hands down to the small of Gillian's back. "When can you leave?"

"I have to type up my report on Baker the Baker, and then I'll be free. What were you thinking about?"

"I was thinking about taking you home, drawing you a bath, and then doing things with and to you until we collapse from exhaustion."

Gillian sighed and brushed her lips over Riley's. "I think I'd be amenable to that. Could I do things to you, too?"

"That can be arranged."

"Mm. Good." They kissed, and then Gillian pulled back. She stepped away but not out of Riley's grasp. "Riley, I can't. I know I said I would try, and I am trying. But I can't just play like everything is normal."

Riley closed the distance between them again. "It is normal, Gillian. I closed a case, we're going to go home and celebrate like we always do, and then we'll go to bed and wake up tomorrow to do it all over again."

"But we're only going to do that a finite number of times, Riley. I don't care how high the number is, because eventually we're going to run out of mornings together." She pressed her lips to Riley's forehead. "I'm sorry. I tried to give you normal, but I just can't. I can't."

"It's okay. It was a lot to ask of you." She stepped back and took Gillian's hands in hers. "So fine... we won't do normal. We'll acknowledge it. We only have a certain number of mornings left, but we also have a set number of evenings. So how about I help you shut this place down for the night and we go home to take advantage of this one? Paperwork can wait."

Gillian smiled. "Sounds good to me. Why don't we get some dinner? We'll find someplace to get some nice simple takeout, and then we can go back home and have a date on the living room floor."

Riley smiled. "That sounds like my favorite plan ever."

"But I really do have to type up my report on the Baker case. If we really do have Finn Burke after all this time, I don't want him to slip through on a technically. I want that guy locked down."

"Fair enough. You're worth waiting for." An idea occurred to her. "I'll call Primo. They always have an hour wait, so by the time you're done the food will be waiting for us."

Gillian cupped Riley's chin and kissed her lips. "This is why I love you. So smart. Call him up. I'll be quick."

Riley let Gillian out of her grasp and watched as she crossed the morgue to her office. Normal was a stretch, and nearly impossible given the information Gillian had to process. But Riley loved that she'd given it a shot. She sighed and rested her hands on one of the empty exam tables. She had ended up on one of them once; most people weren't lucky enough to get back off of it. She supposed every day after that was basically borrowed time. Technically she didn't have two years until she died, she had been given five extra years after being stabbed in the heart. How many people would turn down that deal?

She couldn't complain about how unfair it was. The unfairness, in this case, worked in her favor. She just had to be careful to waste as little of her life as possible.

THE MERCY SEAT

OTIS ROOSEVELT could hear them outside, the protestors and those who had come to stand vigil. He was in a small cell in an isolated corridor, two empty cells on either side of the last room he would call his. His elbows rested on his knees and he was bent forward, palms together and fingers extended with the tips touching. He was utterly still as he listened to the pastor's words. Elsewhere in the prison he could hear voices raised and a clatter of alarms and buzzers. The animals were restless tonight.

At midnight, he would become the first person executed by the State in almost two centuries. Legal battles had raged to determine if it was ethical, right, proper, et cetera, but the night had finally arrived. He thought back to years past, when the ninth of September had rolled around. One year on this date he had been engaged to a sweet woman with a laugh like a cartoon mouse. Another year it was just another day work. He was sure there was a September Ninth in his childhood that he'd spent playing with trucks and getting in trouble for tracking mud through the house.

The prayer ended and Otis sat straighter, inhaling sharply as he flattened his hands to his face and pulled at the skin. When he looked again he saw the pastor was shifting uncomfortably in his seat. Even a man of God was afraid to be alone in the room with him. There was a time when he would have taken pride in that, but now he felt only sadness. The old man had a slight hump to his spine, his ash gray hair falling over his forehead to the top rims of his glasses.

"Was there anything else you would like to confess?"

Otis took a deep breath. "There is something. But I can't say it to you."

The old man nodded and gathered his holy book to himself like it was a shield. "Yes, I assume you have much to say to your family..."

"I don't have any family."

"Oh. They told me you had another visitor scheduled."

"Yeah." He held out one hand, which made the pastor twitch again. After a moment the old man took the hand. Otis squeezed gently. "Thank you, Padre. I can't imagine many of your people were willing to come here to speak to me tonight."

"Yes... well. Those who seek absolution must not be cut off from the path." He paused at the cell door. "For what it's worth, I do believe you feel remorse for what you've done."

Otis smiled ruefully, eyes locked on the far wall of his cell rather than at the holy man. "Do you think that makes a difference in my case, Pastor?"

"In your case," the old man whispered. "No. Perhaps you are right with God, but I cannot forgive you. And for that, God will forgive me."

"Right. Well... thanks for the thought."

The pastor stepped out of the cell and walked back to the door. He called for the guard and was escorted away from death row. Otis stood and walked to the small window that showed him a section of the courtyard. He couldn't see the prison entrance, but he could hear the people there. He imagined the pastor being escorted from the grounds, his identity protected by a hooded cloak so no one would know who had given peace and absolution to such a monster.

Otis looked at the clock. It was just before seven. The cell door was still open; despite his reputation, no one expected him to make an escape attempt.

He walked back to his cot and sat down. His last meal sat heavily in his gut. That was the awful trick of the last meal ritual. The prison allowed the condemned anything he wanted to eat, but five hours before death everything tasted like paste. The food was just another torment. He put his hand over his stomach and massaged it through the coarse material of his jumpsuit. He hoped it settled soon. He didn't want to go to his grave with indigestion.

Soon the guard came back. "Are you ready for your other visitor?"

"Yeah."

The guard walked away and thumbed his radio microphone. "He's ready. Send Detective Parra in as soon as she's cleared."

Caitlin Priest frowned at the file. "Are you certain you want to be alone in a room with this man?"

Riley looked to see what page she was on. They were sitting in uncomfortable plastic chairs, waiting for the warden to come back and escort her down to death row. Her watch, wedding ring, weapon, and all the coins in her pocket had been confiscated. She shifted in the seat and felt as much as heard it protest under her.

"That's why you're here. I figure if things go bad, you'll know faster than the guards."

"Hm." Priest closed the file and closed her eyes. "This is a bad man, Riley. Worse than most in his situation. It's very telling that the legal system decided to put him to death. The last individual given the death penalty in this state was~"

"1834," Riley said. "Gillian looked it up. Jed Elkins, accused of murdering his wife and two daughters. He claimed the Devil made him do it."

Priest nodded. "I must admit I have mixed feelings about capital punishment. Responding to the end of one life by ending another. But I accept that extreme measures are sometimes necessary. And in this particular case..."

Riley didn't need to hear the details again. For the past twenty-two years, Otis Roosevelt had acted as a contract killer. He traveled hundreds of miles back and forth across the state at the behest of his mysterious benefactors and killed anyone he was told to kill. All of his victims were holy men. His death tally included priests, pastors, rabbis, monks, reverends, imams... he showed no preference or discrimination and there were no religious lines he wouldn't cross. His victims were always found in their places of worship, often in sacrilegious poses.

He was finally arrested when he targeted a reverend who had responded to the news reports by hiring a private security firm to keep an eye on his church. Even with the heightened security, Roosevelt had managed to get into the reverend's inner office and had his hands around the holy man's throat when his rescuers finally burst in.

The Holy Terror, as he'd been called before his name was known, had been on the radar for as long as Riley could remember, but he'd never gotten close enough for their department to be on the alert. Now he was set to die in five hours and he wanted to have a conversation with Riley. A detective he'd never met in a city he had apparently never set foot. She couldn't help but feel a little anxious about the situation.

The warden finally appeared, sighing wearily in a silent apology as he opened the door and joined them in the waiting room. He was a small man, a few inches shorter than Riley, with a shock of blonde hair that he obviously tried and failed to tame. He wore a blue dress shirt and matching tie with the knot loosened as if he'd already had a long and trying day.

"Detective Parra?" She held up a hand, and he extended his. "Warden Ramos. Sorry about the wait. You can understand the calls I've been getting today. It's been hectic."

"Of course. This is my partner, Detective Caitlin Priest. She's here for moral support."

Priest took the warden's hand. "I hope you find some peace tonight."

"Yeah, well..." His voice trailed off and he closed his eyes as if he'd smelled something delicious. After a moment he opened his eyes again and let his hand drop from Priest's. "Thank you, Detective. Now that we're getting down to the wire I'm trying to make sure we have everything ready. I don't suppose you have any idea why he's requested to speak with you."

Riley shook her head. "I haven't got a clue. We had a murder in a church three years ago, but we caught the killer in that case. We couldn't find any open cases that match Roosevelt unless he changed his methods."

"Let's hope not. He has more than enough blood on his hands as it is. This way, please."

Priest touched Riley's arm and she felt a brief surge of warmth passing through her sleeve. She nodded her thanks for whatever had been passed to her and followed Warden Ramos out of the waiting area. She heard a buzzer, its sound muted by the solid brick walls.

"Everything okay here?"

"The natives are a little restless. They may not agree on much, but there are a few constants you can count on. Don't expect a child molester to last long in general population, and don't kill holy men. It may sound strange, but a lot of the people in here... religion is the only hope they have left. We've had four attempts on Roosevelt's life the past month, and that's just what I know about. Could've been others. A lot of people want to be the ones who take out the Holy Terror, get the credit with the big guy."

"They must skip the commandment part of the Bible."

Ramos chuffed quietly and she deduced it was supposed to be a laugh. "They go in more for the Hammurabi stuff. More eye for an eye than vengeance is mine sayeth the Lord."

He sighed. "I guess the whole eye for an eye thing is more fulfilling. I can send a guard into the cell with you, but I can't promise he'll stay close. No one really likes being near him, and since he seems to prefer solitude, it works out for us all. Having a little island of space around him means he can't get his hands on anyone. Plus it's made it easier to stop the assassination attempts. We just watch for anyone getting within ten feet and push them back."

"I think I'll be fine."

He led her through a corridor that seemed winding, but she knew it was simply following the shape of the prison's interior. There were areas that were restricted to prisoners, other areas that were off-limits to guests, and never the twain should meet. Eventually they reached an area that felt desolate and far removed from everything else. Two guards flanked a steel door, and Ramos motioned for them to unlock it.

"We originally planned to set aside about two hours for the visitations, but seeing as you're the only person he asked to see... you obviously don't have to stay for that entire period."

"I guess it depends on what he has to say."

Ramos nodded. "And we're all very interested in what that is. If you need anything, just ask Kevin or Anthony here." Judging by when they nodded, Kevin had a military brush cut and a barbed-wire tattoo peeked out from under the short sleeve of Anthony's uniform shirt.

"Okay. Thanks, Warden."

She stepped through the door and Kevin followed her. There were five cells along the left-hand side of the corridor, and the center one was occupied by a large black man wearing a tan button-down shirt and matching trousers. His head was shaved, and he tracked her silently as she approached the open door of his cell.

Kevin spoke softly, even though there was no way Roosevelt couldn't have heard him. "Want me to stay, Detective?"

"No. Thanks."

He walked back to the door and shut it behind him. Roosevelt took a deep breath and looked her over, then smiled.

"You're Riley Parra."

"That's right."

"I was picturing a man."

Riley shrugged. "Sorry to disappoint you."

"Not a disappointment. I haven't seen a woman in person in a very long time. It's nice. Women are beautiful."

Riley rolled her eyes. "All right. Are we done, because I have a pot roast in the oven and all those chores won't do themselves..."

"I apologize, Detective. I didn't mean to imply anything prurient by my observation. I simply received your name without many details. I asked you here because I need to confess a final crime."

"And there's no one else you could unload on? You know how long I had to drive to get here?"

He closed his eyes and tilted his head to the side as if listening. His eyes snapped open and he looked toward the door.

"You brought an angel with you?"

She tensed but tried to keep the surprise off her face. "What are you talking about?"

He took a step forward, and Riley took a step back to maintain their distance. "Your angel is here. Her name..." He listened again. "She's called Zerachiel."

She narrowed her eyes. "I don't know where you're getting your information, pal, but~"

"I'm getting it from my angel. The same angel who told me to call you, to warn you. The final crime I must confess hasn't happened yet, but it will. Tonight, before my execution, someone in your city will be killed in the manner I once employed. You must see that it doesn't happen. It can't be allowed to start again or all my work will be for nothing."

Riley watched him for signs of lying, but he seemed sincere. She stepped closer to the cell door. "Okay, Mr. Roosevelt. You got my attention. Start talking."

The rain caught in the collar of Otis Roosevelt's jacket, pooling before the weight of it created a stream that poured down his back. He didn't notice. A little cold wasn't going to do him any damage. He stood on the walkway of the bridge and looked down. He wasn't entirely sure if it was high enough to kill him on impact; fifty, maybe sixty feet. That had to be enough. But weren't there stories about people surviving falls from ten stories? He cursed himself for not doing enough research on the subject, then climbed up onto the concrete barrier that kept people from accidentally doing what he was about to do.

"Are you sure about that?"

Otis didn't turn toward the speaker, although his sudden appearance made Otis' entire body tense. "This has gone way beyond reasoning with me, man. Just let me do what had to be done. I'll wait until you get far enough away you won't hear, but you gotta go now."

The man was suddenly standing next to Otis on the barrier. Otis took a quick step sideways, struggling to maintain his balance. The new arrival casually looked over at him and tried to conceal the amusement on his features.

"Yes, you do seem ready to greet the abyss. So go ahead. It's your choice, and I've always been fascinated by suicide. I'll feel no guilt since you're obviously determined." He gestured at the air in front of them. "Go. Meet your god. Give me a good show. I like a lot of flailing, but screaming is just being overdramatic."

"I don't want witnesses."

"That's how you've gone through your whole life, isn't it? No one paying attention to you, no one caring. They only care when things are bad, when you owe them something. It's a shame, isn't it? You're a human being, but the only people who know you're alive are the ones who want something from you."

Otis tightened his jaw, debating whether it was worth his time to get off the ledge and kick this joker's ass.

"My only question is why you're punishing yourself. You didn't do anything wrong. You did your level best at every turn, and still the troubles compounded. Your wife left you. You lost your home. And then six months ago, you discovered your daughter was dead. Your wife hadn't bothered to tell you, because you weren't speaking at the time, so you'll never know if you were a bone marrow match. You'll never know if you could have saved her life, and you're afraid to find out for sure because if there was a possibility, she'd just be another failure."

"Who the hell are you?" Otis struggled to make himself sound fierce even though he was fighting tears.

"I'm the man who can give you what you want. You're not

angry at yourself, you don't want to hurt yourself. You're the only one who tried to fulfill his promises. You fought, man, and that's respectable considering everything that was piled on your shoulders. It's not your fault you cracked. It was a fight against a bully who had all the power and used it to bring you to your knees. Don't you want to make him pay?"

"Him," Otis said. "Who the hell are you talking about?"

The man faced him then, and Otis finally noticed his eyes were completely black. "I'm talking about God, Otis Roosevelt. Don't you want to make Him pay for what He did to your family?"

A part of Otis knew that this was his true test, the pass or fail that would determine the fate of his soul.

"Hell yes."

The other man on the ledge smiled. "That's what I was hoping to hear." He put his hand in the middle of Otis' chest and shoved him off the ledge.

"I died. The man from the bridge found me in Hell and brought me back up into my body. I was only down there for a few seconds, but it felt like centuries." Otis had moved to his cot, while Riley was still standing in the doorway of the cell. "He told me his name was Valefar and he had a mission for me. I could feel that I was different, but I didn't understand how. He told me that I could get vengeance on God for everything He'd taken from me. I was angry. I had nothing else, so I agreed.

"I started walking. First church I found, I went inside and found the priest. I was covered with blood, still moving stiff because as it turns out falling sixty-three feet will mess you up right quick. Even with the demon raising me I was hurting. The priest offered me sanctuary and a sympathetic ear. I... killed him in the confessional. I cut off his ears and I~"

Riley stopped him. "I read the report. I don't want a hit-by-hit recap."

Otis pressed his lips together. "Right. Well, you know what happened next. I wandered. Valefar would show up now and then to lend a hand, make sure I didn't get caught, point me in the right direction for the next attack. Now I know he was just making sure I kept my resolve. I don't even know how long I did it or how many people I killed. They told me in court, but I forced myself not to listen."

"Want to know the tally?" Riley said.

"No. Please."

Riley thought about telling him anyway, but something about the man hunched over in front of her made her feel pity. "So what changed?"

"The church with all the security. Everyone on the news said they just got lucky, but that wasn't it. The Right Reverend was tipped off. The security he hired wasn't from this realm. I got into the office, started to choke the life out of him, and suddenly I was surrounded by angels. They pinned me to the floor and then one of them stepped forward and began to speak to me. He told me his name was Barachiel. He had been tasked with stopping me."

"Took his sweet time about it."

Otis smiled ruefully and looked at a spot near the corner of the cell that, to Riley, seemed empty. "Want to know what I think? I think religion was taking a pounding in the news. Scandals with altar boys every time you turn around, church organizers skimming from the tithes... Hell, even the big boy in Rome called it quits for the first time in six hundred years. So as horrible as my crimes were, churchgoing people were the victims. People were sympathetic. Attendance shot up. Mysterious ways, huh?"

Riley rolled her eyes. "Sure. So that's all really fascinating, but I don't see what this has to do with me."

"Barachiel told me to call you. He has been keeping an eye on me until the fateful minute. You think these cells and these rent-a-cops with their little pop guns could stop Valefar if he wanted to get me out? Barry is my real warden. He's spent the past few years trying to get me off that ledge I was standing on when Valefar came into my life. He made me realize that I was still up there, I'm just still waiting to fall. Only a couple of hours left."

Riley looked at the clock. "Yeah. Speaking of running out of time, my time is more precious than it used to be. So if we're done with this~"

Otis stood up so suddenly that Riley reached instinctively for her hip and grabbed the air where her gun usually sat.

"I called you because you're in danger. In all the time I was bouncing across the state looking for churches, I never visited your city. It was too big, too many churches, too many angels and demons floating around for me to feel comfortable. But Barry said that when I get taken out of the picture, Valefar is going to replace me with someone else. He's already got someone chosen, and they're in your neck of the woods."

Riley tensed. "Someone else is going to take over as the Holy Terror?"

"I don't know if it's going to happen exactly at midnight, but sometime before the sun rises tomorrow, Valefar will have someone else in his control if he isn't stopped."

Riley jogged back to the door, slapping her palm against it until Anthony and Kevin unlocked it. "I need a cell phone."

Priest's head was resting against the wall when the phone in her pocket chirped. She unclipped it from her belt and stood as she answered it, moving away from the desk. "Riley? Is everything all right? What? Yes, I know of Barachiel... he's..."

She furrowed her brow and listened to a much-abridged version of the story Otis had just told her. Priest stepped around the corner into an empty stretch of hallway. Her stride didn't change, but the walls around her seemed to bleed into darkness. The floor stretched out and hardened until it became asphalt, and Priest stopped walking when she reached the corner outside of her apartment.

"I'm home now. Do Barachiel or Roosevelt have any idea who the target is? Either the victim or the intended... no, I wouldn't think so." She longed for the time when Good Girls had been stationed on every corner; if anyone would know about a new demon arriving in town with a plan this heinous, they would know. "I'll find them both. But Riley, if I'm not at the prison, you'll be unprotected." She closed her eyes. "Okay. Just be safe, Riley. I'll be back as soon as I can."

She returned the phone to her pocket and scanned the street. *Please, Zerachiel. Point me in the right direction. Valefar is a powerful Duke of Hell. Surely you can feel his presence even in a city this size. Please... help me...*

When Priest opened her eyes, she was inexplicably drawn toward the west. "Thank you," she whispered. She unfurled her wings, stretching them in preparation for flight, and ascended so she could better cover the distance. If anyone happened to glance up and see her, they would have made themselves forget by the time she was out of sight. People were experts at ignoring what they couldn't explain, and she couldn't waste time obscuring what she was doing.

Roosevelt never let a church's size or denomination get in the way of his spree, so any one of the six hundred churches or mosques or temples in town could be the target. She set a northerly course, moving toward the opposite side of the city on a trajectory that would also cut across the affluent part of town.

Otis tracked Riley with his eyes as she walked back to the open cell door. "Was that your angel? She has a cell phone?"

"Yeah. What can you tell me about the target? She may be divine, but even she can only do so much on her own."

"Sorry. Barachiel is pushing the limits as it is. He's not even supposed to know about Valefar's plans, let alone giving anyone the means to stop it from happening."

Riley looked at the empty air of the cell. "Breaking the rules, huh? Well, tell him thanks for the heads-up." She crossed her arms. "So how did Barry know I was the one to call?"

"He says you're the champion, whatever that means. He knew that if anyone had the means and the wherewithal to stop whatever was going to happen tonight. Personally I'd never even heard of you. No offense."

"None taken." She debated whether she had enough time to jump in the car and drive back to town to help Priest with the search, but she doubted it would be worth the rush. If Priest couldn't find and stop Valefar on her own then Riley wouldn't be much help. "So Barachiel helped you see the error of your ways? Fixed all the damage you got from being down where the goblins go?"

Roosevelt smiled. "Not exactly. But he helped me find the man I once was. Have you ever read the Book of Job, Detective Parra?"

"I'm still working my way through Harry Potter."

"Everything Job had was taken from him, all of his riches and his family, his health, all of it stripped away. And the guy just kept on praising God. We came into this world naked and screaming and it only goes downhill from there, so what did he have to complain about, right? God never apologizes to Job for what He's done. He just basically says He's God and he can do whatever the hell He wants to us."

Riley said, "I'm guessing this is the Old Testament."

Roosevelt leaned back, smoothing his hands over his knees. "You might think I wouldn't take comfort in a story like that, but I do. Job was God's most beloved, and God treated him like crap because the Devil told him to do it to prove a point. Bad things happen to good people. It's an indifferent universe. I wasn't anyone special when Valefar found me. Just another bitter soul, someone mad at the world and looking for a way to take it out on... anyone. Valefar just gave me a way to focus my darkest thoughts."

"And now you're ready to die again."

He looked up at her. "After everything I've done? My time can't be up fast enough. I'm ready to pay my penance."

"But it's death. The end, lights out, no curtain call or encores. Aren't there books you want to read? TV shows you want to know how they end?"

Roosevelt chuckled. "I don't watch a lot of TV."

"There has to be something," Riley said. "You can't just sit there knowing you're going to die in a few months and just be okay with it."

He frowned at her. "Months? Lady, I'm looking at minutes here. What are you talking about, months?"

Riley tensed. "I said minutes."

"No, you said months."

"Forget it." She turned away from him and walked out of the cell.

Roosevelt stood up. "I know where I'm going, Detective. I've been there before, and it ain't pretty, but I earned my place. No use trying to fight it now."

"You committed those crimes under a demon's coercion."

"Yeah, but I said yes to him first. You always have to say yes. I don't think it's a rule, I think they just like making us culpable. So I'm scared as hell. I'm sure I'm in for a whole litany of terrors I can't even imagine once I get down there. But what's the point in fighting it now. All I can do is stop it from going further. Maybe if I can stop Valefar from getting someone to take my place I'll get downgraded from an eternity of torture to just a few hundred eons."

Riley managed a smile at that and rubbed her face. "All right. Zerachiel is looking for the demon, but maybe you can narrow it down for her. Who would Valefar go after?"

"Someone like me. I wasn't an evil person when he found me. Hell, I wasn't even particularly bad. I was just vulnerable. He took a lot of joy in pulling me down into the pit. Making me something... well." He gestured at the window with his chin. "Making me the sort of person other people want put to death. I was sad, angry, bitter..."

Riley had been leaning against the wall, but she pushed away and moved slowly toward the cell door. She'd had a thought, but she was too frightened to put it into words.

"Detective?"

She held up a finger to say she would be back, then knocked on the door to get Kevin's cell phone again.

Priest alighted at the end of the block, taking the time to search the area for anyone suspicious. She spotted the dark-clad person halfway down the block, shoulders hunched and a hood flipped up so that Priest couldn't see any identifying details. She felt a pressure at the base of her skull, a sense of wrongness that told her the person wasn't just an idle pedestrian. She started off at a jog, but her steps slowed as she neared the church. The pressure was enough that she was stopped dead by the time she reached the middle of the street.

The dark figure didn't stop to look back before ducking into the church's side door. Priest could see several lights glowing through the stained glass, indicating there was someone inside. She held up her hand and pressed it flat against the resistance, grimacing as the depraved energy coalesced to keep her out. She stepped back, gasping as if she'd held her head underwater. She crouched and launched herself in the air, a passing cab just barely missing her shoes as it sped by underneath her.

Priest spread her wings as wide as she could, her skin glowing as she rose so high that the air grew thin. She twisted into a dive, thinking of those silly superhero movies she had seen with Kenzie and Chelsea, the wind whipping her hair past her face as she picked up speed. She knew the church was surrounded by evil, but the heart of the building was godly. The two should cancel each other out, and her own holiness would be like a hot knife carving through butter. She bared her teeth as she hit the barricade, her skin crawling as she passed through it and into the warm embrace of the church's energy.

She changed her angle and came in through the window, the shattering glass cutting her cheeks and hands. She ignored the stinging and forced herself to stop before she continued through the other side of the building. She dropped her feet onto a pew and jogged to the end, hopping into the aisle and spinning to face the altar.

The reverend was on his knees, and the dark figure Priest had seen outside was holding a gun on the back of his head. Priest's heart sank as she saw Riley had been correct, the phone call she'd been so desperately trying to ignore, the warning she had almost dismissed now realized. She held up her hands, the blood on the back of her hands trickling down to stain the cuffs of her sleeves. Her voice shook when she spoke.

"Please. Stop. Don't do this."

The hand holding the gun didn't waver. The reverend's eyes were closed, his hands clasped together under his chin as he muttered a nearly-inaudible litany of prayers.

"You don't want to do this. Please, Gillian."

Standing on the altar, Gillian Hunt began to cry but she kept the gun trained on the old man's head.

"Who is she?"

Riley looked up into Roosevelt's eyes, belligerent and angry. He was the calming force in the room, and she felt like the caged one. "She's none of your concern."

"If Valefar wants to do to her what he did to me, then yeah. I'm kind of interested. Is she your sister?"

"She's my wife." Riley's voice was weak, and she closed her eyes as she nearly choked on the last word. "Gillian is my wife."

Roosevelt took a deep breath. "I'm sorry."

"Don't be sorry yet. Priest... Zerachiel... she's going to save her. She's done it before."

"Before?"

"Gillian's..." She swallowed hard and turned her back to the prisoner. "She's been through a lot since she met me. She was possessed by a demon... twice. But she survived, damn it. She's stronger than you were." The words came out angry and defiant, and she had to push back her rage reaction. She settled her breathing and began to pace. "Priest will save her."

Roosevelt said, "I hope so."

"She will. I've given up too much... Gillian has been through far too much shit for this to happen now. For it to end like this." She swallowed hard and faced Roosevelt again. Her voice was weak. "Can an angel stop Valefar?"

"I don't know. I was never lucky enough to have one fight for me. But I think if anyone has a chance..."

Riley nodded, eyes closed, and paced away from the cell again. "Come on, Cait. Please. Save her for me. Please."

The reverend finally opened his eyes and looked at the new arrival. Priest's wings were still extended, the outermost feathertips brushing over the pews as she advanced on the altar. She was now close enough to see the sweat beading on Gillian's brow and upper lip. There were minute tremors in her hands, her forefinger tense on the trigger guard. She wore Riley's police sweatshirt, the hood still up to cover her red hair. Her lips were a thin white line, and her eyes were wide with anger, fear, and pain.

"Gillian. Please, listen to me~"

"I can't. If I do this..."

"If you do this, what? What can you gain from this?"

Gillian's face twisted. "I can hurt Him. Hasn't He hurt me enough? He deserves this." She brought one hand up to wipe her face and then quickly resumed the shooting stance Riley had taught her. "He's hurt me so much, Caitlin. He let me be possessed. *Twice!*" She barked the last at the back of the reverend's head, and he flinched. He clenched his hands together and resumed praying. "He's killed Riley. And he brought her back, and now He's just going to kill her again."

"This isn't you, Gillian. This is a demon speaking to you..."

Gillian laughed without humor. "So... again? Going for the hat trick, huh? Please don't come any closer, Caitlin. Please don't."

Priest stopped her slow advance. "The demon is called Valefar. He's manipulating you, just like he did with Otis Roosevelt. Don't let him win. I'm not going to save you."

Gillian's eyebrows twitched. The reverend's prayer halted and then began again.

"What?"

"I'm not going to save you. I can't save you, not if he's already brought you this far. He's in your head, Gillian. If you pull that trigger, he'll have you completely. He'll possess you without ever taking your body. You'll be his tool for the rest of your life. If I try to force you away, he'll keep his hold. You've fought demons before and you won, Gillian. You are the most impressive human being I've ever known. You're stronger than Riley. You're braver than Joan of Arc."

"You knew her?"

"Briefly," Priest said. "We talked a few times. It... kind of went sideways."

Gillian managed a quiet laugh at that.

"Reverend? What's your name?"

He swallowed a few times to work up enough moisture to speak without croaking. "My name is Peter Iasiello. Are you an angel?"

"I am Zerachiel. The woman standing behind you is a good person. Will you pray with me for her?"

"I have been praying for her since she told me to kneel."

Priest nodded. "Good." She crouched next to her friend. "Her name is Gillian Hunt. She's a brilliant doctor, a medical examiner. She brings peace to those who have lost loved ones to violence. She gives relief and succor to a woman who time and again lays her life on the line for this city. She is my friend."

Gillian's lips were parted now, her teeth exposed as she fought back tears. "It's not fair."

"No. It's not fair, Gillian. It's not fair for you to be exposed to such evil, but it makes you strong enough to be there when Riley needs you. And you will be rewarded for your patience."

"With Riley's death?" Gillian thrust the gun at Iasiello's head. "That's how it ends? After all this, after all the last minute saves and rewriting history, she just *dies*?"

"No, in two years she dies. That's your reward, Gillian. You know. You won't be surprised in the night. You won't wake up one morning to simply find her gone. Riley has looked death in the eye every day since she was a child, and she has known that death lurked around every corner. But not anymore. Now she knows when it will happen and so do you. You have the time to cherish her, to show her how much you adore her. And when the fateful day comes, you can be with her. You can hold her hand, and you can kiss her as she leaves."

Gillian closed her eyes. "Help me."

"I'm doing everything I can, Gillian." Priest's voice was almost a whisper. "Please put down the weapon."

Gillian looked at the gun and followed the line of the barrel to the sweat-matted white hair on the back of Iasiello's head. She rocked back on the balls of her feet and swung the gun wide to the right, exhaling sharply as she uncocked it. Priest got to her feet and cleared the steps in a single leap, closing her fingers around the gun and easing it from her friend's hand. The tension evaporated from Gillian's body and she went down, and Priest caught her with her right arm.

Reverend Iasiello fell forward onto his hands and knees, gasping praise for his salvation. Priest lowered Gillian to the altar and lightly kissed her lips in benediction.

"Reverend, she'll be weak and sad when she wakes. She'll likely have a horrible headache so please have some painkillers on hand."

He nodded, dazed but coherent enough that she didn't feel the need to repeat herself. He looked at her, noticing her wings again now that the danger had passed.

"Are you truly an angel?"

Priest nodded. "I am, sir. And I'm sorry." She touched his cheek and his eyelids fluttered closed. In a few moments he would open his eyes and find a woman in need of his care lying on his altar. He would remember a skirmish, and he would know that the redheaded woman in the sweatshirt was a victim. He would take care of her until the proper authorities arrived to take her home.

She rose to her full height and descended the altar. Her skin burned again, and her wings extended high enough that they didn't touch the pews when she passed. The air she passed through seemed to boil with white-yellow energy as she held out a hand to blow open the doors of the sanctuary.

Valefar was standing on the opposite side of the street. Priest faced him from her higher ground atop the church steps. He lowered his protective shield that should have kept her out and walked toward her.

"You should have stayed away from this city, imp."

"I couldn't resist. Getting a new acolyte and breaking a champion in the process? I decided to save the best for last. Pity you had to throw a wrench in the works."

"I'll do more than that. You've hidden behind puppets for far too long, Valefar. I name thee Malaphar. Malephar. Valafar. Valefor. You are Duke of Hell and you stand before an angel of the Lord and I command thee to surrender now or face the consequences."

Valefar laughed and held up his hands, motioning her forward with quick flicks of his fingers. "Bring it on, Wings."

Priest walked down the concrete steps as Valefar crossed the street to intercept her. She extended her arm to push him off balance, but the demon bent at the knee and lunged forward. He brought his fist up into her gut and the air was pushed out of her. She gasped as her muscles struggled to regain their natural rhythm. Valefar straightened and punched her twice in the face, first with the left and then with a roundhouse right that sent her to the ground.

"Wow. I expected more from an angel. From the powerful Zerachiel, the guardian of Riley Parra. But I shouldn't be surprised.

You chose to take human form and with it, you inherited their weaknesses. You've become frail."

He kicked her in the side and Priest threw herself sideways to minimize the impact. She rolled and stumbled to her feet, one arm across her stomach as the other hung limp, her index finger pointed at the ground. She shuffled sideways to escape him and he pursued her slowly. He feinted with his right fist, aiming at her head. Priest flinched.

"I won't even be able to take pride in this. I can't even call it a fight. This is an extermination. Zerachiel once stood guard for the strongest heroines in history. Your name meant something to our ranks. But a few short years as a mortal and you've become *this*? I avoided your city, Zerachiel." He lunged and punched the back of her head and Priest fell again. "You seek to know me by naming me? Then I name thee. I name thee Caitlin Priest." He kicked her in the chest and felt something give against the toe of his shoe. She fell flat on the ground and he stomped on her hand. "I name thee Detective." He kicked the side of her head and, for a moment, thought she was unconscious before she flattened her palms to the ground and pushed herself back up. "I name thee Zerachiel... and I name thee mortal."

Blood blossomed on the front of her shirt. He sighed and shook his head in disappointment. She was already beaten, dripping blood from both hands. He saw black like ink soaked in the cuffs of her pants so that the blood trailed her every time she took a step. He wondered how much blood was actually still in her body. "I intended to enjoy this. But now I think I'll just get it over with. Even a demon can show mercy."

"And even an angel can be vicious." Priest threw herself at him. Valefar crossed his wrists in front of him, catching her on the throat and squeezing. Priest choked and fell backward. He assaulted her with a series of punches, alternating between body blows and hitting her in the face. When he was done her lip was split, one eye swollen shut, and he was certain he had felt a few bones crack.

"Give yourself up, Priest."

She spit a red gob onto the ground and wiped the back of her hand over her lip. Blood poured from each nostril, and her forehead was rubbed raw with road rash. She swayed on her feet, hunched over to protect the trunk of her body, her wings curled protectively inward as she raised her eyes to him again.

"I think that will do it."

"That will..."

His skin prickled as Priest poured her energy into the barrier she had just drawn on the ground with her blood. She swayed as the power was drained from her but she managed to keep her eyes open. Valefar swung at her but his fist refused to pass above the line she'd drawn around him. He stepped back and looked at the asphalt. The circle was in no way completely straight, but it was unbroken.

"Angel blood is extremely powerful, Valefar, even if it comes from a human body. You could slam yourself against it until daybreak and you wouldn't make a dent in it. But that is too kind for you." She forced herself to stand as straight as she could bear, wincing as her muscles pulled against shattered bone. "For your crimes against innocent holy leaders, I could find a way to forgive you. For what you did to Otis Roosevelt, I could find it in my heart to forgive you. I could have simply beaten you and sent you back to your infernal realm. But you were right about one thing. I have been tainted in my time with mortals, and I have grown accustomed to the heart beating in my chest. And what you did to my heart when you attacked Gillian Hunt? Even I can't find it in my heart to forgive that."

Valefar sneered, revealing the teeth of his human host had been ground down to points. "So you'll sacrifice your holy self to seek revenge? You'll rip me apart, rend me limb from limb? If you do that, you'll be a fallen angel."

"I won't hurt you, Valefar. I will only give you gifts that would be blessings in other circumstances. I am going to send you home to your domain of damnation and torment. The pit where you have spent countless eternities subjected to torture so horrific that it turned you into this dark and twisted beast that stands before me. A creature that takes delight in darkening good souls and extinguishing the holy light of good men and women.

"But before I send you there, I will make you forget. I'll take the memory of every ordeal you've suffered at the hands of your brothers. I will take the anguish and sorrow and shame they poured into you century after century so that when you return you will experience it all anew. You will be pure and untarnished so that the pain you feel will once again be unbearable. And when you have acquired your darkness again, when you have been reborn into this vile creature that stands before me, I will find you, and then I will snuff you out."

Valefar spoke so softly that Priest almost couldn't hear him. "Please. Don't."

"You chose your path, Valefar. I am only returning you to it. Walk it well."

The pillar of energy filled with holy flame. It faded to smoke and ash after only a second, and afterward Priest was alone on the street. Her blood had vanished from the pavement when Valefar was sent back below. She tried to take a step forward but instead swayed back, lost her footing and felt the world tilt underneath her as she moved somewhere else. By the time she hit the ground she was inside, sitting with her back against a stone wall. She coughed and pain racked her entire torso, making her wince and spread her fingers over her chest. She felt as if a glass plate had been shattered between her chest and shirt and that any movement would only make it worse. But it wasn't broken glass under her shirt.

She opened her eyes and saw Riley crouching beside her, horrified, and a man in a tan prison uniform looming behind her at the open door of his cell. And behind the prisoner was...

"Barachiel."

Riley turned to see who she was addressing, but he was invisible to her eyes. The angel stood taller than the prisoner, clad in a layered robe the colors of Heaven. His hair, so black it was almost blue, was pinned in a braid at the back of his head.

"You were victorious," the other angel said.

"Was I?" Priest looked down at herself and winced when she saw something poking against the material of her shirt from within. One of her ribs had broken the skin. "Is there a prison chapel or..."

Roosevelt answered instead of the angel. "There's one that no one ever uses. I think the fellow who gave me last rites is still on the grounds."

"I can do better than that." He was gone in an instant and Priest sagged against the wall.

"Where did he go?" Roosevelt asked.

"I don't know." She looked at Riley. "Gillian is safe."

She saw the conflict on Riley's face; she didn't want to look overly relieved when her wife's salvation caused such damage to her closest friend. She touched Priest's cheek.

"Are you going to survive the trip home?"

"Not without help."

Riley nodded. "Whatever you need..."

Priest groaned. "I need to feel worship."

"Here?" Riley looked at Roosevelt, who shrugged helplessly. "Cait, I don't know if that will be possible."

She sagged against the wall, struggling to swallow as she listened.

They had been protesting for hours. Marianne Corbin had knitted during the six-hour bus ride while Pastor Paul led the group in singing and Bible trivia games. They had arrived at noon, twelve hours before the government planned to kill one of God's creatures on the other side of the gate. No matter how horrendous his crimes - and they had been truly terrible - she couldn't stand idly by while anyone was murdered.

Pastor Paul had spoken passionately about their trip the previous Sunday. "If you see a man on the street with a piano dangling over his head, would you first ask if he was a good person before shoving him out of the way? If you encounter a woman being mugged, do you ask what church she's affiliated with before you call the police? No! Evil against one of us is an affront to all of us."

His sermon lit a fire in her, and she'd signed up despite the fact she'd never been more than ten miles out of her home town her entire life. The protest was, dare she say, fun. She enjoyed spending the evening with Sherry and Monica and Blanche. Their dinners were packed in brown paper bags which meant she didn't even have to cook for Martin tonight.

Later on when her friends asked, she would claim one of them had started singing first. They didn't have much of an argument; when pressed none of them was certain which had started it. The melody popped into her head and the next thing she knew someone else was singing the first few words of the song: "On a hill far away..." She felt compelled to join in. "...stood an old rugged cross. The emblem of suffering and shame."

Pastor Paul began singing as well, and others who were further away - under the impression he started the sing-along, raised their voices with him.

Terry gripped the bars of his cell door between his fists, eyeing the tattoos that ran from wrist to bicep on both arms. He was bored with the shouts and cries from all around him, the normally laid-back guards running back and forth trying to keep any uprisings quelled before they began. He didn't like reading, and the guards weren't letting anyone out to watch TV because of the "special event" taking place in a few hours. So he "read" his tattoos, remembering the story of when and why he had gotten each one.

He was nearly to his elbow when he thought he felt someone else in the cell behind him. He spun around and, for a split second, thought he saw someone in a queer-ass multi-colored robe standing by the window. But he was gone too quickly. He narrowed his eyes and walked to the middle of the cell.

The robe reminded him of his grandmother. His breath came out of him in a quick rush, almost a laugh. He hadn't thought of the old bitty in years. She'd always said he would amount to something, had always been proud of him. He looked at the palm of his left hand, the hand she had gripped when he was led out of the courtroom. She hadn't given up on him, even then. Even when she should have. God, how he'd hated those long-ass afternoons in her simmering apartment, forced to watch church shows. People singing all those lame-ass songs... there was only one he could remember and, without realizing it, he began to sing it.

"In that old rugged cross, stained with blood so divine, a wondrous beauty I see." When he went on to the next line, he heard someone in the next cell joining in with him. Ordinarily he would have shouted the man down just on principle, but tonight he didn't mind. He raised his voice and turned to face the cell door again. The guards were singing as well, and their voices rose louder than they ever had on Nana Edmonson's church shows.

Roosevelt tilted his head back and listened as the sound rose. It was like the rumble of thunder coming in from the mountains. "What in the world...?"

Riley said, "Worship." Her hands were red with Priest's blood. As the song grew louder, audible even through the thick stone walls as hundreds of voices rose as one, the color returned to Priest's cheeks. Her hands twitched, and she parted her lips in a silent gasp. She curled her hand around Riley's and whispered her name.

"So I'll cherish that old rugged cross," Riley sang softly. "Til my trophies at last I lay down. I will cling to that old rugged cross, and exchange it some day for a crown."

The swelling had gone down enough that Priest could open both eyes, and she gave a crooked smile with a lip that was still, for the moment, split.

"I didn't know you knew the words."

"I looked up a bunch just in case we were ever in this situation again. You tend to get hurt a lot."

Priest laughed and cried out in pain. Riley looked down and, despite the sticky blood coating the abdomen of Priest's shirt, the bone was no longer poking out.

"I hang out with a dangerous crowd." She looked past Riley. "Otis Roosevelt."

He nodded. "Are you another angel?"

"Yes. My name is Zerachiel. I am Riley's guardian angel." She swallowed a lump in her throat and, when she spoke again, her voice was stronger. "Valefar has been sent back to the pit. He won't hurt anyone else."

Roosevelt swayed on his feet and grasped the cell bars to keep from falling over. "Thank God. Thank you. I didn't know why Barachiel wanted you here, but now I know. Thank you."

Priest nodded and motioned for Riley to help her up. They clasped hands and Riley braced herself as she hauled the slender angel to her feet. Priest swayed and rested her hand on Riley's shoulder until she was steady. She took a step forward and met Roosevelt's eye.

"I could give you a measure of peace for what is coming next."

"I don't want it. The things I did..." He looked down and then shook his head. "No. It's my punishment and I'll bear it."

Riley said, "Do you want us to stay?"

"No. From what your angel here says, it sounds like you need to be with your woman. I'm not going to be responsible for keeping you away from her. Got enough on my soul. But the fact you offered... Well, it's been a while since anyone offered me a kindness. It means a lot to me."

"You saved my wife. If you hadn't called us, we never would have gotten to her in time. I don't even want to think about what would have happened if I'd ignored your call. So maybe you have some karma to spend after all."

Roosevelt nodded. "It feels nice to do something good for a change. It doesn't make up for everything bad I did, but maybe it helps a little bit in the grand scheme. I guess I'll find out soon." He sighed and held out his hand. "I'm glad you and your partner will be the last people I meet, Detective Parra."

Riley couldn't think of how to part ways with a man due to die in a few hours. Best of luck, take care, see you later? Finally she just said, "Goodbye, Otis."

He smiled. "Goodbye."

Riley put her arm around Priest's waist and helped her to the door. Anthony unlocked it and his eyes widened when he saw two people waiting.

"Where did she come from?"

"It's a long story," Riley said.

Anthony stared at the blood soaking Priest's clothes. "Did he do that?"

"No. He helped her after the fact." He looked skeptical. "Look, this woman is my best friend and that man is due to die tonight anyway. What possible reason would I have to lie? Do you have a wheelchair?"

They could still hear the prisoners singing, and maybe the atmosphere helped encourage their good will. Anthony went off to find a wheelchair and returned with it a few minutes later. Riley helped Priest into it while Kevin went to check on Roosevelt. He declared the prisoner to be in good health, so Riley and Priest were escorted back through the maze of corridors.

Riley wheeled Priest across the parking lot with a guard trailing them so he could recover the wheelchair when she was done with it. Priest gestured when they got close to the car.

"Put me in the driver's seat."

"Are you sure?"

Priest nodded. "I can manage the drive."

The guard looked at Riley, one skeptical eyebrow raised, but Riley just nodded. She helped Priest get behind the wheel and waited for the guard to leave before she crouched in the open door. She pressed two fingers against Priest's stomach, grimacing at the feel of her blood. Priest grunted quietly, but her ribs at least felt solid again.

"You're sure you're okay to drive?"

"Absolutely positive. I can heal behind the wheel." She started the engine, then turned on the radio. She scanned the stations until she found a station playing praise music. She breathed deeply and sighed. "I can feel the effects already. You have somewhere you must be, and you shouldn't waste time driving."

Riley nodded. "How bad is she?"

"She'll be doing better in a minute." She cupped Riley's face. Riley closed her eyes; she had always hated the quick trips Priest took her on. The feeling of hands on either side of her face lingered for a moment like a ghost before it faded. Riley was crouching in the nave of a church. She rose and walked down the corridor until she found a room with the lights still burning. She knocked just under a small black panel with white lettering that identified it as the office of Reverend Iasiello.

The door opened a moment later. "I'm Detective Riley Parra. I'm here for my wife."

When Gillian woke, Riley was sitting on the floor beside the couch. Her knees were bent, her hands resting on them, and her head was bowed forward as if she'd fallen asleep. Gillian took a moment to remember where she was and why, and dread clenched in her chest. How could she have listened to that damned... She closed her eyes and pushed aside her self-recrimination. Demons spoke sweetly; that was how they worked. Now she was sleeping in the office of a man she'd gone out intending to kill. The light coming through the window was just bright enough to tell her it was almost dawn.

She reached out and touched Riley's shoulder. Riley rolled her head to the side and Gillian brought her hand up to stroke her hair.

"Hello."

"How do you feel?"

Gillian took a deep breath and tucked her knees up closer to her chest. "Ask me again tomorrow."

Riley turned so that she was sitting parallel to the couch. She took Gillian's hand and kissed each knuckle. "I'm sorry."

"You don't have anything to be sorry about."

"This all happened because of me. I've been sitting here thinking about that. Are you okay? The reverend said you might have a headache when you woke up."

Gillian nodded carefully and Riley retrieved a bottle of pills off the table. Gillian cupped her palm and swallowed two of them with a drink of water from the waxy cup of the cooler in the corner. Riley stroked her hair until she settled back against the pillow.

"Priest was savage tonight."

"She was fighting for a just cause."

Gillian smiled weakly. "I'll have to thank her for it. She saved me. Where the hell was my guardian angel, huh?"

"I think Caitlin's a little more hands-on than most angels."

"Mm. Well, thank God." She ran her thumb over Riley's fingers. "I met him in a grief support group."

Riley's brow wrinkled slightly, but she understood. "You didn't tell me you were going to a group."

"I've only been twice. I thought tonight, with you on your road trip..." She shrugged as her voice trailed off. "I've only got two years to get used to not having you, Riley. Are you upset I was going?"

"No. I just wish you had told me. I wish I could help you." She wet her lips. "And I've been thinking about that, too. I think it's time you and I head for Paris."

Gillian frowned. "What? Paris... I don't want to go to Paris."

"I meant..." She smiled. "Last year after I chose Aissa, you used Paris as a metaphor. You said you wanted me to find out if I could retire one day. Well, I've decided I'm going to walk away. There's always going to be another demon, or another case, or something else pulling me away from you. And we can plan all we want, but the truth is Marchosias or another Valefar or some other threat we can't even imagine right now is going to crop up, and I know that it'll keep me from being where I'm supposed to be. Every fight is going to take me away from you. So while I was sitting here, thinking about your close call, I decided it's going to be the last one.

"I'm going to get rid of Lark Siskin, because I won't leave that mess for Aissa to clean up, but then I'm going to walk away. Not just from being the champion, I'm going to retire from the force. I want you to take a leave of absence and go with me. It doesn't matter where. We'll leave the city and spend whatever time I have left just being with each other. No demons, no murder investigations, just you and me."

Gillian kissed her long and hard. When they parted, she said, "I'm in. But can you do that? Will Marchosias allow it?"

Riley shrugged. "When I defeat Lark, I'll be given the option of letting Marchosias choose a new champion or ending the war for good. I'm going to choose you. From now on, that's the only choice I'm making. If you'll have me."

Gillian caressed Riley's cheek. "I'll take you for as long as I can get."

Riley rested her head on the couch next to Gillian's shoulder, and Gillian stroked her hair until they were capable of getting up to take each other home.

WANDERING STEPS THROUGH EDEN

THE DOORS were open to let the brisk winds sweep across the floor, its force almost enough to knock Aissa and her Mother off their feet. Aissa's hair was pinned back, her robe exchanged for a white sleeveless shirt and baggy tan pants. Her feet were bare, her hands wrapped with tape. Mother was dressed in an identical manner save for a hood that obscured her face so Aissa wouldn't be distracted during their sparring match. The ends of Mother's staff whistled through the air, coming down toward Aissa's head.

The girl ducked and lifted one arm straight up. She caught the staff between her thumb and forefinger, twisting her body to the left as she swung her arm down. She pinned the staff between her arm and body and then spun away, pulling it from her Mother's grip. Mother was pulled off balance by the move. It was only a split second of distraction, but Aissa took advantage of it. She grabbed the staff with her other hand, laid it lengthways across her body, extending it until the end was against Mother's chest.

Mother pushed the staff down before Aissa could bring it up to crack her chin. Aissa shifted her weight so she wouldn't lose balance and let the end of the staff be pushed to the floor. She wrapped her arm around it, hooked it around Mother's right leg, and then pulled. Mother crashed down and Aissa pounced on her. She straddled Mother's chest, pinning her arms down with her thighs, and yanked the mask from the older woman's face.

Aissa's face shined with sweat from their training, chest heaving as she tried to catch her breath. A few stray hairs had escaped her braid and hung around her face.

"I've won."

"You've defeated me, yes. But you forgot..."

A leather loop dropped around Aissa's head before she could counter the attack. It tightened and she was yanked back, sailing almost halfway across the training floor before she landed with a crash. She clawed at the strap cutting off her air, keeping the rest of her body still so as not to waste the oxygen she had left. Flailing would only exhaust her faster.

Mother stood and leisurely picked up her staff, walking to where another Sister was holding Aissa by a long leash. Mother pressed the end of the staff against the center of Aissa's chest to symbolize a killing blow.

"The number of opponents at the beginning of a fight does not necessarily equal the number of opponents at the end. If faced with true violence, you must be prepared for the fight to be joined by reinforcements. Be aware of your surroundings at all times, Aissa."

She croaked acquiescence and the choking grip lessened. Aissa pulled it away from her neck and breathed deeply, gasping on the floor. Mother dismissed the other Sister with a brief dip of her chin as Aissa sat up. She crossed her legs in front of her, staring at the loop of cowhide that had cost her a victory. Another strong gust blew across the floor, chilling the sweat on her flesh. Mother seemed unaware of the cold as she unwound the tape on her hands.

Aissa knew better than to complain the fight was unfair. She knew better than to be angry or pout because victory had been taken from her. She pushed herself up and walked to the edge of the sparring floor. Beyond the walls of their cloisters, she saw the mountains that protected them from the outside world. They were high enough that wispy clouds formed a floor that kept her from seeing the ocean except on the clearest of days.

"Did I hurt you?"

Mother's footsteps were soft on the hard wood of the floor as she joined Aissa at the edge. "Yes, Daughter. But that was the point of the exercise. You're progressing very well. I wouldn't have had to resort to such underhanded tactics with many of your sisters."

Aissa allowed herself a bit of pride.

"We can't remain safe behind these walls forever, Daughter. One day we may be called forth into the dark world. When that happens we must be ready. We do not believe in violence, but when we're in their world, violence will believe in us. I won't send you out unprepared." She touched Aissa's neck to make sure she wouldn't bruise. "Go and take a bath. I'll have Lilou prepare one special for you."

"Thank you, Mother."

She cast one more look outside before she turned to leave. The thought of going outside, being in the secular world, intrigued and terrified her in equal measure. Her sisters often whispered rumors they heard from the acolytes who delivered food and supplies to them at the beginning of every month. She didn't know how many of the stories were true. She wasn't sure she wanted to know for certain.

The Mothers had spoken for generations of one day being called to leave their home. It still hadn't occurred, and Aissa had no reason to believe it would happen during her lifetime. But she would still prepare herself for the day even if it was never to come. She would not be left unprepared when she was called.

Aissa was momentarily trapped within the dream after waking, staring in confusion at the water-stained wall next to her bed. Remembrance flooded back to her and she rubbed her eyes with the heels of her hands before she realized she wasn't alone under the blankets. She stretched and yawned before she rolled over to face her bedmate.

Cerys had stolen most of Aissa's blankets, curled in the fetal position with her back to her sister. Aissa hesitated to wake her but then touched the girl's shoulder. She rubbed in slow circles, humming the song Mother had always sung to wake the Sisters in the morning. The girl gradually woke and then lifted guilty eyes to meet Aissa's.

"It's the third time this week, Cerys. You'll have to stay in your own bed eventually."

"I know. Please don't be angry."

Aissa smiled. "I'm not angry. I'm homesick as well, but we made our decision." She kissed the younger Sister's forehead. "Go say your morning prayers and dress. I'm sure Eddie or Anita need your help today. And Cerys... I know you're still grieving, but Annora wouldn't want you to remain adrift. She would want you to have a purpose to strive toward. Keep her memory alive in good works."

Cerys nodded. "I will. Thank you, Mother." They both tensed at the honorific and Cerys looked away. "It wasn't intentional. I'm sorry."

"It's all right." Aissa was too thrown to be offended or angry. In fact, to have Cerys make that mistake was a high honor to her. She motioned for the door. "Go on. Your day is already begun. Go meet it."

Aissa had been living at the shelter for over a year, so Eddie had insisted on assigning her a semi-private room. It wasn't much, but it offered her more privacy than she had ever known. As a result she tended to leave the door open, and Cerys often took that as an invitation to crawl into bed next to her. The girl was making good strides in getting over the death of Annora, but each morning Aissa woke to find herself sharing the bed was a step backward.

She waited until Cerys was out of the room before she herself rose. She knelt next to the bed and clasped her hands, resting the thumbs against her forehead. Before leaving her sanctuary she had prayed for the well-being of a champion she'd never met in a city she couldn't even imagine. Now she prayed for those she had left behind, the Sisters and her Mother, the Grandmother whom she had never spoken directly to.

When she was finished, she ended her prayer the same way she always did. "I'm safe and I'm happy with my purpose. Amen." She crossed herself and stood up, removing the soft white nightgown that reminded her of the robes she once wore for daily work and exchanged it for the jeans and a T-shirt under a sweatshirt. She had inherited most of her clothes from Eddie or Anita, and the majority of them had a saying or identifying word on them that she didn't understand. Today her shirt advertised a place called Cooperstown.

A few other residents were awake and moving around in the early-morning quiet. The dream was still fresh in her memory so Aissa thought of the mornings back home when she and her sisters would be freshly-woken and quietly joking and laughing with each other in the dark. Mother understood that children needed to be children, so she tacitly allowed the joking and whispering that occurred between their morning prayers and ablutions.

The kitchen was fully lit as it always was at this time of day, but Aissa was surprised to see who was seated at the counter speaking with Eddie. She was dressed for work in a white shirt and gray slacks, the shape of her gun holster visible under her black leather jacket. Her hair was slicked back and gathered in a ponytail that rested between her shoulders. Aissa grinned as Riley Parra turned to face her.

"Good morning, Riley!"

The detective turned and smiled. "Morning, Aissa."

Aissa hugged her. "I didn't know you were coming today."

"It was a little spur of the moment. I got some unexpected downtime, so I thought I'd see if you wanted to spend the day together."

"Oh." Her smile wavered. "I'm not sure I can afford to leave No Man's Land today. With the earthquake and everything that's happened, people have gotten used to seeing me..."

Riley held up a hand. "I meant I would stick around, lend you a hand with whatever you needed. I'd be like your assistant. But nothing too strenuous. It's my day off, after all."

"Then I would be honored to have you at my side. Do I have time for breakfast?"

"Of course. Eddie was just showing off the culinary skills he's picked up since the days when we ran together."

Eddie pointed the stirring spoon at her. "I'll have you know that it takes skill to keep food fresh and hot when you're living on the street. And I'd like to see you heat up a can of beef stew without having it explode on you."

Riley leaned toward Aissa and lowered her voice. "That's a true story, by the way."

Aissa smiled, enjoying the banter between them. She still found it peculiar, even after a year, that she counted Riley among her friends. She had grown up praying for the champion of this city, had spoken the name under her breath thousands of times, but she had never seen Riley's face or heard her voice. She was still trying very hard to see Riley as an ordinary person; maybe spending a day with her would help her along with the process.

Eddie was also hard to get used to. She had seen men before, of course. They came to the sanctuary from time to time as deliverymen or messengers. Occasionally one of the Mothers would have a man in her private chambers to take care of certain physical needs; Aissa tried not to think too hard on those instances when she'd heard the needs being handled. Those men were all blessed and sanctified before they were allowed past the gates. Eddie was the first *man*-man she'd ever met.

She admitted she had false feelings for him. She knew that didn't truly want to be with Eddie, he was just a person she was comfortable with. He was also taken, married to Anita, and all too likely uninterested in a woman as young and inexperienced as Aissa was. But from time to time she caught herself watching him and chastised herself for her impure thoughts. She would never act on them, but they could be a fun distraction.

Breakfast was oatmeal with blueberries, a nice combination of the simple meals Aissa was accustomed to back home and the luxuries that came with living in the real world. She loved orange juice, and the convenience of a gallon of milk in the fridge whenever she wanted a cold glass. She tried not to overindulge, but it was difficult to restrain herself sometimes.

Eddie left while Aissa was still eating. Riley settled in with a glass of milk, waving off Eddie's offer to whip something up for her.

"I already had breakfast with Gillian this morning."

"How is the old ball and chain?"

Aissa was watching, so she saw the brief flash of emotion across Riley's face. "She's had a hard time lately. But we're doing really well. How about you and Anita?"

He nodded. "We're all right. We managed to get through the quake unscathed, so we're counting our blessings. And this one..." He gestured at Aissa. "I don't know where you found her, but she's sort of like a mini-you. Running around, bringing people in, helping people get back on their feet. She's a one-woman force of nature."

Riley smiled. "I'm glad she's working out for you."

"Yeah, besides... it would be hell to try returning her now. I lost the receipt."

"No refunds," Riley said.

He winked at Aissa to let her know they were joking. "Okay. I'm going to go round up the troops, see who else wants some breakfast."

Aissa waited until he was gone to speak. "Are you sure everything's okay?"

Riley nodded and looked over her shoulder at Eddie's retreating back. "We had a little trouble with a demon a few days ago. Gillian..." She winced and shook her head, refusing to go into detail. "Priest went toe-to-toe with it. She used her blood to trap it, but the thing had to make her bleed before she had enough. He beat her up pretty badly. Worship helped heal her, but she still needs some time. So I asked Lieutenant Briggs for a few days off so Priest could heal and I could be with Gillian."

"So why aren't you?"

"Because she doesn't want me to be." She caught Aissa's shocked look and smiled. "It's nothing horrible, trust me. It's just two people cooped up in an apartment for days on end. One is injured, the other feels guilty, so we were just stepping on each other's toes a lot. I thought I would give her a day of peace and quiet."

Aissa relaxed. "Oh. Well, I'm honored you would spend it with me."

"There's actually an ulterior motive involved. But we'll get to that." She finished her drink and took the glass to the sink to rinse it out. "What do you have planned today?"

"I don't usually plan anything. I go where I'm needed, and the city has ways of letting me know where that is."

"That should be interesting." Aissa brought her bowl to the sink and Riley rinsed it for her. "How is Cerys?"

"She's..." Aissa pressed her lips together. "I don't know. She's not well. I'm trying to help her overcome the grief of losing Annora, but they had only just declared their feelings for each other. I'm not sure how helpful I can be on the subject of heartbreak."

Riley said, "If you need any advice, give me a call. I was an expert before Jill. I was usually the one doing the breaking, but I may know a few tricks to help pull her through." She put Aissa's bowl on the rack to dry. "Is that it, or do we have to wash all the dishes?"

Aissa chuckled. "No, we can leave. Eddie will reuse the utensils to cook for anyone else who wants breakfast." She washed her hands and dried them on a towel before she led Riley to the front of the shelter. "There is one thing I wanted to show you. But I'm willing to follow your lead on what we should do in the morning. I've been trying to emulate you since I came here, so I'd be very interested in seeing how you would approach a day."

"Well, it's been a while. And this isn't the same place I grew up. Hell, it's not even the same place I used to patrol. Listening to the city sounds like a good place to start. Do you have any contacts, people who have eyes and ears on the street to let you know what's going on?"

"I have a few people I use, yes."

Riley nodded. "Okay, then. Let's go meet them."

Riley drove while Aissa directed her from the passenger side. Most of the streets they passed were blocked off due to earthquake damage and, while there was evidence of road crews preparing to do work, Riley couldn't see any sign that work had actually taken place. It didn't surprise her since evil's champion was serving as Mayor. With Marchosias' champion calling the shots it was in her best interest to let the city go to hell as quickly as possible.

Aissa told her to pull over when they reached a three-way intersection. They were facing the waterfront across an east-west road, and Aissa leaned forward to look down one arm and then the other. Finally she unfastened her seatbelt and opened her door. "I want to meet with them first, just so they don't get spooked by me walking in with a cop."

"I understand." Riley was a bit distracted by the fact she recognized where they were. "Take as long as you need. I think a friend of mine is around here somewhere. I need to talk to him and now is as good a time as any."

"Okay. I'll be by the waterfront in plain sight."

Riley nodded and got out of the car. Aissa went west while Riley backtracked toward a pool hall. The front door was open and she closed her eyes as she stepped inside the vestibule, opening them again as soon as she was in the hall. Taking the second was enough to help her eyes adjust to the interior darkness so she saw the bartender tense and three people at the bar hunch their shoulders in a weak attempt to hide their faces without moving.

The back of the room was the only well-lit part of the establishment, and it was there that Riley's target was holding court. He had apparently just won another game, laughing as he folded the cash his opponent had just handed over. Riley whistled and every man in the room tensed, relaxing only after she walked past him.

"Muse! Fancy meeting you here."

His smile vanished and he turned his back to her. "You mean my place of business? Yeah, you a real lucky one. You oughta be a detective or something."

A few people chuckled at that. Riley ignored them. "I was just in the neighborhood, thought I'd see what you were packing." She picked up the cue ball. "Is this weighted like the last one? You suckering people again?"

Muse turned and glared at her. "I win fair and square."

"Sure." She dropped the ball, and the man who had just lost looked at it and then looked at Muse with suspicion. Before the man could demand his money back, Riley motioned at Muse to follow her into the back room. "Come on, old friend. Let's have a chat."

"This is bullshit even for you, Parra. Aren't there real criminals you can be hassling? Looters and killers? I think you just have a crush on me."

She rolled her eyes and shoved him into the back room. As soon as the door was shut behind her, Muse relaxed.

"That wasn't cool, man. Now he's going to want a rematch."

"Double or nothing, I'll bet," Riley said. "And since you beat him fair and square the first time, you'll do it again no problem. So I just doubled your winnings. You're welcome."

He smiled. "Good point. So what do you need? I haven't heard much that would help you, but I'm willing to scrounge around today if there's anything specific."

"No, actually. This is sort of a social call. There's something I have to say." She slipped her hands into her pockets. Muse was the first person outside of her immediate family to get the news, and she wasn't sure how to start. "Marcus, I've been using you."

He was thrown by her using his real name. "That's kind of the point of this whole thing, right? I give you information, you pay me... we use each other."

"Yeah, but I've been taking advantage of you. You cleaned up your act a long time ago, but since I needed information, you stuck around. You pretended you were still the person you used to be. I'm sorry. I should have let you go a long time ago."

Muse wiped his hand over his face. "Wow. I don't know what to say to that. I mean... I did a lot of bad things before I met you, Riley. Me sticking around? That wasn't because of you, that was because I felt like I owed it to the other people down here. I'd done enough bad things and I needed to do something good for them. You're giving me that opportunity. I'm grateful for it. If it wasn't for you I'd just take what I found out to random cops at the police station and someone would probably see me going in and out and..." He sighed and shrugged. "What's this about anyway? You firing me?"

"Yeah."

He stared at her and then smiled in disbelief. "What?"

"Muse, you've worked too long and too hard to keep up like this. You're living two lives here. Your old life, and your new life, which you have to hide. It's time for you to let it flourish. You need to be thinking about your grandmother. She doesn't have a lot of time left, and you need to show her how much you've changed while you still can."

Muse looked down at his feet, arms crossed over his chest.

"I wouldn't be saying this except I'm leaving."

He looked up sharply. "Leaving? Where the hell are you going? You're Riley Parra. You've never turned your back on No Man's Land."

"This time I don't really have a choice. I'm dying, Muse."

"What?" His voice was so soft she almost didn't hear it, and he took a backward step so he could lean against the wall. "What happened?"

"It's a long story. The point is, I don't want to be doing this up until the day I die, so I'm going to be leaving town with my wife. I don't want you to keep up this game. There will still be people who watch out for No Man's Land, and they'll still need information, but they'll get it from someone else. You've done your duty, and you've made up for the person you once were. Now you deserve to live as the man you've become."

He finally met her eyes. "I was conning you. When I started? Yeah, I wanted to be a better person, but you were this green rookie cop offering money for info. I thought I would take some of the worst people off the streets and improve my profile at the same time. Clear the way so I could become the big-time. But you really believed in making this city better. You made me really want to help. So if I really am someone Grams can be proud of, then that's down to you. And if you're saying it's time to stop, then... it's time to stop."

Riley nodded. "It's the right time, Marcus."

"Yeah. Still, I don't know what I'm going to do now."

"The same thing you've been doing, only you'll be upfront about it. You'll help the people around you get themselves out of No Man's Land. And if you need help, Kenzie and Chelsea Stanton will be willing to lend you a hand. And there's a young woman named Aissa Good. She's sort of new to town, but~"

"Aissa? I know her. Met her right after the earthquake." He scoffed. "Should've known you were friends with her." He stared at her for a long moment. "You're really dying?"

"Not soon. But... yeah. I only have a few months left."

He blinked rapidly and ran his hand quickly over his cheek. "Damn. I know you've gone into a lot of bad situations, but you always come out of it on top. Kind of got to thinking you would be around forever."

Riley smiled sadly. "Yeah. I kind of felt the same way. We're so worried about traumatizing our kids when really we should be telling them every day that they're not going to be around forever. Might give them nightmares, might give them the incentive to make the right decisions."

"I'm making the right one right now. I'm going to do it." He took a deep breath and ran his hand over his hair. "Wow. Some people might not be too happy with me tomorrow."

"They'll get over it. You're making the right decision."

Muse nodded. "Yeah. Besides, it's not going to be any fun doing this without you anyway. You're not leaving immediately, right?"

"No. There are some things I have to take care of. I'll warn you before I just disappear."

"You'd better." He surprised her with a hug, and Riley patted his back.

"You did more than anyone else to keep me on the right track. Times I got tempted, I thought about how disappointed you'd be. I couldn't upset you."

"Damn right." Riley pulled back and checked the time. "I should probably go check up on Aissa. You've helped me save a lot of people, Marcus."

He winced. "Stop calling me Marcus. Geez."

"New life, new man, new name. You're going to be respectable now. Get used to it, Mr. Skaggs." She slapped his arm and stepped aside to let him out of the back room. He stepped back out into the bar room and looked at the men gathered there. After a moment he turned back to Riley and held out his hand. "It's been a pleasure working with you, Detective Parra."

Riley stared at his hand in disbelief. She hadn't expected him to be quite so blunt. She took his hand, squeezed, and looked behind him to make sure no one was pulling a weapon.

Muse stared at her when he spoke again. "Everyone in this room. This lady right here? She cared about you even when you fought against her. Called her pig and scattered whenever she showed up. Didn't matter to her, no sir. She just kept showing up because she cared about what happened to you. She cared about your sister, your brother, your aunt, your grandmom. When every other cop in this town turned their backs on us in No Man's Land, she kept coming back. Bad stuff still happen? Sure. But she did what she could, and I helped her out from time to time Ôcause I cared, too. To everyone else we were write-offs. To this lady? We're just people who need a little help. We're her neighbors. I'm honored she let me help her when I could."

He finally turned and looked at the other men.

"You want to beat my ass for helping a cop, or you want to show a little gratitude that someone actually cared what was happening here in No Man's Land."

The tension faded from the room. Muse finally let go of Riley's hand before stepping back to the pool table. Once she was certain no one in the pool hall was waiting to jump her, Riley walked past them and back out into the sunlight. Aissa was standing next to the door, hands in her pockets, a slight smile playing at the corners of her mouth.

"How much of that did you hear?"

"Enough. Muse and I have crossed paths a couple of times."

"Well, you know those people you went to meet?" She nodded. "Well, looks like you already knew one of them. Muse was my informant. He gave me a lot of great information over the past few years."

"So why are you cutting him loose now?"

Riley sighed and motioned for Aissa to follow her back to the car. "That's a very long conversation. One I wasn't planning to have until tonight."

"I know something is wrong, Riley. Please, just tell me what it is."

"All right. I..." She paused and glanced at the reflection in the window of a store they passed. "Aissa, I'm really not trying to change the subject, but do you know those punks trailing us across the street?"

Aissa looked past Riley into the window as if looking for a price tag. "Oh, for crying out loud."

"Problems?"

"Irritations. Boys who heard about protection rackets from TV shows and decided to start one of their own. I managed to put a stop to it before they actually hurt anyone, but they've damaged property. Made threats. I talked to them and I thought they had gotten the message."

Riley said, "Looks like the only message they got is that you need to be dealt with." She risked a direct look, but the teenagers - four of them in all - didn't seem to care that they'd been seen. They only started moving faster. "They're going to catch up with us soon.

You want my help?"

"No. If you help, they'll just come back when I'm alone. I'm sick of this. I want it ended. Go on to the car."

Aissa stopped and turned to face them, standing in the center of the sidewalk. Riley kept going, fighting the urge to look over her shoulder to make sure Aissa was okay. She stepped around the corner into an alley where she could watch without being obvious about it.

Three of the punks fanned out around their leader, who stopped in front of Aissa. He brought his hands up and began cracking the knuckles of one fist.

"I thought we had an understanding, David. You four were not supposed to be friends anymore."

The leader, David, shrugged. "I don't have too many friends. I got lonely. We decided that we're going to stick together. If you're the one who has a problem with it then you're the one who is going to have to change."

"The difference is that the four of you combined create a drain on society. I, on the other hand, am not."

"You think you're better than us?"

Aissa shrugged. "I know that I'm better than you. But it's not permanent. You can always improve yourselves."

David rocked back on his heel and brought his arm around in a quick, ugly punch. Aissa took the blow and leaned to one side with the force of the blow. She remained standing, however, and slowly straightened as she brought her hand to her face. Riley's jaw hurt from clenching her teeth, but she restrained herself from stepping in. If Aissa wanted help, she would make it known.

"Jesus said to turn the other cheek. Not to advocate peaceful responses to violence, but to force the attacker to declare he was equal to his victim. Are we equal, David?"

He looked at his friends, one side of his mouth curled up in a sneer. "Yeah. We're equal." He swung at her again, this time using his left hand to strike the other side of her face. Aissa brought her arm up to block the blow, clasping his wrist and wrenching it so that his arm was fully extended. She kicked his hip and knocked him back, knocking him down and jerking the arm out of the socket.

David howled, and the biggest of his three friends pulled something from his pocket as he stepped around his fallen friend. Aissa didn't release David's arm as she spun and kicked the second punk in the knee. He went down with the cry of a wounded animal, dropping the switchblade he'd been wielding. The other two fighters were already backing away, eyes wide.

Aissa turned her attention back to David. He had fallen to his knees from the pain of his dislocated shoulder, and he howled when Aissa wrenched it back.

"The damage I have done to you and your friend is temporary and easily fixed. I have other alternatives and, should you attempt to extend this aggression, you will see just how permanent I can make your pain. Am I understood, David?"

He winced, whined, and cried out as Aissa pulled his arm again. "Yes! Yes, okay, yes, understood. We're done."

"Good." She looked at the two men still standing. "You two. Your friends are in pain. They have behaved like animals, but you don't have to. Take them to get help. See that they get medical attention."

They eyed each other and decided following her order was the wisest course of action. They came back to retrieve David and the knife-carrier. Aissa stepped back as the wounded were gathered up and limped away with their friends. Riley stayed out of sight until the four punks were gone, then approached Aissa.

"Very impressive."

"The first time I asked them nicely. The second time they get hurt."

"What happens if they come back for a third time?"

Aissa sighed. "That is not on my conscience. It will be solely their choice if they want to face me again. At that point I will do what I must."

"Three strikes and they're out, huh?"

"Baseball." Aissa smiled as she started walking back toward the car. "Eddie likes baseball. We watched a game together on TV."

"Yeah? How'd you like it?"

"It was interesting. I can see why he enjoys it."

"Gillian likes it, too."

Aissa watched her. "I won't let that altercation distract me, Riley. Something very big is going on, isn't it?"

Riley sighed. "Yeah. Come on. We'll talk about it in the car."

Aissa watched her warily but eventually admitted she had no choice but to follow Riley and hope she could handle whatever revelation she was about to receive.

Aissa looked dubiously at what she'd been handed, then raised her eyes quizzically at Riley. They were seated on a table outside of a small yellow building shaped like a squat cupcake. Their feet were on the bench and they were facing the street, watching as traffic passed. Aissa looked back at the snack Riley had bought for her.

"Do I lick it or do I chew it?"

"Both. And I know you're not sure about the flavor, but trust me, it's the best one. Can't go wrong with cookies and cream." She licked her cone, pulled a chunk of cookie into her mouth, and chewed carefully. "If you're going to have ice cream for the first time, the safest bet is to go with a classic. If you like this you can branch out into other flavors." She looked to see Aissa had yet to take even a lick. "Come on. It's good, trust me."

"It's normally a hot weather treat, isn't it?"

"Yeah, well. It's good for comfort food no matter what the weather is like" She considered her ice cream for another long moment. "And you can't always count on being around for summertime."

Aissa tensed. "Have I been unsatisfactory?"

Riley looked at her. "What? No. Not at all. You've been amazing, Aissa. Seeing you deal with those punks back there was awe-inspiring. I wish I had half that badass calm when... hell, I wish I had it now. You're going to be an excellent champion when the time comes. The problem is that the time may be coming a lot faster than I thought it would."

"Tell me."

"Eat your ice cream."

Aissa obediently took a bite. It was too cold and she didn't like how it felt in her mouth, but she let it melt on her tongue regardless. The chunks of cookie were good, at least.

"Gillian was hurt, so I made a deal with someone. I got a chance to undo what happened, and in exchange I agreed that my death would become a set moment in time. I have a little over a year and a half left before I die."

"My Lord," Aissa whispered.

"If I die while Lark is still in power, it's going to be a default win for her. You'll inherit the title with a loss under your belt. I won't do that to you. I'll clean up that mess, and then I'll be faced with the same choice I had last time. Continue the war or end it. I'm just going to leave. You'll take over, Marchosias will choose a new champion, and everything begins again. But don't worry. I think Marchosias knows he bit off more than he can chew with Lark, so he'll err on the side of caution next time. He'll pick someone a little less insane. I think you'll actually have a chance against whoever it turns out to be. That is, if you want to."

Aissa recovered from her shock and furrowed her brow. "What do you mean if I want to? The choice has been made. I bear the symbol..."

"Right. But you expected to have some time to get ready to take my place. Neither of us expected the call to come this early. If you want me to find some way to take it away or transfer it~"

"No. When you gave me this honor, you told me that I could be called at any time. You could have died in a day, or in a month, and I'd have been forced to fill your shoes. Now I've had over a year to get used to the city. To adjust from my past life. And I'll have at least another year? I'm ready, Riley. Whenever you go, even if you decide to leave early, I will gladly fulfill the role of champion in your absence. I just hope I can live up to your example."

Riley smiled. "I think you'll do just fine, based on what I saw today."

"Sure, I can fight. I've been training to fight my entire life. But I'm no good with people. Good people who need my help. Living at the shelter has given me some experience, but I fear I'm failing with Cerys."

"Things aren't going well?"

"Things aren't doing anything." Aissa sighed heavily. "I feel the grief of losing a sister, but she has romantic feelings compounding it. She can't get past the trauma, and I fear that if she continues in this way she'll never adjust to life outside of our sanctuary. I think it was a mistake for her to remain when Mother took the others back home."

Riley said, "Is there a chance they could take her back?"

"Someone would have to escort her. And it can't be me, since I turned my back on them as well. She made her decision and now she'll have to live with it. I just fear that she'll soon reach a point of no return. I see her becoming one of those lost souls who inhabit the shelter, stuck in some horrible tragedy rather than proceeding."

Riley had a vision of herself stepping over a faceless,

anonymous homeless woman in a cold alley, felt the twinge of guilt that had lived in her chest since being told the woman was her mother. "You're not going to give up on her, Aissa. I know you. You'll be there for her as long as it takes, and you'll get her through. I have faith."

"I wish I shared it."

"That's one thing you'll have to learn about being the champion, kid. You can't do it alone. I'd have been dead several times over without Jill, Cait, Kenzie, Chelsea..." She shrugged. "It's a team effort. You can't do it alone. Get a support group, people who can take some of the burden off your shoulders from time to time. Even if it's just someone who lets your guard down a little bit and knows that you aren't a superhero."

"Like Dr. Hunt is for you?"

"Exactly like that." Riley smiled. "You'll do fine, Aissa. Just don't try to do it all on your own. You'll be setting yourself up for failure."

Aissa nodded slowly. "I'll keep that in mind. Thank you, Riley."

"It's what I'm here for. As long as I'm around, I might as well offer you what little advice I can. Work with people you trust, don't try to take it all onto yourself, and avoid Pelachinos."

"The restaurant? Is it a stronghold of evil?"

"No. Their food is just inedible. Finish your ice cream."

Aissa smiled and examined her cone again. Some of the ice cream had melted down over her fingers. "How do I... is the cone edible?"

"Yep. Gillian says it's the best part."

"Hm." Aissa bit off one part of it. A little bland, maybe, but the ice cream gave it a little flavor. She would give it a shot. The ice cream was evidence that there was a lot more to living in the real world than just understanding the difference in morals and behavior. She was glad Riley was willing to teach her about the little things like this in addition to the big things. She licked her ice cream around a bit of cookie and bit down on it.

"I like the cookies."

"Aha, a woman after my own heart. Next time we'll try pistachio. That's Priest's favorite."

Aissa nodded slowly and licked the melted trails off her thumb. "This is part of the training, isn't it?" Riley looked at her. "The need to just sit and enjoy a treat from time to time. That's how you keep your head on straight. You take time out for yourself."

"I do what I can."

Aissa nodded. "Maybe I'll give baseball another chance. It could prove to be the distraction I need after a long day."

"That's what most sports are. And if baseball doesn't do it for you, you could always take up... some other activity. Knitting, jigsaw puzzles, jogging."

"What do you do?"

"Uh." She shrugged. "I, uh..."

Aissa chuckled. "You spend time with your wife."

"Yes."

"That's very sweet, Riley. Love is your hobby."

"More than a hobby. It's a way of life." She winked and went back to her cone.

After finishing their ice cream, Aissa asked Riley to take her to the industrial district. "There's something I've been keeping my eye on down there for a few days. It might turn out to be nothing, but I want to keep track of it for as long as I can."

"Should I get out the Kevlar?"

"No. It shouldn't be dangerous."

"Famous last words," Riley said.

She parked out of sight and they walked the last block to the building Aissa was interested in. Aissa pressed against the brick wall at the corner, and Riley leaned forward to look past her. The loading area was blocked off by a tall aluminum fence that was too high to see over, but the gate across the driveway was chain-link and revealed a phalanx of identical jeeps embossed with the logo of the Postal Service. They were lined up along the bays of a large anonymous pre-fab building, and Riley watched as a group of men in identical purple-and-black uniforms carried boxes from the shadowy warehouse to the waiting jeeps.

"Something tells me those aren't official mail vehicles."

Aissa shook her head. "I've watched them make their deliveries. The real mailmen I've seen usually aren't armed, not even in No Man's Land."

"Nope. That's a little much."

"I was waiting for an opportune time to get in and see what they're doing, but it's not exactly a job I could pull off single-handed. Since you're here today..."

Riley nodded. "Right. Happy to lend a hand."

"The last driver usually rolls out around two." She looked at her watch, a heavyweight, thick-banded model she had gotten from a thrift shop. "They only have a few people manning the warehouse while the jeeps are out for delivery. We should wait until then."

"Do you have any idea what they're delivering?"

Aissa shook her head. "I've never been close enough to get a look. I've followed a few of the drivers on deliveries, but apparently they've been instructed not to leave packages unattended. If they don't get an answer, box goes back on the jeep and is taken back to the warehouse."

"Any idea how they receive orders?"

"It must be online. I've never seen a single customer go inside."

Riley scanned the fence. "You said you've been coming here for a couple of days. Have they seen you?"

Aissa looked ashamed. "Yes. Once or twice. They don't seem too concerned by my presence."

"We're going to make them regret that. Can you drive?"

"No. Eddie has been meaning to teach me..."

"It's okay. I'm going to need you to be a distraction."

Aissa said, "Where will you be?"

Riley grinned. "I'm going to get one of those jeeps."

Al wasn't surprised to see Steven standing next to the doors doing nothing; the man took even the smallest opportunity to take a "cigarette break." The fax machine stopped its whirring and delivered a new order into the tray with a gasp that sounded almost like a sigh of exhaustion. He hated the beeps and whistles of the archaic machine, and people preferred doing business online or over the phone. But faxes were less restricted for the simple reason no one bothered looking for them.

He grabbed the new order and left his office, stalking over to where Steven was staring off into the distance. Everyone else was already out on their routes, so Steven would have to do.

"Let me guess. You were just waiting for me to come along and give you something to do, right? Just wanted one more delivery before you finally headed out?"

Steven ignored him, gesturing with his chin. "That girl is back."

Al looked and saw the blonde girl lurking across the street. He shrugged and pressed the order sheet against Steven's chest. "I don't care. If she was going to do something, she'd have done it a long time ago. Customers are waiting. I get any complaints about a late delivery, I'm taking it out of your cut. Understand me?"

Steven rolled his eyes and offered a sloppy salute to Al's back. He glanced at the order form and bared his teeth in a sneer when he saw it was halfway across town. He was going to be driving for hours. Of course, if he complained, Al would just tell him to plan a route like the other drivers did. Like he had time for that. He had another job, so he couldn't just sit and plot addresses on a map all the live-long day.

He turned on the GPS hooked to the dashboard and punched in the first address from his list. Down by the high school, which meant he could stop and maybe score a little weed before getting on with his work. That could take some of the edge off for sure. He put the jeep in gear and crossed the parking lot, using the garage door opener hooked to his visor to make the gate roll out of the way.

As he left, he looked across the street to see the blonde girl had disappeared. Al might think she was nothing to worry about, but Steven wasn't so sure. He had half a mind to grab her, take her somewhere private, and spend a few hours seeing what she found so interesting about their warehouse. He grinned as he pictured it, fantasizing that she wouldn't talk immediately so he could have a little fun.

He was so caught up in his reverie that he almost missed the girl herself running out of the alley and crossing the street a few car-lengths ahead of him. She ran along the sidewalk just ahead of him, picking up speed after she glanced back to see he was coming. Steven smiled and sped up as well, pulling up alongside her. He rolled down the passenger side window with the controls on his door, leaning across the passenger seat.

"Hey, sweetheart. You find our little depot back there pretty interesting, huh? Maybe I could give you a little guided tour."

"No thanks." The traffic at the corner forced her to stop, and she looked for a gap between cars like a cornered animal. "I was just... hanging out, you know?"

"Yeah, sure. I know what you were doing." He put the jeep in park. "Come on over here. I just want to talk."

She smiled nervously. "I don't want to cause any trouble. Please, I'll-I'll stop hanging out by your place. I promise."

He looked at traffic - still busy - and the street behind him was empty, so he opened the door and climbed out. The blonde girl froze, a deer in the headlights, and held her hands up in surrender.

"Please. Don't hurt me. I'm sorry."

"We're just going to talk, all right?" He grabbed her arm and twisted, and she yelped. He felt a thrill at the sound and twisted harder as he pulled her toward him. "That's right, sweetheart. Just a little talk. Nothing wrong with talking, right?"

He heard tires screeching on pavement and turned to see his jeep reversing down the street. A woman was behind the wheel, twisted to watch out the back window so he couldn't see her face. "Hey!" He started to tug the blonde girl down the street with him like a parent forcing an unruly child into the dentist's office. Suddenly his hand was stabbed by four separate blades. He stiffened, almost blacking out from the pain, and looked down to see the blonde girl's free hand was curled into a rake, her fingernails digging into the back of his hand.

Steven couldn't even shriek, his voice caught in his throat by the pain. Finally he managed to bring his free hand up and shoved the girl away from him. Blood welled from the four crescent-shaped wounds in the back of his hand but he didn't have time to take care of it. If Al found out he'd lost an entire jeep of packages... oh, hell.

The jeep turned the corner and sped away as something barreled into him from behind. He was knocked forward, skinning his knees before he fell flat onto the sidewalk. The girl, her voice now hard and unwavering, said, "Don't fight me. I don't want to hurt you any more than I already have."

"You're dead, bitch. I was just going to have some fun, but when he finds out what you did? You're *dead*."

"I'll take my chances." She pulled his arms together and slipped a zip-tie over his hands. He struggled again just before she tightened them. She leaned close to his ear. "Right now I could shove your face into the pavement." Her hand shot past his head and slapped on the ground hard enough to make him flinch. "Want me to do that?"

He grunted and grumbled and she pushed up off of him. "I didn't think so. Come on." She hauled him up, one hand on his arm and the other on his shoulder. He could feel the strength in her grip and knew that it would be a dumb move to try fighting her. Steven wasn't a stranger to dumb moves, but he also liked having teeth.

She walked him a few blocks to the parking lot of an abandoned fast-food restaurant. His jeep was parked at the back, near where the drive-thru had once been. The woman who had stolen his jeep had the rear door open and was going through the packages. "Ah, no... no, no, no..."

"Wish I'd seen you take him down," the woman said.

The girl smiled proudly. "It wasn't anything worth writing home about. He went down pretty quickly."

The woman tossed the box she had been examining back into the truck before she turned to face him. He saw the badge on her hip and his stomach dropped like a stone. He worked his tongue to combat his suddenly dry mouth and tried to remember what Al had told him to stay.

"Y-you can't use anything you find in that against me, because this is unlawful search and seizure and... hey. Yeah. You stole my truck, and you didn't identify yourself, so-"

"Quiet." His teeth clacked together. "I'm Detective Riley Parra. That's Aissa Good. She's making a citizen's arrest right now. She alerted the authorities - me - about a crime in progress and I responded. Here's where you come in. What's your name?"

"Steven."

"Well, Steven, you have a choice. We can either let you go right now and use what's in this jeep to take you down with everyone else back at that warehouse, or you can turn yourself in as a cooperating witness. Which option do you see having the brighter future?"

He looked at the boxes stacked in the back of his jeep. He knew what was in there, and he knew that if the cops were on their way, he wanted to be on the other side of the fences.

"I'd..." He cleared his throat. "I'd like to turn myself in, please."

Briggs stopped on her way to the break room when she saw Riley seated at her desk. "Detective Parra. I thought you were taking the day."

"I am. I'm not officially at work." She kept typing as she spoke. "I'm just writing up a witness report."

"What witness report?"

"Mine. I happened to witness a crime, and I'm officially making a report of what I saw. Like a good citizen."

Briggs pursed her lips. "Hm. Why do I get the feeling it's not as simple as that?"

"Because you're a suspicious person?"

"What was the crime?"

Riley leaned back in her chair. "A couple of goons got their hands on some jeeps, made them up to look like post office vehicles and used them to deliver drugs to clients who faxed in their orders."

"Nice catch."

"Wasn't mine. Aissa's the one who did all the legwork. She's down in Narcotics now making the official report. One of their drivers is even giving a statement listing everyone involved, and I think they're putting together a team to raid the place tonight. If everything goes well, Aissa might even get a reward."

"I'd be surprise if she didn't. Looks like you taught her well."

Riley shrugged. "I meant to. But today I figured out that she doesn't really need much help. I chose well, though. That's for sure."

"That's one thing I can say about you, Riley. You definitely surround yourself with good people. Speaking of whom, Priest and Dr. Hunt. How are they?"

"On the mend, both mentally and physically. We should all be back to work by the end of the week."

"Fantastic. It's not the same without you three around here. Work gets done, nothing catches fire, I don't have to wear holy relics... it's nice." Briggs smiled and continued toward the break room. Riley stared at the computer screen for a moment and then looked at Briggs' back.

"Boss."

"Yeah."

Briggs turned to face her again, and Riley noticed the lieutenant looked exhausted. It was only the afternoon, but she could see it had already been a long day. Briggs was on her way to the break room, obviously in search of something to keep herself awake for the rest of the shift. Riley couldn't pile her personal bombshell on top of everything. She pushed a hand through her hair and shook her head.

"Never mind. It can keep."

"You sure?"

"Positive. I'm not even supposed to be here today."

Briggs chuckled quietly. "Yeah. But I like it better when you are here. It's comforting when I can keep an eye on you."

Riley smiled, sighed, and went back to work on her report. She knew she had to let Briggs know what was going on, had to warn her about the deadline, but there would be a proper time and place.

Aissa expected a long wait after she knocked, but the door swung open before she felt the need to announce her presence again. Priest's hair was much shorter than she remembered, and she was dressed in casual clothing. Aissa resisted the urge to drop to her knees, all too aware of the nature of the being standing before her.

She dipped her chin out of respect, her hands clasped in front of her. "Zerachiel. I know I should have called first, but... I hope I'm not disturbing you."

"Not at all, Aissa. Please, come in." She stepped aside and Aissa entered the apartment. "And you can call me Priest, or Caitlin. I've grown accustomed to it in the past few years."

"I'll try. You have a lovely home."

"Thank you."

Aissa looked at her again, glad to see that there were no longer any bruises marring her skin, and she moved gracefully without the obvious pain that had nearly crippled her after the run-in with Valefar. She was barefoot, and Aissa wondered if skin-to-floor contact helped her absorb the praise seeping up from the church below her apartment.

"You seem to be doing better."

"Much. I'm almost completely recovered. Riley insists I continue my rest until Gillian is also ready to return to work, so I'm trying to keep myself occupied here." She looked toward the kitchen. "Would you like something to drink?"

"No, thank you. I have to get back to the shelter before dark. I just wanted to ask you for help. Riley said that her success as champion is due to having a strong support group. There's no weakness in asking for assistance."

"Not at all. In fact sometimes admitting you need help is the strongest thing you can do. If I can help, I would be more than happy to. Please, have a seat."

Aissa sat on the coffee table while Priest took the couch. "You know that one of the other Good Girls, Cerys, chose to remain behind with me when the others returned home. She wished to be here when we find Annora's killer and bring her to justice." Priest nodded. "She's been having a difficult time adjusting to the outside world. I have been trying my best to help her, but if a blind man leads a blind man, both will fall into a pit."

"Matthew 15," Priest said softly with a weak smile.

"Yes. I thought that perhaps you would have a better insight into what she's facing and how she feels. You know what it's like to leave a holy place and try to exist in this world."

Priest nodded slowly. "It isn't easy. I'm not sure what I could tell her, or you, that would help. But I am willing to talk as often as you want. What you two did was extraordinarily brave. I was very impressed when Riley told me Cerys was staying. Whatever I can do in the time I'm still here, I will be more than happy to do."

Aissa frowned. "Still here? Where are you going?"

"Did Riley... I was under the impression she was going to tell you something today..."

"She did." Aissa realized the connection. "Oh. I didn't think."

Priest nodded sadly and looked down at her hands. "Riley and Gillian are planning to leave the city when Lark Siskin has been defeated. With her out of danger and no longer being champion, and with her death predetermined, there will be no reason for me to remain." She sighed heavily and blinked away tears. "Please don't tell Riley I cried. It's hard enough for her as it is. We've spoken and we're on good terms regarding what happened. I don't want her to think I'm harboring this sadness."

Aissa didn't know what to say. She had come to the angel to ask for help, but now wondered what she could do for Zerachiel.

"May I give you a hug?"

Priest looked up, surprised by the question. "Yes."

Aissa moved to the couch and took Priest into her arms. Now she truly understood Riley's advice about having a group of strong supporters. Sometimes they would help her, sometimes she would help them, and every now and then they would have to help each other. She rested her head on Priest's shoulder and held her, whispering that she would stay as long as she was needed.

FAREWELL HAPPY FIELDS

LARK SISKIN stepped behind the lectern, her aide Emily Simon standing just behind her and to the right as always. "Good afternoon, ladies and gentlemen of the press. As promised, I will get to your questions in a moment but first I would like to make an announcement. I've spoken with Police Commissioner Benedict about the increasing number of complaints being made in regards to looting, property damage, and other assorted criminal behavior that has been on the rise since the devastating earthquake five months ago.

"We certainly recognize the need for a heightened law enforcement presence in some of the hardest hit parts of the city. Commissioner Benedict and I have come up with a plan which will ensure a much more efficient police force. Through a partnership with a local automotive accessory retailer, we will provide every police service vehicle with a state of the art GPS and communication system. This will allow for an immediate connection between the person reporting the crime and the officers responding to it, and the dispatcher will be able to stay in contact with the officers from the moment the call is received until they arrive at the scene.

"These systems will be installed over the next three months, until all of the vehicles in our fleet are fully equipped and all of our officers are able to provide this city with the level of protection it deserves. Any questions regarding this initiative will be addressed at the end of this press conference but for now, the reason we've all gathered here... the steps the city is taking to recover after the earthquake..."

Riley muted the television since she'd already heard the rest of the comments during the late news. This was the replay, but she couldn't make herself ignore it. The television provided the only light in the apartment, washing over Riley as she stood in front of the coffee table.

The news had shown the majority of Mayor Siskin's press conference, followed by a roundtable discussion about what the new camera systems meant. One expert said that it was like Big Brother turning the all-seeing eye on itself; someone was finally watching the watchers. Another thought that it was a nanny-state experiment to keep constant track of people who had been hired to keep the city safe. Riley had no doubt there was some nefarious purpose behind the scheme, and that she would see it if only she looked hard enough.

She was distracted enough that she didn't hear the shower shut off, and only realized she had been busted when she smelled Gillian's body wash. Before she met Gillian, she didn't even know what juniper was, let alone what it smelled like. Now the lemony pine scent filled the room like an aura, and Riley closed her eyes to breathe in deeply and savor it before she spoke.

"Sorry. I know we said we'd turn it off."

Gillian brushed the hair from Riley's neck and bent to kiss her just behind her ear. Riley closed her eyes and felt the tension seep from her shoulders.

"It's my fault. I didn't give you a proper distraction."

Riley smiled. "Well, I like the sound of that." She turned to embrace Gillian, but instead took a step back and ran her eyes down her wife's body. "Baby, you're all kinds of naked."

"I seem to be, yes. I thought I'd dress down for you."

Riley pulled Gillian to her. "I approve."

"Good." They kissed, and Gillian teased Riley's lips with the tip of her tongue. Riley had opened her mouth to accept it when Gillian pulled back. "I'm sorry."

"For what?" Riley looked dazed at the preempted kiss.

"For the past few weeks. Since you told me about..." She flinched and looked down. "I haven't been here for you."

Riley shrugged. "You've had a lot to deal with. I understand.

And after what Valefar did to you..." She let her voice trail off and touched Gillian's hair. She followed the strand down to where it curled against the freckles on Gillian's chest, pressing two fingertips against the moist skin before sliding them up to her neck. "You've had a rough time of it. I haven't felt abandoned. But I have missed you."

"I've missed you, too. And I'm back now." She kissed the corners of Riley's mouth, then offered her tongue again. Riley took it, and Gillian rocked back on her heels to guide Riley toward the bedroom. She moved her hands to the waistband of Riley's pants, hooking her fingers on the belt to tug her closer as she was walked backwards down the short hall.

"What did you have in mind?" Riley asked against Gillian's cheek.

"Oh, I have some very specific things in mind. Let's see if you can guess what they are."

Riley wet her lips and reached out to turn on the light as they entered the bedroom. Before, with other women, she could have counted the number of times she'd made love with the lights on with one hand. But she wanted and needed to see Gillian. When they reached the bed Gillian sat down, and Riley knelt in front of her. Gillian pushed Riley's hair back and bent down to kiss her. Riley ran her hands over Gillian's thighs, keeping them apart until the kiss broke. She kissed Gillian's breasts, smoothing her tongue over the valley between them.

Gillian sighed and rested her hands on Riley's shoulders, bent forward over her as Riley moved lower. She licked one hip, then the other, then pressed a kiss to Gillian's pubic hair. Gillian hissed and moved one hand to the back of Riley's head. She didn't guide her lower, but there was enough tension in her grip to get her point across. She used her thumb to part the smooth, dark hair, twisted her wrist, and wrapped her fingers around the hair. She bit her bottom lip and smiled when Riley looked up to meet her eyes.

"You can pull."

"Yeah?"

Riley nodded and Gillian tightened her grip. Her eyes closed as Riley kissed between her legs, a weak sigh escaping against her will. Riley teased with the tip of her tongue, resting her arms on Gillian's thighs with her fingers spread over her hips. Gillian glanced to the right and tugged a pillow away from the headboard. She wedged it under her ass, pressing against Riley's mouth. Riley pursed her lips and hummed, and Gillian arched her back with a sharp cry of approval.

They had made love in the weeks since Riley told her about the deadline, but it had been as close to perfunctory as was possible with them. Riley knew that she could never be half-present when it came to Gillian, but she could feel the weight of her mortality looming. This time, however, it felt like it had during the early days of their relationship. Riley didn't care about debts owed or demons looming, even Lark Siskin's machinations fled from her mind, replaced with the singular purpose of making her lover climax.

Gillian hunched her shoulders, pulling Riley's hair harder than she intended as her knees came up. She gave a series of slow, staccato grunts and then growled noisily as she dropped her chin to her chest and finally opened her eyes. Riley was kissing Gillian's thighs and looked up with an impish smile.

"Did I hurt you?" Gillian smoothed her hand over Riley's hair.

"No."

"Take your clothes off."

"I like it when you boss me around, Doctor." She stood and quickly stripped off her shirt and pants, kicking the clothes aside before removing her underwear. Gillian watched, enjoying the show but also eager for the endgame.

Once her clothes were out of the way, Riley moved to straddle Gillian, but was instead turned around to face away from her. She scooted back so that there was space on the edge of the bed between her legs, and she guided Riley down. Riley sat, and Gillian pressed against her from behind. Riley relaxed, and Gillian cupped Riley's breasts as they kissed.

"I think I like this."

"Yeah?" Gillian whispered. She brought up one hand and wet the fingers before dropping it between Riley's legs. "I like it too. I like your weight against me. Do you like this?"

Riley inhaled sharply and went stiff. "Yeah..."

"I thought you would. And I know you like it when I talk to you... so..." She licked the shell of Riley's ear as she stroked with two fingers. "I've been thinking about the first time we made love. Not the first time we had sex... not the first time we fucked. The first time I knew you were the last woman I'd be with. It was right after I came back from Georgia. I knew it wasn't about where I wanted to be, it was who I needed to be with. You were my home, Riley, even then. And when you took me to bed to welcome me home." She slipped her middle finger inside and Riley stiffened. "It was like my first time all over again."

Riley moved her hand to cover Gillian's, guiding her.

"I love you, Riley. Every day you have left, and every day after you're gone, I'll love you just as much as I did the day you brought me home."

Riley came quietly, her hand tight around Gillian's, her toes curling in the carpet. She held her breath for as long as she could, then let it go in a series of hitching gasps. Gillian kissed Riley's neck and shoulder, her free hand massaging Riley's breast. She pinched the nipple between two fingers as she stroked Riley's inner thigh, and Riley turned her head to capture Gillian's lips.

They maintained the kiss as Riley twisted, parting only when absolutely necessary, until they were lying side by side across the mattress. Gillian tenderly brushed Riley's hair back from her face and then drew a line over both of her eyebrows. Riley closed her eyes and let her face be caressed, kissing Gillian's palm when it was close enough.

"Don't count the days. Or, if you do, don't tell me the number."

Riley shook her head. "I won't. I promise. Priest worked out the date, but I asked her not to tell me until it rolls around. I don't want to dread it."

Gillian nodded and dropped her hand to Riley's side. "Thank you."

"For what?"

"I don't know." When she smiled a tear slipped free. Riley kissed it away before it could make a trail down her cheek. "You have this huge, magnificent life, and you want to spend the little time you have left with me. Thank you."

"Thank you for staying with me."

"Oh, Riley." She kissed both of Riley's cheeks. "Where else would I be? Hurry up and take Lark Siskin down. I want you all to myself as soon as possible."

Riley smiled. "I'll see what I can do, pretty lady."

Gillian shifted on the mattress, inching closer. Riley wrapped her arms around her, guiding Gillian's head to her shoulder. She kissed Gillian's hair, breathing deeply the scent of her body wash again. "As long as I'm here... I'll be right here."

"Good." Gillian's voice was barely a murmur, and Riley knew she was close to sleep. A minute or so later her breathing had steadied, and Riley followed not long after.

He was waiting when Lark returned home from City Hall. She eyed him as she passed, slipping out of her jacket and tossing it to Emily without looking. Emily caught it, folded it neatly, and draped it over her arm as she followed Lark into the bedroom. After a moment the demon rose from the sofa, straightened his own jacket, and went into the room unbidden.

Lark stood at the wardrobe to remove her suit. She stripped down completely as Emily transferred each item to the hamper.

"Tell me you didn't leave him alone."

Leraje, the demon prince who had been assigned to her once she became evil's champion, smiled. "He's asleep right now. All is well, and all will be well. I thought I would pop up here and see how you were doing. It's been a very busy year for you already."

Lark stretched out facedown on the massage table next to the bathroom door. Emily poured a dollop of oil into a cupped hand, rubbed her palms together, then began to massage the deathly pale skin of the mayor's back.

"Don't worry about us. Just worry about your end of our little project."

Leraje poured himself a glass of brandy and walked to the bedroom window. "Have you come any closer to determining the cause of the earthquake?"

Lark grunted. Whether it was a critique of his question or the result of her massage, Leraje didn't care. After a moment she spoke. "No. It definitely wasn't a natural occurrence, and all the evidence implies the Ladder was indeed the point of origin."

"And yet the Ladder has not been breached. Hasn't been breached for centuries. So how could it possibly have caused damage on such a massive scale? The only possible explanation is that it was breached at a later time and the effects rippled back to this point. Both sides are currently guarding it, but we've seen no evidence of activity on the site." He turned to face her now and saw that Emily's hand was between the mayor's legs. He rolled his eyes and swirled the liquor in his glass. "The other champion, for the angels. Piley or whatever her name is. She's the only possible explanation. She or her angel will do something to harness the Ladder's power in the future. That is what you should be concerned about, not whether I'm a good babysitter."

Lark's breathing was labored now, and Emily's hand moved faster. "We can't afford the distraction... right now. The earthquake was a... nice bonus..." She grunted again. "But if it gave Parra an advantage she hasn't seen fit to use it. We'll... keep... a close... eye on her and her friends. What of Gillian Hunt?"

Leraje sighed. "A complete failure. Valefar nearly destroyed Zerachiel as collateral damage, but the angel was victorious and has since recovered. Dr. Hunt is back to work and shows no lingering effects from her mental manipulation. It was an excellent plan, regardless of the outcome. And we still have Valefar's payment for pointing him in the right direction, so we ended up ahead. It simply wasn't meant to be."

Emily had finished Lark while he was speaking, and she took an extra moment to catch her breath. She pushed herself up on her elbows and looked at him.

"And what about Abby?"

Emily had been washing her hands but froze when her erstwhile partner's name was spoken. Lark didn't notice but Leraje did. The demon watched her as her responded to the mayor.

"She's doing as well as can be expected. She's in withdrawal, as you might expect. It could become an issue. The guards think that she's coming down off a mundane addiction. Cocaine or meth. The rehabilitation treatments are basically the same, so she'll survive."

"Has she spoken to anyone?"

"Not a soul."

Lark rose from the table and allowed Emily to drape her in a robe. She tied the belt herself before she rose, letting the ends of the silk fall around her legs. "If that changes, make sure it's dealt with in an expedient manner. Now I believe our good friend has been left unsupervised long enough. Run along." She gave Emily a pointed look and then went into the bathroom.

Leraje looked at the assistant, a woman who had been surgically altered to look exactly like the woman currently in prison.

"You don't draw the bath for her?"

"That used to be Abigail's job. I do it wrong."

"Hm." Leraje looked into his glass and swallowed the last bit of brandy. "I would have thought Lark would want you to do it wrong. That way she gets a bath, plus she gets the bonus of punishing you."

"She doesn't enjoy punishing me, sir."

He smiled. "Sure." He walked to her and pushed up the sleeve of her jacket. She passively allowed it, looking at the track marks on the inside bend of her elbow. "How are you doing on your doses, sweet?"

"I'm managing."

"With your manufactured paste?"

She slipped free of his grasp. "Please leave. The mayor doesn't like it when you stay."

"Lark doesn't like it when Leraje lingers," the demon sang. He moved his hand to her throat and tightened his grip. She whimpered and closed her eyes and, when he spoke again, his voice was nearly a whisper. "What do you like, little Emily?"

"Please," she moaned. He let go of her throat and stepped back. Emily's eyes opened, flashing darkness. "I said please."

He smiled and chucked her chin. "I believe your mistress is ready for her bath now. And I have a prisoner to attend. Perhaps another time, sweet."

"Bastard," she hissed.

Leraje laughed as he walked out of the room. He took the elevator up to the top floor of the building, the erstwhile penthouse before the mayor had adjusted it for her purposes. Leraje crossed the floor, ignoring the scent of sex and blood that lingered no matter how much time was spent scrubbing. Some rooms simply evolved to fit the purpose they were given; he couldn't see how this room could ever be anything but a den of pleasure and pain.

He waved his hand in front of the cell door and it evaporated. Within, a man lay hunched over himself as if to maintain his dignity. The prisoner was nude, with graven images carved on his back and arms. Heavy iron bracelets weighted down his arms, identical ones linked around his ankles. His arms rested on his knees, the arms out in front of him and his face pressed against the bicep of his left arm. The man was drenched with the sweat of a fever patient, and grime was smeared over his pale flesh. His blonde hair was lank and limp, resting on his skull like a discarded rag.

Leraje walked around the shackled prisoner eyeing his handiwork. The wounds were on their way to healing, but he didn't feel like refreshing the marks. "Are you awake?"

The head lifted weakly. His eyes were lined with red and his lower lip trembled as he gazed upon his captor. Leraje smiled.

"Good. We can begin again."

"No."

"Then stop me."

The man pushed himself up. Wings extended from the middle of his back, stretching so far that they touched the walls at either side of the room. He took one step before Leraje focused on the sigil carved into his prisoner's left pectoral. "Praise to the profane."

It was barely more than a whisper, but it was enough to make the angel recoil. He howled in pain and dropped to his knees. Leraje stepped forward and put his hand over the angel's heart. "Weep, caged bird. You know how I love to hear you weep." Vile energy poured from the demon's hand into the exposed muscle. The angel held back for as long as he could but eventually he gave in as he always did. He cried out in agony as his body was used for wicked worship, his holy body treated as a sacrilegious idol, and all of his wounds began to bleed once more.

Leraje smiled and prepared himself for a long night.

Riley was surprised by the lack of activity around the crime scene. Normally there was a crowd of witnesses or rubber-neckers standing at the limits of the police tape. It was a little past rush hour, but even the stores on either side of the street still seemed to be doing business as usual. The only people milling about were men in hardhats and reflective vests standing by their machines and watching from the corner of their eye as she and Priest walked past.

"Wonder where all the lookie-loos are," she muttered as she pulled her gloves on. "Maybe everyone finally realized how creepy it was to lurk somewhere that a person just died."

"I don't think that's why they come," Priest said. "I think they're affirming the fact that, whatever happened, it didn't happen to them."

Riley considered that as she ducked under the crime scene tape. She soon realized that the lurking voyeurs weren't present because the crime was very, very old.

Gillian and her team were in a pit that the construction crew had been digging. She could see evidence that they were trying to repair a water line when they found a metal container. One side of the container had been cut open, and the skeletons within had tumbled out. Gillian was crouching next to a skull.

"Did you know him, Horatio?"

"Is that a Shakespeare reference or *CSI: Miami*?"

"Whichever one makes you laugh more."

Gillian said, "Alas, I did not know this fellow. Nor any of his eight or ten friends."

"Eight or ten?" Priest asked.

"Or even more," Gillian admitted. "Some of the skeletons are still mostly intact, but some are just a jumble of bones. We'll know more once we get them to the morgue and put them back together."

Riley looked at the jumble of bones scattered around the first skull. There were even more still in the box. "Please tell me this used to be a cemetery and we can all go home early."

"Sorry, hon. The box barely predates the building they're under, which means they were put here when the foundation for the basement was being poured. One of the patrol officers found someone who said that was fifteen years ago, so they've been down here since then. If that earthquake hadn't damaged the infrastructure down here, they could have gone another decade or two without being found." She gave Riley a pointed look, offering her a silver lining.

"So they could have been someone else's problem?" Riley climbed carefully into the pit and joined Gillian. They crouched with the skull in between them. "Can you tell how they died?"

Gillian wiggled her hand. "It'll be difficult. There's a lot of postmortem damage to the skeletons, but..." She pointed with her pinkie. "See here? The hyoid bone is broken, indicating strangulation. And this is just speculation, but given the disarticulation of these other bodies, I would say there's a good chance some of it happened before they died."

"You mean they were dismembered prior to death?" Priest said.

"Yeah. Or they were killed and someone had to fit everyone into a single box. So space saver..."

Riley grunted. "Okay. So we're dealing with a serial killer. Yet another one."

"No," Gillian said. "I mean, yes, he had at least eight victims, but I don't think it's a serial killer. They were all buried in the same place, and they were all killed around the same time judging by the decay. I think all of these people were murdered in a short period of time and then buried together."

Riley raised an eyebrow. "Huh. Somehow that seems worse than a serial killer."

"Yeah," Gillian agreed. "But at least he's not still active."

"That we know of. Maybe this was just his dumping ground for April and the kills for May are buried somewhere else."

Gillian shuddered. "Thanks for the nightmares, sweetie."

"Sorry." She kissed Gillian's forehead and stood up. "Have fun figuring out who these people are."

"Yeah, thanks. If the dental records are helpful, I should have a name or two by this afternoon."

Priest offered Riley a hand out of the pit. She brushed off her pants to make sure she wasn't carrying out any minuscule particles of dead people. "Okay. It's going to take her a while to get the bodies out of the pit, let alone identify any of them. Let's spend the time talking to the business owners. Maybe someone was around back then and remembers seeing something. Want to take that side of the street?"

"Sure."

She blew a kiss to Gillian and set off to talk to the people on her side of the street.

"No, sir, I'm not accusing you of anything. I just want to know if you~"

"Law-abiding citizen. Been here ten years. Cops just waltz in, see brown skin~"

"Sir, that's not what this is. And if you've only been here for ten years, you can't give us any information we might need." She checked her cell phone as she fled the bodega, relieved to see that Gillian had something for her. She walked quickly back down the street. She didn't know what Gillian had found, but whatever it was had to be better than talking to any more grumpy proprietors about a case that had gone cold when Riley was still a rookie.

Most of the bodies had been loaded up, their black bags looking oddly deflated due to the fact they only held skeletons. Gillian came to the edge of the pit and Riley crouched, hooked her hands under Gillian's arms, and lifted her up to the street level. Gillian smiled when she was back on solid ground, leaning against Riley for support.

"Whoa. That was kind of fun."

"Then why are you smiling like someone just told a joke at a funeral?"

Gillian pressed her lips together. "Because I found something. We may have a possible identification on one of the bodies."

"May have and possible... not exactly brimming with confidence."

"You'll understand why when I tell you who it is. Some of the bodies still have clothing that hasn't decayed. Nothing whole, in most cases. But one body was wearing a pair of pants with the waistband still in one piece. There was writing on the inside..."

"Someone wrote their name in their clothes?" Riley went cold. "God... please don't tell me these were kids, Jill."

Gillian shook her head. "No. The bones are all fully formed. However many people were in that box, they were all full-grown adults."

"But..."

"But the name on the pants was H. Keane."

Riley frowned. "I don't get it."

"A person named H. Keane who disappeared fifteen years ago, Riley." She raised her eyebrows, hoping to prompt Riley's memory. "Hayden Keane."

The pieces snapped together in Riley's head and she flinched. "No. You said there were only eight to ten~"

"But there could easily be as many as twelve once we get back to the morgue."

Riley hooked her hand on Gillian's elbow and guided her away from the pit. "Did you tell anyone?"

"No! I didn't even tell Priest. Something this big..."

Riley rubbed her cheek with the back of her hand. "Yeah. We don't want to open this can of worms until we're positive we have to."

She looked back at the pit where Gillian's assistants were carrying the gurneys up over the uneven terrain to be loaded into the ambulance. If one of those bodies was Hayden Keane, and if the other bodies turned out to be the Twelve Apostles, then the city was about to have a very ugly part of its history blown wide open.

Riley and Gillian sat across from Zoe Briggs as she examined the dental reports. Priest was standing beside the door, arms crossed and stoic as if she was carved from marble. The report in front of Briggs wasn't very thick, but she spent ten minutes reading and rereading the scant information before she leaned back in her chair. She looked at Gillian.

"You're absolutely sure?"

"About these results? Yes, ma'am. I visually compared the dental X-rays to the ones we have on file. I was a bit pressed for time since I didn't want to spread the work around. I figured the fewer people who know about this, the better. I was going to check them all but I thought three was a fairly reasonable sample."

Briggs cut her off with a quick nod. "Yes, you're right. If

Hayden Keane, Wayne Carver, and Timothy Gates are buried in a box, it's safe to assume the other nine will be there, too. Shit." She looked at Riley and Priest. "This is immense, ladies. Riley, were you even around when this happened?"

"I was twenty-one. A rookie."

Briggs sighed. "I was still in uniform. Those were bad days."

Priest raised her hand. "I'm not sure what this is all about."

Riley and Gillian twisted to face her. Riley said, "Really? I thought you were... around even back then."

"I was. But before I became Caitlin Priest, I didn't pay much heed to mortal affairs if they didn't directly affect you. I have no idea what the Twelve Apostles are. I mean, other than the obvious..."

Briggs chuckled without humor. "Well, then, allow me to do the honors." She closed the folder of dental X-rays. "The Twelve Apostles were a group of police officers who were involved in a department scandal fifteen years ago. A reporter went undercover and recorded two officers accepting bribes. Victor Jennings and Luke Hale. That would have been a big story all by itself but the reporter was greedy. She wanted a bigger story, so she flipped them. They were part of a bigger group and knew of three officers involved with extortion and embezzlement. She flipped them, too. By the time she got to what she thought was the top, she was dealing with police officers involved in protection rackets and murder for hire. Twelve of them in all.

"She got them all to talk about each other, confirming allegations and cementing the facts before she went to print. But through it all, she kept hearing about someone who controlled them all. They all referred to him as Shere Khan after the tiger from *The Jungle Book*. The reporter wanted to get all of them together to take him down. She had the article ready to go, all she needed was the final piece. Shere Khan's name."

Priest said, "I get the impression that never happened."

Riley shook her head. "The reporter disappeared. Not long after her editor received a box with her severed hands inside. The rest of her was never found, but she mailed one of her friends a key to a safe deposit box. Inside was a copy of her unfinished story and all the evidence she had gathered so far. By then it was too late. The twelve cops had disappeared and their boss was nowhere to be found."

"The press started calling them the Twelve Apostles," Briggs said. "For a while, every other cop in town was considered a suspect for Shere Khan. Public support of the police crashed. It was one of the biggest scandals to ever hit the department, followed a few years later by..." She caught herself but then decided there was no point in not finishing. "Chelsea's incident destroyed any goodwill we'd built back by that point. It was a one-two punch from which we have yet to recover. And now we find out the Apostles have been buried underneath that diner for the past fifteen years?"

"Shere Khan wanted to keep them quiet," Priest said.

Gillian shrugged. "It makes sense. They had already proven they were willing to talk in exchange for a lighter sentence. It never made sense to me that they'd all just been thrown to the wind. But this? I never dreamed anything like this."

"None of us did," Briggs said. "Okay, Dr. Hunt, I want you to finish the comparisons. Get DNA. I'll make sure the department pays for a rush on it. I need to be absolutely sure all of the Apostles are there before I say a word to the press. Considering how many people saw us taking bodies out of the ground this morning, I'd say we have a very small window before people start asking questions I don't want to answer."

"Yes, ma'am. I'll get on it now."

She brushed Riley's hand as she stood up. Priest held the door for her and, once she was gone, took Gillian's seat.

"What should we do, boss?"

She rested her hands on the desktop. "No one ever figured out who Shere Khan was, so there's a good chance he stuck around. He could be a high-ranking member of the department."

"Or he could have been high-ranking then," Riley said. "Fifteen years go by... he could have retired or he could be dead."

"If only we could be so lucky. Someone put those bodies in the ground fifteen years ago. If he is still around, he's going to hear about this discovery sooner or later. He might come looking for you. Keep your guard up on this one, ladies."

"Always do." Priest looked dubiously at her. "Okay, we'll try harder than usual this time."

Briggs dipped her chin in thanks. "That's all I can ask. Good luck." They stood and Briggs cleared her throat. "Just to spare you the time and effort, at the time of the Apostles controversy, I was just a lowly patrol officer. Most of the Apostles outranked me and wouldn't have taken orders from a woman in the first place. Just so you don't worry I was Shere Khan."

"The thought never crossed my mind, boss."

She smiled sadly and shrugged. "Just in case it did at some point. Riley... stick around for a second."

Priest understood that she was being dismissed. "I'll be at my desk."

Riley nodded and watched Priest go, then turned to Briggs once the door was closed. "Everything okay, boss?"

"Yes. I just know that Caitlin has a personal relationship with Chelsea Stanton, so I didn't want to say this in front of her. When Stanton was originally arrested for her crimes a lot of people suspected that she was Shere Khan. The investigation never went anywhere, but given the new evidence..."

"You want me to talk to her?"

"I think it needs to be done, yes. She's a different person now, so I think she would be more forthcoming about the truth."

Riley nodded. "Sure. Are you sure you're okay?"

Briggs raised her eyebrows, then her shoulders sagged. "I'm as okay as anyone else here. It's been a rough few months. We're just starting to recover from the earthquake and now we have to reopen this can of worms. I don't think I've had a good night's sleep in six months."

"Let me know if there's anything I can do to help out."

"Catch this bastard before I have to give a press conference."

Riley smiled. "I'll do my best."

"Keep me informed."

Riley agreed and left the office. Priest was waiting at her desk and stood up when Riley reappeared. They walked to the stairs together.

"What did Briggs want?"

"She wanted to make sure I knew what had to be done. Cait, you can stay here if you'd prefer to skip this."

Priest glanced at her. "I go where you go, Riley."

"Okay. But I warn you, it's not going to be pretty."

Chelsea and Kenzie's desks faced each other across the middle of the room. Two lamps were placed behind Kenzie so that their glow formed a halo around her. Chelsea could still discern the difference in light and dark so the resulting silhouette meant that she could look up and see Kenzie whenever she wanted. At the moment Kenzie was doing a background check for a client while Chelsea dictated a case report into the headset Kenzie had bought her last Christmas. The microphone was sensitive enough that she could speak in a low murmur, but it didn't pick up the music from Kenzie's iPod on the other side of the room.

The sensor on the front door chimed and Chelsea paused the recording. Kenzie identified the guests for her, though Priest's presence was like a lantern in the darkness. Chelsea smiled and rose from her seat. "Riley. Caitlin. To what do we owe the pleasure?"

"Hey, Chelsea. Kenz." Riley was standing in the glow of a lamp, so Chelsea could see her stiff posture. "I'm afraid this isn't a social call."

Kenzie said, "What's going on?"

"Maybe we should speak to Chelsea alone," Priest said softly.

"No," Chelsea said. "Anything you say, I'll just tell her later anyway. What's happened?"

Riley cleared her throat. "Chelsea, what do you know about the Twelve Apostles?"

Chelsea tensed and turned her head away from the light, trading vague silhouettes for shadow. When she was confident she could speak without a tremor in her voice, she looked back.

"You found them."

"Yeah." Riley stepped forward. "How did you know we found all of them? You didn't think one of them came back, you didn't think one of them had been tracked down... did you know we'd found them all together?"

Chelsea offered a grim smile. "No. But it's been so long that if any of them were still alive, one of them would have screwed up before now. It stands to reason they all died, so I assume they were buried somewhere. And wherever that is, the earthquake revealed them. And now you're here to see if I killed them."

Kenzie stepped around her desk. "Riley... what the hell."

"This is an investigation, Kenzie. It's not personal."

"The hell it isn't. You walk in here and accuse my wife~"

Riley cut her off. "Fifteen years ago, she wasn't your wife. Hell, five years ago, you would have told me to drag her downtown on principle. Chelsea, I know you're a different person now. But fifteen years ago you were the kind of person who would have fit right in with the other Apostles. You were a high-profile detective, and the fact you went down so hard just a few years later... you fit the profile of who Shere Khan was."

Chelsea chose her words carefully. "I made mistakes. I was a bad cop, but I paid penance for what I did. I've sought forgiveness

and I've had it given to me. I thought I had changed enough that..."
She closed her eyes behind her shaded glasses.

Kenzie said, "You have. Riley, she's a different person now."

"These crimes happened over a decade ago, Kenzie. She~"

"She's a different person, and if she had been Shere Khan, she would have confessed to it. She would have taken her punishment for that before she started seeking redemption. How dare you think she's capable of hiding the murders of twelve people? Something that huge..."

Riley said, "She covered up her own drug addiction by trying to destroy the careers of good cops."

Chelsea jumped at the sharp sound of skin on skin. Priest lunged forward, stepping between Riley and Kenzie.

"I'm her guardian angel, MacKenzie, so I would advise you against striking her again."

"Maybe you should step aside, Detective Priest, before I decide you're as bad as she is."

Chelsea snapped, "Stop it, all of you. Kenzie, just because we've been together for four years doesn't change the fact you used to hate me. And Ril~ Detective Parra. I know you've accepted me as your friend's partner and wife, but apparently that acceptance had a limit. No. I was not Shere Khan. I do not know who it was, and I have no idea what happened to the Twelve Apostles. I wasn't involved in their crimes and I was not responsible for their deaths. Is that a definitive enough statement for you?"

"Yeah."

"Then get the hell out of our office."

Riley wisely chose not to argue. She turned toward the door and Priest followed.

Kenzie said, "And maybe make yourself scarce for a few months. Both of you."

Chelsea heard Riley stop at the door. Priest looked between the two women. "Riley, perhaps we should~"

"Fine," Riley walked away without looking back. "It's been nice knowing you, Kenz." She opened the door hard enough that it bumped the wall as the detectives left.

Kenzie waited until they were gone before she went to Chelsea. "I'm sorry, baby."

"Don't be." She took off her headset and placed it on the desk. "She was right. If the Apostles had been found five years earlier, you both would have been in here to drag me downtown in chains. The fact that she came here and did it quietly, and that she took my word for it... that was a kindness."

"It didn't feel like a kindness."

Chelsea put her hand on Kenzie's cheek and leaned in. They pressed their cheeks together for a moment before kissing.

"I think I'm going to go upstairs and lie down for a while."

"Okay. Do you want me to come with you?"

"No." She kissed Kenzie again. "But come up later?"

"Promise."

She stroked Kenzie's face again, then pulled away from her and went to the stairs. She suddenly felt very done with the day.

Priest had to hurry to catch up with Riley, who was moving quickly down the sidewalk to where she had parked. "Riley! That was uncalled for."

"It had to be done, Cait."

"You could have been kind. You owe them that."

Riley faced her. "Kenzie and I both forgave Chelsea for what she did. For the awful, horrendous thing she did to us, and to every cop on the force. She paid for those crimes and I am comfortable with her watching my back when I go into a dangerous situation. But she's still the same person who did all those awful things. She stole drugs. She was an addict. And then rather than taking her punishment, she tried to smear the names of other cops. Like it or not, she did exactly what the Apostles did to each other. And if there was even the slightest possibility she was the ringleader, I wasn't about to walk into that room hat in hand."

Priest lowered her head. "You may have burned some bridges back there. Bridges that it will take time to rebuild." She looked at Riley again. "Time you don't have."

Riley steeled herself. "Then that's her choice."

"You can't believe that. Riley, Chelsea is still the same person you've grown to trust over the past few years. And Kenzie... you can't just abandon Kenzie after everything you two have meant to each other."

"I did my job, Caitlin. If they can't handle it, that's their problem." She turned her back and walked to the car. "Get in if you don't want to walk."

The lines in Priest's forehead disappeared as realization dawned. "You did that on purpose, didn't you? It was easier to make them hate you than to tell them you were dying."

Riley rested her hand on the side of the car. "Get in the car, Caitlin."

"This may be the easier way, but it's not the right way. You owe them a proper goodbye, Riley. You can't just walk out on them and disappear."

"Well, I'm going to disappear, aren't I? Maybe they should get used to me not being around early."

Priest walked around the hood of the car. "They'll hate you until the day you die. And then they'll be angry you didn't trust them enough to tell them. Don't throw this away, Riley. You still have time left, and you should spend it with the people you care about." She touched Riley's cheek where Kenzie had slapped her. "Does it hurt?"

"Stings a little. Kenzie always knew how to throw a good slap."

"Go back."

Riley furrowed her brow. "They don't want to see me."

"Go before that feeling can grow roots. Apologize. And tell her the truth."

"Yeah. Okay." She swallowed the lump in her throat and pushed away from the car. She walked back to the agency, wishing the chime over the door was quieter. Kenzie was standing at her desk, bent forward to type something, but she straightened when she saw who had walked in. "Kenzie..."

"I thought I made myself clear. Do you have any idea what~"

"Kenzie. I'm sorry. I'll apologize to Chelsea, too." The fight went out of Kenzie's stance, and she just looked tired and sad. "There's something I need to tell you both. And I should probably tell you somewhere with access to alcoholic beverages."

Kenzie suddenly transformed back into Riley's friend and former partner, her erstwhile lover, the person who had gotten her through so many hard times.

"This is going to destroy me, isn't it?" Kenzie asked softly.

"If it does, I'm glad you have Chelsea to put you back together. She's a good person, Kenzie. She deserves you."

Kenzie blinked back tears. "Stop. Stop talking like you're dying."

Riley put her hands in her pockets and looked at her feet.

"Oh, God. Chelsea... Chelsea is upstairs. Come on up..." She paused to give Riley a hug before she went upstairs. "I'm sorry I slapped you."

"You did it to defend Chelsea. In that case, I'm glad you did it.

I was being a bitch."

Kenzie gave her another squeeze for good measure before letting her go. Riley took a steadying breath and then followed her up to go through the spiel all over again.

Riley managed to escape the apartment after promising to come back with Gillian for dinner that night. She profusely apologized to Chelsea for her behavior, and Chelsea assured her that it was water under the bridge. When she got back to the car, Priest was leaning against the passenger side with her feet crossed at the ankles.

"Are you going to be smug? Say you told me so?"

"Angels aren't smug."

"You're even smug about saying you're not smug."

Priest smiled and got into the car. "So I take it from the length of time you were gone that things are smoothed over with the Stantons?"

"They are. You may want to go back sometime soon just to make sure they don't hold a grudge against you."

Priest nodded. Riley pulled out onto the road and was halfway back to the station before her phone chimed with a text. She took it from her pocket and passed it to Priest.

"It's from Gillian." She read the body of the text. "Dental recs confirmed IDs. Twelve for twelve."

"Damn," Riley growled. "Briggs is going to be thrilled. If we don't close this case quick, she's going to be stuck giving endless updates. She'll be the face in the media, and it'll reflect poorly on her if it drags out. It would be nice if I could hand her Shere Khan all nicely gift-wrapped in time for the press conference."

"Surely there are witnesses and people with information... it was only fifteen years ago."

"No offense, but fifteen years is different to us mere mortals, Cait. People retire, they move, they die. And with a case like this, people are more likely to remember the myth than the real case. There were true crime books, those TV newsmagazines came to do a story on them... whatever we find out is going to be so muddled it'll take weeks just to sift through it all for the one grain of truth."

"The alternative is that after fifteen years, people will be less likely to maintain their silence due to fear of reprisal."

"Hopefully." Riley pulled into the parking garage. "Might as well head upstairs and give Briggs the bad news."

The scene was reminiscent of the mayor's press conference the day before. Riley, Priest, and Gillian were standing just behind the lectern as Briggs stepped onto the stage. The bottom of the screen displayed LIEUTENANT ZOE BRIGGS as she took her place behind the podium. She placed her notes in front of her and took a sip of water before she spoke.

"Thank you everyone for coming. This will be a brief statement of fact in regards to an ongoing case, so we will not be taking questions at this time. And as soon as the case has been closed we will of course allow you to ask whatever you want to your heart's content, but right now it's a matter of keeping the investigation private.

"This morning a construction crew working off Taft and Richmond uncovered what we believe to be a mass burial site. The bodies had fully decomposed by the time they were discovered, so I'll turn the microphone over to Medical Examiner Dr. Gillian Hunt..."

They shifted places and Gillian smiled weakly. "Good afternoon. Evidence found on one of the bodies recovered from the site led us to believe the bodies were the Twelve Apostles." The reporters reacted with gasps and whispers. She glanced up as if surprised that there were other people in the room, then went back to her notes. "Records, ah... dental records confirmed the identities of all twelve men. We are currently awaiting the results of a DNA test, but the evidence seems conclusive that these are the, um, officers in question." She glanced back to see who would rescue her and Briggs stepped forward.

"I'll save you folks a bit of research and identify the officers who were referred to by the Twelve Apostles moniker. Carl Barrett; Wayne Carver; Timothy Gates; Jacob Hagen; Luke Hale; Victor Jennings; Hayden Keane; Philip Lawrence; Anton Maddox; Melvin Stockton; Matthew Welch; Saul Wells. The manner in which these men were found leaves little doubt that they were executed by the individual who has been dubbed Shere Khan. Our investigation, led by Detectives Riley Parra and Caitlin Priest, will focus on finally identifying this individual and bringing them to justice.

"As I said..." The crowd began to speak and she quieted them with one upheld hand, raising her voice to be heard. "As I said, we will not be taking questions as this is a continuing investigation. As soon as we know more, we will share it with you at the earliest possibility."

Riley muted the television; she didn't need to hear Briggs repeat that they weren't taking questions before finally concluding the press conference. They had just gotten home from their dinner with Kenzie and Chelsea, and Gillian was in the bathroom getting ready for bed. After four years together, she knew exactly what was happening behind the closed door: teeth brushed, contacts out, makeup off, shower, hand lotion, then applying face cream if she didn't plan on making love, or shaving her legs if they did.

The bathroom door opened and Riley chuckled when she saw the gleam on Gillian's cheeks and forehead.

"What's so funny?"

"Nothing." On-screen, the news was now showing headshots of the officers who made up the Twelve Apostles. Riley hadn't known any of them personally. Part of her felt a sick appreciation for their betrayal. Losing twelve policemen all in a single day had opened up the ranks. She and Kenzie advanced through the ranks faster because of all the open slots.

Gillian was in the kitchen. "Do you want a bedtime snack?"

"What do we have?"

"Grapefruit and cottage cheese."

"Sure." She turned off the television and joined Gillian in the kitchen.

Gillian was slicing a grapefruit. "You're famous again."

"Hooray." She ran her hands over the hip of Gillian's nightgown, inadvertently lifting the material to show off a flash of thigh. She kissed her wife's neck before continuing to the fridge. "You're the one who got all the screen time."

"Like anyone heard a thing I said over the sound of my knees knocking together."

Riley got two of their smallest bowls out and spooned some cottage cheese into them. Gillian added the fruit, and they sat together to eat.

"So if Shere Khan isn't Briggs or Chelsea...?"

Riley shrugged. "Could be anyone. Maybe Detective Timbale. That would be a fun arrest. He's been around long enough."

Gillian smiled. "Well, maybe he'll be a good source of information. Like you said, he could give you a first-hand account of it."

"His own personal first-hand account, which I guarantee would be filtered through his misogynistic view-finder. I am going to talk to someone who was actually there. Two detectives were originally assigned to track down the Twelve Apostles, and they tried to find Shere Khan at the same time. One of them died a few years ago, but the other one is still puttering around in a nursing home downtown. I called him up and he agreed to meet me tomorrow night."

Gillian nodded.

Riley scooped up a piece of grapefruit with her spoon and offered it to Gillian. She took it and then wiped the juice from her lips with her pinkie.

Riley smiled. "This is what I want. When it gets down to the last days, when we're counting minutes instead of months. I just want to be sitting with you. I don't care what we're doing." She furrowed her brow. "I'm sorry I took that away from you."

"What do you mean?"

"You're going to keep living after I'm gone, Jill. I was selfish. I couldn't live without you, so I'm making you live without me. You wanted to grow old with me, you wanted to get gray and sit in rocking chairs..."

Gillian looked into her bowl. "I have a confession, Riley. I've always known you were going to die first." She shrugged. "Not really a contest, right? You're always throwing yourself at demons. To save me, or Priest, or the city."

"That is the order of importance."

Gillian smiled. "The night you came into my life in a real, forever sense, you needed me to stitch you back together. I fell in love with a woman who had collapsed on my couch, a woman I was afraid would die that first night. Do you remember a point when I went into the bathroom to rinse out the towels you'd soaked with blood?" Riley nodded. "I prayed that you would survive. Not because I wanted you, or I thought anything was going to happen. Because you were such a special person that I knew losing you would be a loss to the whole world. And I was right.

"The past four years, every time I wasn't in your presence, a part of me was always braced. Waiting for Priest or Briggs to walk in and tell me I should sit down. I was just waiting for that moment when it finally happened. I know you were the same way; I could see it in your eyes and the way you carried yourself. Knowing that it's in the future, even if that future is earlier than I would like, it tells me

I have time."

Riley leaned across the table to kiss her. When they parted, Gillian chuckled.

"I got some of my face cream on your chin."

"Want to go wipe it off?"

Gillian was about to answer when there was a knock on the door. Riley rolled her eyes and pushed her jaw out, giving the evil eye over her shoulder at whoever was disturbing them. Gillian used a napkin to wipe the cream off Riley's face.

"Go on. Whatever they need you for. I'll be here when you get back."

"Will you finish my snack for me?"

Gillian nodded. Riley kissed her hair and crossed through the dark living room. She saw Priest through the peephole and undid the latch.

"It's late, Caitlin..."

"I know. I'm sorry, but this couldn't wait until morning. It took longer than I expected to set it up. Will you come with me?"

"Where?"

Priest hesitated. "It's something you should see for yourself."

"I love trips that start like this." She opened the door to let Priest in. "I need to put on my shoes and tell Gillian I'm leaving." She picked up her shoes from beside the door and went back into the kitchen. "Another mystery trip."

"Ooh. Have fun."

Riley said, "The last time Priest dragged me somewhere in the middle of the night, I ended up fighting Gail Finney and a demon in an abandoned building designed to hide the Ladder connecting the mortal realm to Heaven and Hell. I got my ass kicked."

Gillian pushed back her chair, opened one of the kitchen drawers, and held up a large knife. "Want to take it, just in case?"

"Nah." She kissed Gillian once more. "I love you."

"I love you, too. I'll stay up and read for a while just in case it doesn't take you very long. Do try to get back before morning."

Riley saluted and walked back out, motioning for Priest to follow her.

"Was Gillian upset?"

"No. We had a really good talk tonight. That and having dinner with Kenzie and Chelsea, she's in a good place right now."

"Good. I'm glad to hear it."

"How about you? Did you make nice with the Stantons?"

"They accepted my apology, yes."

Riley looked at her. "That seemed very politic."

Priest averted her gaze. "We, um."

"Ah. So you guys really made nice, huh?" She narrowed her eyes. "Wait, when did that happen? I was with you until I came to pick up Gillian for dinner, and then..." Her eyes widened as she remembered offering to do the dishes since Kenzie and Chelsea had cooked. When they were ready to go, Kenzie had shown them to the door with the lame excuse that Chelsea was "already sacking out" in bed. "Were Gillian and I still in the apartment when you three...?"

"We kept quiet."

Riley laughed. "Wow. Kinky girls. So was that during a break from setting up whatever this is?"

Priest nodded, still blushing. "I set the wheels in motion, and I just received word that it was ready."

"What exactly is 'it'?"

"Like I said, it's better if I show you."

Riley shook her head. "Last time you said that I ended up with a couple of broken bones."

"Sariel healed those."

"It's the principle of the matter, Cait. But fine... I'll drive, you be the navigator."

Priest gave her directions through the city. As they drew closer to their destination, however, Riley got the sinking feeling she knew where they were going. She saw familiar stores and restaurants, although some had gone out of business and others were replaced by more upscale buildings. Several times she glanced at her passenger, but Priest kept her eyes on the road and only spoke to direct her.

She finally parked in front of a very familiar building and stared at the road through hands that gripped the wheel tightly.

"What are we doing here?"

"It's the apartment you had before you moved in with Gillian."

"I know. I recognize it. What does this have to~?"

"Upstairs."

Riley waited for a long moment before she got out of the car. She followed Priest upstairs, her head swimming with deja vu. She could hear TVs and radios playing behind closed doors and shied away from them as if she was afraid they would pull her back in. She hadn't realized how far she had come since moving to Gillian's home, and the reminder made her wary of how easily she could be pulled back in.

"Cait, I don't like being here."

"I know. Please, bear with me."

Priest reached for the doorknob of Riley's old apartment, but Riley stopped her. "Hey. Someone else lives here now."

"No. It's been empty since you left."

Riley knew that wasn't possible, but Priest opened the door and stepped inside. Riley was stunned to see that the fire damage was still visible. Her furniture, destroyed by a demon's attack that had fortunately missed its mark, was still crowded in the middle of the living room. She felt a chill as she stepped over the threshold.

"What could possibly be here that I need to see?" She spoke in a whisper, as if afraid of disturbing the ashes.

Someone came out of the hallway that led to the bedroom. Riley looked at the new arrival and recoiled, backing up so quickly that she hit the wall.

Sweet Kara stopped in her tracks and held her hands up. "Whoa, jumpy. Relax. Hey, give me a cigarette."

"What?"

She gestured at Riley's coat pocket. "My cigarettes. You're holding them. I feel like I haven't smoked in ages."

"I don't... I don't carry your cigarettes anymore, Kara."

"Ah, come on. Look at this place. You're really going to lecture me about the dangers of smoking?" She crossed the room and patted down Riley's pockets. Her face fell as she came up empty. "Seriously? Not even an emergency pack?"

Riley could barely think, so she simply muttered, "Sorry."

"It's okay. I should probably quit anyway."

Riley looked past her at Priest. "What the hell is this, Caitlin?"

"You said that anyone we spoke to now would be subject to the passage of time. I thought it would help to have a more contemporary testimony."

"But Kara..." She looked at her lost partner and felt her eyes filling with tears. "She wasn't a cop when this all happened."

"She might remember something useful. And there are others."

Riley jumped as someone came up behind her. She turned and, when she recognized the new arrival, she took three quick steps away.

"Everything all right, Detective?" Nina Hathaway asked.

Riley swallowed. "Stay the hell away from me."

Kara moved to stand next to the deceased lieutenant. "She's

been like this all night, boss. I'm a little worried for her."

"Priest..."

"We required the perspective of people involved in the Twelve Apostle case without the degradations of time."

Riley closed her eyes; it helped center her in the present. "But they... Lieutenant Hathaway was still a uniformed cop at the time." She swallowed hard. "She didn't work on the case."

A third person spoke up, and with three small words Riley was catapulted back to a painful and dark time in her life. "But I did."

"No." Riley didn't open her eyes, didn't turn around. A tear slipped free and rolled down her cheek. "Cait, why did you bring her here?"

"She worked on the case, Riley. She died not long after the Twelve Apostles disappeared. Of the three I called, her account will be the freshest. Her input will be invaluable."

Riley opened her eyes and turned to face Officer Christine Lee. The woman who saved her from the streets, the woman who set her on the path to becoming a police officer, her first lover. The woman who made her the champion. She looked the same as she had the last time Riley saw her, smiling and patient, dressed in her pristine uniform.

"Hello again, Riley."

"Hi, Chris."

Lieutenant Hathaway gestured at Priest as she stepped forward to stand next to Riley. "This lady says we have a new case."

"No. It's an old case. A really old case."

Kara walked over to the burnt couch and flopped down. "Then we don't have the luxury of wasting time. Let's get to it."

Riley looked at the three dead women from her past. One who had died after making Riley the champion. One who had been killed after a fallen angel included her in his plot. And one who had died because she was standing between Riley and a demonic assassin. Despite the circumstances, having them in the room was an invaluable asset. She couldn't pass up the opportunity to pick their brains on the subject.

"Okay," Riley said. "Let's put our cards on the table. What do you all know about the Twelve Apostles?"

HAIL HORRORS

GILLIAN GOT close enough to Riley's face that she felt the warm breath on her cheeks, but she still had to ask. "You're sure she's okay?"

"She's in absolutely no danger." The apartment lights were low, casting long shadows over every surface. Priest was standing behind the couch, her hands on Riley's shoulders. A glow emanated from beneath Priest's hands, as if they were covering flashlights rather than the thin material of Riley's nightshirt. Riley's eyes were half-lidded and focused on nothing despite the fact Gillian was leaning forward far enough that their noses were nearly touching.

"So where is she?"

"That, I don't know. It has to be somewhere Riley considers safe. She had to choose it herself or else her mind would consider it a trap."

Gillian adjusted her gaze to focus on Priest. "But she agreed to it."

"Yes, but she won't remember that conversation until she wakes up. She needs to do it this way, Gillian. Riley has changed so much that she avoids accessing the doors she closed within herself. She has to open those doors to access the missing information. I'm providing a conduit to that information, to the version of herself that has the knowledge we need."

"So she could be standing in her childhood bedroom talking to herself at five different ages?"

"Possibly. I don't know who she chose to represent the past, and I don't know where she decided to hold the meeting. I'm simply a lifeline so that she can make her way back."

Priest had sat with them at the kitchen table to explain what she wanted to do. Riley was reluctant but willing, and Gillian agreed to stand by her for the duration.

Gillian nodded. "Then don't let me distract you." She knelt on the floor in front of Riley and took her hands. "I'm right here, baby..."

Riley flexed her hands, looking down at them as she extended her fingers. It almost felt like someone was holding her hands, but the sensation was comforting rather than alarming. She looked up at the three women standing in front of her. Sweet Kara was still slumped on the couch, her arms extended along the back. Nina was at the door, responding to Riley's obvious discomfort at having her there.

Christine had moved to the kitchen and out of sight. Riley couldn't even think when she looked at her first lover, so Christine had quietly moved to the other room.

"The Twelve Apostles are ancient history, Riley," Hathaway said. "Why bother bringing them up now?"

"We found their remains. They didn't skip town like everyone thought. Shere Khan killed them and buried the bodies."

Kara said, "Ah, so you're not looking into the Apostles. You want Shere Khan."

"If he's still around, he needs to be brought to justice."

Hathaway said, "It was a witch hunt back in the day. Everyone with a badge was suspected to one degree or another. We didn't trust each other, and people picked up on that. The Twelve Apostle scandal was probably the turning point in terms of public distrust in the police department. Even years later when no one remembered the name Shere Khan, we were still tarnished by the fact he'd never been caught."

Kara leaned forward, elbows on her knees. "You really think he's still out there? Still wearing a badge?"

Christine had moved to the kitchen doorway. When she spoke, Riley tensed. "If he is, he'd be rather high-ranking. Who is the commissioner of police?"

Riley stammered.

"Preston Benedict?" Hathaway said.

"Right. Yes, he's... he's still in charge." She cleared her throat, arms crossed over her chest as she tried to subtly put distance between her and Christine. The shift brought her closer to Hathaway, and she countered by stepping over the coffee table to sit on the couch next to Kara. "I've never had any real interaction with the man."

Hathaway said, "An idle king in an ivory tower. He's not actively bad, but he's also not especially good."

"Could he be influenced?"

"Influenced by what?" Hathaway asked. "Money, women...?"

"Demons."

Hathaway laughed. "Demons? What the hell is happening in that town?"

Christine came into the living room. "It was happening long before you were there, Lieutenant Hathaway. You were just never made aware of the war's presence in your city. There was no reason for you to be informed so you were allowed to live in ignorance."

Riley looked to Priest for input, only then realizing that she'd disappeared. "Where did Priest go?"

"Who?"

"My partner. The one who brought you all here. She was standing right over there a minute ago."

Priest tapped Riley's shoulder with two fingers. In a voice that sounded more like an echo than actual speech, Priest said, *"I'm right here, Riley. Can't you see me?"*

Riley relaxed. "Oh. Right." She closed her eyes and, for a moment, the vision of the burnt apartment was replaced by Gillian's face. Riley shook her head. "Sorry. I panicked for a second."

"It's all right." Christine risked stepping closer. "You're under a lot of stress. Let us help you with this case. Now my memory is a little foggy. What are the names of the Twelve Apostles?"

Riley tried to remember the names and began to list them. Christine noted the ones she had heard of and, when Riley finished the list, she had marked five names.

"Gates and Jennings, I'm not surprised. They were like those *Lethal Weapon* movies if Mel Gibson's crazy character had been teamed up with present-day Mel Gibson. They were loose cannons. Anton Maddox, the same. After a while they stopped assigning him partners because, in his eyes, they were just fodder for the gangbangers. He'd send them in to draw fire and take the credit.

If the partner was lucky, they survived to ask for a transfer as soon as they recovered. Saul Wells surprises me, though. He was a good egg. At least I thought he was. What did they charge him with?"

Hathaway was the one who answered. "He was one of the lower-tier guys. Extortion and protection rackets."

"I suppose that makes sense. He was a charmer. He could make people happy to pay."

Kara tapped her finger against her forehead, trying to kick start her brain. "Wasn't there some club that got shut down after the Apostles disappeared? It was a cop club where the twelve of them used to meet, and afterward no one wanted to go there because they thought it would implicate them as being Shere Khan."

"The Geary Club. Yes." Hathaway nodded. "But we went over that place with a fine-toothed comb. We never found any evidence that Shere Khan ever attended any of their meetings in the back room. There was a photo on the wall of the Apostles, all the bartenders swore up and down it was always the same people who went into the back, and there weren't any extras. Shere Khan was either a master of disguise or excellent at staying hidden."

"Or he never existed," Kara said. "It makes sense, right? These guys all get busted by the reporter and they Keyser Soze her. 'You don't want us, you want the big boss.' They offer to flip on that guy for a lighter sentence, then they just have to find a patsy to finger as their boss."

Riley shook her head. "No. Someone killed all twelve of the Apostles and hid their bodies so well that we didn't find them for fifteen years. If it hadn't been for the earthquake they might have stayed hidden for decades. If it wasn't Shere Khan, then who?" She stood up and began to pace. "Someone out there was pulling the strings. Someone had power over all twelve. Patrolmen from two different precincts, detectives, and a lieutenant. Who would have that kind of pull?"

"The commissioner at the time was Michael Carlisle," Christine said. "He spearheaded the task force to find the Apostles."

"What better place for Shere Khan to be than at the head of his own investigation?" Kara said. "All he has to do is ignore anything that pointed to him."

Hathaway shook her head. "Carlisle was a good man. He did the best he could in the job, given the circumstances. I can't see him being Shere Khan."

Kara held out her hands. "Exactly. That's why no one's caught this guy in fifteen years. Whoever he is, no one suspects him so he's been getting away with murder. Twelve murders."

Riley put her hands over her face and growled. "This isn't helping."

Priest sighed. "I'm sorry, Riley. I thought accessing your memories in this manner would allow you insight."

Riley dropped her hands and saw Gillian kneeling in front of her, her head swimming when she realized she was on the couch in their apartment.

"What~"

"It's okay, Riley," Gillian said. "How do you feel?"

"Confused. What just happened?" She winced and massaged her temple. "Oh. Wait. I think I remember..."

Priest came around the couch to sit next to Riley. "Did you learn anything?"

"No. Not really. There's a club, the Geary Club. The Apostles used to meet there. But it's been shut down ever since the case went cold. Can I have a glass of water?"

"Sure, sweetie." Gillian got up to retrieve it.

"Who did you see?"

Riley sighed. "Sweet Kara, Nina Hathaway, and Christine. We were in my old apartment. It had been completely gutted by a fire."

"My goodness. Never let it be said you take it easy on yourself..."

Gillian returned with the water and Riley thanked her softly. She sat on Riley's other side and stroked her hair as she drank.

"So what do we do now?"

Riley licked her lips. "Now we go to bed. Tomorrow, Priest and I will check out the Geary Club. Maybe the other detectives missed something since they didn't have an angel on their payroll. Thanks for the walk down memory lane, Cait."

"I wish it had been more help."

"You went above and beyond." She rubbed her cheek. "Besides, it may have unlocked some things. Maybe the pieces will fall together when I'm asleep."

Priest said, "We can hope. I think I've taken up enough of your time tonight. I should get back to Kenzie and Chelsea's."

"You're spending the night there again?"

"Just for tonight. To make sure all is forgiven."

Riley smiled. "Uh-huh. Say hi for me if they're still up."

"I will. Good night, Gillian."

"Night."

Gillian escorted Priest to the door, then returned to the couch to help Riley up. "How was your little trip?"

"Bizarre. I remember leaving with Priest, but I also remember sitting down and agreeing to the little mind-game. Kind of worries me."

"You think she would ever do something like that without your permission?"

"Her, no. But I'm not exactly Person of the Year with the other angels. If they ever decide they want a more docile champion..."

Gillian put her arm around Riley and squeezed. "They've put up with you this long without putting the whammy on you." She kissed Riley's cheek. "Besides, if they tried they'd have to get through me. I've taken out demons. A couple of puny angels would be no sweat."

Riley laughed. "My hero."

They undressed and got into bed, with Gillian spooning Riley from behind. "So who did you see? I heard you tell Priest, but I couldn't make out the names."

"Kara, Lieutenant Hathaway, and... Christine Lee."

"Wow. That must have been weird." She kissed Riley's neck. "Are you okay?"

Riley nodded. After a moment of silence, she whispered, "I got them all killed."

"Sh. That's not true..."

"Christine gave up the protection of her tattoo for me, because I was young and stupid. Kara... I pulled the trigger myself. I had her blood on me. And Lieutenant Hathaway was just in the way when a demon tried to assassinate me."

Gillian pressed tighter against Riley's back. "You can't blame yourself for not protecting Christine. She gave you her protection because she loved you. If she hadn't, Marchosias and his demons would have taken you out before you became a threat to them. She was willing to sacrifice herself, just like you would for Aissa. Kara was manipulated by a bad angel. You had to stop her. And Lieutenant Hathaway~"

"Don't try to make me feel better about her. There's nothing you can say, because I wanted her dead."

Gillian's hand rested on Riley's stomach. "I know you two didn't get along~"

"No. I wanted her dead because of what she did after Kara's

death."

"No one would hold that against you. What she did was despicable, and you harbored bad feelings about that. But just because you felt..." She swallowed hard. "Riley, you still fought for her in the end. You took care of Kara's family despite what she had become at the end. And Christine... she sacrificed herself for you because she knew that you were the champion this city needed. Come here."

Riley moved onto her back and Gillian settled on top of her.

"You did everything you could for them, Riley. Despite Kara's betrayal, despite what Hathaway took from you, you never gave up on them. Just like you've never given up on this city despite everything it throws at you. Like you never gave up on me when I ran away. Like you never gave up after I was killed." A tear had slipped from Riley's eye and Gillian bent down to kiss it away. "You can't burden yourself with what you couldn't do. You've done more than anyone could ask."

"Thank you."

Gillian smiled and kissed Riley between the eyebrows. "You fight the actual demons, I fight the emotional ones. Get some sleep. If you need someone living to talk to, I'll be here."

Riley ran her hand down Gillian's flank. "I meant what I said. I'm going to end the war. I'm going to make Marchosias agree to let Aissa take over early so we can leave."

"I'm just taking it one day at a time, Riley. I'm going to treasure every day we're together and not think about what's waiting at the end of the road." She kissed Riley's lips. "And who knows? We still have a year and a half. Maybe we have a miracle or two left in the chamber."

"Maybe so. But I think I used up my quota getting you."

Gillian chuckled. "Silly Riley, that didn't cost you anything. But I used up all my wishes to get you in my arms." She touched her nose to Riley's. "Go to sleep."

"Only if you come with me."

"I'll follow you anywhere. You know that."

Riley guided Gillian's head to her shoulder and breathed deep the scent of her hair. She focused on the rhythm of Gillian's breathing, hypnotizing herself with it until she fell asleep.

"She's beautiful."

Riley was in Christine's squad car. She tensed and looked

around with conservative movements, trying not to draw too much attention to her confusion. They were parked on a dark street, the headlights shining out to illuminate a vast field of nothing ahead of them. Christine was in uniform, her hair pulled back in a tight braid. Riley had a distinct memory of undoing that braid their first night together, Christine pulling away just before they kissed.

"I can't do this. You're too young, Riley."

"Everything I've been through... I'm not too young for anything. I've just never been able to choose. Let me choose you, Chris. Please."

"Who is beautiful?" Riley asked.

"Your wife." She smiled but kept her eyes front and her hands on the wheel as if she was driving. "She's not the sort of person I imagined you ending up with, but I know she's exactly the kind of person you need in your life. I'm so glad you found her."

Riley nodded slowly. "Did Priest do this?"

"Inadvertently. The connection should have been broken when you pulled yourself out of the trance. The three of us decided to stick around in case you needed more help."

Riley twisted to look in the backseat. Lieutenant Hathaway was behind her and Sweet Kara was behind Christine's seat. Kara wiggled her fingers in greeting, smiling apologetically.

"So what, you're hijacking my brain?"

"Only while you're asleep," Kara said. "We'll quiet down again once you wake up. And you won't miss out on any rest because you're not really here."

Hathaway said, "While we're on that subject, we're not really hijacking anything. We're manifestations of your own thoughts and memories. We're just the form you chose to represent those parts of yourself that you refuse to revisit. You've made such strides in your life that you think spending any time in these memories will taint the person you've become."

Christine said, "You don't want to be the woman you were when Nina took advantage of you. You don't want to be Sweet Kara's partner who ignored the evil in her city. And you definitely have no intention of devolving into the kid I knew. So we're..."

"Pooka," Riley muttered. "Like Harvey. The big rabbit."

Christine smiled. "I've been called worse."

"All right, dream team... where are we going first?"

Kara said, "Let's see where the bodies were found. Maybe it has some significance."

Riley shrugged and told Christine the address. The city flashed by like shots in a kaleidoscope, illuminated and then gone in a blur. They arrived at the site much faster than Riley anticipated. The water company's equipment was gone and the street was once again intact. After they got out of the car, Hathaway silently split away from the group and walked off into the shadows to see what she could find.

Now that she knew the true nature of her ghostly companions, Riley had restricted Hathaway's contributions to the bare minimum. She would speak only when absolutely necessary, and afterward she would just fade into the background again. Kara watched her go and moved to walk beside Riley.

"Wow. I knew you didn't like her much, but you're treating her like she kicked your dog."

"After I shot you, she found the note you left framing me. She offered to cover it up if I went down on her."

Kara's smile faded. "God. Riley, I'm sorry."

"It's ancient history." The set of Riley's jaw proved it was anything but history, but Kara stayed silent as they approached the building that had served as the Apostles' tomb. Christine was examining the face of the building with a determined expression. She watched for a moment, aware of how odd it was to ask since she knew Christine was just a representation of her own subconscious memories, but she had to go with the illusion.

"Do you recognize it?"

"This building wasn't here fifteen years ago."

Riley nodded. "We think whoever Shere Khan is, he buried the bodies during construction. He had to have access, though..."

"The building next door," Hathaway said. "It used to have office space on the second and third floor above the laundromat."

Kara chuckled without humor. "Clever hiding place for someone who was laundering money."

Riley forced a quiet laugh as she approached the building. "Okay, so. Maybe Shere Khan used this place as a front, or he had office space up above where he kept track of the Apostle business. Shere Khan must have lured the Apostles here when it looked like everything was going bad, then he got them into the vacant lot and killed them all at once."

"One man taking out twelve?" Kara said. "Who the hell are we looking for, Bruce Banner?"

Christine shook her head. "He's too smart for that. He wouldn't go after them as a group. He would gather a few of them at a time and tell them each a different story. For instance, let's say he got Carl Barrett, Phil Lawrence, Anton Maddox, and Saul Wells together and told them they were going to eliminate the others. Those four would handcuff the others and execute them. But then Shere Khan would have told Lawrence and Maddox that they were also taking out Wells and Barrett."

Riley shuddered. "He kept using them right up until they were executed."

"And then there would be one left. All Shere Khan had to do was overpower that man. Not exactly a superhuman feat."

"No, but it is diabolical," Riley muttered. "Whatever happened, the laundromat owner had to have some idea what his upstairs neighbor was up to. He may even have been in on it. I'll see what I can find out about him tomorrow."

"You and, uh, Priest?"

Riley looked at Kara. "Yeah. What, you don't like Cait?"

"She's amazing. I just don't like the idea of someone taking my place. Let alone so much better at the job than I was."

Riley glanced at Christine and moved Kara back toward the street so she wouldn't be overheard. "Kara, you were a great partner. After what happened, I didn't even want another partner. I hoped, like Timbale, that I was senior enough to work alone. But Cait was a special case. It's worked out for the best, but she didn't replace you. No one could replace the great Sweet Kara." She smiled. "You showed me it was okay to have fun from time to time. You made me less dour. Took down my guard just in time for me to let Gillian in. And I'll never be able to thank you enough for *that*."

Kara chuckled. "She's a good one, huh?"

"The best."

She looked at Riley's left hand. "I still can't believe you got married. Is this the love 'em and leave 'em Riley Parra I once found handcuffed naked to her bed?"

Riley laughed. "One night with her is worth a one night stand with every other woman in town. And that includes the woman who does the weather on Channel 89."

Kara's eyes widened. "Wow. I remember her. She's so hot *I* would do her. And I'm straight. And dead." She nudged Riley's foot with her own. "I'm really glad you ended up with her. I saw the way you two were always flirting, staring when you thought you could get away with it... you were made for each other."

"Thanks."

Hathaway approached. "I know this street."

"Yeah?"

She pointed back the way she had come. "The Badge Barracks isn't far from here."

Kara gasped. "Oh, God. I'd forgotten all about that place."

Riley had, too. Twenty or thirty years earlier, an apartment manager decided that the best way to keep his building crime-free was to have police officers living on the premises. He gave them discounted rental rates under the table in exchange for having them keep an eye on things during their off-hours. Most of the officers who took advantage of the discount were separated from their significant others for indefinite lengths of time. The apartments were one step above being slums, but it was better and cheaper than living out of a hotel.

She remembered the Badge Barracks as the place Christine set her up with after she finally left home. She'd never treated it like much of a home, preferring instead to stay on the streets with her friends. But the apartment gave her a safe place to run. It was where she and Christine made love, where she could sleep when the nights were too cold, and it gave her a firm foundation to prepare for real life. Christine was watching her, and Riley knew she was remembering the same time.

Christine finally looked away. "When did they shut it down?"

"Ten years ago," Riley said. "A newspaper article gave up the secret. They said it was a shameful example of kickbacks and 'quiet, shameful bribery.' The commissioner made every cop who lived there move out. The place was eventually condemned and knocked down. If Shere Khan had an office over the laundromat, then maybe he was living in the Badge Barracks. Are there any surviving residential records?"

"We don't know," Kara said.

"By which you mean *I* don't know. Something else to look into tomorrow. This little parlor trick is turning into a really useful tool. I may have to get Priest to do it on all my cases."

Kara snorted derisively. "Hey, if I'm going to be doing your job for you, I'm going to get paid."

"I'm not sure how one would pay a mental manifestation," Christine said.

Kara shrugged. "Stock up on some nice mental images for me. Watch a little hetero porn and let me look over her shoulder." She winked at Riley, who rolled her eyes and scanned the street. Kara sighed and put her hands on her hips. "Fine. At least let me watch you with Gillian. She really is hot."

"She is, Riley," Christine said with a self-conscious smile.

"Can we please focus on the horrific murders here?" She caught Hathaway standing on the sidewalk, grateful that she hadn't ventured an opinion on her marriage. "If we can find the rental records for the office space and match it to someone who was living at the Badge Barracks, we'll actually have a solid lead. So thank you for that. But I think I'm going to work the rest of this case alone."

"Sick of us already?" Hathaway said.

"Some of you more than others."

Hathaway set her lips in a thin line and walked back toward the car. Kara trailed behind her, leaving Riley with Christine in the middle of the street.

"Back to the beginning, huh? The Badge Barracks." She smiled sadly. "You never did like that place."

"Too many cops. I only liked you." She scuffed her shoe on the ground. "Look, I know."

"You know what?"

Riley met Christine's eye. "I know why you couldn't take me home to live with you. I knew back then, I just didn't care."

Christine's face fell and she looked away. "Oh. Well, we..."

"You don't have to explain anything, Christine. I figure if your marriage was anything like mine, you would have been at home with your wife instead of trying to keep a scrawny kid off the streets."

"It wasn't like that. We just had problems. She checked out early on." She looked across the street. "She loved me. But she hated the fact I was the champion. She thought being a cop was dangerous enough. We both hoped her love would be stronger, but it... it never got there. So eventually it was just easier to pretend."

Riley hugged herself. "I'm glad I was able to be there for you. I never thought about the fact you might be getting something out of... what we had."

Christine smiled. "I got so much out of it, Riley. You made me happy. I hope I made you happy, too."

"Yeah." She chuckled. "I'm not sure I even knew what it was at the time, but yeah. I was happy. And you showed me what a normal, grown-up relationship is like. So I have you to thank for the fact I've managed to make it work this long with Gillian."

Christine touched Riley's cheek. "I'm so proud of how you turned out, Riley. That first night, you were barely there in the car.

Barely even a presence. I knew if I put you in prison you would vanish before my eyes. But now look at you. Such a strong woman, so vital and... happy. God, Riley, you smile so much. It's a good look for you. And I hate to risk erasing it, but there's something I have to say. It's about your death."

Riley's smile faded. "We don't have to talk about that~"

"We do. You do. I died quickly, suddenly. I didn't have a chance to say goodbye to you, and I didn't get a chance to tell my wife how sorry I was for everything I'd done to her. I left so much undone. I always knew I could die at any time, but I never let myself think about it. You have a gift, but you also have a sword hanging over your head. You need to stop looking at your death as something that's going to happen and start seeing it as something that has already happened. The car is barreling down on you, Riley, and you need to take advantage of the time you have remaining."

Riley shook her head. "I am. I'm going to stop Lark Siskin, and I'm taking Gillian away from here. We're going to enjoy what little time I have left."

"Then stop putting it off. Lark isn't going down without a fight, and if you find yourself still fighting her on your last day... I don't want you to miss out on the opportunity to say a proper farewell to the people you love. Promise me, Riley. Once this Apostle mess is cleaned up, promise me you're going to focus on Lark. Even if you have to hand in your badge a little early and go rogue to stop her, do what has to be done. Be a champion, one last time."

Riley nodded. "I promise."

Christine kissed her between the eyebrows. "Good girl. Now, I think someone is waiting for you to wake up."

When Riley opened her eyes, Gillian was watching her with a half-smile. She stretched under the blankets, grunting as she shifted closer to her wife. "Was I snoring?"

"You were talking in your sleep."

"Uh-oh."

Gillian pecked Riley's lips. "You said I was beautiful."

"I did?"

"Several times." She stroked Riley's arm. "Who were you talking to?"

"Kara and Christine mostly." She pushed herself up so she wouldn't be tempted to fall back to sleep. "I think Priest left her little pantomime play running when she left. I spent the night running around with them going over the case in my head."

"Did you find anything interesting?"

"I don't know yet. It's all a jumble right now, but I have a few leads I want to follow up on when I get to work."

"Mm. And where did your gorgeous wife come into the picture?"

Riley smiled. "Christine wanted to be sure I ended up with someone worthy. Kara was just shocked to discover I was married." Her expression faltered and she shook her head. "I'm talking about them like they were really there."

"Well, they were. Priest used your memories to bring them to life. The women you were speaking with were basically the people you remember without your preconceived ideas getting in the way." She brushed Riley's hair back away from her face. "I'm glad they approve of me. I remember how much Kara's opinion mattered to you, back in the day."

"She was always pushing me to ask you out."

"Really? Why didn't you?"

Riley rolled her eyes. "Please. You were so out of my league that I wasn't about to make a fool of myself by coming on to you."

Gillian smiled. "So I'm not out of your league anymore?"

"Oh, you definitely are. I just stopped caring about it." She kissed Gillian properly and reluctantly pushed the blankets away. "I should probably get ready. I want to hit the Geary Club early and see if it's worth our while to investigate."

"Okay. I should head in, too. Want to share a shower?"

"Smarter than me, too. You are definitely out of my league, wife."

Gillian grinned and followed Riley into the bathroom.

Briggs was waiting at Riley's desk when she and Priest arrived at work. She tapped a print-out that was resting on top of Riley's keyboard.

"You're in luck. When the commissioner cracked down on residents of the Badge Barracks, he compiled a list of officers who rented there. It goes back five years, so there are a lot of names. We're still waiting on the full list but until we have it, this is the first batch. There's a name on there you should recognize."

"Yeah." Riley picked up the list and flipped through it, skimming the names. They were compiled in order by year of residency, so she focused on the time around the Apostle scandal. "I know about that."

"I thought you might. The laundromat owner is proving a little harder to find, but we're in the process of getting a warrant for the names of who rented the offices from the landlord."

"Thanks, boss. Priest and I were also going to check out the old Geary Club today."

Briggs blinked. "Wow. I would've thought anything worth finding there was found a long time ago."

Priest smiled. "Yes, but I haven't been over it yet."

Riley nodded. "An angelic detective. It's the difference between going to the beach with your naked eye, and going with a metal detector."

Briggs chuckled. "I wish you luck, then. It'll be very nice to put this to bed. It'll be a nice feather in your cap, Riley. I'll have to watch my job."

"Yeah. Boss... can we talk in your office?"

"Everything all right?"

"Sort of. Please."

Briggs looked at Priest and shrugged as she indicated Riley should lead the way. Riley went into the office and waited until Briggs had shut the door before she took a seat. She looked at the framed picture of the stadium behind the desk.

"Why do you have a picture of Yankee Stadium in your office?"

Briggs was startled by the question and twisted to look at it. "My father was a shortstop. Minor league, but the Yankees were his favorite team. I don't think that's what you really wanted to ask, though."

"No. I actually wanted to tell you something." She looked down at her hands. "This is tougher than I thought it would be. I don't want to go through the whole thing again, so I'm going to just head straight for the metaphor. I'm dying."

"You're... dying?"

"It's not a perfect metaphor, but yeah. In a little over eighteen months. Yes, it has to do with the war, and no. There's no cure. Priest and I have played too many Get Out of the Afterlife Free cards and we've run out. Gillian and I have been preparing for it, but I had to tell you so it doesn't come out of the blue when I resign."

Briggs leaned back in her chair. "You're leaving?"

"Once I take care of Lark Siskin, there will be another reckoning moment when I can choose to either end the war or let

Marchosias choose a new champion to continue on. When that time comes, I'm going to hang up my mantle and let Aissa take over for me. And then I'm leaving to spend the rest of however much time I have left with my wife."

Briggs stared into space for a moment before she slowly shook her head. "This is incredible. I can't believe this. I saw you die before and that barely even slowed you down. I guess I just started believing you were invulnerable. How is Dr. Hunt taking it?"

"She's taking it pretty well. She's been great through the whole thing."

"Okay. Well, if you need time off to... deal with everything, let me know. I'll see what strings I can pull." She smiled sadly. "I'm sure Aissa Good is up to the job, but I don't know how this city will survive without you watching over us. I didn't even like you when I took this job."

"You didn't?"

Briggs shrugged. "You had a reputation as a troublemaker. Of course, it makes sense now that I know the truth, but if I didn't know about everything happening under the surface? You'd have given me even more ulcers than I already have."

Riley chuckled. "Sorry."

"Eh, it's not you. It's the job." She smoothed her hands over the blotter. "If I don't get a chance to say it in the future, you're a damn good detective, Riley. I'm proud to have had you in my squad."

"And you've been a good boss."

Briggs looked away. "All right. Now that we're done with that, get out there and do your job, Detective. You're burning daylight."

"Right. Sorry, lieutenant." She stood, sketched a quick salute, and left the office.

Priest was waiting at her desk. She stood up as Riley approached and raised her eyebrows in an unspoken question.

Riley nodded. "I told her."

"How did she take it?"

"I think she's a little shocked, but she'll be fine. Do you have the list of names?" Priest held it up. "We'll start running down the names when we get back from the club. Hopefully by then we'll have the full Badge Barracks records so there's something to compare it to."

Priest flipped through the pages as they walked to the elevator. "I went through it while you were in with Briggs, and I saw several familiar names. Barrett, Gates, Hagen, Keane, Lawrence... it seems as if the majority of the Apostles took rooms at the Barracks."

"Maybe Shere Khan liked to have his followers close to hand. Were they all on the same floor?"

"No. Spaced all over. There's also another name I think I recognize..."

"Yeah, I know. It doesn't have anything to do with the Apostles; it's just a coincidence."

"If you're sure."

Riley nodded. She remembered the dark, cramped apartment where she did her homework, waiting for the sound of Christine's key in the lock that meant they were going to spend the night together.

"It's unrelated. Trust me."

"If you're certain."

"Positive." The elevator arrived and Riley stepped inside. She was hopeful that even if the Geary Club was a bust, they would find what they needed in the paperwork. Once the warrant came through it would just be a matter of finding the match.

The Geary Club had once appeared stately but, in the years since closing, it had fallen into disrepair. The ground floor was a basketball court and gymnasium where officers could work out, and the third floor was a bar that brought to mind the speakeasies of old. Huge circular booths marched along the walls with a sea of tables between them and the bar. Riley and Priest climbed the exterior stairs and pushed through doors that had long ago been compromised by squatters looking for a safe place to sleep and adventurous teens looking for a thrill.

The booths were now filled with detritus that indicated people had been using them as hovels, and the mirrors behind the bar were boarded over. Riley paused in the doorway and Priest stopped next to her.

"Is it unsafe?"

"Huh?" Riley was thrown by something, but she couldn't quite put her finger on what it was. "No. I mean, I'm sure it's safe. Patrolmen have to run homeless people out of here all the time. It's just weird. I recognize this place."

"From your own patrol days?"

"No. I remember when it was still in business." She shook her head. "But I was a rookie when it was shut down. I never would have been invited here."

She was startled when Kara came out of the back room and leaned over the bar in search of something to drink.

"Cait, did you put the whammy on me again?"

"What?"

She indicated her head. "Is this really happening, or is it like last night at my apartment?"

"It's really happening. What do you see?"

"Kara. And..." Hathaway and Christine entered. "God, it's all three of them. What are they doing here?"

"I don't know." Priest scanned the room, but seemed alarmingly unable to see their companions. "They shouldn't even have infiltrated your dreams."

Kara found a dusty bottle and brushed off the front to read the information. "Oh, nice." She uncapped it and walked to where Riley and Priest were standing. "So have you figured it out yet?"

Christine hissed, "We promised we wouldn't push her."

Riley stepped forward. "Figured what out?"

"Riley, take your time. Try to think about the last time you were here."

"You really want to make a difference, kid?"

"You know I do."

"No."

Priest put her hand on Riley's shoulder and she drew strength from its weight. "I was here. Someone brought me here."

"Who?"

"Donald Rafferty. My first partner on the force."

She remembered how he had taken her under his wing, his gut just beginning to press against the front of his uniform shirt. He had gone into No Man's Land to patrol at her insistence, but she could tell he didn't like it. He humored her because she was a rare female rookie, and word from on high was that they needed more women in blue. He spent most of their patrols pontificating about how No Man's Land was falling down a slide, and it was their job to slow its descent.

"We're not going to make much of a dent in them, mind you. New bad guys get born every day, and cops are an endangered species. Especially cops willing to do what it takes to meet the bad guys on their own terms. Like trying to catch every damn snowflake before it hits the ground. You might catch a couple, but before you know it, your boots are buried."

After a few weeks on the job, he pointed out that everyone in the city was imprisoned. "Only difference between us and the criminals is that we willingly lock ourselves into our cells. End of the day, go home, shut the doors and make sure there are bars on the windows. We lock ourselves up by choice, and we lock up those who dare walk the streets without fear."

"So what can we do?"

He had looked at her for a long time after that. Finally he seemed to come to a conclusion. "You really want to make a difference, kid?"

"You know I do."

Riley shook her head to dispel the past. "No. Stop this..."

Christine stepped forward. "Riley, it's important that you remember this. You've blocked it for so long, refused to remember~"

"No. Raff was a good man. He taught me how to survive."

"He did," Hathaway said from the back of the room. "But he was doing it for his own reasons. He saw how strong you were, and he knew you would grow up to be a big player in this town. He wanted you as his student, his successor. So he brought you to this place to show you what you could have."

The decay was gone now, and Riley saw the place as it had been all those years ago. Cops sat in the shadowy booths, some in uniform but most not. Beer flowed freely to anyone regardless of whether they were on-duty or not. Riley felt like a child at her parents' country club as Raff put his arm around her shoulders.

"Don't let them scare you, kiddo. They were all rookies like you once, too."

"What are we doing here?"

"I wanted you to meet some people. Yo, Victor. Where are the others? Got someone I want you all to meet."

She looked to her left and saw Christine watching the scene with her. "You met with them. They told you what they did and then they tried to recruit you. You told them no, and you left. You knew nothing would be the same with Raff after that, but you couldn't bring yourself to join them. You knew it was wrong, but you were just a rookie. Who would listen to you?"

"They were already being investigated by the reporter at that point," Hathaway said. "A few weeks later they were dead. By that time, you and Raff were spending your shifts apart. You told him you just wanted to patrol No Man's Land by yourself, but the real reason was because you couldn't bear to be in a car with him. You wanted to turn Raff in, but then one night he was stabbed by a carjacker. You were saved from betraying him by a random act of violence."

Kara said, "But the damage had already been done. You joined the force because Christine Lee gave you faith that you could make a difference, and Rafferty took it away. It's why you have such a hard time accepting your new partners. You've hated all of us at first. Kenzie, me, Caitlin. Every one of us was another test. Someone else who might turn into a betrayal. The pain of what Raff did to you was so strong that the only way you could deal with it was to bury it. Like you buried my betrayal, like you buried what Lieutenant Hathaway did to you. It wasn't forgotten, but it was locked away like the three of us were."

Christine said, "It's time to let the memory out, Riley. You know Donald Rafferty was Shere Khan. You've always known. It's time to close the book once and for all."

"Riley?"

She turned and saw that time had rushed onward, the rot overtaking the glitz until it was once again the decrepit remnant. Priest was framed by the light coming through the doorway and Riley blinked before she looked around for her ghosts. They had all disappeared, and the room felt oddly empty without them.

"What's wrong?"

"You said there was a familiar name on the list of Badge Barrack remnants. You meant Christine Lee, right?"

Priest frowned. "No. I mean, yes, she lived there as well. But the name I recognized was Donald Rafferty, your first partner. I never knew he lived there."

"He killed them. Oh, God. I have to go..."

Priest put her hands on Riley's shoulders to stop her. "Riley? What happened?"

"Those doors you opened in my mind? I think you opened one too many."

She left the room and all its ghosts, her hand hovering just above the ancient railing to avoid splinters as she flew quickly down the stairs. She remembered the last time she had descended these steps, with Raff following her. He'd remained silent until they were back in the car, watching the traffic streak by.

"So you're thugs."

"Thugs?" Raff shook his head. "We're doing what has to be done. You've been out there, girl. You lived on the streets, so you know how bad it gets. We're hamstrung by the rule book. The criminals sure as shit ain't playing by the rules, so they win. They get better guns, they get more funding, they get stronger. Meanwhile we can't even afford to properly patrol the streets because of budget cutbacks. You know we actually had to fight for Kevlar vests a couple of years ago? Bet you the bad guys aren't doing that."

"You're killing people."

"People who would just fill up the prisons. You know what prisons are? Schools for how to be a better criminal. They go in, then they get shuttled out a few months later due to overcrowding. But now they have new contacts, new skills, and they're not afraid of going back. Hell, it's like summer vacation for some of these douche bags. So yeah, I got sick of it like everyone else, but the difference is I'm doing something about it. The guys in that room are doing the same thing."

Riley didn't know if she was angry or just extraordinarily sad. "You're as bad as they are. You're just doing whatever you want and trying to justify it. You're supposed to be better."

Raff started the car and shook his head. "You're young. You don't know how this job eats at you. One of these days you're going to look back and see that this is the best option. This is how we're going to get our city back."

"I don't know if the city is worth the cost."

"What do you think the cost is?"

Riley shrugged. "Our souls."

"Hah. Small price to pay. Look, Parra, you're a smart kid. You're green, but I can tell you're going to be a good cop. You wanna waste your time with busywork, put in your time, keep your nose clean, and become a lieutenant in twenty years, you go right ahead and do that. We'll always need bureaucrats to ignore. But if you work out here on the streets, you're going to have to decide which of your precious morals you're willing to sacrifice. 'Cause I guarantee you, once you're down here in the shit, you'll understand."

She was silent for a long time before she said, "We should probably go back to the station."

"Right." Raff sighed heavily and shook his head as he backed out.

Riley was brought back to the present by Priest getting into the car and sitting beside her. Riley looked up at the building that now seemed to loom over them like a monolith.

"The day after I turned him down, I started coming down to

No Man's Land on my own. As far as dispatch was concerned we were patrolling together, but then we just went our separate ways. I kept it up even after I became a detective, as much as I could." She rubbed her face. "That's how I ran into Marchosias the first time."

Priest said, "So being propositioned by the Apostles led you to becoming the protector of No Man's Land. It established you as a presence for the people here who had given up hope."

"So you're saying it all worked out in the end, so it's okay?"

"No. I'm saying that even a sordid and awful decision, Donald Rafferty's choice to become a criminal, resulted in something good in the world. It made you the police officer you are now, the dedicated and true protector of the law. You were faced with temptation and you withstood it."

Riley smiled ruefully. "Great. Good for me. I idolized Raff, Cait. I put a Chinese wall around that night and made myself forget about it, and I went on thinking he was a mentor. How could I be so stupid?"

"You weren't stupid. You were protecting yourself. If you had carried the memory of who Officer Rafferty really was, you would have become disillusioned with the job. You would have become the person he wanted you to be. Jaded and fatalistic."

Riley took a deep breath and rested her hands on the steering wheel. "I wish you'd been there that night."

Priest smiled. "I was. I just couldn't take an active part in the events that were playing out."

"Free will," Riley said softly. "I had to make my own decision, for good or ill."

"Exactly."

"Well. I didn't mean you-you. I meant Priest. Kenzie and Kara were both amazing women, and I was lucky to have them watching my back. And Zerachiel has been a pain in my ass since the moment I learned her name. But you, Caitlin Priest, you've been the best partner I could ever have hoped to have. Thanks for being here for me these past few years. I..." She made a face and twisted her lips. "I don't say this often to people I'm not sleeping with. Even then it takes a while. But I love you, Cait."

Priest smiled. "I love you, too. And that's from me, not Zerachiel."

"You can differentiate?"

"Sometimes. Zerachiel loves you, of course, but this feeling is definitely human. It's tension and frustration, and knowing that I would do anything for you. Not because I have to, but because it would hurt to not be there when you needed me. And when it's time for you to leave... when your time is up... I will be there to take you to the next part of your journey."

Riley was surprised by that. "Escorting me... elsewhere... is part of your job?"

"No. But I think I'll make an exception for you."

"Thanks." She didn't think she had shed any tears, but she wiped her face just the same. "Okay. Enough of that... let's go close this damned case."

Once again the press was gathered in the cramped media room on the ground floor of the police station. And once again, Riley and Priest stood beside Lieutenant Briggs as she approached the lectern to give a statement. Riley told her the entire story upstairs in her office, but the official report would be amended to leave out Riley's near-recruitment. Once the warrant came through they confirmed Rafferty kept a small office above the laundromat during the time of the Apostle scandal. He gave up the office around the time the Apostles went missing, and all evidence seemed to point to him trying to cover his tracks when he was killed in a carjacking.

Briggs was in the middle of laying out the case when her speech was disrupted by the unexpected arrival of Mayor Siskin. Riley tensed and glanced at Priest, who bristled and stepped toward the edge of the dais as Lark stepped up to the lectern. Briggs had straightened her shoulders at the mayor's arrival and assumed a business-like expression as she surrendered the microphone.

"Thank you, Lieutenant Briggs. I hope you don't mind me shanghaiing you like this, but I just wanted to take the opportunity to applaud the excellent police work by Detectives Parra and Priest." She looked at them and smiled. Riley refused to even fake the gesture despite the cameras focused on her. "It seems like time and again, when this city has been faced with some horrible crime - be it the Angel Maker or this Shere Khan specter - Parra and Priest have been at the forefront of the investigation. And time and again they seem to do the impossible to protect the people of this city. Now, I know we don't give the police department nearly enough credit for the tough job they do, but Detectives Parra and Priest go above and beyond the call of duty. Not because it's expected, but because they truly care. How about a hand for them?"

Lark faced Riley as the press applauded. Lark winked, and

Riley narrowed her eyes and gave Lark a predatory smile. When the applause ended, Lark faced the microphone again.

"That is why, effective today, I am going to take advantage of their exemplary record and use it to benefit the entire city. I'm establishing a task force wherein Riley Parra and Caitlin Priest will share their skills with other police officers. Now, yes, unfortunately this does mean that two of our finest detectives will be off the streets for the next few weeks, but in the end we'll have a new breed of officers working to the high standard these two detectives have set over the past four and a half years."

Briggs moved closer to Riley and lowered her voice. "I swear, I had no idea~"

"I know." Riley kept her eyes locked on Lark as she forced herself to applaud. When the mayor came over to shake hands, Riley spoke without moving her lips. "Well played."

"I have no idea what you're talking about, Detective. The interests of this city are my only concern." She arched an eyebrow as she stepped to the side to shake Priest's hand. "Detective Priest."

"I won't shake your hand."

"Cait..."

"No, Riley. I won't." She turned to leave, but Emily Simon was blocking her exit from the stage. The room had fallen silent, and Riley was all too aware that the press was listening to everything that was being said on the stage.

"Cait, maybe just for appearances~"

"No."

Lark cleared her throat. "Detective Priest, I assure you that I have the utmost respect for what you and your partner have accomplished. I merely want to extend your good works throughout the city."

Priest faced Lark again. "Your motives are anything but pure."

Briggs stepped forward between the two women. "Let's not do this here, Detective Priest. Mayor Siskin... let it go."

Lark held Priest's gaze for a moment, and then turned her hand in surrender. "Very well. It's unfortunate we couldn't be civil."

The press conference was ended with a few quick words from Briggs, and the press filed out through the main door. Riley and Priest beat a hasty retreat through the back, but Lark didn't let them get very far before she followed.

"Detectives. A word?"

Riley faced her but Priest kept her back turned. "The cameras aren't here, Lark, so I don't have to play nice."

"No. But you have only your partner to thank for what happens next. You see, I'm trying to help the police. I'm trying to give you a better public image. You helped me with that, Riley. You closed the book on a very dark chapter in this city's history and you put to rest one of its biggest bogeymen. And when the time came, you sucked it up and shook my hand. But you, angel... you had to make a spectacle out of yourself. You proved you weren't a team player. It's very sad. But there's no room in my vision of the city for people who don't play ball."

Priest finally looked at her. "What is that supposed to mean?"

"It means that I need people who are willing to put on a happy face for the cameras. I want to usher in a new era of cooperation, a world where the police are our friends. Good, stalwart, trustworthy. And I cannot do that if one of the detectives I just praised turns her back on me rather than shaking my hand.

"Tomorrow, you and Detective Parra will report to City Hall to prepare for your first workshop. And despite what you may think of me, I really do want you to demonstrate your skills. I want you to teach the other detectives in this town how to be better at what they do. You're the best detectives this town has seen in a long time, and I would be a fool not to capitalize on that."

Riley said, "Sure. Benevolence. You're a kinder, gentler champion for evil."

Lark smiled. "When the workshops are complete, Detective Parra, you will return to your regular job. But you, Detective Priest... I can't have you standing as a roadblock in my new police department. So you will be demoted. You will report to dispatch, where you will handle the switchboard until such time as I deem you appropriately contrite for the way you behaved in that room."

Briggs had been lurking until that point. "Madam Mayor, I'm sorry, but you can't do that. You don't have the authority to take one of my best detectives out of my squad."

Lark didn't look at Briggs, her eyes locked onto Priest's. "No. But my very good friend Commissioner Benedict? He has the power to do whatever I ask him to. If I want Officer Priest in the parking authority writing tickets for expired meters, I can make it happen. I would keep that in mind if I were you. Have a nice day, ladies."

Priest didn't allow the fear to enter her expression until Lark was gone. "Riley..."

"It's okay."

Briggs said, "I'll fight it. She can't just laud one of my detectives and then demote her because her feelings got hurt. You'll be fine, Caitlin. This is just a roadblock, a way to distract us from what she's really up to."

"A way to waste time, when time is our most precious commodity," Priest said.

"We'll stop her, Cait. I don't care if she makes me Officer Friendly and makes me go around to every elementary school in town. Nothing she does will change who we are. I'm the champion, you're Zerachiel, and one way or another we'll stop her."

Briggs exhaled sharply. "I'm glad you're so confident."

"Right. Confident. You should never play poker with me."

Priest at least looked mollified. "What do we do now?"

"Paperwork," Briggs suggested.

Riley nodded. "When I get back. Right now there's something I have to do."

"God, this is so trite."

"Hey, I'm the one who is going to look crazy talking to thin air. At least here people won't find it too unusual." Riley looked around to make sure the cemetery was empty around them. Kara stood beside her, hands in her pockets despite the fact she couldn't feel the cold. She had already said goodbye to Christine Lee, and Lieutenant Hathaway had faded on her own without ceremony. There was only one ghost left to say farewell to. Riley looked back at the headstone. "I thought even though you're just a cake-mix of my own memories, you might want to see this."

"Did they have to put my real date of birth on there? All those years of lying about my age, wasted."

"Yeah, but now you'll be thirty forever. You know how many women would love that?"

"Somehow it doesn't quite seem worth the price."

"No," Riley admitted. "Kara~"

Kara held out her hand. "Stop. Right now. Because I know what comes next. You're going to apologize. But save it, Riley. I was turned. I was a bad guy at the end. Sure, I was doing it for the right reasons, but that's a sucky excuse. You stopped me because I was bad, and that's sort of your thing. If you hadn't stopped me, I'd have probably done something horrible. I pulled my gun first. What if I'd just shot you in the back of the head? You would have died that day, and then this city... God, this city would probably not even be standing right now."

Riley scoffed. "Right. I caused a massive earthquake and unseated a small-threat champion who was replaced by evil incarnate. If you'd killed me, Gail Finney would still be around and a lot of people would still be alive."

"Do you ever wonder how many people would be dead if you weren't here? Gillian. Muse. Radio. Kenzie. It's easy to look at the bad things. Focus on the good things, Riley. Focus on the things you've done right. You found a home for Aissa, you've battled the demons in Briggs' past, and you brought together Kenzie and Chelsea Stanton. You gave Muse back to his family and you put Radio on a path to mental health. And me... you made sure my legacy was intact. People remember me as a good person and a good cop, Riley. My family is taken care of. Because of you. You didn't let my final moments define me. I can't repay you for that."

Riley realized she was crying. "Kara, I..." She looked, but Kara had disappeared. This time Riley knew she was gone for good. She breathed in deep, held the air in her lungs, and slowly exhaled. She let go of her pain and regret, her guilt over pulling the trigger all those years ago, and looked down at the name carved on the granite in front of her.

KARA SWEET.

She took the pack of cigarettes out of her pocket, undid the foil, and tapped one out. She stepped forward and rested it lengthwise on top of the stone.

"Last one, Kara." She crouched and kissed her fingers, then pressed it against the carved K. "I still miss you, kid."

As she stood, a stray breeze wrapped around her, kicking up the tails of her coat and knocking the cigarette into the grass. Riley started to replace it, but a smile slowly spread across her face as she straightened up again.

"Finally quit, huh? Better late than never. See you around, Sweet Kara."

She propped up the rest of the cigarette pack against the tombstone, just in case, and took the long way back to the car.

EASY IS THE WAY

"The gates of Hell are open night and day
Smooth the descent, and easy is the way
But to return, and view the cheerful skies,
In this the task and mighty labor lies."
- Virgil, The Aeneid

KENZIE GLANCED toward the bed as she padded toward the bathroom. Chelsea was seated on top of the blankets, legs crossed in front of her to form a table. She was holding a letter in her hand, identical to the other pages draped over her thighs and the bedspread around her. Her head was bowed and her eyes closed for deep concentration as she guided her fingers over the raised Braille lettering. Kenzie had tried to learn Braille, but her mind rebelled at tactile reading.

"Hey, babe. What are you reading?"

Chelsea startled, lifting her head and folding the note in half. "It's... nothing."

Kenzie chuckled. "Love letters from your old flames?" She left the bedroom door opened and ran the sink. "I'm not jealous. In fact, invite them over. Show them who won." She expected a laugh, but Chelsea remained oddly silent. Kenzie splashed the water on her face and looked out to see Chelsea was putting the letters away in the bottom drawer of her nightstand.

Kenzie washed off her minimal makeup and wiped her face on a towel as she stepped into the doorway.

"Hey. You know I was kidding, right?"

"Yes, of course." Chelsea smiled tightly. "I'm just not in much of a joking mood."

"I'm sorry."

"No, you don't have anything to apologize for."

Kenzie sucked on her bottom lip. "I'm going to hop in the shower, then I'll join you. Okay?"

Chelsea smiled. "I'll wait up."

Kenzie undressed with the water running, then stepped around the curtain and ducked her head under the spray. She'd spent the morning doing a background check for a security company. It turned out their applicant hadn't worked at any of the places he'd offered as references, and Chelsea discovered that he had a criminal record in another state. Kenzie delivered the information and received a check, which was currently being processed at the bank. Another day, another dollar. Unfortunately their rent averaged out to more than a dollar per day. Still, they had savings and there was always another client.

She finished her shower and changed into a nightie. She thought of the ribbing she would receive if her unit could see her in the flimsy silk get-up. Even Riley would probably get a few good jabs in. Kenzie honestly preferred to sleep either in the nude or in a T-shirt, but Chelsea once mentioned how much she liked the feel of silk. Kenzie wore a nightgown for her once, and the reward had been great enough that she kept it up.

Usually she only wore it when Chelsea had a bad day and needed to be cheered up. Kenzie didn't know what was in the letters, but she had a feeling it was a silk-nightie kind of night. She turned off the lamp as she passed, crossing the room in near total darkness and slipping under her side of the covers. Chelsea shifted to meet her and rested her hand on Kenzie's stomach. She rubbed the silk between her thumb and forefinger.

"Darling, thank you..."

"It seemed like you needed it." She kissed Chelsea's forehead. "Want to talk about it?"

Chelsea was quiet for a long time. "I'm thinking about what Riley told us. Her deadline."

"Me too." She stroked Chelsea's shoulder. "I can't even imagine what it will be like without her. She's always seemed so invincible. I remember when we were in uniform, the crazy risks she would take. She would try and get me to patrol No Man's Land with her. A lot of times I'd go just because she was my partner, but other times... it was just too damn scary. Never stopped her. She would just go alone if I wouldn't back her up." She stroked Chelsea's arm. "I kept waiting for the news a cop had been killed down there. When it never came I just... I guess I assumed the call would never come."

Chelsea made a quiet noise of consideration. After a moment she said, "I was reading letters people sent me while I was in prison. Mostly other police officers."

"Hon, why would you do that to yourself?"

"I have to remember. Riley coming by here the other day reminded me that no matter how far I've come and no matter how many people say they forgive me, I can never get away from what I did. I wouldn't want to erase it."

"But you don't have to rub your face in it all the time." She looked at the drawer and frowned. "Wait, those letters are in Braille. You weren't blinded until after you got out of prison."

"I had them translated."

Kenzie sat up. "Why would you do that?"

"It would be too easy to forget otherwise."

"Then forget." She took Chelsea's hand and put it over her heart. "Do you want to know what I thought when your scandal happened? I thought you were the worst human being I'd ever met. You made me hate this city, the police department, my work... I couldn't see the badge without remembering what you did, and it made me sick to my stomach. So I threw it away. The uniform and everything. I got a different uniform and flew around the world to do a similar job in a sandpit." She moved Chelsea's hand to her face. "And this happened."

Chelsea's eyes glistened in the darkness as she ran her fingers over the scars.

"And when I came back, I found you. And I wanted to come in here to spit in your face. But as soon as I saw you... I couldn't be angry anymore. No one deserves what happened to you." She touched Chelsea's face. "It was cruel, and I couldn't bear to add to your burden any more. I should have been content to just walk away."

"Why didn't you?"

Kenzie smiled, knowing Chelsea felt the muscles moving against her palm. "Because even then, I couldn't walk away from you. Something in me knew that I belonged with you. So I had to get over my hurt and my anger at the woman you *were* so I could see the woman you had become. You *were* a bitch, a criminal, a liar, and a junkie. You became... the woman I was supposed to be with. Strong enough to fight me back, smart enough to know when I just need to rail a little bit, and with poor enough taste that you settled for me."

Chelsea laughed quietly. "I've been thinking about everything we've been through since I 'settled' for you. This city isn't my home, Kenzie. I struggled here before I found you to be my anchor, and I've stayed because you made it tolerable. But the friends I had before I sinned have never come back. And yes, I won back the only one that matters." She bowed her head and kissed Kenzie's chest. "But I've mainly stayed because I wouldn't ask you to leave Riley or Caitlin. But now they're both... they're going away."

Kenzie had been trying not to think about Priest's imminent demise, but if Riley died there was really no need for her guardian angel to stick around. She dreaded the heartbreak of mourning them both at the same time.

"I would stay here for you, if that was what you wanted. You're my wife, so of course I want to be wherever you are. But I want you to think about the possibility of leaving when Riley's time comes. This city is evil, Kenzie. And I want a fresh start. I want to work with police officers who don't see betrayal every time they look at me. I want you to live somewhere that doesn't require you to defend your choice of partners."

"Hey. Anyone I have to defend you to~"

"Kenzie. You had to defend me to Riley earlier this week. You took my last name when we got married, and that meant... that you were willing to be a Stanton in this city, that meant the world to me. But I want us to live where people know we're both lucky. I'm not saying we have to start packing in the morning. We have time before Riley's clock runs out. But it's something worth considering."

"Right," Kenzie said softly. She brought Chelsea's hand to her lips and kissed the knuckles. "I'll think about it."

"That's all I ask. Good night."

"Good night."

Chelsea rested her head against Kenzie's chest, and Kenzie stroked her hair. She'd left the city once before, and she'd never intended to stay when she came back. The return visit was a necessity; she had to find and protect Radio. She stayed because she felt like it was where she was meant to be. Maybe her purpose in the city was done. She'd been meant to help Riley and find Chelsea.

The idea of a clean slate was tempting. To live in a place where people didn't pity her for ending up with the infamous Chelsea Stanton and, instead, thought her lucky to have such a brilliant and beautiful wife.

She closed her eyes but didn't plan on getting much sleep. She had far too much thinking to do.

But she did sleep, and when she slept she dreamed of reality.

Chelsea in a white satin blouse that fit her well enough to have been tailored specifically for her torso. It billowed away from her arms to cinched sleeves, and the button at the collar was hidden beneath an elaborate bow. The skirt followed the muscles of her thighs down to her knee, where it swept out into a wave of ruffles that would trail behind her when she walked. Kenzie saw her and every doubt she'd ever had about marriage and wedding ceremonies was instantly discarded as childish.

"You look beautiful."

"You're not supposed to see me before the wedding."

Kenzie stepped into the bridal suite. "One of us isn't supposed to see the other one," she said. "For once, your lack of sight is working for our benefit."

Chelsea held out her hands, and Kenzie took them. She was dressed in a black suit with a matching shirt and tie accented by a single white rose in the lapel of her jacket. The rose was from Chelsea's garden, a symbol of the love and care they had taken with each other in the early stages of their relationship. Chelsea's attention had bloomed a beautiful rose, while their combined attentions created a gorgeous relationship.

Chelsea squeezed Kenzie's fingers. "You're sure about this?"

"Positive. I saw how easily I could have lost you in that earthquake."

"This is a dangerous world. Not just the city, anywhere we go would have its dangers."

Kenzie knew that their pre-bed conversation was seeping into the dream; Chelsea hadn't said anything remotely similar on the actual day.

"I know. But you have to admit, the dangers here are pretty singular."

"Yes."

"The truth is, any city and any danger... I'll face any of it as long as you're there with me. Except nowhere warm. I got enough heat and sand when I was overseas, thanks very much."

Chelsea smiled. "Deal."

They leaned in for a kiss. When they pulled back, the room had changed. One wall was missing, replaced by a tall row of glass windows. Kenzie looked toward it as the first snowflakes began to fall, and she let go of Chelsea's hands to move closer. Their property was vast, the green grass sloping downward until it reached the edge of an evergreen army waiting for the order to advance. She could feel the cold emanating through the glass and she hugged herself, hands tucked into the sleeves of her sweater. She curled her bare toes in the carpet and smiled. The skin grafts on her cheek pulled taut, reminding her of the scars she had once worn.

"It just started to snow, baby."

Chelsea embraced her from behind and kissed her neck. "Describe it to me."

Kenzie covered Chelsea's hands with her own to warm them. "Why did we spend all that money on your surgery if you're just going to close your eyes and make me describe things to you?"

"Because I still love your voice."

Kenzie laughed and leaned back against Chelsea's body. "It's gorgeous. There's an old, white-haired woman in a sweater that's too big for her because you didn't want to spoil the surprise by getting my measurements. And she's being hugged from behind by a tall, elegant woman with short gray hair."

Chelsea kissed Kenzie's earlobe. "I meant the snow."

"Snow is just weather." She turned in Chelsea's arms and kissed her lightly. "The reflection was the real beauty."

"You're much too old to flirt, Mrs. Stanton."

"Come into the bedroom with me and we'll take the age test." She kissed Chelsea's bottom lip. Chelsea sighed into the kiss and leaned Kenzie against the glass, deciding maybe they weren't too old after all.

Kenzie woke to a dark, cold bedroom. Chelsea's body was warm against hers and Kenzie cuddled closer against her. She wasn't one to put much stock in the promises of dreams, but she had a feeling she was going to hold onto that one for a good long while.

Riley grimaced as Gillian undid the knot in her tie and redid it properly. "Don't make faces," Gillian said. "Everyone needs to dress up now and again."

"It's not the dressing up. Although I do hate that. It's this stupid, nonsensical diversion the mayor has us on. Cait and I can do so much more good on the streets."

"Well, maybe that's the whole idea. She is the champion for evil, after all. Maybe she's just a better chess player than Gail Finney was. She doesn't have to kill you, she just has to put you out of the way."

Riley glared at her wife. "I hate when you're reasonable and logical."

"No, you don't. You love it."

"I hate when you tell me what I love."

Gillian gripped the knot of the tie. "You love me."

"I do, damn it." She kissed Gillian and pressed against her. "I have sick days."

"I don't. I've gotten beat up a lot recently."

Riley's expression flickered between a few emotions before settling on guilt. "Believe me, I know."

"Hey." She stroked Riley's cheek. "It's not your fault. I didn't mean anything by it." She kissed Riley's lips, chin, and nose.

"I know. I still feel guilty."

Gillian stepped back and smoothed the wrinkles from Riley's shirt. "When you've taken care of Lark Siskin, you and I will go somewhere and be safe for a year. And maybe we'll get lucky and find a loophole. Caitlin said that you'll die when you reach a certain age, so all I have to do is figure out how to retard your ageing process. That way you stay alive, and I have a hot young wife forever."

Riley finally let a smile break through. "You're so selfish."

"Mm-hmm. I can't help it." She kissed Riley again and then stepped away. "You and Caitlin are going to be amazing. This city could use a new fleet of cops trained to think like you. This is going to backfire on Mayor Siskin in a major way."

"Hm."

"What hm?"

Riley checked her outfit in the mirror. "That's not something Siskin would overlook. She's getting me and Priest off the streets for a couple of days, but then we'll be back. And when we come back, there will be a crew of cops who learned from me. Either she has something specific planned for the next week or so and wants to make sure I don't get in her way, or she thinks my training won't make a difference."

Gillian chewed her bottom lip. "I don't know which one of those to root for."

"I'm rooting for the 'something planned.' That way we won't have to wait for the hammer to fall." She put on her blazer and grunted as she caught a glimpse of her reflection. "I look like a college professor."

"I like it." Gillian pressed against Riley, slipping her hands into the blazer pockets. "I really need this credit, Professor Parra. I'm willing to do anything for another chance at your final. Just one more chance."

Riley said, "You think you can bribe me, Ms. Hunt?"

"I was hoping."

Riley kissed her softly. "See me after class. We'll discuss it."

"Hooray." She grinned and stepped back to let Riley go. "I'll miss seeing you at work. Do you get a lunch break?"

"We get fifteen minutes at eleven. It's inhumane."

"I'll bring something by. We'll have a snack together in the courtyard."

Riley smiled. "It's already the best part of my day." She kissed two fingers and held them out to Gillian as she headed for the front door. "What does it say about me that I'd rather be heading off to fight demons?"

"That you're the hero everyone claims you are?"

Riley blew a raspberry. "Yadda, yadda, yadda."

Gillian chuckled after Riley left, then went back to getting ready for work.

In the morning Kenzie dressed in pinstripe slacks and a white dress shirt, still buttoning the cuffs as she came downstairs into the office. She noticed the intruder in her periphery at the same time he spoke. He was a wraith-thin man in a nice gray suit, with a birdish head balanced on top of a thin neck. His receding hair was feathered and blond, making him look like a well-off accountant rather than an intruder. Kenzie instinctively took her gun from the shoulder holster and aimed it at him before he'd managed to say three words.

"Don't be alarmed oh my and now there's a gun in play." He held up his hands and smiled sheepishly. "Please..."

"How did you get past the security system?"

"I, ah-ahem. I have my methods. First, there's a red piece of chalk on the edge of your partner's desk. Do you see it?"

Kenzie glanced quickly down and then locked her gaze on him again. "Yeah."

"If you would kindly take that chalk and complete the circle, I think you could put the gun down and we'd all be much more at ease with each other."

"Circle?" Kenzie looked at the man's feet and saw he was standing in an ornately-drawn circle of chalk. She recognized it from The Cell as a devil's trap. It was complete save for a space of about three inches where the circle was broken. "What the hell. You drew on my floor?"

"With chalk!"

"I don't suppose you're going to clean it up."

"I'll... be happy to pay the charge for the carpet cleaner. You can add it to my bill."

Kenzie frowned. "Bill?"

"I'm hiring you. At least, I hope to hire you. But in order for us to have a pleasant conversation, you must holster your weapon and complete the circle."

"Why didn't you finish it?"

"Then I would be unable to get out. The circle must be broken by the one who drew it, and it can only be opened from the outside. You can see my conundrum. Besides, by allowing you to finish the circle and trap me, I'm giving you the power in the situation. It's a show of faith. I only wish to talk and, should you agree to my offer, we can proceed as allies. On your terms."

Kenzie narrowed her gaze. "And when I kneel in front of you, you bash my head in."

He winced as if he'd smelled something disgusting. "Please, Mrs. Stanton. Such chicanery is well beneath me. I would never resort to such ridiculous tactics. I circumvented your security system and I've spent enough time down here this morning to draw the circle. If I wished you harm, certainly I could have done it while you were orally pleasuring your wife or during your shower or~"

Kenzie raised the gun to his face and he swallowed his words with an audible gulp.

"You're really not good at this 'get on my good side' stuff, are you?"

"No. Not... exactly well-practiced. I'm a demon, you see."

"I figured from the drawing. Why are you here?"

He cleared his throat and pointed at the ground. Kenzie sighed and used one hand to pick up the chalk. She held the gun on him one-handed as she crouched and finished the circle. She felt a tingle as she connected the lines, a sort of static fuzz similar to holding her hand in front of an old television set, and the demon shuddered and rolled his shoulders.

"Whooo, how I hate that." He cleared his throat and smacked his lips as he addressed her. "Thank you, Mrs. Stanton."

Kenzie straightened but kept her gun at her side. "Okay. Speak."

He cleared his throat. "My name is Ziminiar, and I have been a guest of your fair city for near a century. It's been mostly hospitable. I've made friends, and I've made a decent living. But recently things have become unsettled. There are things brewing, very big things, and I have decided that my time on this mortal plane should come to an end. I wish to return to the Hellish landscape of my birth, and that is where you come in."

"I think you have us mistaken for the travel agency down the street."

He smiled. "Believe me, if I could simply book passage on a tramp steamer, I would be wishing you bon voyage from the quarterdeck as we speak."

"Quarterdeck?" Kenzie muttered.

"It's unimportant." He noticed red chalk on his fingertips and took a handkerchief from his pocket to daintily wipe it away. "What is important is that returning to Hell is hardly a simple undertaking. Not to mention the fact that, ah, ahem." He adjusted his tie and averted his gaze. "One does not simply choose to live among mortals without reason. My initial choice to relocate was due to an unfortunate misunderstanding with some associates in the Underneath. We demons have long lives and sometimes it seems as if we have even longer memories. Certain forces do not want me returning. I cannot go through the same channels other demons have when they wish to quit this world."

Kenzie rolled her eyes. "Where do I come in?"

"You are associates of Riley Parra and the angel. You have access to the Cell. Take me there, entrap me, and exorcise me back to Hell. You know the saying... when you have nowhere else to go, home is the place that has to take you in? The same goes for Hell. If I am exorcised by a knight of goodness, I will be allowed back. They won't be happy, but it's Hell. They're never exactly 'happy.'"

"I take it the demons who don't want you back are in town?"

"Yes. They've already renovated my office and replaced my car with a new Ferrari."

"Those bastards."

He glared at her. "They're trying to entice me to stay. I've feigned contentedness thus far, but I can only keep it up for so long. And once they see I'm taking steps to leave they will up the ante. It will be a very dangerous undertaking should you choose to help me."

Kenzie raised an eyebrow. "Somehow I don't think our standard two-hundred-a-day plus expenses will be enough to cover this. So sorry Samovar, but I think I'll have to pass."

"I never intended to pay you with money, Mrs. Stanton. Should you do this for me, I would repay you in a manner befitting the danger you would be putting yourselves in. Should you successfully convey me to the Cell, my last act on this earth will be to heal your wife's sight."

Kenzie had to tighten her grip to keep from dropping the gun. "Shut up."

He shrugged. "I've thought long and hard about what the proper payment would be. You have no reason to oblige my request and, if you did, you would have no incentive to ensure my safety. This way you have a vested interest in my continued survival."

"No."

The demon blinked. "You would refuse—"

"I would refuse whatever bullshit devil's bargain you try to pull. You'll restore Chelsea's eyesight but take mine. You would let her see but take away her reasoning. I know the whole genie myth. There's always a catch, there's always a loophole... and besides. Even if it was straightforward, I'd still refuse. It's not up to me to decide something that huge. I love Chelsea as she is. I won't change anything about her."

"Then your scars. Surely you would like to be returned to normal..."

"Normal?"

He rolled his eyes. "Humans are so precious about that word, as if being abnormal wasn't the norm." He pinched the bridge of his nose. When he spoke again, his voice was harsher and carried more frustration. "I can undo the damage caused to both of you. It would come at great cost to me if I wished to remain on this plane, maywant to go home it's a moot point. So I am willing to expend enough energy to permanently restore your flesh and your wife's eyesight. No hidden costs. I would be repaying a debt to you. You wouldn't be indebted to me. You can have it writ in my blood if you wish, but I'd prefer not to cut myself while wearing this suit."

"You expect to be in Hell by the end of the day, and you're worried about the suit?"

"It's a Hermes. Discuss the terms with your wife. Decide what an appropriate payment would be, and I shall pay it. Just please, do not dally. The longer I spend here, the more likely it is those who oppose me will discover my intentions. Your work will only get harder the more you wait."

Kenzie started for the stairs, then pointed at the circle with her gun. "You're stuck in there, right?"

"Yes, yes."

"Good. Sit tight, Zimmy."

"My name is~"

"I know what your name is. Just don't make too much noise. We have neighbors."

She went upstairs where Chelsea was just getting out of the shower. Her hair was slicked back, her eyes unprotected by her mauve-tinted glasses. She wrapped a towel around herself and smiled at the sound of Kenzie's entrance.

"Did you forget something?"

"No. We have a... potential client downstairs."

Chelsea said, "I trust you to take the meeting."

"Not this one. It's a demon."

"A demon?"

Kenzie stepped into the bathroom and closed the door. "It's okay. He locked himself in a devil's trap. He made me close it so only I could break it down." She picked up an eyelash curler and turned Chelsea to face her. Chelsea could manage the small amount of makeup she usually wore, but sometimes Kenzie liked to do it for her. As she applied the lipstick and eye shadow, she explained what Ziminiar had said.

"And then he offered... the payment."

Chelsea looked dubious. "What's he offering?"

Kenzie wet her lips. "Your sight and my scars."

Chelsea went very still. After a moment she said, "And what's the catch?"

"He says the catch will be how hard it is to get him to the Cell. Apparently a lot of demons want him to stay right where he is, stay out of trouble, that sort of thing. They don't want him moving back into the old neighborhood." She looked down at the makeup kit. "I said no."

"You did?"

"It's not my place to make that decision for you. Chels, he's asking me to change you. He's trying to make me say I want you to change. I won't say that no matter what he wants to do. Maybe if he made you less of a blanket-hog, that I might consider..."

Chelsea dipped her hand in the sink and flicked the water at Kenzie's face. Kenzie chuckled and wiped the droplets away with the cuff of her shirt.

"If you say you want your eyesight back, then fine. But I like our life the way it is. I love you as you are. I will only say this... if you're still using your blindness as a punishment for what you did in the past, maybe the offer is a chance to set yourself free. You don't have to prove yourself to anyone anymore. You don't have to continue suffering." She touched Chelsea's cheek. "I love you, Chelsea. If you decide to be sighted, I can learn to live with it."

Chelsea smiled and touched Kenzie's scarred cheek. Kenzie hated for anyone to look at it, but she only allowed Chelsea to touch it. She closed her eyes and leaned into the caress.

"What are you punishing yourself for, Mac?"

"Lots of things."

Chelsea sighed. "Maybe we should both think about getting a clean slate. We're married. Riley is going away... this offer could be our chance at having a real life."

"From a demon."

"I'm considering that," Chelsea said. "I wish we could ask Caitlin her opinion."

Kenzie nodded. "I'll give her a call. I think she'll take any excuse to beg off that seminar the mayor has her and Riley doing today."

She had crossed the living room in search of her cell phone when the floor shuddered under her feet. A second later the security alarm began its clarion call. Chelsea braced herself in the bathroom door.

"Another earthquake?"

Before Kenzie could answer, she heard Ziminiar shouting from downstairs. "Mrs. Stanton! Your presence would not go amiss!"

"Damn it. Chelsea, stay here." Kenzie drew her gun and half-flew down the stairs, her free hand skimming over the banister until she hit the landing. The front door of the offices stood open, blown off its hinges, and three demons stood in the entryway. Their leader had crossed to the space between Kenzie and Chelsea's desks to examine the devil's trap. Ziminiar cowered against the far curve of the chalk outline, the extent of his ability to run and hide.

The leader turned at the sound of Kenzie's arrival. He regarded the gun for a moment and then gestured lazily at the trap.

"Did you do this? It's awesome work. You don't usually see this kind of technique in a mortal. They're usually all about the shortcut and the clo-snuffs. You know what the clo-snuff is? It's when you do something half-assed and you just say, 'eh. Close enough.' Which Stanton are you? The new one or the blind one?" He laughed at himself. "What am I saying? Way you're aiming that gun, you're sure not the blind one. I'm Furfur."

Kenzie couldn't help herself; she laughed. "You're kidding."

"It's Latin. Well, a corruption of Latin, which is only natural considering it was used to name a demon. My full name is Furcifer. Mortals tend to mumble it, so I accommodated. Unlike you, who chose your moniker because you thought it sounded sharper. You thought Kenzie would be more dangerous than Mac or Mackenzie. And you wanted to be dangerous, didn't you, little Mackenzie Crowe. The child who was backed into a corner and beaten by the boys on the Rez? The boys who tied your hair to the flagpole~"

"Mrs. Stanton, don't listen to him!"

Ziminiar's voice cut through the fog threatening to overtake Kenzie's vision. She pushed back the image of herself tied to the flagpole while the boys pulled down her jeans and laughed at her. It was just teasing, boys and girls dealing with Their Changing Bodies in the only way they knew how, but she'd been humiliated. It had taken her ages to trust anyone, and now she suspected it was due to that one morning on the playground when Billy Redcrow had shown the entire school her panties. She was the only girl in the class, the only girl her age on the entire reservation.

Her cheeks flushed red and she tightened her grip on the gun, focusing on Furfur. She realized the memory had threatened to overwhelm her, blinding her to the situation, and she couldn't risk that with four demons in the room. "I gotta keep an eye on you, huh?"

Furfur shrugged and looked at the trap again. "How did you even manage... ah. I see. Ziminiar helped you." He focused on the quaking demon. "Pathetic. You snared yourself to earn her trust? He needn't have bothered, Mrs. Stanton. You have very little to fear from this pantywaist. He's lived among your kind for so long that he's more human than devil."

"Yeah, well, call me paranoid."

Furfur faced Kenzie again. "Release him from the trap and we'll be on our way."

"And if I don't?"

Furfur shrugged and held up his hand. A moment later Kenzie was back in the hospital, half of her face burned off, screaming as the medics tried to piece her back together. She threw herself back without thinking, slamming her shoulders against the wall to ground herself back in reality. A sob was torn from her throat as she crossed her arms over her face to protect herself from the memories as they rushed back.

"And my weapon doesn't have to be reality."

Again, only this time the burns covered her entire body. She slid to the floor, trembling as the pain covered her body like a wave.

She heard a shrill beeping noise and thought it was part of the illusion, but then she was sprayed with the fire-suppression foam they'd had installed after the earthquake. The false memory vanished in a flash, and she found herself on the floor in the fetal position while the demons crowded into her office were covered with the thick white goo.

"What... *argh*!" Furfur cringed and hunched over, wincing as the foam began to sting. "What is this?"

"Water-based." Kenzie coughed so her voice lost its tremor. "Holy water-based, to be a little more precise. It's sinking into your skin and your clothes, so I figure you've got about a half hour of pain ahead of you unless you get it washed off pretty quick."

Furfur's demonic nature flashed across the face of his human host. "You've made a powerful enemy today, Mackenzie Crowe Stanton."

"You're a demon. You're my enemy no matter what, so why not have a little fun at your expense? Now get out of my office."

Furfur gestured at the goons he'd brought with him and they crowded out the doors. Kenzie got to her feet as Chelsea came downstairs.

"Kenzie?"

"They're gone. Thanks for tripping the system."

Chelsea nodded. "Of course." She turned toward the trap. "I can see energy... over there. Is that the demon?"

"Yeah. Ziminiar."

He swallowed a lump in his throat and nodded rapidly. "Yes, ma'am. I am so terribly sorry to have brought those demons to your doorstep."

"We've had clients bring worse," Kenzie said.

Ziminiar started to nod, then realized what she had said. "Client. I'm your client?"

"Yeah. Let's send you back to Hell. Maybe if we're lucky we can send Furry there right behind you. But first I want to make sure we have an understanding about your payment. Nothing happens without our okay."

Chelsea said, "I'll accept it."

Kenzie looked at her. "Are you sure?"

"I want to see you."

Kenzie blinked to hold back the tears and nodded once. "Okay. But you fix Chelsea's eyesight, full-stop. No strings attached, no extra touches. It's a strict escort-for-vision exchange."

"I concede. And your facial scars. I'll heal them as well. It's the least I can do for bringing this down on your heads before you even took the case. You will both be... whole again."

"And nothing else will change?" Chelsea said.

"No. This I avow to you, for whatever worth you give the word of a demon."

"Very little," Kenzie said. "Before you do anything, we want Cai- - Zerachiel to be present to serve as an official. A holy notary public, I guess."

"Understood. Very smart." He looked warily toward the door. "Now can we please, please begin? Sooner begun, sooner done."

"If you try anything~"

"I will be on my best behavior. Again~"

"As much as that means coming from a demon. Right." She looked at Chelsea to make sure she was ready, then stepped forward to where Furfur had been standing. She took a moment to curse her own stupidity as she swept her foot across the chalk line and broke the circle.

Chelsea hung up the phone on her desk. Across the room Kenzie was slipping into a Kevlar vest, a pair of guns with blessed ammunition resting on her desk blotter. "Caitlin will meet us at the Cell. I still don't know why she can't help us transport you."

"She's an angel. If she helped me get back to Hell, even if she was acting on my wishes, it would stain her purity."

"She's sent your kind back to Hell before," Kenzie said.

Ziminiar nodded. "Yes, demons who meant to do her harm or to do harm to those in her protection. I am no threat to her. It's the difference between a human killing in self-defense and randomly shooting a passer-by in the head. She can be present to ensure my intentions are good when I make recompense, but I will not have her righteousness darkened by lending a hand in my damnation."

"A demon with a heart of gold," Kenzie muttered. "Okay. Let's go."

She checked to make sure Furfur wasn't lying in wait outside before she motioned Ziminiar out. Chelsea followed, shutting the door as well as she could given the circumstances before following them to the car. Kenzie put Ziminiar into the backseat, Chelsea in the front beside her. The Cell was most of the way across town; provided they didn't run into any problems they could be there in twenty-five minutes.

Unfortunately she didn't think they would be lucky enough to make it without a few hiccups. She also wasn't going to risk taking the most direct route. If Furfur knew Ziminiar's intentions, then he more than likely had contingency plans set up. She didn't know how widely known the Cell's location was to the city's demon population, but she knew last year's incident with Falco had seriously compromised its security.

Ziminiar settled in the center of the backseat and fastened his seatbelt. Kenzie looked at his reflection in the rearview and gave a shudder.

"What?" Chelsea whispered.

"Just a movie flashback. 'I just shot Marvin in the face.' I saw Seminar back there and it's the first thing I thought of."

Ziminiar looked from one woman to the other. "I don't understand the reference."

"Be glad you don't." She started the car. "We're going to take a little detour. If Furfur is following us, we're going to give him every opportunity to slip up and show himself."

She pulled away from the curb and drove north before turning west toward the waterfront. She mentally tried to keep track of the time she was adding to their journey by taking a roundabout route, but she quickly gave it up as a lost cause. It was still early enough to deal with traffic of people on the way to work, but the actual rush hour was long over. The sun glinted off the fetid stretch of the waterfront, making it look more beautiful than it actually was. In the mirror she saw Ziminiar crane his neck to look at it as she turned north.

"Homesick? Remind you of the River Styx?"

"I'll actually be homesick for this city, if you must know. I first came here as an actuary. It was my job to ensure people were ill-prepared in the face of a natural disaster. I assured them risks were low, pushed them toward low-yield insurance policies, and ignored their venomous recriminations when they were left with nothing." He smiled almost wistfully, rubbing his palms together. "It wasn't a flashy job, but ah... ah, I loved it so. And this city! So many wonderful things just waiting to go wrong. I could never have predicted the earthquake, though. A splendid little surprise that none of my clients were properly prepared to face. Hm."

Chelsea said, "I would call you heartless, but I fear you would take it as complimentary."

"I would." He lifted his chin and considered the buildings they passed. "But I was corrupted. I discovered that I loved this world. Being mortal, walking the earth as a human... eating food, listening to music. Music! You humans take it for granted. The simple pleasure of a voice and instrument joined together in harmony." He closed his eyes and held up his hand as if following a note. "You have no idea how special it is, while at the same time you surround yourselves with it. When was the last time you went an entire day without hearing music?"

"People in the seventies went an entire decade without hearing music. They tried to replace it with something inferior. Like New Coke."

Chelsea smiled. "Hey. I had my fair share of disco albums."

"Marriage over," Kenzie muttered. "Irreconcilable differences."

Ziminiar laughed. "And this... love. It should come as no surprise that my kind has nothing even remotely similar to love. The love of another person or the love of a barbecue sandwich." He closed his eyes and then snapped them open. "Could we possibly stop for a barbecue sandwich? I'll pay, of course."

"We're not making any detours," Kenzie said.

He sighed. "I suppose I understand. It's just that I didn't quite realize everything I was giving up before I made this decision."

Chelsea pressed her lips together, and Kenzie eyed her for a moment. "What?"

"He's giving up his life, and he's doing it willingly. If we're giving Fervor a chance to make a mistake, perhaps stopping for an early lunch would make him tip his hand."

"So you're good cop?"

"I'm at the very least Missed Breakfast Cop."

Kenzie sighed. "Okay. Demon wants some barbecue, wife wants breakfast. I'll see if I can find a vegan-barbecue fusion restaurant around here."

"It would be a miracle," Ziminiar said.

Kenzie and Chelsea both told him to shut up.

Kenzie stared. Ziminiar finally looked up from his meal, one cheek bulging with a bite of his sandwich, and he swallowed delicately before asking, "What?"

"Who raised you? Wolves?"

His suit was protected by a wide bib, but his chin and either side of his mouth was smeared with thick brown barbecue sauce. The restaurant didn't have any truly vegan options, but Chelsea wasn't a true vegan. She sufficed with a spinach veggie wrap, which she was picking at as Ziminiar tore through the first of three sandwiches he'd ordered. He sheepishly picked up a wet-nap and tried to clean up the majority of the damage, but succeeded only in smearing it around.

"Did I get it?"

"No. But never mind. It's a lost cause." She was seated across from him in the booth, turned toward Chelsea so she could see out the window behind them. So far there were no signs that Furfur was pursuing them, but she had no doubt he could go unseen if he wanted to. She turned back to see Ziminiar assaulting his second sandwich, adding to the smears on his lips and cheeks.

Chelsea said, "If you're so enamored with this life, enamored enough that you've stayed a century after your assignment ended, why are you suddenly so eager to return to the infernal realm?"

"Did you just say 'the infernal realm'?" Kenzie whispered.

Chelsea shrugged.

Ziminiar swallowed his mouthful and shook his head. "Not eager. Lesser of two evils. If you live on Nantucket, you may hate Boston. But you'll definitely head there when a hurricane is brewing." He straightened up and considered the sandwich in his hands. His fingers were slick with the sauce, but he seemed to be waiting until the meal was done to tidy up. "This city has seen its share of cataclysms, don't get me wrong. As an actuary I was able to see most of them coming. This earthquake surprised even me. So I started looking for cracks."

"You'll find no shortage of cracks these days," Kenzie said.

"No, not actual cracks. Do you know what an actuary does, Mrs. Stanton?" She glared at him and he cleared his throat. "I'll assume that you do. The earthquake shook me awake, quite literally. I was knocked out of bed. Sleep! God, I'll never sleep again." He cast a melancholy gaze at his sandwich, and Kenzie snapped her fingers to get him back on track. "Right. So I started reading the tea leaves, as it were. Examining the patterns and reading the possibilities. You can imagine, thanks to my origins, that I am *very* good at my job. And it is thanks to this skill that I know without a shadow of a doubt that something big is going to happen. And it will happen soon. I want to be safely away when it occurs."

"And Hell is your safe haven?"

He looked at her without blinking. "Yes. And that should tell you everything you need to know. I may not have specifics, but I can read the signs as sure as any meteorologist. The earthquake will be a footnote compared to what happens next."

Chelsea put down her wrap. "I believe I've lost my appetite."

"All right, Zimmerman. Take the rest of your breakfast to go."

He finished off his second sandwich in two bites, then gathered up the third as he scooted out of the booth. Kenzie stood and stretched, glancing toward the kitchen as Chelsea disposed of their trash. She was using the white cane she despised bringing out in public, mainly because the way it made everyone treat her like a delicate china doll. The thought of her never having to use the cane again, of looking into her wife's eyes and knowing she was being seen in return... She furrowed her brow and forced herself not to want that too much.

A flash of white drew her attention to the front counter. She could see into the kitchen, and the light had come from the alley entrance being swung open and then quickly shut. No one was at the cash register, and the prep tables were equally empty. Alarms sounded at the back of her mind and she straightened, moving her hand to her hip for the gun hidden under her jacket. "Chelsea, crouch."

She did as she was told, utilizing the paltry protection of the trash bin. Ziminiar was suddenly alert, whipping his head from side to side to spot the threat.

"What? What is it, what did you see?"

"Maybe nothing. Shut up."

There were two other customers in the restaurant, and neither seemed to have noticed the shift in tension. She grabbed a handful of Ziminiar's suit jacket and pulled him out of the booth. She immediately pushed him down so that he was almost crawling on his hands and knees. She knew she was backlit by the sun coming through the front windows, and she hoped it was enough. "Chelsea, can you see where I am?"

"Well enough."

"Come toward me. Carefully."

As soon as Chelsea moved, the front counter exploded outward. The other customers hit the deck, and Kenzie rose to her full height as she stepped forward. She brought out her gun and fired as Furfur emerged from his hiding place. He was human-sized, but something about the rage in his fury made him seem larger. The bullets hit him in the chest but only seemed to agitate him further.

"Holy bullets, my ass."

The ding of bells over the door was incongruous given the circumstances. She looked back and saw Chelsea ushering Ziminiar outside, both of them staying low. When she looked back, Furfur had closed the distance between them. He swatted her gun away, grabbed her throat, and squeezed. Kenzie's lungs immediately protested the lack of oxygen, a situation that was only slightly less worrying than the fact her feet left the floor.

"I gave you the opportunity to stay out of this, mortal. Why would you sacrifice your life just to stand in my way?"

"Seemed... fun," she croaked.

Furfur sighed. "You'll die for your fun."

Kenzie had both hands on his forearm, her entire body dangling from his fist.

"I could tear you limb from limb and leave you alive to endure the agony. I could make you do horrible, awful things, unable to stop yourself. Or I could just squeeze until your head pops off. Did you know human heads could pop off?"

Kenzie bared her teeth, her face burning from the blood trapped there. She dug her fingernails into his forearm until they drew blood, but if he noticed he didn't pay it much attention.

"Maybe I'll take over your body just long enough to kill that beautiful wife of yours."

Kenzie's eyes flashed with anger. She swung her body back, and Furfur twisted his hips so she couldn't kick him in the crotch. If she'd been aiming for that, her plan would have been ruined.

Instead she swung forward again, planted her sneakers on his hip, and walked up his body. She pushed against his stomach with both feet and he staggered backward. He blindly reached back to stop his fall, and his grip loosened just enough that Kenzie was dropped hard to the tile floor.

The wind was knocked out of her, but she scrambled for her discarded weapon before he could regain his balance. Spilled barbecue sauce made the whole floor slick, which alternatively worked for and against her attempts to move.

"Kenzie, baby, you high or low?"

"Floor!"

Chelsea was standing in the doorway with her gun. She fired twice, hitting Furfur in the head and neck. He was thrown backward by the impact and Kenzie was given time to retrieve her gun. She rolled onto her back and saw Furfur had one hand against his right eye. Blood poured around his fingers. He sneered at her as she aimed for his still-good eye.

"See you 'round."

She fired and Furfur's head rocked with the impact. Kenzie got to her feet and motioned for the other two customers to leave first. Chelsea ushered them out the door, then grabbed Kenzie's hand to pull her outside. When Kenzie looked back she saw Furfur lurching toward the back of the store rather than pursuing.

Ziminiar was curled tightly in the foot well of the car's backseat, hands over his head, shaking like a kitten. Kenzie and Chelsea got into the car and squealed the tires as they pulled away from the curb. It was a half a block before Kenzie got her breath back, the adrenaline manifesting as violent tremors as it evaporated.

"You owe me a shirt," she growled.

"Sure... sure," Ziminiar mewled from his position on the floor.

Kenzie swallowed the lump in her throat and reached for Chelsea without looking. Chelsea found her hand, and Kenzie squeezed it in gratitude.

"No more pit stops."

Kenzie was aware of cars pursuing them through the city, and she evaded them as best she could with defensive driving techniques. She cut through a parking garage, slipped through a red light at the last possible moment, lingered at intersections until the cars behind her began to impatiently flow around her. She ignored their one-handed signals as they passed her, waited until the road was clear, and then took a side street that looped back around to her original route. She kept them on the road until lunchtime when the traffic was at its peak to make the final run toward the Cell.

Riley and Priest were there when they pulled up on the overgrown back lawn. Priest was dressed in a sweater vest over a white dress shirt, and Kenzie bit her bottom lip as she approached. "My teacher fantasy has just increased twenty-fold."

Priest ignored the jibe, focusing on the demon behind her. "Are you certain you trust him?"

"He's mostly harmless," Kenzie said. "But no. I don't trust him at all. That's why you're here." She looked at Riley. "Hi. I don't recall inviting you."

"I'm like a bad penny," Riley said with a grin. "Figured you'd want the extra backup if there were demons involved."

Kenzie's manner became more serious as she nodded. "It's appreciated."

"Any time, Kenz."

Priest craned her neck and looked at the buildings across the street. "We're about to have company."

"Shit. I thought we'd lost them."

The squealing of tires announced the arrival of two cars, one from either side of the street leading to the Cell. Kenzie stepped between Ziminiar and the road, urging Chelsea to take the demon inside. He hunched over, arms crossed over his head as Chelsea ran for the storm doors. The cars screeched to a halt and Furfur got out of one. His face was still blood-red, but his eyes had healed into a pair of small black beads. He and his cronies stalked toward the group, but Priest stepped forward.

"You're not welcome here."

Furfur bent at the knees and squatted quickly, slapping both palms against the ground between his feet. Priest grunted as if she'd been punched and was thrown backward. Riley tried to catch her and was bowled over by the impact. Kenzie brought her weapon up and aimed at Furfur's eyes.

"Feel like losing three eyes in a single day, pal? You lost."

"You think just because you got him here in one piece the game is over? It is far from over." He gestured at the church that held the Cell in its basement. He extended two fingers and twisted them as if scooping a chip in dip. The ground exploded upward in a fountain of dirt and grass. Kenzie ducked at the sound of the explosion and Furfur launched himself at her. He grabbed the wrist of her gun-hand, twisted, and Kenzie howled in pain as the bone was broken.

"Go get the prick," Furfur growled to his men.

"That won't be necessary," Ziminiar said. He stepped over Kenzie and slammed himself into Furfur's chest. If Kenzie hadn't seen the behemoth knocked on his heels by Jiminy Cricket, she would never have believed it was possible. She cradled her broken wrist against her chest as Ziminiar and Furfur rolled, ending with the actuarial demon on top of the biker demon. Ziminiar reared back for a punch and, when it landed, his fist continued through Furfur's chest.

"I may have forgotten a lot about my true nature," he said, "but I remember the important things." He jerked his arm and Furfur's limbs twitched violently. "I so did not want to resort to this. He pulled something black and steaming from Furfur's chest and twisted at the waist to hurl it at one of the other demon's followers. When it hit, it exploded in ichor and knocked the demon on its ass.

Furfur took advantage of the distraction and wrapped both arms around Ziminiar. He squeezed with all his strength and, even from a dozen feet away, Kenzie heard a series of crackling pops that left Ziminiar's upper body limp. Furfur rolled and slammed the rag doll actuary down against the ground, rising on shaky legs as he looked down at him. Ziminiar tried to retreat, but his body refused to cooperate.

"You always were weak, brother."

Ziminiar coughed, and blood spattered his chin. "The weak have an advantage the strong ignore. We choose our friends wisely. Botis, Caim?"

Two of Furfur's associates suddenly grabbed the hulking demon from either side and hauled him backward.

"What..."

Ziminiar groaned as he prodded his crushed midsection. "You've fulfilled your end of the bargain as well as you could. You kept him away from me for far longer than I anticipated. And for that I thank you. Your families will be well-compensated." He cried out and dropped back to the grass.

Priest had regained her senses and crossed the lawn. She held her hand palm out, and light seemed to flow from within the sleeve of her sweater.

"Be gone from this place."

Furfur howled, and black smoke poured from his eyes and

mouth. "You haven't won, Ziminiar! You've only changed the battleground!"

"Yes, yes," Ziminiar murmured. "I'll see you in Hell."

The body slumped, and Priest dropped her hand. She eyed the two remaining demons, the ones that had apparently been in cahoots with Ziminiar from the beginning. "Leave now, while I feel generous."

They took her advice. Priest knelt next to Kenzie and wrapped her fingers around her wrist. As the white light spread, the angel smiled at her occasional lover. "I seem to be spending a lot of time mending the bones of Stantons."

"We'll try to keep it to a minimum from now on," Kenzie said, then gasped as her bones knit together again. "Damn, that felt nice."

Priest kissed Kenzie's temple and helped her up. Chelsea had come out of the cellar with Ziminiar and, now that the sounds of battle had ceased, she ran forward. Kenzie caught her, kissed her cheeks and lips, and whispered in her ear. Riley brushed off her clothes, looked at Priest and the Stantons, and pretended to wave off the people who weren't coming to help her.

"No, no. I'm fine, you guys. Really, stop worrying about me."

"For a champion, you sure are whiny," Kenzie said.

Ziminiar coughed. "Zerachiel... if you have a moment...?"

Priest warily approached the dying demon. She stood well out of his reach and peered down at him. "You're not long for this world, Ziminiar."

"That was the plan, wasn't it?" He smiled through the pain, then winced. "I considered this moment very carefully, Zerachiel. I was shrewd. I knew that no associate of the champion would accept my offer without having you present. The offer was made honorably, I assure you, but I needed you here so I could warn you."

Priest sighed. "Save your warnings, demon. You~"

"No. I'm not threatening you, Zerachiel. I wish only to alert you to the forces at work in this city." He swallowed and grunted. "Pahaliah."

"The angel? What about him?"

"When was the last time you heard from him?"

Priest knelt on the grass beside the demon. "I've been out of touch since coming to the mortal realm."

"He is being abused. He was captured, and his body is being subjected to unspeakable sacrileges. His morals, the seeds of his strength, are being carved away an atom at a time. He is being turned into an abomination; an angel not allowed to fall but too tainted to be allowed back into Heaven. He is being crafted into a weapon to be used against you."

"Why are you telling me this?"

Ziminiar smiled, his eyes closed. "Often we forget that good and evil are human ideals. In truth there are only sides in a war. And as in any war, occasionally soldiers come to believe their side is wrong." He wet his lips and coughed. "I would never wish to be dragged kicking and screaming to the gates of Heaven only to be refused entry. To see the reverse done to someone else twists within me like a blade, even if it is an angel. I could only make amends by warning you."

"Thank you."

"Now... there is a matter of payment. I need to speak to Mackenzie and Chelsea."

Priest called them over, and Ziminiar looked at them with true sorrow in his eyes. "I'm very sorry. I didn't expect to be damaged so severely in the battle. I expected my cohorts to step in much earlier than they did." He coughed and cried out as something within him snapped. "I can fulfill my obligations. But only for one of you."

Priest said, "It was your plan all along. You gave them both hope, only to make them choose now. You son~"

"No," Ziminiar said. "You must believe me, I never intended to deceive."

Kenzie said, "It's okay." Her voice was soft, and she squeezed Chelsea's hand. "We made our decision. Thanks, but no thanks."

He frowned at her. "What?"

"I don't care how free of strings you claim it is, we're not going to take a gift that extravagant from a demon. But you did make us talk about it for the first time in... well, for the first time ever. We're not punishing ourselves by keeping our scars. We're reminding ourselves of who we are and how we found each other. So thanks. But no."

Ziminiar closed his eyes and laughed softly. "A century in this skin, and I'm still no closer to understanding humans..."

Kenzie looked at Priest. "Cait... he said you can't be involved."

"He was wrong," she said. "This is a mercy." She rested two fingers on Ziminiar's forehead. "I release you. Go where you wish, and find relief from your pain."

Ziminiar's body went rigid and collapsed against the dirt. His face relaxed but, for an instant, Kenzie could have sworn he was smiling.

Riley joined them. "Well... not bad for a lunch break, huh, Cait?"

Priest smiled, but her spirits were too weighed down by what Ziminiar had told her for it to be very convincing. Kenzie and Chelsea embraced each other, grateful that the day was over.

Chelsea sniffed the air and smiled. "Barbecue. In honor of the fallen?"

Kenzie put the veggie sub sandwich in front of Chelsea, then took her own sandwich out of the bag. The wrapper was stained with the sauce. "Is it odd? I mean, the guy was a demon."

"A demon who sacrificed himself to save you. Whatever he was, I'm grateful for him. He fought his way free of me and returned to the fight of his own volition. For that, I will honor him. At least a little bit. I'll honor the man he was, rather than the demon he overcame."

"That, I will drink to. Come on. Let's have dinner upstairs." She took Chelsea's hand, guiding her up to their apartment.

Chelsea squeezed Kenzie's fingers. "Are you certain about your decision?"

"Yeah. The whole internal debate I had going on was finding reasons to accept. I finally realized that if it was that much of a struggle, then the right answer was to say no." She stopped at the head of the stairs and turned to face Chelsea. "I'm not ashamed of my scars. Feel them."

She reached up and touched Kenzie's cheek, then spread her fingers. "Is your hair up...?"

"It is. I tied it back before I went out to get dinner. I got a few stares, but nothing I can't handle. These scars are mine. I earned them. I'm not going to let some demon take them away. And your eyes..."

"I feel the same way. It's strange to feel precious about what I've used to punish myself all these years, and it partly stinks of martyrism. But I can't allow it to just be taken from me with a wave of a hand. If I do get my sight back, the restoration will be earned."

"Yeah. And that brings us to the other question we've been batting around. Leaving the city when Riley is gone."

"Mm. Yes..."

"I want to stay."

Chelsea smiled. "Me too. The city will need us more than ever with Riley gone."

"And today we proven we can go up against demons."

"Ignoring the angel-ex-machina at the end there, yes." She chuckled. "We can't leave just because Riley is leaving. I think us being here is one of the reasons she feels comfortable leaving. She knows she's leaving the city in good hands."

Chelsea nodded. "Yeah. So it's settled. Scars and all, Stanton Investigations will be a No Man's Land institution for the foreseeable future."

"As far as I'm concerned."

Kenzie kissed her wife, then looped an arm around her elbow to guide her into the dining room so they could have their dinner.

THESE TROUBLESOME DISGUISES

MY NAME is Gillian Eleanor Hunt Parra. I was born in Georgia and went to school there studying pathology. Then I accepted a job with the Office of the Medical Examiner here, in a city with one of the nation's worst crime rates, because no one else wanted the job. It was a way to get my foot in the door, a way to ascend quickly in the ranks simply because the people above me weren't sticking around. Now I'm forty, the Chief Medical Officer, and I'm married to a woman who will die in one year, three months and eight days.

When Riley told me the date, I tried hard not to put up a countdown clock in my head. Trying to ignore it only made it stronger and brighter, and every morning I wake up and subtract a number from the end. I have one year, three months, and eight days left with my wife. The woman I waited my entire life to meet, and we only get six years together. I know I shouldn't complain; some people only get a few hours of true happiness, but I'll have had the better part of a decade. Riley and I have had our dust-ups, but we're also each other's safe place. I know what she goes through, and I'm proud to be the one she comes to when she needs a shoulder. When she needs to let her vulnerability out.

I looked over at her, watching her sleep on Day 463. Her back was to me, and I could see the tattoo on her shoulder split in half by the strap of her top she wore as a nightshirt. If she hadn't gotten that tattoo all those years ago, she wouldn't have become champion.

She would have been an ordinary cop doing extraordinary things, but she wouldn't be dying right now. Of course, if she never became champion, she might never have come to me that horrible night.

I still remember how horrified I was by the sight of her on my doorstep. Torn up, dripping blood, weak. The dread I felt as I tended to her injuries, as if a part of me already knew that her death meant I would miss out on something glorious. That night she spoke of demons and angels, of a war taking place right under our noses. Anyone else might have laughed at her, could have counted it as a delusion caused by trauma and blood loss. But I believed in angels, even back then, and I believed in Riley. I believed her.

I let her stay in my apartment that night. I watched her sleep, and I knew I would never let her go. She needed somewhere to run to, someone waiting who would catch her. I swore to myself, long before I made the promise to her, that I would be that person. I may not have loved her on that morning - it was still far too early in our new relationship for me to claim that, no matter how I may want to - but I respected her.

To every other detective, coming down to my domain in the morgue was a chore. An unseemly and daunting task that disgusted them. They were uncomfortable, smearing scented lotion under their noses so they wouldn't have to smell the myriad of chemicals used in my work. They referred to the people I worked on as "the vic" or "the body," and they lingered as close to the door as possible even when I tried pointing out minute pieces of evidence.

Not Riley. She stood right next to the table, she looked in the face of the victim, and she would ask, "What happened to her?" or "Who did this to him?" She didn't see the cadaver; she saw the person it had once been. Though I may not have loved her then, that first or second or fifth time I'd met her, but the respect she showed made me appreciate that she was someone special.

Riley began to stir, and I moved onto my side to greet her. She rolled onto her back and stretched in the rigid way she had, shifting under the blankets before she turned to look at me. She blinked her eyes into focus and I smiled so it would be the first thing she saw. She smiled and leaned in to kiss me, whispering, "Good morning, beautiful," in the moment before our lips met. I moved my hand under the blankets and stroked her hip as we moved toward each other under the blankets. She murmured questioningly, and I moved my fingers under her top in response.

I only had four-hundred and sixty-two other opportunities to make love to my wife just after waking up; I wasn't going to squander any of them. I felt her smile as she deepened our kiss, her tongue teasing my teeth before retreating and making me chase it. I pressed my elbow into the mattress and twisted up over her, easing my leg between hers as I settled on top of her. She moved to sit up, but I pushed her back down.

"Uh-uh."

"Oh, it's going to be like that, huh?"

"Yeah." I pushed my hair back and hooked it behind my ears, smiling down at her in the pre-dawn gloom of our bedroom. I put my hands on her again, stroking her stomach through her shirt before I gripped the material and pulled it up. She lifted her arms and let me remove it, letting me toss it aside before I cupped her breast. I bowed down and took the nipple into my mouth, teasing it before moving to the other.

She twisted under me, pushing down her underwear as much as she could before she pushed my nightgown up over my hips. I lifted myself just enough for her to get the underwear off and I took the opportunity to doff my nightgown. Skin to skin, I lifted my head to her lips as I settled my thigh against her sex. She reached past me and found the covers I had displaced, drawing them up over my shoulders. I bowed down and let her cover us both.

I could barely see her in the shadows, but I could feel her. Her warmth, her skin, the puff of warm air as she exhaled against my cheek. I slid my hands over the curve of her, from her breasts down to her hips, pulling her to me as our lower bodies moved against each other. Riley arched her back and I pressed my thigh against her, closing my eyes as the feel of her. Her hand was on the back of my head, fingers splayed as her breathing became rougher. Then she grunted my name, her entire body tense, and I kissed the shell of her ear as she came.

After a moment she dragged her fingers over my hip until she found the hair between my legs. I sat up enough to break the cocoon of our blanket, letting in enough light to see her face as her fingers entered me. My eyes narrowed, but hers stayed wide open and locked on me. I settled against her palm and rolled my hips in a gentle rhythm until I came.

She sat up again, and I didn't push her down this time. We kissed, and the blanket fell back from us to let the morning light in. Riley touched my cheek and extended her thumb to brush it over my lip. I kissed the pad and nipped at it, and Riley grinned before leaning in to kiss me again.

"You're pretty," she whispered.

I chuckled. "You're not so bad yourself." I combed my fingers through her hair away from her face. "I think I might love you."

"Ah. So that whole getting-married gamble paid off, huh?"

"Yes. Safest bet I've ever made."

We kissed again, lingering this time until Riley dropped her hand to my hip and squeezed gently to let me know she needed to get up.

"As much as I'd love to stay here and repeat as needed, crime never sleeps in."

"You're so noir." I climbed off and let her out of bed, sitting on the edge of the mattress as she went into the bathroom. After a moment I got up and went in after her. She showered with the curtain half-open so we could talk, and I brushed my teeth before I spoke. "How is Caitlin dealing with her exile in Dispatch?"

"Bored as hell," Riley said from the other room. "Lieutenant Briggs is working on getting the punishment lifted. Cait did nothing to justify a demotion like this. It's just petty politics. She'll be back soon enough."

"I hope so. I hate the idea of you out there solo without an angel watching over you."

"Me too. I just miss having her around. She's a good partner."

I joined her in the shower and took the shampoo from her. She obediently bowed her head so I could wash her hair. She soaped her hands and washed my body as I rinsed the shampoo from her hair, trying not to think of how many solo showers I would face after she was gone. I'd made a decision after she revealed the truth to me; I wasn't going to be a weepy victim, I wasn't going to play the martyr. The sacrifice was Riley's to make, and she'd made it so I could live. Every day I had was a gift, and the fact I got to spend more than four hundred of them with her was part of that gift.

We embraced after all the soap and shampoo was gone, the water raising goosebumps on our skin as we held each other.

"I'm going to miss you."

"It's just a ten hour shift," Riley said, deliberately missing my point.

I smiled. "Yeah." I kissed her temple.

"Jill..."

"Don't." I kissed her again. "Let's just pretend it's an ordinary day in an ordinary year. Okay?"

Riley nodded against my shoulder. "Okay."

After our shower we dressed for work, and Riley made me breakfast. Scrambled eggs that she served onto the plate so that it was in the shape of a duck. Well, a Rorschach version of a duck, but it was the thought that counted. We were almost finished eating when Caitlin arrived, looking stiff and miserable in her clothes. Instead of her standard three-piece suit, she wore a V-neck sweater over a shirt and tie. Instead of slacks, she wore a knee-length black skirt and white stockings. The sweater had a patch with DISPATCH sewn onto the breast.

"Hey, Priest," Riley said as she rinsed out her milk glass. "First day at private school?"

"I feel ridiculous."

"You look fantastic," I assured her. "I'm sure that when people call in for help, they appreciate having you on the other end of the line. I know that if I was in trouble I would want to hear your voice."

Priest smiled. "Only because it would mean Riley is right behind me."

I couldn't deny that. "That too."

Riley said, "I'm almost ready to go."

"Go," I said. "I'll finish the dishes."

She kissed my cheek, whispered that she loved me in my ear, and followed Priest out of the apartment. I finished with the dishes not long after and gathered my things to head in myself. I hoped toxicology had sent back their results from Delgado's case. His investigation was on hold until we knew if the victim had been drugged or not. I was almost to the door when my cell phone rang, and I had to stop so I could fish it out of my bag.

"This is Dr. Hunt."

"Dr. Hunt! I'm so very glad I caught you. This is Warden Quinn Mackintosh from the prison. I was hoping you might be able to assist me in a sensitive situation."

I frowned. "The prison?"

"Yes, Doctor. There was an incident this morning in the Infirmary. Our doctor was mortally wounded by an inmate who then proceeded to attack several other patients."

"My God. How many were killed?"

"Six dead, another four badly wounded. The attacker was killed by guards. We were hoping you would be able to come to us rather than shipping the bodies to your morgue. We want to keep the situation as contained as possible until we have a better idea of what the hell happened this morning. Ordinarily we would have our own physician do the examination, but..."

I nodded. "Yes, of course. Um... yes. I'll find someone to fill in for me at the morgue." I tried to remember where exactly the prison was and how long it would take me to get there. "Give me an hour to get my assistant."

"Thank you, Dr. Hunt."

I hung up and stared at the phone. Six people dead at the prison, another four wounded. I tried to tell myself it had nothing to do with Riley, but I couldn't quite make it believable. I took out my phone and started down the stairs again. I called my assistant Gabriel and asked him to get the van ready to go for an on-site examination. He promised to have it ready to go by the time I got there, and I was in the car before I could dial Riley.

"Have you heard the prison attack?"

"Yeah, Briggs just called me about it. I guess you got a call, too?"

"Yeah. I'm heading in to pick up Gabe and the van. Any chance you'll be assigned to investigate? I know you're on light duty since Priest has been reassigned..."

Riley said, "I'll do what I can to get myself put on it."

"I appreciate it. And Priest?"

"I asked Briggs, but no matter what happens she's stuck in the basement. I'll call you when I know for sure who is coming. Be careful, baby."

I smiled. "Why? Just because I'm going into a gated building full of people you put there? I'll be careful, I promise. Talk to you soon. Love you."

"Love you, too."

I hung up and started the car, hoping it would turn out to be just an ordinary day. An ordinary day investigating six victims of a brutal attack at the prison.

The Hobbes Correctional Facility was a ten-floor tower with four wings radiating from a central column in the form of a cross. I had been there before, responding to shiv attacks or suicides, but I always felt a little odd pulling up to the gate and figuratively knocking to be let inside. It didn't matter what I was there for, a part of me always worried they wouldn't let me back out. Gabe and I showed our credentials at the front gate and waited as drug dogs sniffed the undercarriage of the ME van.

After a brief glimpse into the back of the truck, the guard pointed us in the right direction. Gabe was driving and I noticed he had a bit of a white-knuckle grip on the wheel as he guided us toward the garage.

"You've never been here before, have you?"

He shook his head and smiled self-consciously. "Kind of hoped to go my whole life without getting inside these walls."

"Well, you're here as one of the good guys. Take comfort in that." I patted his arm and got out of the truck to meet Warden Mackintosh. He was new to the job, having recently taken over for the warden I was used to dealing with on these trips. The new warden was a few inches shorter than me with thick white hair that matched his seersucker suit. He reminded me of Ben Matlock without the folksy accent.

"Warden Mackintosh? Dr. Gillian Hunt. This is Gabriel Leighton."

"Thank you for coming. Right this way." He turned and led us toward the elevator. "We've kept the med center completely blocked off since the attack. No one in or out, but we moved the survivors to a nearby surgical theater where they could continue to receive medical care without compromising the scene over-much."

The elevator took us up to the third floor, where a uniformed officer again checked the tag clipped to my collar before motioning us through. I suppose getting to that point and standing beside the warden wasn't enough of a clue we belonged there. We ducked under the tape that cordoned off the entire infirmary and I saw why the crime scene had been extended so far. Blood was smeared on the wall just inside the entrance, and everything on the admission desk was knocked to the floor.

"What the hell happened here?"

Warden Mackintosh motioned over one of the men guarding the stairwell. He looked shell-shocked to me, eyes on the floor as he approached and then drifting from point to point to avoid settling on anyone in particular. The warden seemed not to notice.

"This is Tyler Conrad. He was on duty when it happened and he was fortunate enough to avoid injury. Tyler?"

"Shouldn't I wait for the detectives?"

"Just give them the basics."

He sighed heavily, thumbs hooked on his belt, and he

shrugged. "At about 0530, a patient was complaining of stomach pains. Doc said it was appendicitis, brought him in here. He was doubled-over, looked like he was about to pass out. But then, soon as he got through the doors, dude went ballistic. He grabbed a pen and stabbed the nurse with it, then he jumped one of the guards. Took his gun. Shot him." He swallowed hard, his Adam's apple bobbing as he composed himself.

"Seems he kept upgrading," Mackintosh said as the guard composed himself. "He went from the pen to the gun, then he got hold of a scalpel."

"He went from a gun to a scalpel?" I asked.

"Wanted to spend more time with his victims," Tyler said quietly. "He kept the gun, though. I'd have drawn on him immediately, but he kept waving the gun around with his other hand... I didn't want to risk it."

Mackintosh put a hand on the poor kid's shoulder. "We know, Ty. It's all right. You did what you could."

"Who finally stopped him?"

"One of the patients. She grabbed the gun and got sliced up real good until she twisted the gun around and used it on him."

"Did she survive?"

"Yeah. Our nurses are keeping her in one piece..."

I nodded. "I'd like to see her first, if I could. All of the survivors, in fact. If there's anything I can do to help them, I think they've waited long enough."

"Of course. This way."

He led us through the bloody public area. Several of the beds in the emergency section were painted with streaks of spattered blood. We reached the operating theater where the survivors of the attack had been gathered, a half-dozen beds dotting the perimeter of the room like a scene from a refugee camp. One female inmate had both arms bandaged from her fingers to the elbow and a gauze pad covered her cheek.

Something about her red hair struck me as familiar, but still I sucked in a breath when she turned to face me. I recognized her, but refused to react. She was paler than she'd been when she was arrested and, though she had always been thin, she was now swimming in the small-sized hospital gown they had put her in. She smiled when she saw me and chuckled.

"Ever get the feeling some things are just meant to happen?"

"Hello, Abigail. Looks like you ended up on the wrong side of the knife this time."

Abigail Shepherd, former mayor's aide, had taken the fall for the murders of a Good Girl and an undercover detective. And, as Riley found out, also planned to take part in my murder. I felt cold as she stared at me, knowing the mind behind those eyes had planned how to kill me and, if not for Riley making the ultimate sacrifice, would have succeeded.

"Doc?"

I looked at Gabriel and shook my head once. I would be fine. I put my bag on the table and opened it.

"So you were the one who stopped the rampage?"

"Yeah. Not exactly surprising. He took the time to talk to me, gave me the opening I needed to get the jump on him."

"He stopped to talk to you? What makes you so special?"

She smiled with one side of her mouth, the side that wasn't encumbered by the gauze on her cheek. "Because I was his target. I'm the only person he was supposed to kill. I wouldn't talk to him, but if you're willing to hear what I have to say... let's talk."

I could hear the siren on Riley's car through the phone. She'd signed out a squad car since they commanded more respect and could get her through the early-morning traffic faster. "If she wasn't so torn up, I'd agree with you," I told her. "It stinks of a set-up. But she was hurt very badly. The cut to her face goes straight through her cheek. Even if she'd made that sacrifice, the cut was hasty and clean. No hesitation marks, no sign that it was anything she would have willingly had done to her."

"She's a psychopath, Jill." Riley sounded hollow and faraway, a result of using the speakerphone as she tore through the street. "She could have just gotten someone and told them not to pay attention if she said stop."

"I understand that. But there's something different about her. She was originally taken to the infirmary for withdrawal symptoms. The doctor has no idea what she was addicted to because there's no sign of anything in her system, but the reactions are too intense to be faked."

Riley thought for a moment. "Possession? It has to be an option. Maybe a demon hopped into her body to make her look ill—"

"I can't find any evidence of that. I used those sigils Caitlin gave me, but they never reacted to her presence." Well, other than making the bitch laugh while I drew on her bed sheet with my eyeliner. "I think she's... well, as up-and-up as she can get. She's putting on a brave front, but she's scared, Riley. She's acting tough, and she's putting on a good show, but the strongest thing I'm getting from her is *fear*."

"Okay. I'll trust your judgment on that. I'm still about twenty minutes away."

"I'll see you then." I hung up and left the office I'd used to make the call. Gabriel was tending to the other survivors, but I'd given him strict instructions to stay away from Abby's bed. She was watching him stitch a wound on another patient's hand and she slowly turned her head toward me as I returned to the room.

"Well. Done asking your girlfriend if we can play together? Hope she said yes!" Her derisive smile never reached her eyes, which were still the eyes of a frightened little girl. I hated this woman for what she had done. I knew that she had either killed Annora Good or Wanda Kane, and I despised her. But at that moment my instinct was to hug her and tell her everything would be okay.

"She's not my girlfriend, she's my wife." I stood next to her bed. "Why did Mayor Siskin send someone to kill you?"

"Hm." She smiled at some inner joke, then raised an eyebrow. "Maybe it was my winning personality?"

"Okay..." I lowered my voice for the next question. "Why were you having withdrawal symptoms? Doctors couldn't find anything in your system. Maybe it was something you couldn't tell him about but I would believe. What were you addicted to before you came here?"

She gave me another half-smile. "A charming little concoction of Emily's devising." Her gaze became distant, and she looked sideways at me. "Emily. Is she still...?"

"Mayor Siskin's aide? Yes. Is there a reason she wouldn't be?"

"Hm. Wishful thinking."

I held up my tools. "I'm going to suture the injury to your cheek. Will you let me do it, or do I have to worry about you biting me?"

"Go ahead." She looked at the needle. "Will it scar?"

"At least a little... probably a lot. A wound that grievous doesn't tend to heal without leaving a little permanent damage."

"If there's any way to make it scar worse, will you do it?"

I was offended at the implication. "No. I may be a medical examiner, but I'm competent to work on live patients. And I would never scar a patient out of petty~"

"No. I'm asking. If there's a way to make it scar more, will you do it?"

For the first time, her face seemed to match what I sense brewing inside her head. She looked scared, hurt, angry... she looked like a completely different person.

"I'm sorry, no. I won't scar you any more than I have to." She pressed her lips together, shrugged, and looked away from me. "Abigail... when Riley gets here, please let her help you."

"Do you think she can?"

I nodded. "I've lived in this city for a very long time. I've seen a lot of people try to make a difference, and I've seen all of them disappear. They don't go in blazes of glory, they just vanish. They go away. But Riley keeps coming back. Sometimes she wins, sometimes she loses, but she always gets back up and starts fighting again. If there's a way to help you, she'll find it. And even if it's near-impossible, she'll get closer than anyone else."

"Lark is so strong," she said softly.

"Riley is stronger."

"You don't know that."

"I do. Trust me, I do. Lark Siskin fights dirty, and she hits below the belt. She plays on her opponent's emotions. Do you know who does that? Weak people. People who have nothing else to rely on. She went after the Good Girls and another cop and me because she couldn't come at Riley head-on. She was scared of Riley. And with your help, we can make her terrified."

Abby stared at her and then, slowly, she began to nod. "Are you going to sew up my cheek or what?"

I held eye contact with her for another moment and then nodded. "Hold your head still."

I had just finished suturing her wound when a guard arrived with the warden. "Dr. Hunt, the detective assigned to the case has just arrived. I'll leave Michael here with you and escort them up. Will you be all right?"

"Yes, I'll be fine. You said them... there are two detectives?" I was still hoping that Riley had found a way to bring Caitlin along, but the warden shook his head.

"No, apparently Detective Parra arrived at the same time as Mayor Siskin."

Abby tensed. "Lark's here?"

Warden Mackintosh nodded. "It seems she was concerned about you. It doesn't seem to be a publicity stunt, either... no camera crew, no press. It seems like a sincere welfare check."

I wasn't so sure and, judging from the fear in Abby's eyes, she wasn't either. For a moment I put aside my animosity and touched her hand. She wasn't a cop killer, and she hadn't killed the lover of Aissa's friend. She was just my patient, and she was frightened.

"She won't do anything with Riley here."

"You're wrong. She'll find a way to get you and Detective Parra out of the room and when you come back I'll be dead. A poison, or smothering me with a pillow, or..." She clenched her jaw and I saw the tendons rise in her neck. She looked at my kit and somehow I knew that she didn't intend to harm me if she grabbed a scalpel. I knew that any weapon she took would be used against Siskin... or against herself. I picked up the bag and moved it away from her.

"Why are you so scared of her?"

"Because of what she made me into. Because of what she is. Don't let her in here, Dr. Hunt. Please."

I heard the bell announcing the elevator. There was an anteroom where Riley and Lark were forced to sign in, separated from us by the bloody corridor. I left Abby's bedside, cursing myself as I hurried through the space between us. Riley signed in and glanced up to see me coming as Lark bent down to add her name to the visitor's list. Riley was missing her holster, most likely checked in at the front desk before they let her into the building.

"Hey, Jill," Riley said.

The door to the admissions area was glass, so I could see her smile of greeting turn to confusion as I slammed it in her face.

Warden Mackintosh stepped between Riley and the door as I locked it. "Dr. Hunt, what is the meaning of this?"

"I'm sorry. I can't let you in."

"Why in the world not?" Mackintosh asked.

Lark stood behind Riley, tall and elegant in a black pantsuit. Her ash-white hair was pulled back and smoothed down, giving her a deaths-head visage that I would have found unsettling even if she wasn't lurking over my wife's left shoulder. Riley looked back at Lark, looked at me, and stepped forward.

"Jill, is this about~" Her voice was made hollow by the thick bullet-resistant glass between us.

"I just want to talk to the patient in private."

"Who is the patient?"

"They didn't tell you? Do you know why the mayor is here?"

"I have suspicions."

I said, "It's Abby Shepherd. She doesn't want to see... anyone... at the moment. She's been traumatized. I want to give her a few minutes before I subject her to anything as exhausting as visitors."

Mackintosh huffed. "And for that you have to take my entire medical center hostage? Honestly, Dr. Hunt, there's no call for this."

"Actually, sir, there is." I wet my lips, unwilling to call the mayor out in front of a stranger. I looked at Riley. "I know this detective, sir. She can be an ornery bitch who insists on getting her way. Even if she promises not to speak with the patient, one way or another I know she'll find a way."

Lark rolled her eyes. ÒWarden, these two are married."

ÒYes," I admitted, Òand that puts me in a special position to know just how devious she can be. Right now I'm not her wife, I'm a doctor. And it's my professional opinion that Detective Parra not be allowed to visit the patient until I'm finished with my work."

Riley seemed to be biting the inside of her cheek to prevent herself from smiling. "What if I gave you my word that I'd be on my best behavior?"

"I only need a few minutes, Warden. I'll complete my treatment of Ms. Shepherd's wounds and when I think she can handle the stimuli, I'll let the detective and the mayor in."

"This is highly unusual, Dr. Hunt."

"I'm aware of that, sir, but it's an unusual set of circumstances. Maybe Detective Parra could investigate the culprit's cell in the meantime. There might be evidence that points to why he did what he did."

Mackintosh considered the suggestion, and Riley finally took the choice away from him. "If the witnesses aren't ready to talk, I don't want to force them. I can take a few minutes to check out the cell. I'd hate to be ornery." She glared playfully at me and I fought the urge to wink.

Siskin said, "Warden, I'd like to remain here if that's all right. I have no reason to take part in the search, and I would very much like to speak to my former aide as soon as the good doctor decides she's capable of receiving visitors."

"Fine by me," I said. "But you stay out there."

She stared at me, unblinking. I shamefully lost our staring contest and locked eyes with Riley. I saw trust there, confidence that I was doing the right thing even if she didn't understand it. She nodded very slightly, just enough that I'm sure only I noticed it. She turned to the warden and indicated for him to lead the way back to the elevator. He hesitated before following.

"I expect full access to my med center when I get back, Dr. Hunt. You have half an hour at the outside. Understood?"

"Yes, sir."

When he and Riley had left, Siskin stepped closer to the door. Her breath fogged the glass when she spoke.

"Gutsy move, Dr. Hunt."

"Have a seat, Madam Mayor. Read a magazine." I turned my back on her and walked back to the theatre.

Gabriel had been seeing to the other patients while I tended Abby's wounds, and he'd stopped to watch the confrontation at the doors.

"Is everything all right, Dr. Hunt?"

"Yes, Gabe. Everything's fine."

"The... ornery detective. That was your wife, wasn't it?"

"Yes. And she has been known to be ornery in my experience. We only have half an hour before these people have to be questioned, and I'd like them to be comfortable when it happens. If you don't mind taking up the slack..."

"Not at all, Doc." He smiled as he turned back to the next patient.

I stood next to Abby's bed and crossed my arms. "I bought you a half hour. I know it will be difficult to speak with that injury, but if you want Riley to go out on a limb for you and protect you from the mayor, she's going to need a damn good reason. She's proven to be very... vindictive recently, and I don't want Riley taking the risk without reason. Convince me."

She stared at the wall for a long moment, then reached up to touch the bandage over the cheek I'd just sewn shut. She held her hand there, as if holding it together, as she began to speak.

"My name isn't really Abby Shepherd. Lark gave me that name as a... joke, I guess. I was born Abigail Ross. I was a pastor at a church in a town south of here. I was married... we were trying to get pregnant. Then one day Lark Siskin walks in and asks for a private consultation. I told her that our church didn't have confessional, but I was more than willing to offer her advice if I could. God, if only I'd just sent her away."

She looked wistfully toward the front of the med center. From her position she couldn't see Lark, but I could. The mayor was pacing in front of the locked door, arms crossed over her chest, eyeing the ground as if counting off the seconds in her head.

"She asked if I ever had a crisis of faith. I told her that I was only human, so of course... of course I had crises. It's why it's called faith; challenging it can sometimes strengthen its core. Faith isn't blindly following the Scripture but examining it and... hm." She closed her eyes and tilted her head to one side. "I'm sorry."

"Don't be," I said.

"We became friends. Or at least friendly. And then one night she came to my home and said she had proof. Of everything. God, Satan, angels, demons. She said that I could replace my faith with certainty. I let her. God help me, I let her show me the truth. She took me to meet someone she said was Ôfrom the other realm,' and we talked until the morning. I didn't call my husband to tell him where I was because I hardly noticed any time had passed. I thought it was an angel. I had no reason to think otherwise. He spoke to me of true closeness, of a true communion, and I fell for it. I was naked before I understood what he was doing, and by then it was too late to stop him. He and Lark... he..."

I let her voice trail off. After a moment, she began again.

"Afterward they told me the truth. He was a demon, and I was pregnant with his child. I didn't believe them until I got a positive pregnancy test, and I immediately aborted it. I told no one what I had done, I even drove two hundred miles and told my husband I was at a conference. I went to some back-alley shithole to have the procedure. The next time I stood in front of my congregation, I began to bleed. My husband and a couple of parishioners took me to the hospital, where the doctor confirmed my ovaries had been damaged due to the abortion. My congregation shunned me. My husband demanded to know why I would terminate, and I was forced to tell him the baby wasn't his. He left me. I was considering suicide - yet another of my basic beliefs abandoned - when Lark returned to me.

"She wanted me for something. She told me that she had broken me down in order to build me back up into what she required. She apologized for everything... bathed me... made me feel loved again. Everyone in the world had abandoned me but Lark gave me peace and comfort. At that point I would have followed her anywhere, even though it was her fault I had fallen so far. I made love to her as a way of punishing myself, showing myself that I was no longer the woman I'd once been."

I turned around and looked at the woman in the anteroom. She looked up and met my eye, and I felt as if I was going to be sick when she smiled as if she knew what I was hearing. Maybe she could tell from the look on my face how much she disgusted me.

"A few months later she gave me an opportunity. She said that I could do to someone what had been done to me. I refused, but she told me that it was someone I had once considered an enemy. Emily Graves, who you know as Emily Simon. She lived in the town where I had my church. An atheist and a chemist, she believed in the physical world. We went to school together and we'd butted heads in the past. It was a small town, and we were both large personalities. Lark gave me the opportunity to destroy the foundations of her beliefs. I was eager. It seemed like retribution. So I helped Lark. We shattered everything she believed in and left her a-shambles. And I was so goddamned proud of it."

She touched her cheek again. She had been speaking from the undamaged side of her mouth and gently worked her jaw to alleviate the soreness.

"Lark took Emily in as another pet. She started making minor suggestions to us. We cut our hair the same way, wore matching outfits... we let her change our names. Shepherd because I used to be a pastor. Emily was named Simon after the man who was forced to carry Jesus' cross in the Bible. After a few years Lark suggested more drastic changes. She wanted my chin to be narrower so that it matched Emily's, and she wanted Emily's cheekbones to be higher to match mine. One procedure, then another. Then one day I looked in the mirror and saw the face I recognized as Emily's, and she saw the same thing when she looked at me. We weren't people any more.

"Somehow that made everything... easier. I wasn't a fallen pastor who had given up everything I'd worked for. The woman doing such sinful things with Lark and Emily was a different entity. Abigail Ross died and I was just some thing that had taken her place. After that Lark told us she had another plan that she required us for. She showed us a vial and told us that she'd been injecting it for years. It gave her vigor, heightened intelligence, maintained her youthful appearance... she sold it as a cosmetic aid, so we didn't argue when she said she wanted to inject us with it."

She was quiet for so long that I was forced to speak. "What was it really?"

"Oh, it was what she said. It gave us strength and let us go days without sleep. It took us a while to notice, but we didn't age. We became addicted to it, begging Lark for even the smallest injection.

That's when she told us what it was. Angel blood. She'd gotten it from the demon that impregnated me, but the supply was running low. She needed a source of her own. She had brought Emily into the fold to make a synthetic, but she wanted me to help her summon an angel so she could have a steady supply of her own."

I stepped away from the bed. "Tell me you didn't."

"I was her puppet by that point. She told me to have sex with Emily while she watched, and I did. Not because I wanted to, but because Lark wanted me to. Once she had us hooked on the blood, we would have done anything she asked just to get a fix. Eventually we did whatever she asked just because she asked. When she told me to kill Annora Good, I had no feelings about it. It was just another task put before me by my mistress. And when I was done, I was so *proud*."

"So you're still hooked on the blood?"

"Mm. No. A synthetic Emily created. But we did summon an angel. We did it the day after Lark became mayor. She closed off a room of her loft and set aside a four-by-four square in the center. She then had... she forced..." She trembled violently, her eyes closed as she recoiled from the memory. "She made Emily and me do awful things everywhere else in the room. Debauched things. We desecrated every inch of that room except for the space in the center. Then she summoned the angel and I snared him. Since then she's been siphoning off his blood a little at a time while her demonic handler tortures him every hour of the day."

"Why do you still need the angel's blood if you have the synthetic?"

"Because of how powerful it is. She's building up a storehouse of it and when the time is right, she will unleash it on No Man's Land. She wanted me and Emily to be the distributors, to create the foundation of addiction in the city. The criminals would become unstoppable monsters. The remaining police would buckle under the strain. The police would be crushed and then, when the criminals go into withdrawal because their supply dries up, they'll just die off as well."

I was stuck on one word. "Why did you say 'the remaining police'?"

She looked at me. "I didn't."

I closed the distance between us and put my hand against the wall, leaning in close to her face. I tried to channel Riley's indignant spirit. "You said 'the remaining police would buckle under the strain.' What does that mean? What's going to happen to the police force?" She continued to stare at me. "Look, you wanted to talk to me. You wanted to tell me about what Lark made you do. You went into withdrawal because you didn't have your drug, and she tried to kill you to keep you silent. Don't protect her now."

"She..."

I noticed her look past me but didn't think anything of it until a pair of very strong hands grabbed my shoulders and hauled me away from the bed. I was spun around, too stunned to react as someone shoved me against the wall. I was dazed enough that I didn't even block the blow to my stomach, bent over and retching as my attacker straightened me up and pressed me flat against the wall again.

"Dr. Hunt!" Gabriel's voice was shrill, but all I could see was Lark Siskin's face, pink with rage, her eyes wide as they stared into mine.

"Stay where you are, boy, or I'll have you working in a vet's office cleaning up after the neuterings." Lark grabbed my face, squeezing my cheeks until my lips were pursed. "What has my little pet been telling you, Doctor?"

"The truth."

"The truth as she remembers it. She's a very ill young woman. A junkie. Her memory can't be trusted."

I twisted away from her grip, but she had me pinned to the wall. Angel blood strength, I supposed. "Cut the bullshit, Lark. You and I both know what we're dealing with here. Why beat around the bush? I know what you are, and I know what you did to get to this point. You're one sick bitch, you know that?"

She smiled. "That's a matter of opinion, Dr. Hunt."

"I also know what you're wondering. I know what makes you wake up in the middle of the night and think about how vulnerable you are."

"And what would that be."

"You're wondering why I'm still here. You had it all planned out, didn't you? No one could stop you. And then suddenly I was still alive and one of your pets took the fall for a botched plan you *knew* should have been successful. Riley was suddenly the winner, Marchosias gave you a spanking, and you didn't understand why. Or how. And you still don't. And that terrifies you. It makes you wonder if Riley is too strong for you."

Lark tried to smile, but our faces were too close for her to fake it. "And what makes you think I'm frightened of her?"

"What you do in the next ten seconds will prove you are."

She started to say something else, but she was cut off by Riley. Her voice was dark, cold, and brooked no argument as she spoke six short words.

"Get your hands off my wife."

I saw the fear in Lark's eyes, and the anger a moment later when she knew I'd seen it. There was a crack in the ice queen. She released me and took a step back, and Riley grabbed her shoulder to pull her the rest of the way off. Lark stumbled, tripped over her right foot, and went tumbling onto the ground. She landed hard on her ass, with me and Riley standing over her. The warden stared at the scene in shock, an expression matched across the room by Gabriel. Riley stepped over Lark and put her hand on my shoulder. Our eyes met, and we spoke without speaking.

Are you okay?

I'm fine.

Are you sure?

Yes. Fine.

She accepted that I was unhurt and finally looked down at the mayor. "You may want to watch your step next time, Madam Mayor."

The warden helped her stand, and she angrily brushed off her suit. "I would like to speak to my former aide now, if you don't mind. In private."

"I don't think that's a very good idea," I said.

Lark glared at me. "Why don't we let the warden decide?"

He didn't look happy to be put in the middle of what was obviously a very tense situation, but he cleared his throat and ran a hand through his thick hair. "Um. I-I don't see any reason to deny the request. Dr. Hunt, were you finished with your examination?"

I wanted to say no, but one look at Abigail revealed she would contradict me. The woman I'd been speaking to was nowhere to be seen, replaced by a sycophant in the presence of her leader. She was looking at Lark, the rest of the people in the room having disappeared as far as she was concerned.

"I'll leave it up to the patient."

Abigail smiled with one half of her mouth. "Lark... I've missed you."

"I've missed you, too."

That was enough for the warden. "There's a prep room just

through here where you can get a little privacy. Dr. Hunt, would you help get Ms. Shepherd out of her bed, please?" I helped Abigail stand, letting her lean against me until Riley brought over a wheelchair.

I knelt next to her and made eye contact with her. "You don't have to do this, Abby. You don't have to speak to her."

"Yes, I do. I want to." She leaned in and, for a moment, I thought she intended to kiss me. I tensed, but she continued past my cheek to my ear. "Her demon is Leraje. The angel he is torturing is Pahaliah. They are on the twelfth floor of the penthouse in a warded room. Though Emily is your enemy, she is also a victim. Will you tell Detective Parra to remember that when the time comes?"

"I will."

I stood and Lark took a position behind the wheelchair. She led Abby into the side room the warden had indicated, away from the other patients. The door closed and I returned to Riley, and she put her hands on my cheeks and made me look at her.

"Are you really okay?"

I gripped her wrists and nodded. "I am. She sucker punched me, the bitch, but I'll recover." I looked over my shoulder to see the warden was speaking with Gabriel. I lowered my voice so he wouldn't overhear. "We have to talk in private. She told me a lot before Lark broke in. Names, locations..."

"Okay. We'll talk about that later on."

"Riley... you know what Lark is doing in there. She's finishing the job."

Riley nodded. "We'll talk later, but yeah. Evidence is pointing to that."

"We can't just let Lark kill her."

"It's not that simple, Gillian." She took my hand and squeezed, and I stepped into her embrace. I closed my eyes and waited for the inevitable.

Less than a minute later, it happened. An alarm began to sound at the nurses' station, and Lark opened the door we had just closed behind her.

"Dr. Hunt, I think something is happening."

I shoved past her and ran into the prep room. Abby's wheelchair had fallen on its side, dumping her on the floor where she had started seizing. Her limbs were stiff as boards, and a fine froth forming on her lips. I did what I could to save her, but I knew

I wouldn't be able to get her heart started again. I finally surrendered to the inevitable and rested my hand on her unbandaged cheek.

"What the hell did you give her?" Lark didn't respond, so I stood up and lunged at her. I got into her personal space, bullying her like we were teenagers in a schoolyard. "What did you give her?"

Warden Mackintosh put an arm between us, a move that was about as effective as one might expect. Lark reeled back slightly but managed to stand her ground. I didn't know what I planned to do, if I wanted to fight her or just knock her down, but I was saved from making a decision by Riley. She grabbed my shoulders and hauled me off, walking me away and putting her lips against my ear. When my anger faded, I heard her speaking in a soft whisper.

"Stop. Stop, Jill. Let it go."

"She killed her, Riley."

"I know. There's nothing we can do now. There's nothing to do. Don't make it worse for yourself. Just let it go, sweetheart."

I leaned my weight against her and fought back my anger and sadness. When I trusted myself not to attack her again, I stepped back and touched Riley's arm as a show of gratitude. I held on to her like an anchor and looked back to Abigail Ross. I wouldn't... and couldn't... think of her by that other name now. The warden looked prepared to try and stop another assault, while Siskin was trying not to look overly pleased with herself for my outburst.

"Warden, I'd like to begin the autopsy as soon as possible, please."

"Of course."

Lark said, "I hope you find something," in a way that told me she knew I wouldn't. Whatever she had used would be untraceable, but I had to try. I owed her at least that much.

I left the prison at dusk. The backup doctor had arrived, freeing me and Gabriel to do our work on the deceased prisoners. As expected, Abby's autopsy didn't reveal any foul play. I found nothing to indicate Lark had poisoned her. I was forced to label the cause of death as inconclusive, but I took a little solace in assigning the manner of death as "suspicious circumstances." Riley remained much longer than I expected her to, and I assumed she would catch a bit of grief from Lieutenant Briggs, but there wasn't much for her to investigate in this case. The killer's identity was undeniable, his motivations clear, and the crime scene was a contained environment. Case closed.

I asked Gabriel to drive the van back to the morgue. In the garage, I touched Riley's shoulder. "Can I ride with you?"

"Sure." She put her arm around me, kissed my cheek, and I felt the emotion of the day wash over me. I sagged against her as we walked to the car. She got me into the passenger seat and we sat silently until my tears dried up. She was twisted in the seat to hold my hand, her other hand on the back of my neck to massage the tension away.

"Thanks," I whispered.

"Hey, you've held me enough times. It's your turn."

I smiled and brought her hand to my lips. I kissed the knuckles and brushed the back of her hand against my cheek.

"I can't believe she got away with it."

"Yeah. But sometimes there's nothing you can do. If Lark hadn't killed her, she would have just tried again, or Abby would have tried again, and~"

I looked at her. "What?"

"Abby would..." She looked at me for another moment. "She didn't tell you?"

"Tell me...?"

Riley took an evidence bag out of her jacket pocket and handed it to me. Inside was a folded sheet of paper, folded so that I could only read one quarter of it. "~cut her face as badly as you want. Make sure she's disfigured." I was sickened by that little bit, glad I couldn't read the whole thing as I handed it back. "That's disgusting."

"I found it in the attacker's cell. I compared the handwriting, sweetheart. It matches Abigail Shepherd. For some reason she not only ordered her own assassination, she specifically asked to have her face cut up."

I closed my eyes. "I know why."

"Do you want to talk about it?"

I swallowed hard and looked out the window. "Drive. Maybe by the time we get home I'll be able to talk."

"Okay." She stroked my cheek again and started the car.

As we pulled out of the garage, I was grateful we had a long trip back home.

This is why I love my wife:

She called her boss to put off the paperwork on the case and drove me home. She undressed me, put me in a bath, washed my skin, and then put me to bed. When I woke, she was sitting on the floor next to the bed. Asleep and holding my hand. I cradled her head until she woke and climbed into bed beside me. She spooned me from behind and we lay in silence until I chose to speak.

"I know you hate her. I know she was a bad person, and she killed good people, but I~"

"You felt for her. I don't know what she said, but she made you feel compassion for her. I won't make you feel bad for that. You found something to mourn in a woman the rest of us wrote off as irredeemable." She kissed my neck. "It makes me love you more."

I took a deep breath. "She told me so much awful shit. I don't want it in my head."

"Then give it to me."

"I don't want it in your head, either. There's too much already in there."

She stroked my hair away from my face and kissed my cheek. "I'm not just the city's champion; I'm yours. In fact, I'm your champion first and foremost. I can handle it."

I took a deep breath and began to share. When I got to the names of the captive angel and the demon torturing him, Riley took out her phone and made a note. I loved her for not interrupting and for making a note so I wouldn't have to go back and repeat any part. I shifted onto my back when I was done, and she looked down at me.

"I know why she did it."

"Want to share?"

I inhaled and looked at my hands. "Lark took over her life. The drug, even the torture, became a part of her existence. She didn't know who she was without Lark. So when they were separated, she felt like a non-entity. That's why she told the attacker to cut up her face. It was a reminder of what she'd lost every time she saw it in the mirror. She didn't want to wear it anymore." I looked into Riley's eyes. "I've felt the same way."

She looked horrified, and I was sorry for dropping it that way.

"Not... not in any real sense of planning or anything like that. But when I met you, my life completely changed, Riley. In an instant, in a heartbeat, I became your partner. When you asked me to marry you, saying yes felt like a foregone conclusion. We were meant to spend the rest of our lives together. So when this deadline came along, and I started counting down the days you had left, I thought... about if... I wanted to go on afterward. You're giving your life so I could live on, but part of me wondered if life would be worth living after you were gone. Please don't..." I wiped the tear off her cheek. "Don't cry."

"Tell me you changed your mind."

"I did. Well... not officially. I never actually said I was going to end my life when you were gone. But it was a possibility. But I wouldn't squander the gift you gave me." I reached up and touched her other cheek. It was wet, but I hadn't seen the tear because that side of her face was in shadow. "I'll wait. And one day I'll see you again. And I know that no matter how long it takes, it'll be worth the wait."

"Wherever I end up, I'll find you."

I smiled. "I love you, Riley."

"I love you, too." She kissed me, and I held onto her for a good long time before I let her go. She settled against me again, and I kissed her forehead.

"Priest probably should know about those names."

"Yes. But it can wait until tomorrow."

I smiled. "Yes. I think it probably can."

That night I dreamt of angels and demons, of Riley bleeding on my couch when she was still just one detective out of many that I worked with. But that was a lie. Riley was never just another cop. She had always been special, and I had always been a little more thrilled when she showed up at a crime scene instead of Timbale or Harding. Because I was attracted to her, yes. But also because... she was a special person. Something in me sensed that. And, in my dream, I wondered if maybe this was part of a cycle. If we'd lived other lives and found each other in this one because of the remnants from that past existence.

I hoped so. I hoped there was a continuous circle of life waiting for us when this life ended. And I hoped that when this life was over, I was given a chance to find Riley so I could love her all over again.

I remembered waking at two-thirty and feeling mostly awake due to falling asleep early. I used the bathroom and took off Riley's clothes without waking her. I pulled the blankets over us both and fell asleep even as I mentally discounted the possibility of getting any more sleep that night. The next time I woke Riley had shifted in my arms and had her head against my chest. The clock told me it was too close to the alarm to get any more sleep or to wake Riley with sex, so I just held her and looked over her shoulder at the sunlight cutting through the window.

Four hundred and sixty-two days left.

And counting.

WORMWOOD

ZOE BRIGGS eyed Riley and then looked back at the report in front of her. After a moment she carefully put it down and folded her hands on top of it. "I accept a lot of things from you, Riley. You've proven yourself too many times for me to doubt much of what you say. I believe Lark Siskin is your opposite number for the... bad guys." She glanced at the office door to make sure it was closed, but she still kept her voice low. "But this is a little out there, even for me. I don't think you're contesting the autopsy report, unless you think Siskin manipulated your wife's findings..."

"No. I know the autopsy report says Abigail Shepherd was killed by complications from surgery. And I know that doesn't mean anything. Mayor Siskin has unique resources. She could easily have killed her without leaving any evidence. Abby had started talking to Gillian, giving up secrets. Siskin couldn't let that happen, so the second she got Abigail alone, she killed her."

"I believe you. But I can't justify opening a case, no matter how quiet I try to keep it. Word will get around that I have a detective investigating the mayor. She slapped Priest down to dispatch for refusing to shake her hand. What the hell do you think she'll do to you if... no. She won't do anything to you, because that's not her style. She'd do it to me. Where do you think I'd end up, Detective Parra?"

Riley leaned back in her seat.

"I've given you a lot of leeway in the past, and that won't change. But going against a reporter like Gail Finney is very different from trying to take down the mayor. Especially when she's proven herself to be a vindictive bitch."

"Yeah. Is there any progress on getting Priest back?"

Briggs grunted and shrugged. "It took a couple of weeks but I finally got a face-to-face meeting with the commissioner. Turns out Mayor Siskin is crafty as well as vindictive. She used Priest's incident reports to justify the move, as well as my own performance reviews of her. According to anyone who was asked, Caitlin Priest is a compassionate, kind, soothing presence. What better representative to have manning the phone lines?" She made a face. "I'm working on it. But right now Commissioner Benedict likes the idea of having detectives do a stint in the coalmines now and then."

"Great. I'll brush up on my phone skills when it's my turn to suffer."

"Maybe you'll get lucky and die before that happens." Briggs tensed suddenly. "Good God. Riley, I'm so sorry. I didn't~"

Riley held up a hand. "You're under a lot of stress. Besides, I was thinking the same thing. Everyone else is tiptoeing around the fact I'm not long for this world." She smiled. "I kind of like the blunt approach."

"It was uncalled for. But I'm glad you weren't offended. I just haven't been sleeping very well."

"Everything okay?"

"As okay as it can be. You and Priest gave me hope, Riley. I was a bad detective, and I think I'm just a mediocre lieutenant." She lifted a finger to stop Riley from speaking up. "I'm not fishing for compliments. For the best part of my career I was a pawn of a criminal organization, so anything you say would come off hollow. I came here and you gave me hope for the first time in a long time. You and Priest seemed capable of doing anything. Now you're both leaving, and I'm... depressed and sad. I'm actually kind of happy Priest hasn't been here for the past few weeks because it's helping me adjust to the idea of relying on people like Timbale or Lewis."

Riley shrugged. "Lewis is a good cop."

"Right," Briggs said, smiling weakly. "You know... no one has ever loved me enough to do what you did for Dr. Hunt. It's humbling. And I wish there was a way I could take your place."

Riley chuckled. "Hey, in about fourteen months Gillian's going to need a shoulder to cry on..."

Briggs laughed softly. "As beautiful as she is, I'm straight. No. I meant I wish there was a way I could pay your price. If what Priest said is true, and I have no reason to doubt her, you already died once to save Gillian. If there was a way I could pay your price instead so the two of you could live happily ever after, I'd do it. You deserve happiness."

"I... so do you, boss." Riley had no idea how to respond to that. "Thank you. But I made the deal, and I have to accept the consequences." She stood up and paused before moving to the door. "What I said, about fourteen months from now. Gillian is going to need someone in her corner. Someone she can count on~"

"I'll make sure she knows I'm here."

"Thanks, Zoe."

Briggs smiled and dipped her chin, and Riley headed for the door.

"Oh, Detective. I heard Priest didn't show up this morning."

"Yeah. She's under the weather."

Briggs raised an eyebrow. "Can angels get sick?"

"Physically, no," Riley admitted. "But trust me, she really was sick of dispatch. I'll let you know what Gillian has on the Allison case as soon as she tells me."

"Thank you."

Riley shut the door behind her and looked at Priest's empty desk. She couldn't stand that emptiness, so she turned and decided to see if Gillian was ready with the report. She took the stairs down to the morgue and passed the row of bodies covered by sheets. She glanced down at them as she walked by, unwilling to treat them like furniture, and raised her fist to knock on Gillian's office door. She stopped in position, staring at the new nameplate next to the door.

Chief Medical Examiner - Dr. Gillian Parra.

She moved her hand, extending a finger to trace the lines. They had briefly discussed whether or not they would exchange surnames. Riley briefly considered taking Hunt, Gillian offered a hyphenate, but neither of them were overly keen on changing their names. Gillian liked hearing of Detective Parra's exploits, and Riley was used to speaking to Doctor Hunt. So they decided to keep their professional names while assuming the other's surname as a third name. Sort of an unspoken middle name.

The office door opened, startling both Riley and Gillian. "Oh! God, I didn't know you were down here. Why are you lurking?"

"Gillian Parra?"

"Yeah." She turned so she could look at the label. "I thought about it for a long time. I decided after... you're gone... I'll want it to remember you by. And I thought if I was going to make it official, why wait until you're not around to see it? And I want to be Gillian Parra as long as possible. So... what do you think?"

"I think it was silly of me to hang on to Dr. Hunt because I liked how it sounded. Dr. Parra sounds so much better." She put her arms around Gillian and squeezed. "Thank you."

"You're very welcome. I told everyone to keep it quiet. Who spilled the beans?"

"Hm? Oh. No one. I was down here for a completely different reason."

Gillian waited. "And that reason was...?"

"Give me a second." She finally looked away from the placard. "Oh. The Allison case. Have you finished the autopsy yet?"

"Not yet. I was about to put the finishing touches on it. Give me a half hour?"

"Sure." She let Gillian out her embrace. "Mind if I stick around? I hate going up to my desk when Cait's not there to keep me company."

"I'd love the company. Just let me get a coffee first."

Riley held out her hand for the mug. "I'll be your go-fer."

"Well. There are advantages to a bored Riley after all."

"You should see what a bored Riley would do to fill time if we weren't at work." She winked and headed for the carafe.

"You sure you want to hang out here and watch me type? Did you finally get bored of hanging out in Dispatch with Caitlin?"

"She's not here today. Called in sick."

Gillian was taken aback. "Angels get sick?"

Riley smiled as she poured a cup of coffee. "Let's just say she got a better offer."

"How do you feel?"

Priest looked away from the road to look. Kenzie's hair was pulled back to keep the wind from catching it, exposing the scars on the side of her face and along her neck. Priest's hair was too short for a ponytail since she'd cut it a year earlier, but she enjoyed the feel of the wind whipping through it. She smiled and pushed up her sunglasses.

"It's enjoyable!"

"You've heard of damning with faint praise, right? Come on.

Two hot chicks on a road trip, we've got Huey Lewis blasting and a couple of sandwiches in a lunchbox... this, right here, is a fine-ass time, angel face."

Priest couldn't help laughing. "You have a point, I suppose. The company could only be improved by Chelsea's presence."

"Yeah." She sighed. "I guess someone has to stay behind and hold down the fort."

"I still think the car was an unnecessary expense. I could have gotten us to our destination in a fraction of the time."

Kenzie laughed. "It's a convertible. Ninety-percent of the fun is how unnecessary they are. I figure if we're driving all the way to Old Seneca, we might as well go in style. Besides, we both needed to get away from the city for a few hours. I needed the company, you needed the escape, and driving is a good way to decompress." She looked over. "By the way, if I didn't say this before, I'm glad you agreed to come. I really wanted you there to snoop around all angel-style and see if you can pick up any traces of what's going on."

Priest nodded. They were en route to the small town in the south corner of the state to track down the origins of Mayor Lark Siskin. If what Abigail Shepherd claimed was true, they would find evidence of a summoning. They could at the very least confirm Abigail and Emily Simon's identities. If that part was true, then the rest of it was more likely.

As soon as Gillian reported what she'd been told, Priest left to reconnoiter the mayor's building. She circled the penthouse level but never picked up any indication of her fellow angel being held captive within. If he was there, the room had been warded well. She also didn't like the implications of Abigail Shepherd's story. If Lark Siskin had indeed been injecting angel blood for years, she would be a formidable opponent. She had no doubt that Riley would eventually emerge successful, but how long would it take? She feared the quest to stop Lark would take up the rest of the time Riley had left.

"Hey. No furrowed brow when 'Power of Love' is on. That's a human rule."

"There are so many rules," Priest sighed. "Why not just do what you like and what makes you happy?"

"I think your boss is the one who decided people should feel guilty about the good parts of life. But let's not worry about that. You want to listen to something else?"

"No, this is fine." Kenzie was driving with one hand on the

wheel, so Priest reached out and covered the hand resting on her thigh. Kenzie turned her wrist and laced their fingers together. "Perhaps on the way back we could spend the night at a hotel. Do you think Chelsea would mind?"

"Not if it's you." She lifted Priest's hand to kiss her fingers. "A night in a hotel, huh? Another human experience you want to cross off your list?"

"Perhaps."

Kenzie sighed. "Well, in that case, Zerachiel, I am happy to be your human guinea pig. Crank it up."

Priest let go of Kenzie's hand to turn up the radio, leaning to one side so that the wind coming around the windshield could catch her hair. She closed her eyes and felt the passage through the world. Despite the mystery ahead of them and the danger behind, she smiled.

Aissa hadn't necessarily been avoiding Riley, but she still tensed when Eddie held out the receiver to her. "Something wrong? I can tell her you're not here if you don't want to talk."

"I assume that works better if you don't announce it while holding the telephone with the line open." She smiled to let him know she was only teasing, and he shrugged.

"I'll make her believe me."

Aissa had no doubt, but still she held out her left hand and took the receiver from him. "Hello, Riley."

"Hi. Why wouldn't you want to talk to me? Is this a bad time?"

"No, it's fine. I've just been busy lately."

"Okay, then I do have something I want you to do. Take the day off."

Aissa furrowed her brow, but the corners of her mouth curled into a smile. "Pardon?"

"It's been a hectic year. For you more than most. Eddie hasn't been giving me progress reports or anything, but from what he's said when I called implies you've been going full throttle. So take a day or two. Cait's out of town, I'm hiding out in the morgue, so there's no sense in you being out there alone."

The offer was tempting, but she couldn't help but think of the consequences. If the forces of Good were all on stand-down, then the Mayor's forces could operate with impunity.

"Has Eddie spoken to you recently? Did he give you reason to say this?"

Riley was quiet for a moment. "Why? Would he have? What happened?"

"Nothing. He's just been overprotective of late. I will... I will not look for trouble. Is that an acceptable compromise?"

"Yeah. I think I'll have to be satisfied with that. Aissa, you know that if you ever need to talk... just talk, not coordinate plans or ask for help... you know Jill and I are available."

"Thank you, Riley. I appreciate that. I'll keep the offer in mind."

"Okay. Aissa Good's Day Off. Go see a movie, read a book... take a nap. The world is yours, for now. I feel bad that you've spent two years outside of the convent and you've barely had a chance to see why the world is worth saving. I recommend ice cream. Don't save the world for the people, save the world because it's the only place in the universe that has ice cream."

Aissa smiled. "Thank you, Riley. Goodbye."

When she hung up, she turned and saw Eddie standing behind her. "Sorry. I didn't mean to eavesdrop. So, uh, she doesn't know, does she?"

Aissa adjusted the strap of her sling and shook her head. "I would prefer if we kept it that way. The arm is almost healed. Telling her now would only worry her unduly."

"Look, you're embarrassed..."

"I am *not*~"

"Hey. I've been there, playing the tough guy... I know how badly you were hurt when those punks jumped you."

Aissa turned her face away to hide the bruise on her right cheek. In the past three days it had faded from a vibrant purple to a sickly yellow. She'd gotten it three nights ago when she'd pursued a purse snatcher into a blind alley only to be attacked by his friends. They overwhelmed her in the darkness, knocking her to the ground before they began kicking her. Her arm had been broken in the fall, a sloppy attempt to catch herself, and the bruises came from the boots and fists of the goons. She had been left broken and weeping in the alley when her assailants simply ceased the assault and walked away. Somehow that was even more humiliating than the beating; the fact that she hadn't run them off or regained the upper hand. They simply left her where she lay. Like she wasn't worth the effort of finishing off.

She finally made it home to the shelter where Eddie tended to her wounds. After he went to find some painkillers, Anita sat next to her and held Aissa's uninjured hand. She spoke softly and asked if the men had done anything else to her besides the beating. It took Aissa a moment to realize she meant something sexual, and she realized how close she had come to a truly horrific experience.

Eddie spoke softly, pulling her back from the moment she'd been replaying for three days. "I know you're scared that they're still out there. It's why you've been hiding out here the past few days. If you told Riley~"

"She would run in here with Zerachiel and Kenzie Stanton and fight for me. Then every other group would see that I can't fight my own battles. I would be fair game to them. I've made too many enemies in No Man's Land to show weakness now."

"You've made a lot of enemies, but you've made a lot of friends, too. Let them help."

Aissa sighed. "When the time is right, I will tell Riley. That time will be after I'm healed and I've found the people who did this to me."

She started to leave and Eddie put a hand on her shoulder to stop her. "Don't look to exact vengeance, Aissa."

"Not vengeance. Justice. If I'm to be the champion when Riley leaves, this city has to learn to respect me."

"And no one will respect you if they know how easily they can trip your berserker switch. I'm not saying you should let them get away with this, but be reasonable about how you react. You've been smart about trying to clean up No Man's Land so far. Don't let one group of assholes scare you. And if you don't want to go to Riley for help, then come to me. Promise me, Aissa."

She thought about just walking away, but she couldn't be that rude to Eddie. Finally she nodded. "I promise."

"Good. Now, what did Riley want?"

"She told me to take a day off."

Eddie smiled. "She's a smart woman." He squeezed her shoulder. "A little tip. They left you intact, so they have to expect you to retaliate. They're going to be on high alert. Make them sweat a little. Make them wonder when you're going to pounce. Then, when you're fully healed and rested, they'll be twitchy and exhausted from days of anxiety."

Aissa managed a smile at that. "Thank you, Eddie."

"There are books in the common room. I'm sure you can find one that will hold your interest."

She nodded and left the office. Once she was in the hall, she moved her hand to touch the material of her sling. She would rest, and she would let the bastards who hurt her stew for a while, but when the time came she was going to go after them alone. She was going to show them that Aissa Good wouldn't be a champion they could trifle with.

Old Seneca was a surprisingly idyllic town that instantly put Kenzie in mind of Mayberry. She parked at a curb in the town common, facing the triangle of green grass that fronted a tall clock tower. There were only a handful of people on the street, and the closest offered polite smiles and head-nods of greeting as they passed. Kenzie took off her sunglasses and squinted up the street as Priest joined her on the sidewalk.

"Doesn't really seem like the sort of place to spawn a champion for evil, does it?"

Priest shrugged. "If she was born with the capacity of evil and the need to commit atrocities, this would be hellish for her."

Kenzie could see that. "Okay. There's a diner right over there."

"I thought the sandwiches we packed were for lunch."

"We're not eating. We're going to see what people have to say."

"Oh. In that case, I think I may be of more use at the police station. Perhaps my badge can provide a few leads."

Kenzie nodded. "Good idea. Meet me back here in about twenty."

Priest agreed and, after a moment to gain her bearings, headed north. Kenzie jogged across the street and went into the diner. Sleigh bells hanging from the push bar announced her entrance, but only one waitress behind the counter at the far wall acknowledged her. She lifted her hand in greeting and then swirled a finger to indicate the whole dining room. "Sit anywhere you like, darlin'. Be with you in a tic."

It was between the breakfast and lunch rushes, but one table in the middle of the room was still filled with elderly men and women who seemed to be doing an American Gothic re-sitting of The Last Supper. Kenzie sat in a booth close enough to the coffee klatch for conversation but not so close she was intruding. She ordered an ice tea when the waitress came over, and one of the men at the table glanced over during a lull in conversation.

"Visiting or passing through?"

"A little of both. I was hoping to catch up with a family who used to live around here. The, uh, Siskins?"

The people at the table all seemed to shift a little away from her, spines suddenly straighter and eyes fixed on their coffee. The waitress came back with Kenzie's tea and, sensing the environment, didn't linger to make small talk. Once she was gone, Kenzie moved to a closer booth. One of the men had his sleeves rolled up just enough for her to make out the USMC tattoo on his arm.

"Listen, I'm just trying to help. One soldier to another."

He glanced over, and she tugged on the chain around her neck to free her dog tags. He looked at them, then at the burns displayed on Kenzie's face.

"You get those overseas?"

"Roadside IED. Afghanistan. Major Mackenzie Stanton. I've been out for a couple of years~"

"No one's really out," he whispered. Kenzie nodded and waited. He took a drink of his coffee, everyone else at the table looking to him for how to respond. Kenzie knew that his decision would be the final word, so she prepared to be thrown out on her ass. Finally he wet his lips and put his cup down. "People in this town don't like to talk about the Siskin family. You understand that? Some things don't get easier with time, and some things need to just be allowed to settle. Fade to gray."

Kenzie nodded. "I understand. I wouldn't have come here digging for skeletons if it wasn't necessary. We think a member of the Siskin family is planning to do something bad. If we know a little bit about her history, there's a chance we can stop it from happening. Save lives."

A woman at the other end of the table softly said, "Her."

Another man nodded to confirm. "That means Lark."

"So where's Lawrence?" the Marine asked.

Kenzie shook her head. "There's no Lawrence that I know of. Who is that?"

"Lark and Lawrence were brother and sister. Parents died when they were young, so they lived with an aunt. Died in some big to-do, so the government gave them a check to make up for it." He picked up a napkin and dabbed at his mouth. Kenzie could tell that, despite his reluctance, part of him wanted to tell the story again. She didn't risk interruption. "They lived outside of town. Big house, big enough they got lost in it and never really made much commotion until the kids got to high school age. Living up there all alone, 'course, kids made up all kinds of stories about the Spooky Siskins. Said the brother and sister were bein' unnatural with each other, communin' with the devil, all that sort of stuff and nonsense.

"Lark was in high school when she decided to throw a party up at the house. All the parents were told the aunt would be supervising, but all the kids were told that she'd be gone. Lot of room up there for drinking and carryin'-on. Plus they all wanted to say they'd been inside the fence. So of course the kids showed up. Party went well for about three hours or so, well into the night at any rate, and then right around midnight, lights cut out."

One of the women shuddered. "Like Poe or something. Like straight outta Poe."

The Marine nodded. "Kids laughed it off at first. Spooky Siskins. Then people started screaming. 'Course after that, everyone made a mad dash for the doors. They got outside and a couple of people had been cut across the hands, ears had been sliced almost off, slashes all up and down people's legs. Town doctor had a damn mess on his hands that night. One man pulled out of bed to deal with thirty or forty kids with knife wounds."

Kenzie said, "I assume the cops were called out?"

"Oh, sure. They walked up to the Siskin house and demanded to see the aunt. Girl admitted she'd lied, but said she hadn't had anything to do with the knife. Said someone was just trying to make her look crazy."

"They believed her?"

The woman at the other end of the table said, "They had to believe her. She and her brother was cut up, too. Hands, legs, arms. Lark's brother had a cut on his neck that made Abe... that was the ol' sheriff... it made him step outside for some fresh air. They searched the house but they never found the knife, so there was no way to prove one way or t'other who'd done the cuttin'. Kids had been pestering the Siskin family so long, it made a kind of sick sense that someone decided to blame the Spooky Siskins for being knife-wielding maniacs."

Kenzie shuddered but tensed so the klatch didn't notice it. "Wow. School must have been fun for the Siskins after that."

The Marine shook his head. "They stopped going after that. People say Lark got her GED and moved away. Lawrence went around the same time, leaving the aunt alone up in the big house."

"Is she still up there?"

"Far as anyone knows," the talkative woman said. "She wasn't exactly keen to come down here and mingle with us. It was our kids who accused her niece and nephew of being slashers, so she decided to cloister herself off. Far as I know," she looked at the people around her for confirmation or denial, "she's still up there."

Priest entered the diner and Kenzie nodded to her. She took out her wallet. "Thank you for speaking with me. I know it probably wasn't the conversation you wanted to have over breakfast, so let me treat."

The waitress had reappeared and took the hundred before Kenzie could put it on the table. "Excellent. A buck for your tea, and ninety-nine toward these fools' tab."

The Marine cackled, assuming a completely different persona from the man who had told her the story about the Siskins. "A drop in the bucket, isn't it? Take a couple of bucks for yourself."

"I've more than earned it."

"So you claim," the talkative woman said.

The waitress offered to put Kenzie's tea in a to-go cup, and Priest made her way over. The people at the table eyed her as she passed. Kenzie liked seeing new people react to Caitlin Priest's presence. People could tell there was something unique about her, some special something they couldn't quite put their finger on. It was like spotting a celebrity in a crowd without knowing exactly who they are, or seeing a long-lost friend who had aged just enough you didn't recognize them anymore.

Priest offered a friendly smile and approached Kenzie. "The sheriff wasn't in, but the deputy told me where the Siskin house is."

"Great. These fine folks shared a little story with me. I'll tell you on the way." She took the tea from the returning waitress, thanked her and the group, and led Priest back outside.

"What did you find out?" Priest asked.

"People here in town aren't our new Mayor's biggest fans. Auntie Siskin apparently still lives up on Mockingbird Lane."

Priest shook her head. "The deputy told me she lived~"

"It's a reference to a TV show. Forget it. C'mon. Let's go see what the dowager aunt has to tell us." She took out her phone and opened the maps. "What's the address? I'll see if I can found out how to get there from here."

Gillian came into her office, where Riley was sitting at the desk with her feet up. Gillian's keyboard was on her lap, and she paused typing and moved as if to get up.

"I'm not coming in to work, I just had to grab something." She patted Riley's knee as she passed, glancing at the screen. "Arrest reports. You must be bored."

"Your fault for finding out Drew Allison died of an undiagnosed condition."

"Next time I'll be less thorough."

"I'd appreciate it."

Gillian smiled as she opened a file and thumbed through it. "Did you call Aissa? How is she doing?"

"She sounded weird. I might go by there and check up on her later."

"Why not now?"

"Because now I'm bugging you and getting in your way." The desk phone rang, and Riley grabbed it to answer before Gillian could. "Dr. Parra's office. May I ask who is calling?" She rested the receiver against her shoulder. "Are you in for a Lieutenant Young?"

Gillian made a 'give me' gesture for the phone.

"One moment, please."

Gillian took the phone. "You enjoyed that too much."

"Impossible." She ducked under the cord and abandoned the desk so Gillian could sit down.

As she was leaving the office, she smiled when she heard, "This is Dr. Parra," and she knew she'd never get used to hearing it. At least she hoped she never did.

She decided she had to go back to her desk whether she wanted to or not, even if she didn't have much to keep her occupied. She knew there were days coming when she would relish being bored. But as she pressed the button and waited for the elevator to respond, and even though she knew she was jinxing herself, she hoped the excitement arrived sooner rather than later.

The front yard was separated from the sidewalk by a tall white fence, and this had been topped by chicken wire festooned with signs warning against trespassing and threatening a dog on the premises. Kenzie checked the rusty mailbox hanging off the gate and, crammed inside along with bills and circulars, was a bag that smelled as if it hadn't been sent express delivery. She pinched the least-soiled corner of the bag and lifted it out, holding her breath as she deposited it on the street next to the sidewalk.

"Feel like risking a guard dog?"

Priest nodded, and Kenzie lifted the latch and stepped inside. The lawn was yellowed and overgrown, but no barking beasts zeroed in on them as they approached the overgrown porch. Kenzie had just put her foot on the lowest step when the window next to the door was lifted with a loud protest of warped wood.

"I'm not interested in what you're selling or what you want me to sell you. Please, just leave me alone." The woman's shape was just barely visible through the thin curtains, hunched over and leaning to one side so that the sun didn't fall on her face. Her voice was weary and defeated, all the strength and anger long since drained from it.

"Ma'am, we're not here to sell you anything. My name is Mackenzie Stanton. This is Caitlin Priest. We were hoping we could come in and talk to you for a few minutes."

"You want to talk about those children. I'm sorry, but I've said all I can ever say about them. And no one ever believes me anyway, so why should I waste what little breath I have left on you two?"

Kenzie shrugged. "Because we came all this way? Because we might believe what you have to say more than most?"

"Because I'm an angel."

Kenzie blinked in surprise, staring for a moment before she turned to Priest and whispered, "You lead with that now?"

Priest shrugged. "Time is short. Please, Miss Siskin."

Silence from within the house. Kenzie was about to declare it a lost cause when she heard the locks on the door being thrown. The door swung open a moment later and the old woman stepped out. Kenzie tensed at the sight of her face, the series of scars running along both cheeks and across her forehead. The wounds were long since healed over, blending with the road map of wrinkles that came with age.

"Are you really an angel?"

"Yes, ma'am. My name is Zerachiel, but my earthbound name is Caitlin Priest. We came a very long way because we believe Lark Siskin is planning something that we need to stop."

The woman looked at Kenzie's face. "Did she do that to you?"

"No, ma'am. War wound."

"You really think you can stop her?"

Priest nodded. "With the right information, I think we can put up a strong defense against her. We'd like to try."

"A lot of people have tried to stop that girl. Me among them." She looked back into the house, then sighed and motioned for them to follow her. "Excuse the mess. I haven't had anyone inside in over a decade, so there's no reason to tidy up."

"Thank you," Kenzie said.

The house had a distinct odor; not necessarily bad, but not something Kenzie wanted to experience for longer than necessary. When the door was closed the only light came filtered through the thick curtains on the ground floor windows, blending with the smell to make it feel like some underground den. The old woman shuffled around a stack of books in the doorway between the kitchen and living room, nearly toppling a stack of Styrofoam containers marked with Meals on Wheels stickers.

"You say she's up to old tricks?"

"Or new ones. We're not entirely sure what she did here, other than the story about the blackout and the knife."

"Mm. Yes. That night." She found a spot on the sofa and gingerly sat down. "That was the beginning of it all. She decided she was going to get revenge on those kids who treated her and Lawrence so badly. I never thought she would go to such lengths. Those poor children. Some of them are still scarred. All grown up and scarred forever, just because they went to a party."

"You started home-schooling Lark and her brother after that, Miss Siskin?"

She waved off the name. "Call me Agatha, please. And yes. I couldn't very well send them back to that school. Not that I would have. That night, after everything was settled... I saw Lark. She wasn't manic or frightened or in shock. She was just content. Scared the life out of me when I saw her just casually smiling with all that blood on her."

"So you think she was the cutter?"

Agatha fixed a rheumy-eyed stare on Kenzie. "Look at my face, dear. I know she was the cutter. But I couldn't just turn her in. She was my sister's daughter. And besides, by that time I was... I was scared of her. It was easier to just let people wonder."

"What happened when Lark finally left town?"

She was looking at Priest now. "You're really an angel?"

Priest nodded, and the light in the room increased tenfold. The light seemed to pour from all around her, through her pores and wiping away any shadows near her. Kenzie saw a brief hint of wings unfurling, a ghostly flex of feathers before they folded back against her shoulder blades. Then the light faded, and Priest smiled.

"Why did you believe her on the porch?" Kenzie asked.

"Something about her," Agatha said. "Something I couldn't put my finger on. But then she said that and I..." She looked down at her hands. "Besides, I saw the other side plain as day. It was good to know this house might get to see the bright side as well as the dark. And it did see the dark." She cleared her throat. "Dear, would you mind getting me a drink of water? The kitchen is right through there. You should see the glasses as soon as you go in."

Kenzie stood. "Of course. I'll be right back."

Once she was gone, Agatha leaned close to Priest. "You can feel it, can't you?"

"I can feel something. I can expel it if you so wish."

Agatha sighed. "I've lived with it so long I almost don't know what I would do without it. House would be so quiet by myself. But if I can get rid of it before I die, I suppose I would like that. If it's not too much trouble."

"None at all." Priest stood and placed her hands on the old woman's head. "I assume Lark used you as the focus point for her early rituals. The more powerful ones require blood sacrifice. And your wounds." Light poured from Priest's hands, making the old woman's scars and wrinkles stand out in stark relief.

Kenzie returned with the water but remained at the threshold. Priest closed her eyes, and the walls of the house seemed to groan.

"Caitlin..."

"It's almost gone."

Agatha gasped, her body suddenly becoming rigid. Kenzie hunched her shoulders as the temperature in the house dropped by several degrees in an instant, then snapped back up. Priest lifted her hands and stepped back, the light fading. After a moment Agatha opened her eyes and gasped. Tears filled her eyes and she sagged back against the afghan draped over the back of the couch. "Oh. Oh, my. Thank you."

"I'm pleased I could help."

Kenzie handed Agatha the glass. "What was that about?"

Priest took her seat. "Lark and her brother were involved in profane rituals in the house. They were young and inexperienced, and the easiest way to prepare is to use human blood."

"So they..."

Agatha nodded. "They used me. The first time they drugged my tea. When I woke Lark was cutting me. And after that I was bound by whatever dark evil they summoned. I became a puppet for whatever they wanted." She drank half the water, then ran her tongue over her lips. "After the first few times I was physically incapable of resisting."

"How often did they perform the rituals?"

"As often as they could. Lark made it a hobby. The first thing they summoned told her where to look for more information, she got the books, and she began doing more and more rituals. It was like piano practice when I was a girl. Repeating it over and over again until she got it right."

Priest said, "The demons she summoned spoke to her?"

"As far as I could tell it was only the one demon. Leraje." She shuddered violently as she said the name, an involuntary tic in response to saying the name. She tightened her grip on her glass. "She would summon him while Lawrence stood in the circle. The thing used his body as a vessel whenever he was on this plane. Poor Lawrence was so sickly and frail. God help me, but when the demon was in him, he was strong. He was vital. It was almost worth it to see him standing firm and tall without trembling."

Priest whispered something under her breath. Kenzie looked at her, but she seemed lost in her thoughts.

"When Lark left, did she say what she planned to do?"

"She wanted power. It was why she summoned those evil things into our home."

"So why didn't she let Leraje take over her body?"

"Her brother needed the power more. And he served as a guide, showing her how she could gain more power than she'd ever dreamed." She finished her water glass and leaned forward to put it down on the table. "I was glad when they finally left. I knew they would just keep doing their evilness once they left the house, but at least I was free." She looked at the room around her and smiled sadly. "Well. As free as was possible."

Priest suddenly inhaled, straightening her shoulders and staring at Agatha. "Father, no."

Kenzie looked at her. "What is it? What's wrong?"

"We have to go. Agatha, I apologize~"

"No. You stayed much longer than I could have hoped. And I hope you don't expect me to walk you to the door..."

"That's all right. Thank you, Agatha. Kenzie, we must go now."

Kenzie thanked Agatha for speaking with them and followed Priest outside. She waited until they were on the other side of the fence before she spoke again.

"Caitlin, what the hell? What was all that about?"

"We have to get back to the city now."

"I kind of got that impression. Why?"

Priest closed her eyes. "Lark Siskin is seeking power. More

power than a simple demonic possession could afford her. Ziminiar, the demon you and Chelsea escorted back to Hell, warned me that Lark was holding hostage an angel named Pahaliah. Torturing him, pushing him to fall but never allowing him to make the final step to true damnation. I didn't understand why she would do that, but now... Father, oh, Father, I think I know what she plans."

"What? Don't keep me in suspense, Cait."

"When an angel falls, it expels a great amount of energy. Humans don't always feel it, but it's the spiritual equivalent to an explosion. But it's supposed to happen quickly, in the blink of an eye. What Lark is doing is building up that power, storing it. I'm stunned I haven't felt the vibrations of so much energy being held back. The penthouse must be warded even more than I thought it was."

Kenzie said, "So this angel is a bomb?"

"No. Not in the destruction sense. There will be no property damage and, as I said, most mortals likely won't even notice it happening. But the strength of the energy... well. You saw what happened when I was caught in the wake of an angel's death, and what happened when Riley was in proximity at the moment of Falco's death."

"Lark wants to become a fallen angel?"

"No. That's why she's building up so much energy. When she finally allows it to release, it will wash over whoever is nearby like a tsunami. It will flood them with unimaginable power. Lark wouldn't be happy as an ordinary demon, and she wouldn't be content with simply being another fallen angel. That's why she allowed Leraje to take over her brother. That's why she's been defying Marchosias and treating the war like a game. She's using Riley as a distraction as she works toward her real purpose."

Kenzie said, "So if this happens, Lark becomes an uber-demon?"

"In a manner of speaking. She'll be more powerful than any demon in the depths of Hell. If this is allowed to happen, Lark will become Satan."

Kenzie stared for a moment, then started jogging toward the car. "Get back to the city. Warn Riley. I'll be there as soon as I can."

She heard a strong flap of wings followed by an updraft, but when she looked into the sky Priest was already out of sight. She hoped that even the supernatural mode of transportation would be fast enough to warn Riley of the threat she was now facing.

Mayor Siskin looked up from her tablet as the doors to the council room were unceremoniously thrown open to admit Emily Simon. Councilwoman Leeds squared her shoulders prissily. "Miss Simon, we are in the middle of a budgetary meeting. You can't just barge in here~"

"She can barge in wherever she likes," Lark said. "What is it, Emily?"

"You have a phone call, ma'am. One that I very strongly believe you should take."

Lark capped her pen and pushed her chair back from the table. "Excuse me, ladies and gentlemen. I've learned to trust my aide's judgment in cases like this. We'll take a brief recess and reconvene in twenty minutes."

She ignored Catherine Leeds' contemptuous sigh as she stepped around the table. Emily fell into step just behind Lark as she left the room, shutting the door behind them. Lark held out her hand for a cell phone, but Emily shook her head.

"It came through on your private line."

Fear flashed across Lark's features, there for an instant and then gone. "Old Seneca?"

"Yes, ma'am."

Lark picked up her pace, forcing Emily to trot in an effort to catch up. She burst into her office and stood on the guest side of her desk to pick up the phone with a number only a handful of people knew. If any one of them was calling, things were very bad indeed.

"Who is this?"

"This is Sheriff Bailey, Miss Siskin. You wanted to know if anyone ever showed up asking questions about you or your brother. Seems like we entertained a couple of guests today. One of 'em came to talk to my deputy, and he pointed her toward your aunt's place." Lark tightened her jaw, eyes closed as she fought the urge to scream into the phone. "The other one got the old folks down at the diner talking. Tried to figure out how much they told her, but no one was spilling. So I thought I'd let you know anyway."

"It's much appreciated. The people who came. Describe them."

"The one who came to see my deputy was blonde, hair cut real short. Said she was a cop up your neck of the woods. Deputy Alec said she was real... calming. Like the whole time she was in the office he just felt happy."

Caitlin Priest. "And the other? Hispanic, surly?"

"No, no. Indian, one lady said, Native Am'rican, you know. But I suppose she could'a been mistaken. Said she had burns all up and down one side of her face. Said she got 'em overseas and had the dog tags to back it up."

"Mackenzie Stanton," Lark said under her breath. "Are they still in town?"

"Sorry, no. If they'd stuck 'round I would have found a way to hold them here. Speed trap or plant something in their car. But 'fore I knew it they were up there to talk with your auntie, then hightailed it out of here. Figure they're on their way back up to you."

And depending on what they had been told, Lark knew there was a very real chance Zerachiel had taken the "short way." She was likely already back, giving her report to Riley. Lark bared her teeth as she struggled to remain calm.

"Thank you, Sheriff Bailey. You've been most helpful." She hung up and put her hands on her hips, walking to the window and looking out over the city. She had several people back in Old Seneca working as her eyes and ears, blackmailing them either with information or money. Whatever their poison was, Lark made sure they had a steady supply. The sheriff had a taste for something so despicable that it put a bad taste in her mouth to provide him with it. But forcing herself to keep him under her heel had finally paid off.

Emily hovered nearby, silent but present. Lark considered her options. If Riley knew about Pahaliah, then she would likely do something foolish like attempt to free him. And if Priest figured out her goal, well... they would stop at nothing. She had run out of time. It had all gone so perfectly, from positioning herself in City Hall to catch the eye of Marchosias, to offering herself as a potential champion when Gail Finney died... it had taken some convincing before he finally agreed, as if he could sense she wouldn't be the good soldier he'd employed in the past. But she had the tattoo, and she got the demon to agree on Leraje being her handler. Everything would be perfect if Zerachiel and Stanton had stayed away from town. Now she was going to be rushed.

The office door opened and Leraje strolled in. Lark saw his

reflection in the window, the hazy image of him seeming to stand on her shoulder. She no longer thought of the demon as her brother, though he looked the same as he had on that long-ago day when Leraje finally took up permanent residence. He looked at Emily and then regarded Lark before he spoke.

"I got the feeling I was needed up here. Have we run into problems?"

"Perhaps." She turned to face him. "How long before the angel is ready to be put out of his misery? The bare minimum."

Leraje pursed his lips, his hands clasped behind his back as he considered the question. "Three days. Perhaps two, but I wouldn't recommend it. He's come a long way, but for the power you require... we really should take the full regimen."

"Unfortunately that's not a luxury we have. Damn it. All this time, and it comes down to three days. Well. We anticipated the problem." She sighed and looked at Emily. "How soon can we implement Wormwood?"

Emily's eyes widened and she checked her tablet. "We could activate in four hours."

"Good. Do it."

Emily hesitated, but then she nodded. "Yes, ma'am."

Leraje watched her leave, then moved closer to Lark. "Are you sure this is wise? You'll only make Detective Parra land on you even harder."

"This isn't about Detective Parra or the blasted war. This is about our plan. The thing we've been working toward since those days up in the attic. We're finally in position."

"And if we rush the process, we'll have to start over again at square one. Do you believe Marchosias will be lenient if he discovers your true motives for becoming champion?"

"If this all goes well, my first act as the Dark Queen will be to crush Marchosias. So I'll waste no time worrying about his precious feelings."

Leraje sighed. "I hope you know what you're doing, Lark."

"I always know what I'm doing. The time has come."

"I think you're just overeager. You're using this as an opportunity speed up the schedule. If we wait~"

"We've waited long enough, brother. Three days. I will wait for three days before the ceremony. But we have to distract Riley. We have to enact Wormwood now, this evening."

Leraje met her stare for a long moment, then held his hands

out in surrender. "As you wish, my sister. I'll proceed with the treatments."

"Keep me apprised," Lark said.

The demon left, and Lark prepared herself a drink at the mini-bar. Soon. Soon the plans she made, the small careful steps she had taken, it would all come to a head. She was going to win. She sipped the drink and savored it, knowing that once she was transformed alcohol would lose a lot of its pleasure. A small price to pay for infinite power.

Three days...

She could wait three days.

And Wormwood would ensure that Riley Parra and her flunkies were too distracted to do anything to stop her.

The sun was setting as Kenzie drove back into the city, one hand on the wheel and the other dialing Chelsea. For the third time, the call went direct to voicemail. She grimaced and this time let the message play before she put the phone to her ear. "Hey, Chelse. Hopefully you're with Riley and Priest getting caught up on this insane theory. I'm on my way home. Should be there in about fifteen or twenty minutes." She was about to say goodbye when red and blue lights began flashing in her rearview. "Damn. I think someone's trying to pull me over for using my phone. Shit. Laugh at me later, babe."

She hung up and sighed as she guided the car to the curb. She rolled down her window, took our her license and registration, and drummed her fingers on the wheel as the patrolman took his sweet time walking up to start the lecture about what she'd done wrong.

He finally showed up, and she smiled apologetically at him. He was a young officer, a bit of peach fuzz visible on his shaved head, and he leaned forward to look into her backseat as he approached. His nametag identified him as Officer Daniels. "Evening, ma'am. License and registration, please."

"Hi." She handed him her info. "And yeah, I know. Cell phones are a nuisance. I can't imagine how many idiots you've seen wreck because of those things. Luckily they weren't really so popular back when I was on the beat."

"You were a cop?"

"I was subtle about it, huh?" She winked. "Mackenzie Stanton. I was Crowe back then, though. Listen, I'm a private investigator and I was calling my partner with an update. We're kind of working against the clock here, so I thought I could get away with it. I'm not trying to get out of a ticket. I deserve it. I just... if you could just give it to me without the lecture and the sitting and waiting, I'd really appreciate it."

He sighed, but she could tell he was going to be kind. "Just 'cause you used to wear a badge doesn't put you above the law."

"I know. I'll pay the fine like a good little citizen. I just really need to get back to town."

"Understood. It'll just be a second."

Kenzie nodded and settled back against her seat. Nothing she could do now but wait and hope he didn't keep her too long.

"She wants to be the *Devil?*" Gillian looked at Riley and then back at Priest. They were in Lieutenant Briggs' office with Chelsea. "She's insane."

"It would seem Lark Siskin is a much more disturbed individual than we anticipated. If there is an angel being held in her building for this obscene purpose, we have to do whatever we can to stop it. I can enlist some of my brethren to help. They don't like stepping in, but in this case... this is blasphemy and it must be stopped. We cannot allow one sick woman to upset the balance in such a catastrophic way."

Riley said, "So the angels are the cavalry. Boss, we're going to need a reason to get into that building."

"Find one. I'll go through my list of soft-touch judges and see if any of them will give us a warrant. Give me a reason and I'll push it through."

"Thanks. Right now we need to play it cool. We don't want to tip her off before we're ready to move."

Gillian cleared her throat. "Emily Simon." Everyone looked at her, and she shrugged. "I promised Abigail Shepherd that if there was a way to protect Emily, we would. She's a victim in this whole scheme. She's been held prisoner, tortured both physically and mentally. We need to treat her as a hostage even if she's acting like a coconspirator."

"Right." She looked at Chelsea. "When is Kenzie due back?"

"According to when Caitlin said she left, she should be back in town any minute now." She took out her cell phone and pressed a button. A mechanical voice said that she had a new message, and she played it for them.

Riley tensed when she got to the part about being pulled over.

"She would be coming into town from the south. Anyone know who is patrolling down there?"

Briggs leaned down over her keyboard and tapped for a few seconds. "Officers Franklin, Brewer, Winger, Daniels, and Palmer. We have no way of knowing which one of them stopped her, or if any of them are in the mayor's pocket."

Chelsea said, "I'll call her back." She dialed and turned the phone on speaker.

Kenzie looked down at the phone display, smiling, and answered the call. She kept the phone tucked between her thigh and the seat. "Hey. Sorry, I know I said fifteen or twenty, but this cop is being a real bonehead."

"Which cop is it, honey?"

"Daniels. Why, what's wrong?"

Riley spoke this time. "I don't like the timing. You find out this info about Lark, and suddenly you're pulled over? Did he seem on the up-and-up?"

"Yeah, he seemed fine." She looked at the squad car in her rear and side mirrors. "I asked him to speed things up a little. I think he took umbrage, wants to make me... oh, hold on. He's coming back. Mute your side, ladies." She tucked the phone farther under her leg so the light wouldn't be visible from his vantage point.

Officer Daniels returned and held out her cards. "Sorry about the wait, Mrs. Stanton. I honestly tried to make it fast, but our computer systems are all on the fritz. I knew this would happen as soon as they put in those damned GPS systems. Now nothing works." He sighed and shook his head. "Anyway, you were a good sport and it's my busted equipment's fault you've been stuck here, so I'm going to give you a break. Don't take advantage of my kindness, now, start doing it all willy-nilly."

Kenzie saluted him. "Sir, no sir. I've learned my lesson."

"Glad to hear it."

In Briggs' office, Riley said, "Sounds like he's a decent sort of fellow. Just bad timing he pulled her over now." She looked at Briggs. "Boss~"

"Hey, on stuff like this, I defer to you, Detective Parra. Take the lead."

"Thank you. Okay, Chelsea, I need you and Kenzie to keep an eye on the mayor's home. If Priest and I did it, she might panic. But

I don't think she'll be as alarmed seeing the two of you."

"Riley~"

It took Riley a moment to realize Kenzie was speaking to her over the phone. "Kenz? What's up, babe?"

"Something's wrong with Officer Daniels' car. I'm going to see if I can lend a hand. I'm going to keep the phone on in my shirt pocket."

Chelsea said, "Is everything okay?"

"He said he was having some computer problems relating to the GPS. It might just be a mechanical issue."

Riley wasn't sure. "Okay... boss." She looked at Briggs. "I want you to take Gillian somewhere safe and stay there with her."

Gillian said, "You want me to sit this out? Riley~"

"I want you safe. You've done enough for the cause, and Siskin already got her hands on you once. I won't risk that again." She and Gillian stared for a long moment before Riley's expression softened. "Please. I'm not saying you can't handle it, I'm saying that I won't put you in harm's way if I can help it. Please, please don't fight me on this."

"Okay."

"Thank you. Is there anywhere you can think of to take her?"

Briggs nodded. "There's a safe house not far from here, but it's pretty far from the mayor's penthouse. If that's where this is going down, it should be out of the way."

Riley said, "Okay. Take her, now. I'll call you when I get justification for a warrant."

Briggs came around her desk and put her hand on Gillian's arm, guiding her out of the office. The others followed, and most of the detectives in the bullpen gravitated toward them.

Timbale was the first to speak, as usual. "Lieutenant, what the hell is going on? Closed door meetings with Chelsea Stanton? You guys all look like death warmed over. Something's obviously up."

"Everything is fine, Detective Timbale," Briggs said. "When it becomes necessary for you to know what's happening, we'll fill you in. Until that time~"

Her explanation was cut off my something exploding. Something big, close, and something followed by a duet of similar explosions.

Kenzie kept her hands up where Officer Daniels could see them. "Hey. Just want to lend a hand, if I can. Computer problems, right?"

Daniels lowered his head, obviously embarrassed to have a woman helping him with car problems. But to his credit, he nodded and held his hands up helplessly. "I can't get it to do a damn thing. First the mayor forces this GPS shit on us~"

Kenzie tensed. "Mayor Siskin ordered these systems?"

"Yeah. 'Bout half a year ago."

Kenzie motioned him toward her. "Get out of the car. Officer, trust me, get out of the car right now."

Riley and Priest moved toward the windows, watching as plumes of smoke began to rise between the buildings of the city. There were more explosions, too many to count, coming from all corners of the city. One of the explosions sounded like it was inside the room, and Chelsea dropped her phone. Gillian scooped it up off the floor and held it in front of her face. "Kenzie? Kenzie, are you still there? Kenzie!"

"The GPS," Riley said. "The Mayor tied the GPS to an explosive device."

Briggs said, "She put them in all the squad cars."

Riley went cold. "How many cars are down in the garage right now?"

Briggs went pale. "Oh, Christ."

"Everyone out! Right this second, everyone to the~"

Her last words were cut off by what seemed to be a break in reality. The floor arched up under their feet and the walls bent outward like bellows. Everything snapped back to true a second later, the sudden reversal causing the windows to shatter. Riley and Priest were showered with broken glass, knocked to the floor as every sound was muted by an explosion so loud that it could only have been the end of the world.

SPIRITUAL WARFARE

THE RINGING in her ears faded only to be replaced by the wail of emergency klaxons. She lifted her head enough to see the swirling red lights in the stairwell through a scrum of smoke. She coughed and tasted blood in her mouth as she took a mental inventory of her aches and pains. It seemed like she'd escaped without breaking anything, and she focused on the people around her. Gillian was sprawled on the ground a few feet away and Riley got to her hands and knees to crawl to her.

"Gillian..."

Gillian's body convulsed once as she came to, like someone startling themselves out of a nightmare. She started to rise off the floor, but Riley put a hand on her shoulder to keep her down.

"Hold on. Stay down for a second. Are you hurt?"

"I don't think so. No. I don't... Riley, what the hell."

"I don't know yet." Riley examined the length of Gillian's body, grateful there didn't seem to be any physical damage other than a scrape on her forehead that was bleeding more than Riley liked. She pulled her sleeve up over the heel of her hand, pressed it to the wound, and looked around the room.

The windows had all been shattered, a gaping maw that seemed to breathe with the rush of wind. Priest was up and moving toward a body slumped over a desk. The front of her shirt was shredded to reveal her chest and brassiere, the pale skin smeared with blood from wounds her divinity had already healed. The other cops standing near the window hadn't been so lucky.

Gillian put her hand on Riley's arm and nodded toward the injured. "Go. Help them."

"Not until I know you're okay."

"I'm fine. Go." She was already sitting up, hands on the floor, searching for anyone who needed help.

Riley kissed her, and Gillian replaced the pressure on her wound as Riley stood and moved toward Priest. Briggs had been sat up by Priest before she moved on to other casualties. The right leg of her suit was dark with blood and her face was pale, but she motioned for Riley to keep moving. Riley reached out and gripped the lieutenant's hand before she continued on. Chelsea was unmoving on the ground, and Riley knelt next to her.

"Chelsea? Hey, come on... you with us?"

Chelsea rolled her head to the side and opened her eyes, blinking wildly for a few moments before she reached out. Riley caught her hand, held it tight.

"Kenzie."

"I don't know. We'll find out as soon as we can. Are you hurt anywhere?"

"No. I don't feel anything."

She did a visual scan of Chelsea's body and didn't see any awkward twists or worrying blood pooling on her clothes. She helped Chelsea sit up and propped her against the desk.

"Okay. Stay here until we figure out what's next."

Chelsea nodded, and Riley stood to cross the room. The building groaned and she could have sworn she felt it shift from east to west. She braced herself against a desk and hoped the detonations were finished. She doubted the building could take another blow. Detective Timbale had fallen next to his desk, and Priest had two fingers on his throat when Riley reached her.

"Is he gone?"

"Yes." Priest looked around the room. Other detectives were up, checking on their fellow officers. The majority of them were motionless, sprawled where they had fallen. "What happened?"

"The GPS devices Mayor Siskin put in the squad cars. I think she included some sort of detonator. So we had about two dozen car bombs driving around tonight, and she set them off. There were another ten downstairs in the garage." She looked around. "We have to evacuate these people." She looked over and saw Gillian tending to Briggs' wound. "Is Briggs okay to move?"

"Yes. She has a laceration on her right calf, but the other damage is superficial."

"Okay. Find everyone who can walk and let's start getting them to safety."

Priest put a hand on Riley's arm. "The Mayor wouldn't do this on a whim. It's a distraction."

"Oh, I know. But I'm going to make sure these people are safe before I worry about what she's trying to distract me from." She patted Priest on the shoulder and then clapped to get everyone's attention. "Okay, people. The building is still standing for the moment, but I don't think we can count on that lasting for long. We have to worry about secondary explosions. We... we need..."

Gillian waited for her to recover, then stood up and took over. "We need to get the injured people out of here as soon as possible. We're going to need everyone who is still mobile to play doctor. Stabilize what you can, and anything you can't stabilize come find me. You, Detective Lewis. Go down to the morgue and get whatever first-aid they can spare. Detective Delgado, I want you to go floor-by-floor and see who needs help and where."

Delgado looked at her, then looked at Briggs. "Boss?"

Briggs shook her head from her position on the floor. "I'm not the boss right now."

"She's the corpse doctor," Lewis said.

Gillian said, "Right now I'm the only doctor you have, and you're going to listen to me. Am I understood, Detective?"

He hesitated, but then he nodded and moved toward the stairs. A few seconds later, Delgado followed.

Riley crossed the room to Gillian and quickly embraced her. "That was hot. Thanks for the help."

Gillian chuckled and patted Riley's hip. "Hey, it's a medical emergency. You deferred to my wisdom, which *I* happen to find hot. And as much as I love you and rely on you, right now you'll be much more help elsewhere. Go."

"I can't leave you~"

"Riley. Don't make me order you."

Riley considered it for a second. "Maybe I want you to order me around."

Gillian pressed her lips to Riley's cheek. "Wrong time and place. But I'll keep it in mind. Go. Take Priest. I would love to have you both here for the triage, but that's like having Superman work the soup kitchen during World War III. They need you more than I do. Go."

"You're a good boss."

"Don't forget it."

Riley stepped away from her and motioned for Priest to come with her. They went to the stairs and Riley allowed herself one lingering look at Gillian, standing amidst the destruction and creating order from chaos. Bloody, one side of her scrubs pale with plaster dust, her hair askew, and backlit by the shattered windows, she looked like a hero come to save them all. She seemed to feel Riley's attention and turned to look at her, smiling and lifting her hand in farewell. Riley blew her a kiss and turned around, following Priest to the stairs.

Afghanistan, Land of Sand. Kirby, smiling under his helmet, looking back over his shoulder at her from the front seat of the Humvee. Kenzie felt the sun on her face. She felt the weight of the gear. And then, like a rubber band snapping back into place, she was out of it. The heat was from a fire, not the desert sun, and she was lying on the pavement. She opened her eyes and her eyes were drawn to the part of her body in the most pain: her left wrist was twisted in an utterly wrong way. Her stomach lurched at the sight but she fought the urge and looked away.

The car she had been standing beside was engulfed in flame. *Another roadside bomb*, she thought. She saw the officer sitting behind the wheel, dead before he even had a chance to escape. All around her people were screaming, and she could hear the hollow sound of nearby sirens. She saw her cell phone lying shattered on the ground beside her and kicked it away, knowing there was no hope of salvaging it.

She managed to get onto her feet, cradling her broken wrist against her side as she looked around for a hint at what she was supposed to do next. It was obvious that the other side had just drawn first blood in a big battle. She hoped her side was ready to counter-attack.

Riley and Priest found a group of uniformed officers milling around without direction and gave them orders.

The detectives had the patrol officers barricade the streets around the police station and had them only allow emergency vehicles in or out. Priest directed the other officers to begin setting up a triage center across the street so Gillian wouldn't have to worry about it when she started getting patients out of the building. She saw that at least some squad cars had escaped the destruction and commandeered one for herself and Priest.

They paused long enough to let a fire engine through. Riley watched with relief as a team of EMTs came off the truck and hurried into the building. She was sure Gillian had the situation well in hand, or at least as much as possible, but she was glad there would be backup for her.

Priest found a windbreaker in the backseat and pulled it on, zipping it up over her shredded blouse. "Where are we going?"

"We're splitting up. First, you're going to find Kenzie and make sure she's okay. Then you're going to find Marchosias." Priest stared at her, and Riley shrugged. "The last time Lark went end-of-the-world, Marchosias was surprised as anyone. According to you, he even helped make things right. Somehow I doubt he okayed a plan to blow up half the police cars in the city. I doubt he agreed to anything she's been up to lately."

"The angel blood," Priest said. "Riley, this could be the moment. She could be using this moment to ensure she won't be disturbed during the final preparation."

Riley flexed and relaxed her fingers on the steering wheel, debating her options.

"You need to go to Marchosias."

"Me?" Priest's voice was shrill. "Riley, I can't~"

"You have to, Cait. White flag, peaceful summit. Champion or not, March and his pals may still decide to have some fun with me. But an angel walks in... they'll behave."

"I don't know. I understand your logic, but I don't like the idea of you going to the mayor's office alone. Lark is strong."

"But for the moment, she's still human. And she's the champion for evil. It's my job to take her down. For now, we need to focus on getting our people together. We're going to need all the help we can get if Lark is really trying to become Satan." She laughed and shook her head. "I can't believe I just said that."

"It's just a metaphor. She wants to embody complete evil. If she succeeds, no one will be able to stand against her. Not me, not Marchosias... not the two of us and all of our armies backing us up. If she gains this power, it won't be a matter of fighting her. Fighting isn't..." She pressed her lips together. "Lark will be able to erase her enemies from existence with a thought. There won't be a battle, there will be an instant of blood between Lark deciding what she wants and when she gets it."

"Right. So we stop her. Go find Kenzie, find Aissa, and tell Marchosias what you found out in Seneca. I'll go to the Mayor's offices."

"And fight her alone?"

"Not yet. First I have to at least try fulfilling my promise to Abby Shepherd. If Emily Simon is there against her will, I'm going to do everything I can to get her out of the line of fire."

Priest nodded. "Okay. Good luck, Riley."

"Thanks." She looked into the passenger seat and saw Priest had disappeared. "I'm definitely going to need it."

For once a lack of police presence in No Man's Land turned out to be a good thing; they suffered very little damage when the city's police presence went up in a series of fireballs. Eddie had organized volunteers from the shelter to lend a hand, driving them closer to the carnage and dropping off two or three at a time before moving on to the next site.

So far they had seen three flaming husks of police cars. Thankfully the damage seemed to be confined to a relatively small area around each vehicle. The cars that had been in motion when they detonated had turned into flaming projectiles, crashing into poles or jumping the curb to mow down pedestrians before crashing into the first object solid enough to stop their forward momentum. The elevated track supports had been damaged at several points, so all the trains were currently frozen where they stood. Aissa looked up as she passed under one trestle, watching as emergency workers walked down the tracks to help the people stranded in the frozen cars.

Aissa approached one of the crash sites, the flames from the destroyed squad car having spread through the diner it had rammed. As she approached, she caught movement from the corner of her eye. At first she thought they were random punks taking advantage of the confusion to loot, but when she looked again she recognized them as the group who had overtaken and beaten her so badly a few days earlier.

She slowed to a stop in the middle of the street as they recognized her. One, the boy who seemed to be the leader, rolled his shoulders and moved to intercept her. He smiled and rubbed his hands together.

"Looks like we hit the jackpot. You better run, girlie."

Aissa met his eye, looked at his friends, and turned to face him fully. "No, you'd better run. Look around yourself. This is your city. This is your home, and someone just came and kicked your doors in. This is where you live and you're just letting them destroy it. A piece at a time, one injustice at a time, you're letting them pick away at it. I wasn't born in this town and I can leave whenever I want, but I'm going to stay. I'm going to stay, and I'm going to fight assholes like you because there are still good people in this city. If you want to fight me, then let's get it over with right now. Because I have a lot of damn work to do and I'm not going to waste any more time than necessary on you. The choice is yours. You can either beat me down again, or you can help me make this city a better place to live. But you have to make the choice right now."

She turned her back on them and started to walk. She braced herself for the sound of running footsteps and, when they came, she moved her hand to the switchblade concealed on her belt. She followed the trajectory of the sound and relaxed when whoever was running moved to walk beside her rather than colliding with her. She glanced over and saw it was one of the boys who had attacked her.

"You really think you can make a difference?"

"I think enough of us working together can do amazing things."

He shook his head. "You're delusional."

"Then why aren't you beating me up right now?"

He looked at her for a moment, and then looked at the flaming wreckage. "What do you need me to do?"

"Help," she said. "Help whoever needs it. And when they're set, move on to the next person."

"How many people need help?"

Aissa sighed. "All of us. So let's get to work."

Riley was still crossing the lobby of City Hall when the elevator doors opened to reveal Emily Simon. She looked coiffed and collected despite the late hour and the crisis happening outside. She wore a charcoal gray suit, and had a tablet tucked into the crook of her left arm. It was uncanny to see her after seeing Abby Shepherd's identical face in Gillian's morgue. Emily tapped the screen of her computer and took a breath as she positioned herself between Riley and the elevator doors.

"Detective Parra. As much as Mayor Siskin enjoys the interplay with you, surely you understand that she has more important things to deal with at the moment."

"That's okay. I'm here to talk to you."

Emily blinked. "Me? What business do we have with each other?"

"Abby wanted me to make sure you were protected. She went to a lot of trouble to tell my wife about you two and how you came to be Lark's lackeys. You're victims here, as much as the officers who died tonight in those car bombs. So this is it, Emily." She pointed at the door behind her. "Come with me. If you want me to put handcuffs on you to make it look like you're going against your will, that's fine. But if you refuse, and if you're here when I come back to take Lark out, then I'm not going to pull my punches."

Emily narrowed her eyes and offered a pitying smile. "Detective, I'm sorry. I'm afraid you're not making much sense. Abigail Shepherd was disturbed. She was addicted to drugs--"

"The angel's blood? The synthetic drug you created using a real angel's blood so Lark could be juiced up? You're addicted to it, too."

"So said the junkie." Emily looked at her tablet again. "If you'll excuse me, I have to prepare for Mayor Siskin's press conference. The press is arriving upstairs and she doesn't like making them wait."

She turned, and Riley spoke to her back.

"Didn't you love her?"

Emily stopped by didn't turn around.

"I mean, didn't you even care about her a little bit? You two started as enemies and you were forced together, but something had to change between you in all the time Lark was holding you prisoner. Abby risked everything to warn us about what happened to you. She died because she wanted to give you a chance to live. And you... you call her a junkie and ignore it? Is that really how you want to repay her sacrifice?"

"Detective Parra... Abby was..."

"She was a fellow sufferer. She was brought here against her will, just like you were. Lark took away your face, just like she took Abby's. Now every time you look in the mirror, you're going to see Abby looking back at you. Are you going to be able to face that every morning? It'll drive you crazy if you dismiss her now."

Emily's voice was steady, but in the slow and measured way that revealed the turmoil in her mind. "The Mayor is very busy today, Detective Parra. We don't appreciate you trying to disrupt things on this tragic day. Please leave."

"This is going to end soon, Emily. You need to decide if you're on the right side."

Emily walked on to the elevator without another word. Riley waited until the doors closed before she turned and left the lobby. She took out her cell phone and dialed Priest's number as she got back into the car.

"Cait. Did you find Kenzie?"

"I did. She's hurt, but nothing that won't heal in time. Where are you?"

Riley closed her eyes and whispered a silent prayer of thanks that Kenzie was in one piece. "I'm at City Hall. Emily refused to even listen to me, so I don't think we're going to be able to convince her to switch sides. But the important news is that Lark is preparing to give a live press conference at City Hall. That means she won't be at her penthouse. If we can get in and free the angel she's holding captive, we won't need Marchosias. We can just cut her off at the source."

"I'm all for any plan that saves me from making the demon an offer. I'll meet you there."

"Bring Kenzie."

Priest hung up and finished wrapping Kenzie's wrist in gauze. "You're certain you don't want me to just make this go away? I would only take an instant."

"You're going to need all the mojo you can spare to fight Lark. I can handle a broken wrist." She flexed her fingers as she stood up, leaning on Priest as she looked down the street toward the destroyed car. The rental car she'd been driving had been partially caught in the blast. "Good thing I splurged for the extra insurance."

"Indeed. Do you know where we could find Aissa?"

Kenzie shook her head. "I doubt she'll stay in one place for too long. Even if we found her, I doubt she'd come with us. She'll argue that she's needed here."

"And she wouldn't be wrong. Okay. We'll let her do her work here."

They started walking, and Kenzie tapped Priest's arm. "Can I borrow your phone? I know you told me Chelsea was okay, but I want to hear her voice."

"And I'm certain she'll want to hear yours." She handed the phone to her and Kenzie dialed. The phone chirped loudly in her ear and she winced, pulling it away as an automated voice began telling her that service was currently unavailable. "Damn it... how did Riley get through to you?"

"Oh, sorry." Priest put her arm around Kenzie's shoulders and put two fingers against the shell of the phone. The robotic voice cut off mid-sentence and she heard the line ringing. "A little divinity cuts through the clutter, even with modern technology."

Kenzie smiled. Priest was pressed against her side and she turned to put her free arm around Priest's hip as the line connected. She hissed at the pain in her wrist, but Priest touched her fingers and the pain lessened to a manageable degree.

"Caitlin?"

"No, baby. It's me."

There was a pause on the other end of the line, and then a shaky exhale. "Mackenzie. Thank God. Are you okay? Were you hurt?"

"A little. I think I broke my wrist, but Cait wrapped it up. I knew you wouldn't settle for someone telling you I was okay, so I thought I'd take a second to put your mind at ease."

"Thank you. I'm at the police station, helping Dr. Parra with the triage. Are you going to team up with Riley and Caitlin?"

"I'll go wherever they need me. Stay safe, sweetheart. Sometimes blasts like these can be followed by secondary explosions to take out people trying to offer assistance."

Chelsea said, "Same to you. I'm glad you'll have the champion and an angel looking out for you. I'll see you when the dust has settled."

"I look forward to it. I love you."

"And I, you. Be safe, sweetheart. Kiss Caitlin for me."

"I will." Kenzie reluctantly hung up and slipped the phone into the front pocket of Priest's jeans. "Thanks."

"No problem." Priest kissed Kenzie's cheek, then tilted her head to meet her lips. Kenzie leaned into the kiss, smiled, and leaned back. "I may have overheard her telling you to do that."

"Eavesdropper." She pecked Priest's bottom lip. "Come over when this is all settled, okay?"

"I've been thinking about our arrangement, actually. Now that you and Chelsea are married, I'm not sure it's proper for me to infringe."

Kenzie shrugged. "We're married, we're settled... we miss you. And I may need an extra pair of wrists lying around until I'm fully healed."

"Okay. For now we should meet Riley at the mayor's penthouse."

"Right. Priorities."

Priest put her arms around Kenzie and, in a flicker and a flush of air, they were standing on a different street. Kenzie stepped back and looked up at the building rising next to them, a black-glass tower that seemed to radiate evil. She looked at Priest, whose expression had darkened considerably.

"Cait? Everything all right?"

"No. Things are most assuredly not. The wards are down."

Kenzie looked at the entrance to the building, even though she didn't expect to be able to see anything. "Isn't that a good thing?"

"Ordinarily, yes. But Lark has thrown down the gauntlet. She's drawing attention to herself and then leaving her inner sanctum vulnerable. It's beyond foolish." She held her hand out, palm flat, and tested the air in front of the building's entrance. "Nothing. She wouldn't do this."

Kenzie looked up and down the street to see if Riley had arrived yet. "Well, we can't just stand here on the street looking at the place. If there's some kind of angel trap in place, maybe I should go in without you."

"No. I won't send you in without backup, especially not with a broken wrist." She pressed her lips together. "I'll be on my guard. If I tell you to run once we're over the threshold, don't hesitate. Just turn around and run. Understood?"

"You got it."

Priest ran her eyes along the edges of the building's entrance again, then whispered, "Okay," and stepped forward. She tapped her fingers against the door's silver handle before she gripped it, ensuring it wasn't warded or otherwise protected before she pulled.

The lobby was decorated in shades of black, white, and gray, with darker colors dominating the higher levels. The elevator doors were gleaming silver, separated by waist-high potted plants. The front desk was empty and still, with the security monitors blank and the phones sitting silently. The building seemed frozen in time. There were no sounds echoing down from the upper levels, no chimes sounding as the elevators moved from one floor to the next. Kenzie couldn't even hear the hum of an air conditioner.

"This place is unusually quiet, right? Even with the explosions, this place shouldn't be so dead."

Priest said, "I think Lark has abandoned the pretense that she's just an ordinary mayor. Stay behind me."

They crossed to the elevators. Priest pressed the up button and scanned the lobby again. Something passed through the air, subtle enough to feel but not strong enough to identify. The hairs on the back her neck stood up as she searched for the source.

Kenzie put her hand on Priest's arm. "Cait? If you're feeling anxious, we should probably leave. Riley will be here in a second~"

"They must be using massive amounts of will to imprison an angel, even a weak one. I'm sure it's just bleeding through from that."

The elevator chimed as it arrived. The doors slid open, and a man emerged faster than even Priest could react. His left arm went up and dropped like a piston, the object he'd been clutching in his fist slamming into and through Priest's chest as if it was no thicker than tissue paper. Priest's lips parted in an "O" of shock, flickering blue light pouring from her mouth and eyes as her legs buckled under her.

Kenzie lunged at the man but he countered her attack with a blind backhand. She was thrown back as if she'd been hit by a truck, landing on her shoulder and tumbling until the wall stopped her. The man released the twisted piece of wood that now jutted from the right side of Priest's chest, blood welling around the entry point. He put his hand on the butt of it and shoved until the point pressed against the back of Priest's shirt from the inside.

She dropped to her knees, hands curling into agonized talons as she stared up at him.

"Fe-fi-fo-fum," he sang, "I smell the blood of a seraphim." He smiled. "Good timing. The other one was almost all used up. I've been eager for some fresh blood for a while now. I almost don't know where to start. But don't worry, little angel. I'll figure it out."

A shard of broken glass had sliced through Briggs' calf in the initial explosion. One of Gillian's interns had sewn it up and, despite the doctor's insistence that she stay off of it, she managed to find a pair of crutches so she could help with the triage. So far the death count at the police station alone was fourteen, while thirty-two officers who had been out on patrol couldn't be contacted. An officer from Robbery/Homicide was gathering names and badge numbers of those who were MIA, while Gillian was struggling to keep some semblance of order to the makeshift hospital they'd created outside.

Briggs saw one of the medical examiner interns searching helplessly for a bed to put an injured detective. She seized the opportunity, balancing on her left leg as she got her crutches underneath her. The bloody detective - she thought she recognized him as Vice - thanked her as the intern began working on his head wound.

Briggs said, "Trust me, detective. You're doing me a bigger favor by taking the bed. Rest well." She crossed the tent area, weaving through the injured and those who were tending to the injured, until she reached the folding table where all the medical supplies Gillian could finagle had been dumped. She was opening boxes, moving items from one to the other so she could have one full box of bandages instead of two that were only half-full. A strand of hair had fallen down across her cheek, tangled around the earpiece of her glasses.

She looked up when she saw Briggs hobbling over and sighed with resignation. "Lieutenant, I thought I told you to rest and stay off that leg."

"The leg is in the air, Dr. Parra. I'm not doing anyone any good just lying on my back."

"You're doing yourself good. You're healing. That's enough, trust me."

Briggs shook her head. "Not today. Even if you just need me to get gauze or mop the sweat from your brow like in all those old hospital shows. I have to do something. Prop me up and let me take people's temperature."

Gillian sighed. "Well, you are persistent. Okay. You can be my assistant for now. I can always use an extra pair of hands."

Briggs moved closer, angling her crutches so she wouldn't trip Gillian up. "How have you been coping? I know living patients aren't really your purview."

"I'm dealing with it as well as I can. Some of my stitches may not be pretty, but for the most part they won't scar. And really, the important part is that the bleeding stops. And that part always happens no matter how good a job I do."

"That's the spirit, doc," Briggs said with a smile.

"Dr. Parra?" One of her interns had approached, looking harried and overwhelmed.

"I'll be there in a second, Diane."

The woman nodded thankfully and hurried back to her

patient. Gillian sighed. "Dr. Parra. I wish I'd taken it as soon as we got married. I really like how it sounds."

Briggs smiled. "It suits you."

Gillian squeezed Briggs' arm and then went to help one of her assistants. Briggs looked at the table where Gillian had been working and began organizing the supplies. Someone brushed past her, nearly knocking her crutches off balance. She twisted to admonish the person but the words died in her throat when she realized the man was muttering, "Parra... Parra..."

He was wearing a dirty zip-up jacket with the hood pulled up over his face. Gillian's back was to him as he approached, so she didn't see him slip the knife out of the pocket of his hoodie. Briggs put her weight on her good leg and pivoted toward the attacker. "Gillian!" Gillian turned and saw the man, too late to react as he brought the knife up and started swinging it down in a wide arc toward her face.

Briggs swung her crutch up into the man's crotch, swinging the other around to hit him in the side. He stumbled and twisted toward her and she saw that his eyes were glowing with inhuman light. Briggs dropped one of her crutches and pulled her weapon. The demon bared his teeth and lunged at her, slamming both hands into her chest with all the strength he could muster. Briggs felt something vital crunch as she was propelled backward. When she hit the ground something else within her broke. Air rushed out of her mouth and she felt something hotter and thicker than saliva spattering her lips and chin.

Dazed, she saw the demon turn back toward Gillian. He brought his blade up again and lunged with it, but Gillian had taken advantage of her attacker's distraction to arm herself. She heard Gillian's voice as if it was coming from the far end of a tunnel.

"You know holy water is basically just salt water? All you have to do is believe, you asshole. And you assholes kept attacking me in the morgue, so I asked Priest to help me take precautions. Ever wonder what an ME needed saline solution for?" She used a scalpel to pierce the bag she was holding and squeezed. A jet of blessed water squirted through the tear and splashed the demon's face. It recoiled with a pained howl, dropping the knife as it brought both hands up to protect itself.

Gillian closed the distance between them and pressed the bag tight against his face. She squeezed until the demon's face was drenched with it, and he finally twisted away from her and ran. He stumbled and fell over anyone that got in his way, fleeing from the tent as tendrils of smoke lifted from his face.

Gillian ignored the murmurs of shock and confusion from everyone around her as she rushed to Briggs. She knelt beside her and cradled her head, looking down at the obviously horrific concave destruction of her chest. Briggs coughed again and felt more of that warm not-spit on her lips.

"Hold on, Zoe... hold on."

Briggs closed her eyes, her mind reeling from one topic to another. She thought about her father's dream of seeing a perfect game, but her own opinion was that perfect games were boring. The thrill came from give and take, a combination of awe-inspiring plays and mistakes. It wasn't the mistakes she sought out, it was the recovery that made the game exciting.

She thought about all the bad things she had done as a cop, and the good things she'd done with Riley that maybe countered that a little bit. She had thought her leg would keep her from helping now, when it was really needed, but now she knew that it put her in the right place at the right time to be one of the most instrumental weapons in the final fight.

She tasted blood. It was getting harder to breathe; she was fairly sure her chest wasn't moving anymore and air was wheezing through her parted lips. She squeezed Gillian's hand, and Gillian looked at her. She looked helpless, terrified, and Briggs managed a smile.

"Have a... great year with her."

After that she heard Gillian shouting for someone to help her, desperate pleas for her to hold on that sounded hollow in her ears. The pain was too much but she could see a way away from it. There was a way out, like flipping the pillow to its cool side because the other side was too warm. She let herself go, felt the pain recede like the tide, and her grip on Gillian's hand weakened. Gillian clutched at her desperately, but she was beyond noticing.

She didn't know if her eyes were closed. She knew that if they weren't someone would close them for her soon.

Riley parked in front of the Mayor's penthouse and got out of the car, popping the trunk to take out the item she'd packed away a few weeks earlier. It was a Super-Soaker, the largest capacity water weapon on the market, and she tucked the butt of it against her side as she approached the front of the building. She would have felt ridiculous carrying the toy if she hadn't known how effective the holy water within it was against demons.

She stepped into the lobby and brought the gun up, giving herself a split-second to assess the situation before she opened fire. The water arced across the space and hit the demon dead-center in the chest.

He was in front of the open elevator doors, standing over Priest with his hand wrapped around something that was penetrating her chest. Priest's lips were red with blood, and Riley could see more blood pooling around the object being used to stab her. The holy water splattered on the demon's shirt, making him hiss. He twisted away from the stream as Riley quickly crossed to a potted plant and ducked behind it for the meager cover it would provide.

"Cait!"

Priest said, "Just a second." With the demon's focus divided, Priest harnessed her energy for a single burst of outward power. She brought her hands up, palms out, and pushed. Her divinity knocked the demon back on his heels, giving her the chance to rise and shove him physically back into the elevator. She spread her wings, the right one slightly askew from the chunk of wood pressing out of her back. Riley felt the wave of energy making the floor tremble as the demon decided to retreat.

"See you upstairs, angel... with all my toys."

Once the elevator doors were closed, Riley moved to Priest's side. Priest had sagged slightly when the danger was past but was still upright. "You okay?" She examined the jagged piece of wood that was still protruding from Priest's chest.

"I was meant to survive the attack. He wished to spend a lot of time torturing me before I finally died." She touched the hole in her shirt and then twisted. "Kenzie."

Riley followed her gaze and felt her heart drop. Kenzie was lying against the wall like a discarded toy, her back to the room, her legs twisted around each other. Riley left Priest and crouched next to her former partner, lightly touching her shoulder. "Kenzie..."

"Ow..."

"Thank God. How badly are you hurt?"

Kenzie allowed Riley to roll her onto her back, wincing as she flattened herself out on the floor. "Pretty bad. Think I need a doctor. I'll be fine."

Priest cried out and Riley looked over her shoulder. The

wooden shard was no longer in her, and blood spurted onto her shirt in a vivid red wave before Priest covered the wound with her hand. Divine light poured around her fingers as she healed herself, limping over to kneel next to Riley. Kenzie looked up at her and smiled weakly.

"Cait. Sorry. Wasn't very good backup, was I?"

Priest smiled. "No. But I love you anyway."

Kenzie chuckled. "I love you, too."

"Get her to the hospital, Cait."

Kenzie grunted. "No. I'll be fine..."

"No, you won't. Cait, you're weak, too. You both need to back up and recuperate. I'm not going to lose either of you because you kept going when you should have stopped."

"What about you, Riley?"

"I'm fine. Haven't been touched yet. I'm sick of these bastards coming after the people I care about instead of facing me head-on. Get Kenzie some help, spent a few minutes in a church, and then come back here to bail me out when I've gotten in over my head."

Priest couldn't fight back her smile and nodded. "I'll be here."

Kenzie grunted as Priest helped her up. "Are you sure you'll be okay here? That demon knows you're coming. He'll be ready."

Riley nodded. "Yeah. And the longer we spend saying goodbye, the more time he has to get ready for me. So Cait, get her help."

"The angel is being held on the sixth floor," Priest said. "At least that's where the strongest wards were present. Good luck."

"Thanks."

Riley stepped back as Priest embraced Kenzie and wrapped her wings around them both. They vanished in a flash and a rush of air, and Riley adjusted the water gun's position on her hip. She held it against her left side, using her dominant hand for her actual gun as she crossed to the emergency stairs. Using the elevator would be foolhardy; it would be like delivering herself to the demon in a ready-made cage. Using the stairs would at least give her a chance of defending herself. She looked up the central spiral of the stairs, trying to see a visual indication of what was awaiting her on the sixth floor. She exhaled sharply, set her shoulders, and began to climb.

Gillian didn't look up at the sound of approaching footsteps, her face buried in the crook of her elbow. She was seated on the ground, her back against the brick wall and her arms resting on her bent knees. Whoever approached touched the top of her head, and Gillian tried to fold deeper into herself. "Please, let someone else take care of it."

"I want to take care of you. What happened?"

Gillian looked up and saw Priest. She pushed up her glasses and wiped away her tears, exhaling sharply as Priest crouched in front of her. Priest cupped Gillian's face with both hands, her eyes tender as she waited for Gillian to be ready to speak.

After a few seconds of deep breathing, Gillian trusted her voice. "Lieutenant Briggs is gone. I tried to help her, but it was... the damage was too great."

"The other doctors told me. Gillian, I'm so sorry."

"She died saving me. How many more people are going to die because of me, Caitlin?" She noticed the blood on Priest's shirt and closed her eyes. "God. Not you, too."

"No, this was something else. I'm fine now."

Gillian sniffled. "You're a terrible liar."

"I'm an angel. I'm not supposed to be good at lying."

Gillian smiled at that, and then took off her glasses. "Riley trades her life for mine, like that's... normal, like it's a fair trade. And I've accepted that. But now Zoe... Zoe steps in so I have a chance, and she dies so I can live. What's so goddamned special about me? And where the hell was my guardian angel? Why can't I have an angel like you who swoops in to save the day? Why can't I... why can't I just get hurt so I don't have to see the people I love getting hurt in my place?"

"It's your burden," Priest said. "You love heroes and champions, and their job is to be the ones running toward danger. Your job is to heal. Your job is to be there when they fall so you can help them back up. You're a precious commodity, Dr. Parra. That's why the powerful warriors around you are willing to lay their lives on the line to keep you safe. Because as long as you are alive, there's hope in the world."

"I'm just..."

"You're not just anything, Gillian Eleanor Hunt Parra. You're beloved to a champion, and you're getting a pep talk from an angel of the Lord." She smiled. "You must be something pretty special. Lieutenant Briggs was a conflicted woman. She did many things in her life that she wasn't proud of. I think if she gave her life to save yours, it may have helped balance the scales in her mind. It was her redemption."

Gillian leaned forward and rested her cheek against Priest's unbloodied shoulder. "Thank you, Caitlin."

Priest kissed Gillian's temple. "You injured him with the saline pouches I blessed for you?"

Gillian chuckled. "Yeah. Good thing I asked you to do that. Hopefully it's an isolated incident. It was so bizarre. He was just muttering 'Parra' over and over again."

Priest frowned. "He was saying 'Parra'?"

"Yeah. I guess he overheard the interns calling me Dr. Parra."

"Parra. Not Gillian, not Hunt..."

"No." She leaned back and frowned. "You don't think he had me confused with Riley, do you? It was just some random demon on the street, but even they're too smart to randomly attack the champion."

"They should be." Priest thought for a long moment. "They are. Gillian, I have to leave you. Kenzie is here with Chelsea."

"We'll be fine. Go. Save the world. But if you can't save it all, just bring Riley back to me."

Priest smiled. "Will do. Would you like me to help you up?"

"Yes, please." Priest stood and offered Gillian a hand. Gillian stood and looked at Priest's wounds again. "Do you need anything? I may not be a warrior, but I can offer you a bandage or painkiller." She smiled. "Not that I think you really require either of those things."

"No, but thank you. I would take a change of clothes, but I'm stopping by my apartment anyway. I'll change there." She kissed Gillian's cheek. "Be safe, Gillian."

"You too."

Priest vanished in a flash, something Gillian was never quite prepared for, and she was left standing alone. She wiped her cheeks again and went back into the tent where the injured were still being treated. She found Kenzie and felt her heart seize at how beaten up she looked. Her face was bruised, her wrist bandaged. Chelsea was standing next to her bed, holding her hand. Gillian smiled as she moved to the other side of the bed.

"Mackenzie. You've looked better."

"Thanks, Doc. You know, once you get married, you just start letting yourself go."

Chelsea smiled. "Are you all right, Dr. Parra?"

"I'll be okay. I just wish there was something more we could do to help. I hate sitting around here waiting for word. I don't think I'd be very helpful in a fight. Hell, I'd probably just get in the way. But I just want to do something."

Kenzie said, "Well. No one's ever accused me of being overly religious, but I know Caitlin feels it when we pray for her."

Chelsea squeezed Kenzie's hand. "I think she could use all the prayer she can get today. Her and Riley both."

Gillian took Kenzie's hand and then reached across the bed to take Chelsea's. "Can't hurt, I guess. I'm a little rusty. It's been a while since my mama and grandma dragged me to Sunday school. But I'll do what I can."

She closed her eyes and bowed her head.

Priest discarded her soiled blouse and jacket in her building's incinerator, knowing now just how dangerous even a drop of angel blood could be in the wrong hands. She changed into a black T-shirt and jeans, recovered her sword, and took flight from the window of her apartment. She didn't want to waste time going to the roof; Riley was already in peril. Night now gripped the city, and she could see fires still burning on dozens of streets. Several blocks were dark, whether by choice or due to power outages, she couldn't tell. The destruction was worse than it had been after the earthquake.

She flew to No Man's Land, ignoring her soul's reluctance to be so near such thick demonic activity. She followed the air currents to a familiar hotel, a place where Riley had first made a foolish stand against Marchosias so many years ago. The soles of her shoes had barely touched pavement before she propelled herself forward and through the door. She didn't bother with the latch; there was enough power in her lunge that she knocked the door off its hinges. It flew into the lobby of the building like debris from a hurricane, and Priest extended her wings to their full span as she stepped inside.

Demons emerged from dark rooms and hidey-holes, scurrying toward her like kids trying to prove to their friends that they were brave. Priest held her sword with one hand, eyeing the demons with enough guile that they knew not to test her. She walked toward the stairs, forcing the demonic horde to part around her.

"Marchosias, show yourself!"

He appeared on the landing as if he'd been waiting for her cue. She'd expected cockiness, a confident smile, but instead he looked weak and wrung-out. His clothes looked slept in, and his face was pale and wan. He rested his hands on the banister and peered down at her.

"What do you want, Zerachiel?"

"Your pets are out of control. A demon attempted to harm Dr. Gillian Hunt Parra this evening while she tended to the wounded. I don't know which would be more disappointing... if you approved of Lark Siskin's bomb plot, or if she once again went off without your permission. Which is it, Marchosias?"

"A demon attacked Dr. Parra?" Marchosias looked away from her and scanned the group of demons. "Who knows anything about this?"

Silence loomed.

Marchosias moved to the top of the stairs. "Someone here knows what she's speaking of. If that imp does not speak up now, I will give her carte blanche to begin carving her answers out of you. Speak!"

"The champion's friends are fair game."

Priest and Marchosias both turned toward the speaker. The demon was lounging in one of the chairs in the lobby, not looking at either his superior or Priest. He was gaunt but with lean, wiry muscles that indicated he would be good in a fight. He stared at his hands and then slowly turned his head to watch Marchosias descend the stairs.

"Penemue," Marchosias said. "Did you arrange this?"

"Something had to be done. The champion had already defeated us once. Lark Siskin has the potential to succeed, but only if Riley Parra is distracted. I distracted her."

"You fool," Marchosias said. "We are demons, evil incarnate. We are the bane of existence, we exist to bring bad things in this world. But in this war, we abide by the rules set down at the beginning. We pull our punches so that the other side will pull theirs."

Penemue stood and seemed to expand laterally, widening as he extended to his full height. Though he towered over Marchosias by at least ten inches, Marchosias was still obviously the one in charge. Judging by the tension in the room, Priest couldn't help but wonder how long that would last.

"Zerachiel. Has Detective Parra lost anyone?"

"Yes. One of our friends has fallen."

Marchosias tightened his jaw and pointed at Penemue. "You have my permission to destroy this demon in retribution."

Priest met Marchosias' eye and frowned.

Penemue's eyes flashed with indignation and disbelief. "You would allow an angel to wield her strength in your home?"

"An eye for an eye. Dr. Parra's death was not sanctioned, so I allowed it to be rectified. This is more of the same. Zerachiel... dispose of him. Send him back below."

Priest held up her hand. Penemue lunged at her, but black smoke rose from his clothing before he could take more than two steps. The smoke built until the shape of his body was obscured by it, then it dissipated to reveal he had vanished.

Marchosias spit on the floor where Penemue had once stood and turned to address the entire room. "We fight this war by the rules, or I will remove the restrictions that prevent the angels from doing the same thing to each and every damned being in this room. You will be sent back to the depths of Hell with a flick of their wrists. You will writhe in torment for centuries before you even realize what has happened. The rules balance the scales between us, and you believe that weakens us? It gives us an advantage. Breaking the rules is our nature... but when Good breaks the rules, it makes them stronger than us.

"Gillian Hunt Parra. Mackenzie and Chelsea Stanton. Zoe Briggs. They are untouchable. This war will be fought between our champions, as it has been since the conflict began. And if you cannot abide by this, then I will allow the angel to repeat her banishment on each and every one of you. And I will ask her to do it slowly. Leave my sight."

The demons scurried back into the darkness, most of them looking cowed if not obedient. Priest watched them go and then approached Marchosias.

"Why did you make me do that?"

He smiled and shrugged. "Consider it an Xmas present. Leave before you have to burn your clothing to get rid of the stench."

He started to ascend the stairs again but Priest followed him. "An insubordinate demon challenged your authority in front of all your followers, and you allowed an angel to dole out the punishment. Why would you do that?"

"Maybe I was feeling generous." He stopped on the stairs. "Which of Detective Parra's friends passed away?"

Priest considered not answering, but decided he would know sooner or later. "Lieutenant Briggs. She died stopping the demon that was sent to kill Gillian."

"Hm. I had high hopes for her once. She could have been an effective player for our side. Real flip of the coin, that one. She was a minor victory for your side."

"Don't change the subject. Why would you allow me to send Penemue back to Hell?" She instantly followed her question to the only logical answer. "Because you couldn't do it."

Marchosias glared at her. "I am in my sanctum, angel. You would do well to watch your tone."

"Banish me. Kick me out of your building."

He turned and began climbing the stairs again. "Leave whenever you want. Hell, rent a room. Rates are actually quite reasonable."

"It's Lark, isn't it? She's siphoning your energy somehow." She thought for a moment and then her eyes widened. "The wards. She's found a way to use your profane energy to power the wards holding the angel hostage in her penthouse. How could you allow her to get away with this, Marchosias?"

He laughed and stopped at the head of the stairs. "I met a woman. She was strong, and she knew spellcraft like no one I had ever met before. Her brother was already host to a demon. She was delightfully blasphemous. She took joy in being evil in a way I'd never seen before. I wanted to see her face Riley Parra. I wanted to see how they would butt heads and I knew the battles they waged would be epic. So when she asked for a taste of my power, I was eager to see how she would use it. She was an amateur, but I had the power to make her go pro. But once she got her hooks in, I couldn't shake her. She's been drawing off me for months." He sighed. "I underestimated her hunger. I was right, you know. The city is in flames! Lark Siskin is a grand master at evil, Zerachiel. I thought I was using her as a tool. But I was her tool. She used me to access arcane information, and she used what she learned to become more powerful than me.

"Lark Siskin is going to defeat Riley Parra. She's going to win this battle and, with it, the war. When the dust settles, she will have defeated me as well. My advice, and I offer this sincerely... bid farewell to your friends, hold a wake for Caitlin Priest, and then kill her. Do it peacefully and return to Heaven. Warn them that Hell is about to become a very, very bad neighborhood. Because once Lark Siskin has become Satan, the next step will be to overtake God."

Priest bristled. "That would be impossible."

"Perhaps so. But she will raze Heaven to the ground in the

attempt. Have a good war, Zerachiel. It will most likely be over by dawn."

"Then help us."

He shook his head. "The rules, remember. Without rules, there is chaos." He looked around the empty lobby. "I wish you luck. But I am preparing for the end of my reign. It has been an extremely good run." He winked at her and turned his back to walk away, leaving Priest alone on the stairs with her sword unsheathed and her wings still extended.

Riley stopped on the sixth floor landing and paused next to the door, listening for sounds of an ambush on the other side. She waited a moment and then reached for the doorknob. She twisted the knob, pushed, and then retreated back to the stairs. She brought the water gun up and aimed it at the open door. She waited. Finally, she heard a chuckle from the other side of the door.

"Clever. You don't want to box yourself in the door like a target, and I'm not foolish enough to present myself as a target by coming to look for you. We seem to be at an impasse."

Riley agreed with him if that had been her intention. As soon as he spoke, she knew exactly where he was in the room. She rushed forward, standing up straight since he would be expecting her to present a smaller target by crouching. As soon as she cleared the door an arc of flame passed by her, burning her thigh as she brought the gun around and opened fire on him. Leraje was hit in the chest and twisted away from the burst of holy water, raising both hands to protect his face.

"I've brought down demons, I even took out an angel right before he fell. You think I'm scared of you, Leraje? I think you've gotten a little too comfortable in your human body."

She entered the room, releasing pressure on the gun until she was close enough to hit him point blank. Leraje dropped his arms, saw how close she was, and tried for another assault. Riley countered by dropping to one knee and firing from a kneeling position. The holy water splashed his throat and chin and Leraje stumbled backward. He nearly tripped over his feet as he moved toward the back of the room.

"I should have started believing in this stuff a long time ago. It's handy."

Leraje glared at her, second- and third-degree burns appearing on his neck and face. She saw the pink, blistered skin was already starting to heal itself, the energy required preventing him from casting another attack on her. Riley aimed the barrel of her water gun on his face and teased the trigger so that a single drop of holy water dripped from it. Leraje flinched and looked away, ashamed of his weakness.

"As much fun as this is, Leraje, I have bigger fish to fry. And you've been on the wrong side of reality for far too long." She searched her memory for an incantation that would be appropriate. "*Milum posteritisti vostrum vatissime.*"

Black smoke poured from every orifice, swarming around him like the dirty kid from Charlie Brown, swirling in a charcoal haze until his features were blurred.

"You've taken down angels and demons," Leraje said, "but can you kill a human? Lark may be evil, she may be a twisted soul, but she is still a human being. Can you kill her in cold blood? You may think you're ready for her, but when the time comes you'll have a moment of hesitation, and you will flinch. And in that moment, she'll have you."

Riley finished the spell - "*Ex lacrimamur.*" - and Leraje's body went rigid before he slumped backward against the wall. She moved to kneel next to him to check for signs of Lawrence Siskin's survival. She'd seen Gillian's reports of what happened to bodies subjected to prolonged demonic possession, so she wasn't hopeful. His eyes opened briefly when she felt for his pulse, startling her, but they stared unfocused for a moment before shutting again.

She stood as the elevator bell chimed to announce it had arrived on the floor. She brought up her water gun and her service weapon, training both on the elevator doors as they parted. Lark Siskin, still dressed in a black pantsuit over a white turtleneck, emerged with her hands raised to shoulder-height. She stopped just outside the elevator and smiled reassuringly.

"Detective Parra. I think the time has come for us to talk."

Riley raised an eyebrow and tossed down her water gun. "Talk... what exactly do we have to talk about? You just killed half the cops in this town."

"A third, actually. Granted, I'll admit the true casualty count will be a bit higher. Chaos theory... can't turn dozens of police cars into fireballs without a little collateral damage."

Riley narrowed her eyes. "So what is there to talk about?"

"I'm not interested in the war."

"I got that. You just want power for yourself."

Lark smiled. "Exactly. And I'm well aware that a balance is necessary. So I have an offer for you. You walk out of here in one piece, allow me to finish my plan, and I will deify you. You'll be a goddess, Riley. And goddesses don't age. Your little deal to die when you reach a certain age will be null and void because you'll never reach that age, and you will be God. Capital-G. You and Gillian Hunt could be the new Zeus and Hera. And hell, you can make your friends gods, too. Create a new pantheon. Hasn't this war gone on long enough? It's time a few new faces got put in charge."

"I've never really had delusions of grandeur. I just wanted to be a cop. I wanted to be a good cop. Not a hero, just someone who helped people."

Lark shrugged and moved deeper into the room. Riley moved to keep the distance between them. "But you could be so much more. Help so much more. You have, what... a year left? Think of how many people you could help in ten years, or a hundred years. And a century would just be the beginning for a goddess."

Riley said, "You know, I really like this offer."

Lark smiled. "I thought you would."

"No, not... I'm not taking it. But the fact that you're making it shows me how desperate you are. Lark Siskin, I'm placing you under arrest for suspicion in the squad car bombings. You have the right to remain silent~"

Lark spotted Leraje's crumpled body on the floor and her eyes flashed. "My brother. You killed him."

"He was dead a long time ago. I just evicted the parasite wearing him like a suit. Anything you say can and will be used against you~"

Lark interrupted her with an inhuman howl, charging across the space between them with her arms extended. Riley had a clear shot for most of the advance but Leraje's warning passed through her mind. She changed her aim from Lark's chest to her leg before she fired, hitting her in the thigh and forcing her to stumble. She recovered and lunged for Riley again and Riley's only option was to shoot Lark in the chest or face. Instead she chose to lower her weapon and twist her body so that Lark slammed into her shoulder.

They fell to the ground together, Lark's fingernails digging into Riley's arms through her sleeves. Lark hit the ground and immediately swung her fist in a wide arc. She clipped Riley on the chin and squirmed out from underneath her. She dug her fingernails into Riley's hand, trying to get her to drop her gun, but

Riley swung her other hand up and hit Lark in the side of the head. She pushed herself up, grabbing Lark's collar with one hand as she reached for her handcuffs with the other.

Lark pulled away from her, tearing her coat in the process. She dropped to her hands and knees, her bleeding leg extended out behind her like a dead limb as she pushed herself to her feet. She looked down at her leg, the blood pumping out and darkening her slacks, and she laughed quietly before she met Riley's eye.

"This could be our mythology. When the Goddess and the Devil finally stood face to face. Their last moments as mortals spent locked in combat."

Riley was gasping, enough adrenaline surging through her to keep her standing upright. Her breath was rough and she blinked to clear a droplet of sweat from her eyelashes. "I'm not really up for worshippers. Do you remember where I left off with your rights? Was it the right to have a lawyer?"

Lark smiled. "You've got this all wrong, Riley. We're not enemies. This has nothing to do with you and this little war. When I ascend, this war won't exist anymore. Hell, if you don't want deification, then I'll scrub your debts. No more dying. You can live out your puny existence as a mortal. I have worked too hard to let you stop me because of some goddamn ancient pissing contest. Champions... they mean nothing. Do you honestly think you have a hope of defeating Marchosias?"

"That's not what the champion is supposed to do. We're not soldiers. We're representatives. We stand for humanity, good and bad, and we remind the people pulling the strings what's at stake. I'm willing to fight for the woman I love. I'm willing to risk my life to take you down because I know this city will be a better place without you in it. And that proves to the angels that we're worth the trouble."

Lark laughed and limped forward. "And I show the demons that the shiny happy people can be corrupted? I got a pretty easy job, don't I? I've never been one for easy jobs. This is the purpose of my life, Detective Parra. From the moment I heard about Satan in Sunday School, I knew my path. I learned everything I could. I sacrificed. I used the people close to me as tools, instruments to achieve my goals. Everyone born to this world spends their meager life span trying to make a difference. Trying to be something, to make a mark so they will be remembered. This is my mark. It's time for a change. It's time to end the world as it is and begin a grand new existence for everyone."

Riley said, "Believe me, Lark. People are going to remember you when you're gone."

Her smile was manic when she held out her hands, wrists together. One hand was bloody from where she'd been holding her wound. "Do you really think you can arrest me, Detective Parra? Do you really believe you can hold me?"

Riley stepped forward with her handcuffs. "I'm going to do my best."

Lark grabbed the cuffs with her bloody hand, thrusting her other hand forward. She slammed her palm into the bridge of Riley's nose with all the force she could muster. Riley heard the crack and felt a rush of warm blood coursing over her top lip, dazed by the blow as Lark shoved her backward. Riley fell, and Lark kicked her in the side as she went down.

"It's a little early, but it'll just have to do. I have an angel to kill."

Riley rolled onto her stomach, ignoring the flashes of pain in her skull as the blood continued to pour over her face.

"Siskin! Don't do it."

She stopped without turning. "You're right. I can't do this with another living being present... the angel may send its soiled divinity into you and then where would I be?" She limped back to where Riley was lying, her hand braced against her injured thigh. Riley managed to get to her feet and centered her gun on Lark's chest. At this point it wouldn't be cold-blood; pulling the trigger would be self-defense.

"Do it, Detective," Lark said.

"You don't deserve to die, Lark."

"If I don't die, then I'll never stop. This is my purpose in life, Parra. I'm meant to ascend. Whether it happens today or three days from now or three years from now, if you leave me alive I will succeed. And if it takes longer than a year, I'll come back and find your grieving widow, and I will make her my consort. I'll make her grovel at my feet for my attention before I grant her my attention."

Riley fired. Lark was hit in the shoulder, her eyes wide as the force from the extreme close-range shot knocked her backward. She landed on her ass, tilted backward with one elbow on the ground and the other hand coming up to cover the wound.

"You shot me."

Riley held up her handcuffs again. "You know, I really can't remember where you interrupted me. I think I just have to start over. Lark Siskin, you have the right to remain silent. If you give up this right~"

Lark suddenly threw herself forward, grabbing Riley around the waist and propelling her backward like a football player with a tackling dummy. The backs of her legs hit the table and knocked them both off balance. Riley hit the ground and Lark rolled away from her to end up perched on her hands and knees. She looked up, her blood splattered across the front of her blouse and dripping from her chin.

"You know, without the angel blood, that might have really hurt. But now that my heart's pumping... I'm feeling no pain. Can you say the same, Detective?"

Riley aimed for Lark's head this time without qualms. Before she could pull the trigger Lark knocked the gun away from her. She brought her arm up and pinned Riley's arm against her side, holding her in place as she punched her in the head again. Riley sank down but couldn't fall completely due to Lark's hold on her arm. Lark punched her twice more, and Riley's sense of up and down suddenly became fluid.

"You put up a good fight, Parra. And I assure you, this will be part of my mythology. The day I defeated the last thing standing in my way. You'll be idolized, in your own way. The Cult of Riley. Unfortunately, it will be a posthumous adoration." She pulled Riley to her feet and hurled her at the large picture window.

Riley hit hard enough to make the entire wall shudder, her blood smearing the glass that remained unbroken. She lacked the strength to get up at that moment, her cheek and hands flat against the window.

"Damn it. In the movies, that would have shattered. You'd have fallen to your death... it would have been beautiful." She walked forward. "Oh well. I suppose real life must always be more mundane." She put Riley in a headlock and squeezed. "I'll have to settle for just breaking your neck. Not exactly artistic or original, I know, but I imagine it will be satisfying to actually feel you die. Goodbye, Detective Parra."

The elevator doors chimed again. Lark smiled. "Your angel is a little late, isn't she?"

"Lark. Stop."

She froze and then twisted at the waist, forcing Riley to turn with her. Emily Simon stood in front of the elevator, looking surreally ordinary in her suit with the ever-present tablet computer still tucked against her side.

Lark spit blood on the floor and said, "I thought I told you I would be out of the office for the rest of the night. I'm not ready for the press."

"Let her go, Lark."

"Um." Lark looked at Riley, pretended to consider it, then shook her head. "No."

Emily smiled sadly. "You made me love her. She was my enemy, but you made us love each other. You took away everything until all we had was each other. We had no choice but to fall in love. And then you killed her. Why would you do that to me, Lark?"

Lark glared at her. "You haven't been taking your injections, have you?"

"I've been weaning myself off of it ever since Abby died. Ever since you murdered her."

Lark sighed. "Sorry, Detective Parra. I should probably deal with this." She shoved Riley away and stepped over her. Riley gasped in great mouthfuls of air, her arms trembling from the effort of holding herself up. She rubbed her throat and watched as Lark calmly approached her aide. "Emily, you're fired."

"No, Lark. You are. You changed everything about us, brainwashed us, but you couldn't change our souls. You couldn't change the people we were deep, deep inside. That's why there's another bomb. When I designed the bug that turned those GPS devices into explosives, I made another one. Just in case. I thought it was a last-ditch escape hatch in case Detective Parra got too close, but now I know why I did it. I did it to stop you."

Lark tilted her head to the side, her curiosity casual. "Where is the last bomb, Emily?"

She smiled. "Apologize to me for killing Abby."

"I am very sorry. She was lost to us. She wouldn't have been the woman you loved anymore, so I took her out of her misery. She was peaceful at the end, I promise you."

Emily pressed her lips together. "You're lying."

"Of course I'm lying, you whore. Where is the last bomb? Is it in the angel's cell?"

Riley had gotten herself off the floor, still dizzy but clear-headed enough to know where the last bomb was. "Emily... don't."

"You were right, Detective. Abby and I were both victims. You showed me what I had to do. I wish you weren't here right now. I'm sorry."

Riley summoned what little strength she had left and ran. She stumbled for the far side of the room as Lark ran toward Emily. Emily ignored them both and looked down at her tablet computer. She swept her finger across the bottom of the screen to unlock it. Lark slammed into her as she pressed her palm against the face of the computer, clutching the computer to her chest as Lark collided with her. Emily went limp and collapsed like a wet noodle. Riley jumped the counter that separated Lark's living area from the kitchen. She slid across the slick top as Emily's computer detonated, the force of the blast picking Riley up and dumping her on the hard tile floor on the opposite side of the counter.

Riley heard the windows breaking, saw debris from the main room turned into shrapnel. She covered her head with both hands, deafened by the force of the blast. She wasn't certain how long she was unconscious, but when she came to she was drenched from the fire-suppression system and sprinklers. Her entire body was trembling as she forced herself into a sitting position to examine her wounds.

She heard footsteps on the debris on the other side of the counter and closed her eyes. "You've gotta be shitting me." She scanned the floor for her gun but realized she had dropped it near the windows. She looked at the drawers, wondering which of them was most likely to hold a knife, knowing she didn't have the time or the energy to search.

"Riley?"

She smiled and relaxed at the sound of a very welcome arrival's voice. "Over here."

Priest stepped around the corner and sucked air through clenched teeth when she saw Riley. She crouched and touched the side of Riley's head.

"You said you'd get here at the last minute."

"Looks like my watch is slow."

Riley smiled. "Lark?"

Priest looked around the counter into the living room. "I believe I can see... parts of her."

"Ew." She swallowed and grunted. "The angel she's holding... Pahaliah. He's..."

"I can feel him. Will you be all right here?"

Riley nodded. "Yeah. I just want to sit for a few... months..."

Priest kissed Riley's cheek and then stood and went to find her captive brother.

The pain was good because it meant he was still alive. The pain was bad because it meant he was still alive. Worship was a foul thing to him now, worship the thing that could have saved him once a long time ago. It tore at him. He hated himself. He was wrapped up in these thoughts when the door opened again and he looked away, anticipating more of the same. But there was something different about the person who stepped into the room with him and he raised his eyes to see a holy angel.

"Zerachiel."

"Pahaliah." She cupped his cheek. "I am so sorry you have been through this trial, brother. I'm here to set you free."

He wept. "I don't... I can't go back to Heaven. I've become... I've... what they did to me..."

"Heaven and Hell aren't your only options, Brother. I've been in this body for five years. I've lived as a mortal, and I've found it..." She searched for the right word and smiled. "Interesting. These blasphemous things done to you... they made you more than demon but less than angel. We have a word for that. Mortal."

He closed his eyes. "The temptation to fall..."

"...is something that mortals deal with every day. You have the benefit of knowing the truth, of knowing what you gain with faith. I can't take you back to Heaven. And I will not condemn you to the pit. But I will free you, if you wish, and you can bring a bit of Heaven to this realm. You can help them heal from the wounds your tormentor has caused."

"Will you help me?" he said softly.

Priest smiled. "For as long as I'm here, Pahaliah. You have my word."

He nodded slowly, tears streaking down his cheeks. "Please, Zerachiel."

She rested her forehead against his. Light grew between them, and she set him free.

Medical teams from surrounding cities arrived shortly before dawn, and Gillian was relieved from duty to be replaced with actual trauma doctors. She gratefully handed over her duties to them, and her final act as crisis manager was assigning someone to drive Kenzie and Chelsea home. She was utterly exhausted, but she couldn't bring herself to stop moving. She relegated herself to being a go-fer, taking orders from the "real" doctors and nurses who actually took the time to praise her for keeping things as calm as they were. They told her the tragedy would have been much worse without someone holding back the tide.

She was about to fall over when something near the roadblock caught her eye. It looked like something out of a zombie movie, a shambling and shuffling being who didn't know it was supposed to lie down and pass away. Blood was smeared across the woman's blouse, and dried blood had darkened on her jaw and throat. Gillian was running even before she acknowledged recognition, tears burning her eyes as she ran out of the medical center.

Riley saw Gillian breaking away from the group and smiled. Life returned to her movements and she picked up the pace, too exhausted to run but holding out her arms to catch her wife. Gillian collided with her, sobbing against the side of Riley's head. Riley clutched Gillian, digging her fingers into her back and sighing with relief.

"You're okay," Riley said.

"*I'm* okay? Of course I'm okay... I've been going crazy."

"It's over now."

Gillian pulled back and tried to wipe away the blood on Riley's jaw. "It's over... she's gone?"

"Yeah. Priest and I are going to find Aissa and go see Marchosias now. I'm going to hand the mantle over to her. This is it, Jill."

Gillian nodded. "Be safe. Keep your guard up. Don't ruin things by dying now."

Riley smiled. "I've got more than a year left. I plan to get every minute I'm owed." She kissed Gillian softly, and Gillian cupped the back of her head. When they finally parted, Riley touched her cheek. "Go home. Get some sleep. You had a long night."

"Look who's talking." She blinked back her tears. "Wake me when you come home, okay?"

"Yeah. I'll see you soon."

They kissed once more, and Riley whispered something in Gillian's ear. Gillian returned the sentiment and finally, reluctantly, pulled away from her.

She saw Priest waiting a few feet away and waved, and Priest dipped her chin in acknowledgement. Riley let her hand linger on Gillian's arm and then walked away from her. Gillian watched them go and then began looking for someone who could drive her home.

They found Aissa in an empty storefront, the windows covered with brown paper and the door propped open by milk crates. She was seated at a card table with a laptop open in front of her, and she looked up when Riley and Priest entered. "My people are hearing rumors that Mayor Siskin is dead. Are they true?"

"Your people?" Riley said.

Aissa nodded. "I shamed them a bit. Reminded them that crimes committed against No Man's Land amount to self-harm. I may have reminded them what pride felt like."

"Well. The rumors are true. The witch is dead."

Aissa smiled. "Congratulations."

Riley shook her head. "I didn't have much to do with it. But this set-up... this is nice. Too nice for a champion-in-training." Aissa looked away from the screen again. "How do you feel about a promotion?"

Aissa shot to her feet. "Now? Today?"

"Unless you're too busy running your army."

Aissa grinned.

Marchosias was waiting in the lobby of the building when Riley arrived with Priest and Aissa. "Well, here we are again, Detective. You've defeated me twice. That doesn't exactly put you on my good side."

"Darn. Because I have to ask you for a favor."

Marchosias raised an eyebrow. "That's not the way this goes. You come here, we meet, and you decide~"

"Yeah, yeah," Riley waved dismissively. "The war continues, and you can pick your new champion. You're not taking Gillian away from me again. Just try to choose better this time, huh? Lark Siskin was a real shitty choice."

Priest said, "How are you feeling, Marchosias? Lark Siskin's death should have returned some of the vigor she stole from you."

He breathed deeply and then nodded. "Yes. I feel as if the dark clouds have passed. Not quite fully up to strength, but I'm getting there." He looked at Aissa. "What is she doing here?"

"She's part of the favor I want to ask you. Right now the war is on hold until you choose a new champion. You're going to want to take your time so you don't make the same mistake again. My time is up in a year. I already have my successor chosen so the war won't have to take a break when I die. I want a clean slate. My protection as champion gets transferred to Aissa now, and in a year we don't have to deal with making another transition."

Marchosias tapped his chin. "And what do I get out of the deal?"

"Riley won't beat you a third time," Priest said.

Marchosias smiled and looked at Aissa. "She's awful young."

"And she's already a better champion than I ever was. You should be worried about her Marchosias. I chose really well."

"Then I shall have to really take my time to choose Lark's successor. Perhaps a year. And if hostilities are relaxed, it really doesn't matter to me which one of you has the protection of champion." He waved his hand dismissively. "Do as you will, Zerachiel."

Priest put her right hand on Riley's shoulder, her left on Aissa's, and closed her eyes.

Marchosias smiled. "The next stage of the war has begun. Detective Parra, you were a worthy adversary, but I can't say I'm sorry to see you bowing out early. Aissa Good. We're going to have some fun together."

Aissa smiled. "I can't wait."

The demon's smile wavered and he raised an eyebrow. "Hm. Yes, well. I have some post-game analysis to go over, where we went wrong and how we can do better in the future... you can see yourselves out."

They walked outside together. Riley stopped on the sidewalk and touched her shoulder. Though she couldn't stretch enough to touch her tattoo, she could almost sense that it had changed. "So that's it? After all this time, I'm just... not champion anymore? Just a normal person."

"A mortal perhaps," Priest said. "Never normal."

Riley grinned. "How do you feel, Aissa?"

She took a deep breath. Tears shone in her eyes, and her voice shook when she spoke. Riley couldn't help but smile when she saw the joy in her successor's eyes. She knew Aissa understood the challenge, but her expression at that moment assured her that the girl was ready. "Like my life has been building to this moment. I can't believe it's finally here."

"Believe it," Priest said. "Don't take Marchosias lightly."

"Oh, I won't." She held out her hand. "Thank you for this honor, Detective Parra. I'll do my best to live up to your example."

"Forget living up to it. Exceed it. You're already on the right track."

Aissa nodded. "I should get back to No Man's Land. Eddie wanted me to check in before lunch, and the kids get restless when I'm away for too long."

"Can't have that," Riley said. "Take it easy, Aissa."

"Will you come see me again before you leave town?"

"You know I will."

"Good. Goodbye, Zerachiel."

Priest nodded and shook Aissa's hand. She turned from them and put her hands in her pockets, hurrying down the street. Riley and Priest watched her go.

"She's going to change the world."

"Yes, she is. You chose well, Riley."

"Yeah. At least I did one thing right as champion."

Priest looked at her. "What do you mean?"

Riley indicated No Man's Land all around them. "The earthquake, the car bombs... the city is a mess. The police force has practically been decimated. This place was bad when I came in, but it's barely standing now."

Priest thought for a moment. "Riley, you are one of the greatest champions I have ever seen. Did you honestly believe you could fix everything in five years? This city was spoiled at its core. It was blinded to its own downfall. When you became a police officer, you were the only one willing to enter No Man's Land. Now there's Kenzie, Aissa, Chelsea, Muse... Radio is helping to clean up the Underground.

"Even Mayor Siskin's plot, her heinous decision to kill so many good police officers, will ultimately change this city for the better. She tried to distract us a few weeks ago by having us teach a class of new recruits. Those recruits will now be brought up through the ranks quickly to fill the gaps that have been created. Recruits who were taught your style of policing, who listened to your wisdom and took it to heart. Soon this city will be crawling with police officers you molded, Riley."

Riley stopped on the corner and looked down at her shoes. "I didn't have anything to do with that. Kenzie and Chelsea, they... a- and Radio. It was his choice."

"Kenzie chose to stay because she was curious about your actions. Her love brought Chelsea out of her cocoon of shame and made her the righteous warrior who has been helping us these past few years. Your forgiveness also helped her forgive herself. And you ventured into the Underground to save Radio when he first arrived. You may not have realized it, Riley, but you've been setting this city back on the right course with every action you've taken over the past five years. Every life you've saved, every heart you gave peace, has helped to heal this city. You created ripples, and they'll continue long after you're gone. You've turned the tide against No Man's Land. You've given hope where once it was a foreign concept."

Riley forced a smile. "Huh."

Priest put her hand on Riley's shoulder. "Enjoy your life, Riley. You've earned a little peace."

Riley looked at her and, after a moment, nodded. "Thanks, Caitlin."

"Of course. Do you want me to take you home?"

"Yes. I really, really do."

Priest dropped Riley off outside her apartment. "Want to come in? I'm sure Gillian wouldn't mind a celebratory cocktail."

"I promised Kenzie and Chelsea I'd come over."

Riley grinned. "Give them my love."

"I will. And mine to Gillian."

"Yeah." She held out her hand. "Thanks for coming to find me, Cait."

Priest nodded. "Any time."

When she was gone, Riley went into the apartment. The adrenaline was wearing off, and she stood just inside the threshold for a moment and let the weariness wash over her. She took a deep breath and looked at the couch, expecting Gillian to be there under an afghan waiting for her, but she wasn't. The light over the stove was on, giving enough light for her to see, and she paused to take off her shoes.

"Honey?"

Gillian came out of the bathroom and paused on the other side of the couch. "What happened?"

Riley sighed. "It's done. Aissa is the champion, I'm free. We're free."

Gillian hurried to her, embraced her, and hugged her hard. "Sorry..."

"No. Big hugs are good." She clutched Gillian. "Tighter is good. God, you feel good." She smelled Gillian's hair and sighed.

"I drew a bath for you."

"And they call me a hero."

Gillian kissed Riley's neck and took her hand. "Come on."

She led Riley down the hall and into the bathroom. The overhead light was off, but the half-dozen candles lining the sink and the far edge of the tub cast enough flickering light to see. Gillian stroked Riley's arms and pressed against her from behind as she examined the layout.

"Thought you deserved a little pampering."

"Thank you. But I'll only take the bath if you share it with me."

Gillian groaned. "You drive a hard bargain, Detective Parra."

"I'm a good negotiator, Dr. Parra." She reached for the buttons of her shirt, but Gillian stopped her.

"Let me undress you."

"Talk about your hard bargains."

Gillian stepped around her and undid the buttons of her shirt. She peeled it away from her, ignoring the dried blood and scorch marks. Riley's arms and chest were bruised, but Gillian ignored those as well. They would heal. Riley lifted her arms so her undershirt could be taken off, then turned around so Gillian could unhook her bra. The underwear fell away, and Gillian dragged her fingers over Riley's back so lightly that the touch made her shudder. She paused on the tattoo and circled it with her middle and ring fingers.

"Hm."

"What?"

"The tattoo looks different. I mean, it looks the same, but it's... there's something about it."

Riley smiled. "It's just my old tattoo. Nothing special."

Gillian bent down and kissed the ink, then finished undressing her. Riley returned the favor, grateful for how easily scrubs could be pulled off of a willing body, and they helped each other into the bathtub. Gillian settled against the curve of the tub and Riley reclined against her, eyes closed as she let her feet drift. She liked baths, liked the feeling of weightlessness. And she enjoyed the slick, strong weight of her wife underneath her.

Gillian wet a washcloth and gingerly dried the blood from Riley's face. She ran it down to her chest, wiping away the grime until only clean skin remained. She draped the washcloth over

Riley's chest and then crossed her arms over it. She kissed Riley's cheek and nuzzled her temple.

"So," she whispered. "What now?"

"Now we finish the bath," Riley said. "We can figure everything else out tomorrow."

Gillian kissed her cheek again. "Sounds good to me."

Riley lifted her feet out of the water and rested them on the edge of the tub. She may have had a finite amount of time left before her debt came due, but the war was won and the battle was done. She could spare a single night to soak in the bath with her wife before she thought about where they would go when they woke up in the morning.

For the moment she was just going to enjoy the wide range of possibilities that had been opened to them.

lay down on the bed, and Riley shifted top to bottom and settled on top of her, straddling Gillian's head as she kissed her thighs. Gillian sighed, one hand on Riley's ass and the other between her legs as Riley kissed along the inside of her thigh. At the first touch of Riley's lips, Gillian felt herself peaking again. This time neither of them called for a retreat, and Gillian pressed her cheek against Riley's thigh as she came. Her head swam as she returned the favor, running her hands over Riley's flanks until her body tensed twice, then relaxed.

Afterward, when the bed was silent and their rough breathing filled the room, Riley twisted so that her head was on Gillian's hip instead of between her legs. She licked away the sweat there and Gillian sucked in a breath.

"Good morning."

Gillian patted Riley's ass. "Good morning."

Riley rolled off of her then scooted close so that they were pressed together. Gillian rolled onto her side, looped her arms around Riley's waist, and kissed her thighs. Riley kept her head on Gillian's hip and closed her eyes.

"It's a big day today. We should get up."

"I will if you will."

"Deal."

They remained where they were for a few minutes before they reluctantly moved. Riley led the way into the bathroom and climbed into the shower. Gillian joined her a moment later, whispering an oath that they would keep things strictly confined to bathing.

They managed to keep the promise, for the most part.

Afterward Riley put on her dress uniform while Gillian curled her hair. Gillian came out of the bathroom, hair done but wrapped in a towel, and paused to appreciate the sight of her wife. She walked over, pinching the collar and taking away the job of knotting the tie. Riley let her do the knot and smiled when Gillian exhaled sharply.

"My lady."

"I look good?"

"You look damn good." She kissed the corner of Riley's mouth. "You need to cry?"

Riley shook her head and looked down at the cuffs of her shirt. "I'm not going to cry."

"You liked her. She was a good boss. She died to save my life." She touched Riley's cheek. "It's okay if you want to let it out."

Riley smiled sadly and shook her head. "Briggs... Zoe... was complicated. She made some bad choices, and she did her best to make up for them. I'm sad she's gone. The police department is going to be weaker without her. But you told me what her last words were. I think she knew exactly what she was doing when she attacked that demon. I never told you, but she said she wished there was a way she could give her life for yours. To spare me from having to pay the debt. I think she found a way to make it happen."

Gillian blinked back her own tears. "I wish you people would just let me be normal."

Riley shrugged. "Human nature. We save what's precious to us."

"So how do I save you?"

She kissed the corner of Gillian's eyes, tasting the salt of her tears before they fell. "Remember me. Keep my name alive. Live."

Gillian took a deep breath and brought Riley's hands to her lips. She kissed the knuckles, squeezed the fingers, and said, "One year, two months. I'll get fourteen more months with you."

"Yeah."

"It's not enough. But I won't be greedy."

Riley smiled and kissed her properly. "Get dressed. Chelsea and Kenzie wanted to take us out to breakfast before the service."

"Yes, ma'am."

She dropped the towel and Riley let herself be distracted for a few seconds before she focused on donning the rest of her outfit.

After the dust settled, the final death count stood at one hundred and three police officers dead in the Mayor's attack. Over three hundred people had been injured, with many of them still hospitalized in critical condition. The city was full of funerals that week, private ceremonies orbiting around the mass public service held for all the officers lost. Lark Siskin's official cause of death was listed as accidental, a side effect of the as-yet unexplained terrorist attack.

Zoe Briggs' memorial service was held in a small church near the waterfront, with Riley and Priest serving with the pallbearers. The sun was out, and a cool breeze was blowing off the water as the mourners said their final farewells. Riley, standing with Gillian in the crowd of mourners, found her wife's hand and squeezed it. Gillian returned the squeeze and rested her head on Riley's shoulder. Riley found her attention drifting during the Scripture recitation and the performance of Briggs' favorite song.

She looked at the headstones that surrounded them, the rolling length of almost unnaturally green grass, a golf course dotted with small stone placeholders. She imagined what hers would look like, what Gillian would put on it. Riley Jacqueline Parra. Beloved Wife, Dedicated Police Officer... Foolhardy Deal-Maker?

Gillian lifted her head, her lips grazing Riley's ear in a deliciously intimate way when she spoke. "You okay?"

Riley nodded and pressed tighter against Gillian's side.

After the service was finished, Kenzie and Chelsea found them in the crowd. Kenzie wore a dress, the ultimate sign of respect for their fallen comrade, and Riley honored the gesture by not mocking it. Kenzie sat on the trunk of Riley's car and watched as the crowd dispersed. Priest remained by the gravesite longer than anyone else, finally walking away only when the cemetery workers moved in to begin filling in the hole.

"Everything okay?" Riley asked her.

Priest nodded. "Just saying a few extra blessings over her."

"Good. She deserves it." She looked out over the headstones again, tensed so that she wouldn't shudder, and reached up to loosen her tie. "So, everyone over to our place for drinks?"

Kenzie clapped once and slid off the car. "I'm in. We just have to stop by our place first so I can change."

"Okay. Cait, you in?"

"Sure. There's just something I have to do first."

Gillian said, "So half an hour, we reconvene at our apartment?"

"Sounds good," Riley said. "We'll see you then."

They parted with hugs, the Parras and Stantons going to their cars while Priest walked away on foot.

The church was colder than she expected, and she was grateful that she was still wearing the heavy dress uniform jacket. Her hair was braided, but she reached up to let it free as she walked down the aisle toward the altar. It was the place where she'd been born, an angel in a brand-new human body kneeling in worship before she rose and joined the mortal world. She remembered those days clearly, although sometimes they felt as if they had happened to someone else.

Priest stopped at one of the first few pews and took a seat. A priest - lower-case p - appeared through a side door, drawn by the sound of her entrance, and crossed to stand unobtrusively near where she was sitting. He waited until she looked at him before he smiled and held up his hand in greeting. He was a small man with a stooped back, his thick white hair combed back away from his face.

"Hello. I'm Father Garret. Were you attending... well, I suppose that's a silly question. Of course you were at one of the many funerals."

Priest nodded. "My boss. My friend. Lieutenant Zoe Briggs."

"I'm sorry for your loss."

"Thank you."

"I didn't want to disturb your peace. I simply wanted to let you know I was available if you needed to talk."

"Thank you." He started to walk away, and Priest said, "I was born here."

He paused. "Here in this city?"

"This church."

Garret frowned. "I've been here thirty years... don't mean to guess at your age, miss, but I haven't heard anything about a birth. Are you certain it was this church?"

Priest nodded. "Yes. I remember it well."

"You... remember it?"

"Very clearly."

Garret considered her for a moment and then, deciding she wasn't crazy or lying, decided there was a logical explanation for what she said. He stepped closer and joined her on the pew.

"So why have you come back here today?"

"Things are changing for me. Rapidly. Someone I've known my entire life is... leaving. I don't know if I'll be able to survive without her. But I know that letting her go is the right thing to do. I just worry about..."

Garret waited for her to continue. When she didn't, he said, "You worry she won't be able to take care of herself?"

"No. I worry about who I will be without her. Knowing her has changed me, and I fear that without her in my life I'll change. I don't want to change. I want to be the person I am now, even though I know that's impossible."

He nodded thoughtfully. "You feel this person has changed you. Is it reasonable to assume that you've changed her as well?"

"Oh." Priest chuckled. "Yes. I would say so."

"And this... separation you're going through. Is it acrimonious?"

"No. If we had a choice, we would probably still work together. It's just... not an option. For reasons far too complicated to go into."

Garret nodded. "I see. Well. You needn't worry. The changes caused by the people we love don't go away just because the people aren't there anymore. You've left indelible marks on each other. You've put each other on different paths, you've traveled them together, and now... you couldn't find the original path even if you wanted to. Just keep moving forward and honor the changes your friend has made in you. And accept that, just maybe, parting company is just the next step in your journey."

Priest smiled. "Thank you. You've been very helpful."

"I like to do what I can. And thank you. This has been a very trying time for the city, and for the police force specifically. Thank you for what you're doing for us."

She nodded and Father Garret stood. He walked to the aisle, then paused and turned around. "You said that you were born here. It wasn't a, um... usual birth, was it?"

"No, Father."

"Hm. When your eyes are open and your mind welcomes the impossible, you see all sorts of things other people miss. Especially in this city."

Priest nodded. "You are not wrong."

"Say goodbye to your friend, Officer. Let her know how much she's meant to you. And then... let each other go."

"I will."

Father Garret left, and Priest slid off the edge of the pew. She folded her hands, resting her elbows on the back of the pew in front of her, and rested her fists against her forehead.

"I can't go with her. And you can't not go with her. I've been thinking about this, and it's the only solution. We need to say goodbye, Zerachiel. I wouldn't exist without you. But I've experienced life as a mortal, and I think now... as my choice... I think I can handle it. I want to live. I want to be human, I want to hurt and feel. I want to have a life that isn't centered around Riley's. I love you, Zerachiel, but you and I haven't been the same person for a long time now. We've been two separate lives sharing a body. You've been trapped in it, and I'm letting you go. You deserve to be an angel again.

"All I ask is that you leave the pain. The pain of losing Riley, the mortal love I feel for her. You need to let it go so you can move on when the time comes. I know I've fought you on this in the past, I know I've harbored anger at the other guardian angels who allow grievous pain to befall their charges, but that's the mortal taint in my soul. I know that it's necessary. I know sometimes you have to be able to step back and watch the atrocities happen. So give me that love. Let me feel the pain." She smiled. "We've always thought humans were better equipped to handle heartbreak and sorrow, right?"

She felt warmth that spread down the length of her spine and expanded outward.

"Goodbye, Zerachiel."

She thought she heard a voice echoing, but it faded before she could make out the words. She smiled at the sentiment and then started to stand. Her head swam and she dropped back onto the pew, one hand on her temple as pain shot through her body. She ached tremendously, trembling as she wrapped her arms around herself.

"Oh, God," she gasped, biting her bottom lip as her body clenched around itself.

The moment she thought she couldn't bear the torment any longer, it faded. The relief was almost orgasmic, and she held out her hands to look at her palms. There was an empty, hollow feeling between her shoulder blades, and she rolled her shoulders.

"No wings," she whispered. She smiled and raised her eyes to the rafters, scanning for any visual evidence of the other part of her.

She was mortal again. She took a deep breath and held it until she hurt, then exhaled. She coughed, tears in her eyes, and laughed as she got to her feet and smoothed down the front of her uniform jacket.

"Goodbye, Zerachiel," she said again. She picked up her hat, placed it on her head, and walked down the aisle of the church. She didn't want to be late for the wake, and she had just given away her primary mode of fast transit.

She had to find someone to give her a ride.

Riley washed her face and then dried it on one of Gillian's duck towels. She ran her finger over the yellow embroidery and smiled. Ducks. The apartment was full of ducks, but she'd stopped noticing it ages ago. Gillian bought soap shaped like ducks, she bought shampoo because there was a duck on the bottle, and the dishes they saved for special occasions had small yellow ducks marching around their borders. It was so quaint and domestic, something so ordinary. Ducks.

The towels in her old apartment had been dollar store brand, threadbare and falling apart before she bothered to replace them. The old apartment where she'd gone to sit in the dark, alone unless she stopped at the bar to pick up a one-night stand, and she watched game shows on an old flickering TV set. It wasn't a home, it was the place she'd gone to wait for the next shift to start.

Gillian knocked softly. "Hon? Do you know if Chelsea prefers beer or soda?" Riley opened the bathroom door. "We have enough beer, I think. But I was planning to run downstairs and get some soda. I just don't know how much to get."

"I love you."

Gillian blinked at the sudden change of topic. "I love you, too."

"Thank you."

"You're welcome. Soda?"

"I think she likes tea. Diet soda would be fine."

"Okay." She kissed Riley's lips. "Everything okay?"

Riley nodded. "Everything's fine."

"I'll be right back."

"Okay."

"Are you? Okay?" She tucked Riley's hair behind her ear. She'd taken it down when they got home and had yet to put it into a ponytail.

"I'm fine. Do you need cash?"

"No, I have my card."

"Okay. Hurry back."

Gillian gave her a thumbs-up. Riley turned off the bathroom light and went into the bedroom. It was the same bedroom where Gillian had put her battered and broken body after that first disastrous assault on Marchosias' stronghold. She'd been dripping blood, torn apart, delirious, and Gillian Hunt had been the only safe harbor she could imagine. Gillian, God bless her, had taken in the husk of a coworker and brought her back to life.

Back then she'd been too distracted trying to not die to think about what an amazing leap of faith that had been. In the five years since, she still couldn't make any sense of it.

"Brave woman," Riley said softly. "Brave, crazy woman."

The doorbell rang. She abandoned her reverie and went to answer it, glancing through the peephole before she let Kenzie and Chelsea in. Kenzie had changed into jeans and an Army T-shirt, while Chelsea wore a skirt and sleeveless top. Gillian arrived a few minutes afterward with a six-pack of diet soda and two large bags of chips. They were just getting things set up when Priest arrived.

She entered without knocking, and Riley motioned for her to come inside. She paused mid-motion and furrowed her brow. "Cait? Everything okay?"

Priest nodded. "Everything is fine."

Chelsea stood up. "Caitlin is here?" She looked past her, taking Kenzie's hand. "I can't see her."

Riley moved closer, cautiously. "Cait, you look different."

"Well." She looked down at herself. She'd changed into a V-neck sweater and jeans, her hair down and still wet from the quick shower she had taken. "I wanted to ease into this, explain it in my own time. But after the funeral, I said... I said goodbye to Zerachiel."

Gillian moved to stand next to Riley. "Said goodbye to her...?"

"You and Riley are leaving town soon. I couldn't very well tag along as the third wheel, and Zerachiel couldn't just stay behind. Riley needed her guardian angel. And I wanted to... I needed to live. I needed to survive. So I parted ways with Zerachiel. She's ascended once more, and she'll be a silent observer in your life as she was before. And I will... stay here."

Riley reached out and took Priest's hand. "And you're okay with that? I know how bad it was last time you were mortal."

"Thank you for worrying about me, but this is my choice. Zerachiel is freed from the human frailty that was making her reluctant to move on, and I will live on even when... a-after..." She cleared her throat. "When Zerachiel has taken a new charge, I can remain here as Caitlin Priest. I can have my own life."

Riley smiled. "Congratulations, Caitlin."

"Awesome news, Cait," Kenzie said.

They each embraced her in turn, and Chelsea gave her a kiss on the cheek. Riley was the last to hug her and, when she pulled back, she squeezed Priest's shoulder.

"So you're one of us again. How does it feel?"

"I'm hungry. I'm very hungry."

Gillian smiled. "I have chips. Unless you want something more substantial."

"Substantial would be... yes. I need substance."

"Come into the kitchen," Gillian chuckled. "I'll see what we can scrounge up."

Kenzie watched her go and shook her head. "So, Cait is mortal again."

"Seems like it." Riley smiled. "It fits."

"Yes," Kenzie agreed. "It does."

Priest and Gillian returned from the kitchen with leftover pizza, which Priest was in the process of folding into her mouth. They gathered in the living room, with Kenzie, Chelsea and Priest on the couch while Gillian took her favorite armchair. Riley sat on the arm of Gillian's seat and reached down to take a beer off the coffee table.

"A toast. Lieutenant Zoe Briggs. She always tried to do right by the people she cared about. She was the best boss I ever had, and she deserves credit for letting me pull my shit whenever I needed to. And she died saving Gillian's life, so I'll always owe her for that."

Gillian looked down into her drink, pushing through her shame and embarrassment that it was her fault Zoe wasn't there anymore.

Everyone lifted their drinks. "To Zoe Briggs."

They drank, and Riley ran her thumb over her bottom lip. She still had a mouthful of beer when Chelsea raised her drink again.

"To the woman who brought all of us together, and who has saved the life of everyone in this room over and over again. To a champion in every sense of the word... to Riley Parra."

"Hear, hear," Kenzie said.

Riley sheepishly accepted the toast, and then cleared her throat to change the subject. They spoke of Briggs, her love of baseball and her dedication to redeeming herself as a police officer. Riley recalled the time she'd noticed Briggs was wearing weirdly blue socks at the morning briefing. Her explanation was that her team was in the Playoffs and she had to wear the socks until they either got eliminated or won the World Series. They'd gone on to win it, so the next year Briggs wore them again from the start of the season.

They eventually moved on to dinner, ordering Chinese and eating it around the kitchen table. Priest fell asleep on the couch, exhausted from a half-day as a human being since Zerachiel had made sleep mostly unnecessary. Kenzie and Chelsea quietly slipped out, and Gillian draped Priest with a quilt. She managed to get a pillow under Priest's head without waking her, and when she turned she saw Riley was quietly chuckling to herself.

She lowered her voice so that Riley could barely hear it. "What?"

"The quilt has ducks on it."

"All the best quilts do."

They left the kitchen light on so Priest wouldn't wake in the dark, then went to their bedroom. Riley had never changed out of her dress uniform, so she let Gillian take it off for her.

"I love watching you when you undress me."

Gillian smiled. "Oh, yeah?"

"Yeah. You have an intense look on your face."

Gillian laughed softly. "Well, there's a lot to take in." She leaned down and kissed Riley's breast just above the bra. "Shower tonight?"

"No, I'm too tired. Straight to bed."

"I concur."

"Motion is passed."

Gillian chuckled and walked Riley to the bed. Riley pulled back the blankets, let Gillian crawl under them, and then joined her. They found each other in the center of the mattress, kissing each other goodnight in the darkness before Gillian rested her head on Riley's chest.

"Big day tomorrow. Ready to go back to work?"

"As ready as I'll ever be. Two more weeks. Then we can go."

"Mm-hmm. Can't wait."

Riley stroked Gillian's hair and stared at the far wall until she couldn't keep her eyes open any longer.

Construction was still under way at the station, but the building had been declared fit for everyone to return to work. Commissioner Benedict released an edict that several departments would be combined in order to make up for the loss of manpower. Homicide had temporarily been blended with Robbery, and several detectives were being shuffled from one precinct to another in order to fill gaps.

The morgue was even worse, charged with officially reporting the cause and manner of every death in the city. Part of the burden was lightened by the fact other cities in the state were providing her with medical examiners, doctors, and others who could take up some of the slack. Most of her first morning back was spent herding her new army where they needed to be. When lunchtime arrived, she found her assistant Heather and took her aside.

"I have something I need to do. It shouldn't take too long, but I may need you to cover for me if I'm late."

"Okay. Lunch with your wife?"

"No, this is something else. And if..." She bit her bottom lip and considered what she was about to say. "If she comes down here looking to have lunch with me, can you tell her I was called to another precinct?"

Heather stared at her for a moment. "Is everything okay, Dr. Parra?"

Gillian managed a smile. "Yes. There are just some last-minute things we have to take care of before we leave town, and I don't want her to stress over it."

"Okay."

Gillian went into her office and took off the smock that covered her scrubs. She took the back elevator to the garage so she wouldn't run into Riley and checked the glove compartment to make sure everything she'd hidden was still there. She transferred the items to her pocket and whispered a quiet prayer before she pulled out of the garage. She knew that Riley and Priest had met her guardian angel; she hoped the invisible protector was paying attention as she drove through town and into No Man's Land.

Riley never intended her to know where the building was, but Gillian insisted she point it out once. Now she parked in front of it and pulled the totems out of her pocket.

A cross, a small medallion with the Lord's Prayer engraved on it, and a vial of holy water. She wet two fingertips with the water and dabbed it behind her ears, drawing a cross on her forehead for good measure. She closed her eyes and said a prayer under her breath before she got out of the car and walked purposefully to the front door. She didn't allow herself any hesitation as she pulled the door open and went into Marchosias' stronghold.

The lobby was run-down, but no more than most other buildings in No Man's Land she'd seen in the course of her work. A few transients lounged on couches near a pair of vending machines under the stairs. She felt a sense of foreboding, but otherwise the building was utterly normal. She didn't relax, and she gripped her cross hard enough that she knew it was leaving an imprint in the center of her palm.

There was a front desk. The man in a dirty button-down shirt behind it cleared his throat to get her attention and offered her a gentle smile.

"Can I help you, ma'am?"

"I'm looking for Marchosias."

Someone tapped her on the shoulder. She jumped to the side, bringing up the hand holding her cross, and Marchosias smiled. He held out his hands to show he meant her no harm. He was dressed in a nice suit, his blonde hair nearly styled and swept down across his forehead. He looked like the poster boy for a business school.

"What a pleasant surprise, Dr. Parra."

"Thanks." She looked around the lobby. "From Riley's description, I expected something a little more... Grand Guignol."

He shrugged. "You see it as the world does. And why not? Your wife is no longer champion, her partner is no longer an angel. For the first time in a very long time, you are one of the mundane. I'm told that's not something to be sad about, but..." He shrugged. "And that begs the question of why you're here. Why now, without Riley or Zerachiel to rescue you, would you choose to finally come and see my home?"

"Because you almost got away with it."

Marchosias raised an eyebrow. "I'm not scheming to get away with anything."

"You are. Because you owe Riley a debt. And I'm not leaving here until you repay it."

He didn't move a muscle, didn't take his eyes off her, but his entire demeanor shifted to menacing. He took a deep breath and exhaled through his nose.

"If you want to make a deal~"

"No. No deals, no bargains. I owe you nothing, demon. This is a debt you owe to Riley, and you're going to balance the scales before we leave town."

"Or what?"

"Or you'll be indebted to a human forever. You will owe me, demon. Can you live with that mark on your ledger?"

He regarded her for a long moment. Then finally, he came to a decision. He squared his shoulders and relaxed his posture. Gillian felt the tension fading and allowed herself to relax before he spoke.

"Okay, Dr. Parra. You've intrigued me. Speak your piece."

The days passed quickly, and Riley passed the hours with her final case. She and Priest closed it the day before Riley was due to hand in her badge and gun, arresting the killer with an hour to go before quitting time. Riley sat at her desk and stared at the computer screen, constantly distracted by everything going on around her. New detectives to replace those who had died or were still recuperating. The windows had been replaced, and the entire bullpen was undergoing renovations. It felt like a completely new office. It felt like the scenery was moving on and all that was left was for Riley to leave.

Priest watched Riley for a long moment and then cleared her throat. "Let me finish the paperwork."

"Are you sure?"

"I find the monotony soothing. Besides, all the times you took care of me... it's my turn. Tomorrow is your last day. Go."

Riley pushed back her chair and put her jacket on. "Jill and I are having a farewell dinner tomorrow night. Will you be there?"

"Of course. And I want to be there when you leave Saturday morning, if that's all right."

"Definitely." Riley kissed the top of her head when she passed. "I'll see you then."

She looked back at her desk, at the office where Lieutenant Briggs' things were still on display. She took the time to look at each detective still at work, the familiar faces she'd worked with for the past few years and the new ones replacing those who had been lost. Priest looked up and saw she was still standing there.

"Riley..." She smiled knowingly. "Gillian is probably waiting for you."

"Yeah. I'm going. Don't stay too late, Caitlin."

Priest waved before she went back to filling out their report, and Riley headed downstairs to retrieve her wife.

The apartment looked looted, with only the larger items still in place. The living room, kitchen, and bedroom were still furnished, but the small personal items that had made it a home were all packed away. The heavier bags were already downstairs in the car, while the bags with their clothes and other more portable items were waiting in bags by the door like pets eager to be let out for the night. Riley was standing against the kitchen counter staring at the desolation when Gillian came out of the bathroom. Her face had been scrubbed of makeup, her wet hair held out of her face by an elastic band. She glanced at Riley and stopped where she was standing, trying to gauge Riley's mood before she spoke.

"Hey," she whispered. "You okay?"

Riley nodded slowly, then gestured at the couch. "Hand me that pillow."

Gillian picked up one of the pillows off the couch and handed it over. Riley calmly put it against the wall and then began to pound it mercilessly. Gillian yelped, startled by the sudden violence, and stepped forward. She wrapped both hands around Riley's elbow and finally exerted enough pressure that Riley had to stop.

She was breathing heavily when she let the pillow drop, flexing her fist and looking down to examine the reddened knuckles.

"What the hell was that?" Gillian asked, more concern than anger in her voice.

"I don't want to die. Not in a year, not in a decade, not in three decades. I want to live." She touched the side of Gillian's head. "I want to see your hair turn pale and then white, and I want to see you get wrinkles. I want to buy you a little farm where we can retire, a farm with a pond on the back where you can feed the ducks in spring. I don't want to fit everything we have to do together into one damn year. It's not enough."

Gillian cupped Riley's face with both hands. "Even if we had a hundred years, it wouldn't be enough. But at least we know, and we can prepare. We can take full advantage of the time we have." She kissed Riley's lips. "You know, last time you died, when the Angel Maker stabbed you... I was late. I ran as fast as I could, but when I got to that room you were gone. I don't think you know how much that devastated me. That I couldn't say goodbye. I thought I'd missed my chance. Now I have a whole year. I consider that a gift."

Riley turned her head to kiss Gillian's hand. When she pulled back, she noticed a small red cut near the center of the palm.

"What's that?"

"Oh. I don't know. Just a cut."

Riley looked at it a little longer and thought she could see smaller, almost-healed marks extending out from the main one. It almost looked like a cross.

"You sure?"

"Yeah. Nothing to worry about." She kissed Riley's nose and between her eyebrows. "Come on. Last night in our bed. Let's make it memorable, okay?"

Riley smiled and slipped her arms around Gillian's waist, walking her backward toward the bedroom. They kissed as they crossed the threshold, and Riley undid the belt on Gillian's robe. As she'd hoped, there was nothing but supple, soft skin underneath. She spread her fingers over Gillian's hips and guided her down onto the edge of the bed. Gillian moved her legs apart and pointed her toes, leaning back on her elbows as Riley knelt in front of her.

Gillian ran her hands through Riley's hair and, when Riley looked up at her, she said, "Whatever happens a year from now, I am so lucky I have you. I'm lucky to have had you at all. And I am so glad I found you."

Riley stretched up and kissed Gillian's lips, pushing her back onto the bed and moving a hand between their bodies. Two of her fingers took over the job her hand had abandoned, and she straddled Gillian's thigh to press down against her. Gillian gripped Riley's arms and met her thrust for thrust, taking Riley's tongue into her mouth as they rocked against each other.

"I'll love you longer than a year," Gillian whispered just after she came. "I'll love you for the rest of my life."

Riley bowed her head, burying her face against Gillian's shoulder as she shuddered and came as well. Gillian stroked the back of Riley's head and whispered against the shell of her ear, rocking her back and forth. Soon Riley got up long enough to undress, and Gillian took off her robe and gathered Riley's naked body to hers. They covered themselves in the blanket, but neither slept. They spent the rest of the night talking in hushed tones, their aimless stroking sometimes turning into another session of lovemaking.

Gillian finally dozed off an hour before dawn. Riley stayed awake, watching as the room slowly lit with the rising sun and illuminated Gillian's face. It started on her left ear, the glow, and spread across her face with excruciating slowness. Her nose made a mountain range, her slightly parted lips the Grand Canyon. The light brought her back to consciousness and she blinked her eyes into focus - or as much focus as she could achieve without her glasses or contacts - and smiled at Riley.

"Did you watch me all night?"

"It's my job now." She lightly kissed Gillian's top lip, then the bottom.

"What time is it?" Riley told her. "Mm. The ladies will be here soon."

Riley nodded and reluctantly pulled away from her. They got up and moved their clutch to the shower, finally parting when it was time to dress. Gillian put on comfortable clothes - cargo pants and a lightweight shirt - since she planned to do most of the driving for the first day. She pinned her hair back and wore her glasses instead of contacts, and she walked barefoot to the front door to receive their first guest.

Caitlin Priest had bags under her eyes, but she was chipper when she greeted Riley. She kissed her on the cheek and then ran a hand through her hair. "Eight hours a night. It's hard to find so much time, and waking up is terribly difficult."

"Get used to it, human girl."

Chelsea and Kenzie arrived next. Kenzie gave Riley a thin, flat package shaped like a thick envelope. "What is this?"

"E-reader," Chelsea said. "In case you get bored on the road and need something to read. We already put a few dozen books on it to get you started."

"Thank you."

Aissa came with Muse, who hesitated on the threshold of the apartment. He had dressed for the occasion in a second-hand suit and a loosely-knotted tie. Riley finally stepped forward, grabbed the front of his shirt, and hauled him inside. "Come on, Marcus. It's not going to swallow you whole."

"Never been to your apartment, Detective. It's a lot nicer than I expected."

"I don't know if I should be insulted or complimented on behalf of my wife."

He turned to see Gillian smiling at him. "Mrs. Dr. Parra. The lady who tamed my favorite cop. I don't know how you did it, but it makes me a little scared of you."

Riley patted his shoulder. "Good call. Grab a drink."

"Don't mind if I do."

Riley closed the door and got a drink of her own. She was alone in the kitchen with Kenzie, so she touched her arm and moved closer so she could lower her voice.

"You were a great partner, but I'm glad you left. I'm glad you figured out your place in the world. Chelsea is... definitely not the person I would have chosen for you." Kenzie chuckled. "But you guys are amazing together. I can't imagine you without her now, and she's been so good for you, Kenzie. You're almost like a grown-up."

"I wasn't told this was going to be a roast."

Riley lightly slapped Kenzie's cheek. "I love you, Kenzie."

Kenzie looked at her for a long moment. "Wow. You never even said that when we were dating. I mean... not really."

"Well, I mean it more now. And to be honest, I haven't said it enough. I wouldn't be alive right now if it wasn't for you. So thank you, Kenzie."

Kenzie hugged her. "Thanks, Riley. For everything. I'm going to miss the hell out of you. I don't know what we'll do without you."

"You'll figure something out. Go on."

When she left, Muse inched into the kitchen. "I heard some of that. Don't go pulling any of that mushy stuff on me. I'll leave right now."

Riley smiled. "No. I didn't do anything for you, Muse. Everything you got, you got on your own."

He smiled. "Well, that's just a damn lie." He held out his hand. "It's been a pleasure, Detective."

"I handed in my badge and gun. Call me Riley."

He took a breath, wrinkled his brow, and then said, "Mrs. Parra."

"Ri-ley."

"I was taught to be respectful."

She raised an eyebrow. "To your elders? If you say 'to your elders,' I'll punch your lights out right now."

He smiled. "To people who are above me. To people I respect, and people I aspire to be like. I'll call you by your first name when I feel equal to you."

Riley took his hand and squeezed. "I guess I can live with that, Marcus."

"And whyn't you know more dudes?"

Riley laughed and slapped his arm. "You're all the dude I need or want, pal."

"Fine, fine. Guess I can't complain about spending the morning with so many lovely ladies." He nodded once and looked around the kitchen. "I'll, uh... go help with the... bags."

"Thanks."

When he picked up one of the larger bags, he grunted and mock-staggered under the weight. "Geez, ladies, what you got in here?"

Gillian moved quickly and held the door open for him. "Be careful with that. It's fragile."

"Noted," he said, nodding to her as he passed her.

After a bit more socializing, Riley managed to arrange to be in the kitchen with Chelsea. She touched her arm so she wouldn't be startled when she started talking.

"Years ago, I idolized you. Then I hated you, and then I had to tolerate you because my best friend was dating you. I never thought it would rise above just simple tolerance but now... I respect you, Chelsea. I respect what you've gone through, and how difficult it must have been to keep going. I don't think I could have done it, and the fact you not only kept at it but succeeded? I'm honored, and glad, that I got a chance to really know you."

Chelsea wet her lips and turned her face away. "Wow. That

means... you think you know what that means, coming from you. But you don't. You were a prodigy, Riley. People said I broke the glass ceiling, and when I saw you charging up in my wake I knew they were right. I just blazed the trail. You were the real symbol, the icon of women on the force. I'm just glad I was there to make it easier for you. Well... not easier."

Riley smiled. "It was plenty easy." She wrapped her hand around Chelsea's and squeezed. "Good luck. Take care of her for me, okay?"

"I will."

Riley saved Priest for last. When Gillian and Kenzie were preparing lunch, Riley motioned Priest into the bedroom and shut the door behind her.

"I don't even know what to say to you," she said after a long silence. "You were more than my partner. You were more than my friend. Caitlin, you changed *everything*. And the idea of not seeing you tomorrow hurts. There was a time when I wouldn't even have said this to someone I was sleeping with, but now I've said it to Kenzie and I'm going to say it to you. I love you, Caitlin. I never had a real family, but you showed me what it was like to have a sister. You drove me crazy sometimes. But you also put yourself on the line for me. You made me laugh. I wish I could stick around to see you figuring out this whole human thing, but I know you'll get the hang of it. So instead I'll just say... I love you. And I'm very glad to have known you."

"I'm very glad I got to know you, too, Riley. Zerachiel thought she knew you, but we met... when *we* met. But she didn't. She didn't know how funny and infuriating and loving you could be. I'm glad that I got a chance to meet the real you. It was an honor and a privilege. And I love you, too. You were my mother, and my sister, and my best friend. And if I succeed as a mortal in any way, it's because of the example you provided me." She stepped forward and hugged Riley. "I love you so much."

Riley smiled against her shoulder. "Take care of everyone."

"Will do."

Gillian knocked softly on the door and waited for Riley to let her in. She looked at Priest and touched Riley's arm. "You two okay?"

"We're fine."

Gillian nodded. "Okay. Food's on the table."

They started to leave, but Gillian held up a hand to stop Priest.

"Caitlin. Thank you. All the times you bled for Riley, all the times you stood between her and death, thank you. Thank you so much." She hugged Priest and kissed her cheek, and Priest rested her head on Gillian's shoulder. Gillian stepped back, sniffled, and put her fingers under her glasses to wipe the tears from her eyes. "Okay. Um, Riley... did you want to give Aissa the...?"

"Yeah. Now's as good a time as any."

They returned to the living room, and Gillian took her keys out of her pocket. "Aissa? Could you come here for a second?"

The girl stood up from the table and crossed the room. "Yes, Dr. Parra?"

"God, I love the sound of that," Gillian said softly. "Um, right. I don't know what's going to happen in the next year. Where we'll end up, if I'm going to stay there after Riley is..." She swallowed a lump in her throat and shook her head, moving on. "Anyway, if I do come back to the city, it would be very nice to have a home to come back to. And you're going to need someplace safe and warm to come back to. Nothing against Eddie's shelter, but a champion needs a home. So..." She held up the key. "I want you to have our apartment."

Aissa looked at the key, and then looked around the room. "Your home...?"

"Just for a year, with an option to renew if I don't show up to take it back. Don't worry, even if that happens I won't just evict you. We'll work something out. But for now..." She held the key out to her. "I think it's time you had a place to call home."

Aissa reverently took the key and held it in the palm of her hand. "I would be honored, Dr. Parra. Thank you so much." She looked around the room again and smiled. "This place has seen much love. I think I'll be very comfortable here."

Riley smiled. "Welcome home."

When they moved to the table for their farewell lunch, Kenzie surprised them by standing up with her glass extended.

"When I met Riley, she had the potential for greatness. She was a good cop, but she had no focus. She had no drive. No ambition."

Riley pointedly cleared her throat. "I hope you're going somewhere with this."

Kenzie winked and blew her a kiss. "The day she decided to go for it with the beautiful medical examiner she'd been lusting after since the moment they met, something changed. I came in late, but I saw it even when Gillian was gone from the city. The Riley who was with Gillian was not a Riley I recognized. She was calm. Cool. She had turned from some wild child into a real weapon. The love of a good woman can do amazing things, but the love of a great woman can work miracles. To Gillian Parra."

"To Gillian Parra," the others echoed.

Riley tapped the side of her glass against Gillian's and leaned in to kiss her.

Over lunch, they laughed and shared stories of the past five years. Kenzie brought up a few anecdotes from their time in uniform, a few of which Riley censored from Aissa's innocent young ears. When the dishes were removed from the table and put away - Aissa insisted on washing them, since it would soon be her responsibility anyway - the others moved into the living room. Muse had left a few bags next to the door, and Riley picked one up and slung the strap over her shoulder.

"I guess we should probably hit the road. We want to be well out of the city before rush hour hits. Thanks for coming over today."

"We had to say goodbye," Kenzie said, eyes wet with tears.

They all hugged again, and Chelsea opened her bag and withdrew two white roses. "These represent purity and innocence. I wish you peace in your final days."

"Thank you." Riley took one and tucked it behind Gillian's ear, then threaded the other through the lapel of her jacket. She looked at the group and then focused on her successor. "Aissa. A little tip. You might be called the champion, but it's not a one-woman job." She extended a finger and pointed at the others in the room. "Rely on your support team. More often than not, they'll pull your ass out of the fire."

Chelsea smiled and leaned against Kenzie. "Do you want us to come down and see you off?"

"No, thank you," Gillian said. "It'll make it easier to not look back."

Chelsea nodded. "Then have a safe journey, Dr. and Mrs. Parra."

Riley adjusted the strap on her shoulder so that it wouldn't crush the flower in her lapel, waved, and then took Gillian's hand. They left the apartment without looking back, making it all the way downstairs before Gillian sniffled and bumped against Riley's arm.

"I'm going to miss them," she said.

Riley stopped and faced her. "We don't have to do this. You

don't have to give up your life just because I'm~"

Gillian put a finger on Riley's lips. "I'm getting my year with you, Riley."

"Just thought I'd give you the out." She kissed the tip of Gillian's finger and then went the rest of the way down the stairs. They found places for the last few bags and then Gillian got behind the wheel. Riley got into the passenger seat and took one last look at the building before the car pulled away from the curb.

"Are we leaving from the east?"

"Take Eastern Gate, yeah," Riley said.

The road cut through neighborhoods and business parks that soon gave way to sprawling neighborhoods. They passed through the worst of No Man's Land and emerged on the other side, the waterfront and the sparkling water of the lake visible through the sparse signs of civilization that made it out this far.

They were still technically inside town limits when Gillian sucked in air through her teeth and began to slow down. Riley looked out the windshield and saw Marchosias standing in the middle of the road ahead of them.

"Want me to hit the gas?" Gillian asked.

The demon held out his hands to show he was unarmed. Riley took a deep breath and let it out as a sigh. "No." She unfastened her seatbelt. "If he wanted to hurt us, he would have done it. I'll go tell him to get out of the way."

"Be careful."

Riley squeezed Gillian's hand before she got out of the car. She walked toward Marchosias, and he clasped his hands in front of him with a smile. Riley stopped a few feet in front of him. They were close enough to speak without shouting, but not so close he could reach out and grab her.

"We're done, Marchosias. I'm just a citizen now."

"I'm well aware of that, Detec~ excuse me. Mrs. Parra. But I couldn't let you leave town without saying goodbye! And you didn't invite me to your little farewell party. I won't pretend that didn't hurt, by the way, so I'll just assume my invitation was lost in the mail." He cocked his head to the side to look past her. "Your wife looks lovely, as usual."

"Leave her out of this."

"Hm. Hm-hm-hm." He rocked on his heels and looked down at the asphalt. "I've been alive for a very long time, Mrs. Parra. You're grieving the fact that you're dying when you're only in your fourth decade of life. I don't blame you. Four centuries wouldn't be enough for me. There's just so much to do!" He chuckled and shook his head. "But I was in the same situation you find yourself in now. I was faced with the end of my time. I wouldn't have grabbed a new body, I wouldn't have been cast back into the pit, I'd have been *gone*. It's a terrifying thought. And it was my own doing... choosing Lark Siskin was... nearsighted of me. But you stopped her nefarious plan. You saved my life."

"It was an unintended consequence, believe me."

He smiled. "I'm sure it was. But it was brought to my attention recently that by doing so, you put me in your debt. I don't like that. Not one bit. And now you're leaving town? Just running away, leaving this on my ledger? No. No, no, no. I will not let this hang over my head for the rest of my sure-to-be long life. So I want to make it up."

"Save it. I don't want any gifts from you."

"Not a gift. But a window. I'm opening a window, just a crack." He looked toward the water. "One of my minions recently told one of yours that there is no good or evil. Just two sides with mutually exclusive goals. Sometimes good can appear to be doing evil, and evil can appear to do good. Mysterious ways and all that claptrap. All that matters is that we're throwing a wrench in the other side's plans. You made a deal with Heaven to save your wife's life. I am repaying your debt by mixing things up a little."

Riley advanced on him. "If you do anything to undo the promise I made, if you cause Gillian one second of-"

"Calm. Down." He growled and rolled his eyes. "So dramatic. No. I couldn't erase the promise if I wanted to. You entered into the agreement of your own free will. Hell, it was probably your idea. Your life for hers... such a human concept. My hands are tied there. In one year and... pft, I don't know, a few days, your heart will stop and you will cease breathing."

Riley felt a tightness in her chest to hear it put so bluntly.

"What I'm offering comes afterward. A moment. An opportunity if anyone is nearby, willing, and able. I'm saying there is a chance that once you die, you can be revived. And if the opportunity is taken, you will live on. You gave me a moment, Mrs. Parra. You freed me from the siphon of Lark Siskin and returned my life to me. I'm just returning the favor. If, and it's a big if, there is someone who can take advantage of the opportunity."

He looked past her again, and Riley turned to look at Gillian.

"Your wife really is quite spectacular."

"That was a cross on her palm," Riley whispered. She looked at Marchosias. "What did she give you?"

"Nothing. I took nothing, she gave nothing." He winked. "Good luck."

Riley was suddenly alone in the road. She looked at the empty space where the demon had just stood, then slowly turned and walked back to the car. Gillian was still staring straight out the window when Riley got back in. After a moment she twisted to look into the backseat, trying to find the heavy bag Muse had taken out. She looked at Gillian, admiring her profile.

"What did you do?"

Gillian shrugged and then looked at Riley. "I saved you."

She remembered the heavy suitcase Muse had lugged downstairs. "What's in the bag?"

"Medical equipment. Portable defibrillator, adrenaline shots... routine stuff."

The corners of Riley's mouth curled into a smile and she chuckled. "Routine stuff. Right..." She fastened her seatbelt again and looked out the windshield at the straight of the highway stretching out ahead of them.

"So where are we going? Now that we're this far out, I kind of need a direction to point us in." She looked at Riley. "Any ideas?"

Riley thought for a moment and then nodded. "Yeah. I really want to meet your mother and your Grammy. I didn't get a chance when I went down to Georgia to bring you back."

"They'd love to meet you, too." She started the car again. "So South?"

Riley nodded. "South."

Gillian smiled and started driving again.

A few minutes later, they passed a large green sign at the edge of the city. "Now Leaving Royal City. Come Again Soon." Riley smiled at the name. It had been years since she'd heard anyone say it out loud; even police officers reduced it to R.C. or just "the city." It had been ages since the 'royal' felt anything but ironic, but Riley understood it now. The city still wasn't anything special, but the people she was leaving behind... the people she had risked and sacrificed so much to save were what made it royal. But the real thing that made it royal, the thing that made it special, was sitting beside her in the car.

"Maybe on the way we'll find a farm," Gillian said. "A little farm outside of town, with a little pond in the back."

"We can stop and feed the ducks."

"Sounds about perfect." Gillian took one hand off the wheel and took Riley's hand, squeezing it. Riley smiled at her and looked in the mirror at the receding city.

Just about perfect. Close enough, anyway, that she really couldn't complain.

ABOUT THE AUTHOR

Geonn Cannon is the author of over fifty novels, including the Riley Parra series which was adapted into an Emmy-nominated webseries by Tello Films. He's also written two tie-in novels for the television series Stargate SG-1. He was the first male author to win a Golden Crown Literary Society Award for his novel Gemini, and he won a second for Dogs of War. Information about his other works and an archive of free stories can be found online at geonncannon.com.

CPSIA information can be obtained
at www.ICGtesting.com
Printed in the USA
BVHW051342041021
618092BV00011B/693

9 781944 591960